The EAR,
the EYE
and
the ARM

A Richard Jackson Book

Also by the Author
DO YOU KNOW ME

The EAR, the EYE and the ARM

a novel by

NANCY FARMER

orchard books • new york

Orchard Books
95 Madison Avenue
New York, NY 10016

Manufactured in the United States of America
Book design by Mina Greenstein
The text of this book is set in 12 point Fournier.

2 4 6 8 10 9 7 5 3 1

Library of Congress Cataloging-in-Publication Data
Farmer, Nancy.
The Ear, the Eye and the Arm : a novel / by Nancy Farmer.
p. cm. "A Richard Jackson book"—T.p. verso.
Summary: In 2194 in Zimbabwe, General Matsika's three
children are kidnapped and put to work in a plastic mine,
while three mutant detectives use their special powers to
search for them.
ISBN 0-531-06829-3.   ISBN 0-531-08679-8 (lib. bdg.)
[1. Science fiction. 2. Zimbabwe—Fiction.
3. Blacks—Zimbabwe—Fiction.] I. Title.
PZ7.F23814Ear 1994 [Fic]—dc20 93-11814

to
DANIEL FARMER
born in Resthaven

The EAR,
the EYE
and
the ARM

Someone was standing by his bed, a person completely unlike anyone Tendai had ever met. In the predawn light his features were unclear. He was simply a presence of darker blue than the sky behind him. But there was about him a scent of woody smoke and new leaves and the honey of far-off, unseen flowers. The presence pointed at Tendai and said, "You!"

The boy woke up at once. The first rays of dawn were sliding over the garden wall, and the window was empty. What a strange dream, thought Tendai. He pulled the sheet over his head as he tried to remember it better. The image faded away, leaving a strange sense that something important was about to happen. His ancestors must have felt this way before a big hunt.

Tendai imagined them lying on the warm earth of their huts, feeling it tremble with destiny. Their shields and spears lay ready by the door. Not like me, he thought. He snuggled into a soft bed in one of the finest mansions in Zimbabwe. Around the house were a large garden and a wall studded with searchlights and alarms. The automatic Doberman growled as it made a last tour of the lawn before retiring to its kennel.

Any tremble of destiny would have had to struggle through the concrete foundations of the house. It would have had to work through inlaid wooden floors and thick carpets, to creep up the grand staircase to the second floor. Only a whisper could have found its way to his waiting ear.

Yet find him it did.

He heard the robot gardeners clipping the grass along a walk. Hoopoes called from jacaranda trees, but a microchip went on with a far better selection of birdsong. It was certainly beautiful, but Tendai felt a pang of regret at not being able to hear the real birds. The mynah—a living creature smuggled in by the Mellower—stirred in its cage. *"Mangwa-nani,"* it said. "Have you slept well?"

Kuda, Tendai's little brother, sat up and answered, "I have done so if you have done so."

The mynah paid no attention to this polite reply. *"Mang-wanani! Mangwanani!"* it shrieked, rattling the door of its cage.

Kuda hopped out of bed and released the bird. It fluttered to a table and snapped up a crust of bread from last night's supper. Tendai could hear the crumbs showering over his books. He pulled the covers more tightly around his ears to keep in the light, happy feeling of excitement.

A house robot purred as it went from door to door with tea. It entered and placed two steaming cups on the table. The mynah squawked as it was pushed aside. "Good morning," said the robot. "It's September second, 2194. The time is six-fifteen A.M. Breakfast is at seven. Be on time if you know what's good for you."

"Go away," muttered Kuda as he blew on the hot tea.

"Anyone who oversleeps is a big fat booboo head," retorted the robot as it glided out.

"Rita programmed it to say that," Tendai said as he threw back the covers.

"I know. Well, are you going to ask him?" Kuda swung his short legs off the edge of his chair.

"I'm not promising anything."

"You're a wimp."

Tendai didn't bother to argue. Kuda didn't know how difficult it was to ask Father anything. That duty fell on the eldest brother. Besides, when Kuda got an idea in his head, it took an earthquake to dislodge it. "I had the funniest dream this morning," Tendai began.

"The mynah just knocked over your tea," Kuda remarked. Tendai grabbed a towel and cleaned up the mess. Then he quickly took a shower and dressed in his Scout uniform. Breakfast was at seven, not a minute earlier or later.

The two brothers stood outside the dining room door, where they were joined by Rita. She was also in a Scout uniform. A hundred years before, Boy and Girl Scouts had belonged to different organizations, but now they were lumped together. Father approved of them because they taught the virtues most revered by the people of Zimbabwe: loyalty, bravery, courteousness and reverence for *Mwari*, the supreme god.

Kuda had no Scout uniform because he was only four. He did his best with a sand-colored shirt and pair of shorts. "Breakfast!" chimed the door as it swung open. The children trooped in. They lined up in order with Tendai, age thirteen, first and Rita, eleven, second. Tendai was secretly embarrassed that he and Rita were the same height. Kuda was last.

Mother smiled at them from her chair. She looked cool and elegant in her long white dress. She toyed with a slice of cantaloupe on a blue plate.

"All present and accounted for," said Father. "Rita, stop slouching." The children stood as tall as they could manage as their father marched from his great chair at the head of the table. He wore a general's uniform with gold braid on his massive shoulders. His chest was covered with medals. Since it was breakfast and he was home and it was a warm day, he left his cap on a hat rack.

"Shirttail out, Kuda. Five push-ups for you. Rita, pull in your stomach. You are not a watermelon. Tendai—" Father stopped, and Tendai felt sweat prickle on his forehead. He loved his father, but sometimes he wished he wasn't so—so military. He suspected Father would like to have Mother at the end of the line, tall and perfectly groomed. But even Father could hardly order her to do push-ups if he detected a loose thread.

"Tendai passes inspection," said Father, and he stalked back to his chair. Tendai relaxed, not letting it show. Passing inspection was as close as Father ever got to praise. Perhaps he could ask the question after all.

They were allowed to sit down, but things began to go wrong at once. The maid robot spooned porridge on the tablecloth. She had to be sent to the kitchen for readjustment. The butler took over the serving. He wouldn't give Rita extra sugar, and she sulked. The holophone trotted up to Father's chair and clamored until he answered it.

A report began to feed in: pictures of fire engines and ambulances flashed across its screen. Tendai watched idly because he had nothing better to do. The Masks, the only gang remaining after Father's war on crime, had set off a bomb in a shopping center. Bodies were taken out of the smoking ruins. Statistics rattled across the bottom of the screen. Tendai turned away. It was all remote, of no interest.

"Accursed Masks!" shouted Father at the holophone. "Get me the police chief!" The phone bobbed and dialed. Father and the police chief made plans while the omelets on everyone's plates got cold.

Of course no one thought of eating until Father was ready. He was an elder and head of the family.

"Lizard eggs," muttered Rita, poking at her omelet.

"Don't start," Tendai said in a low voice.

"Chickens are descended from reptiles. I read it in a book."

"Be quiet."

"Nasty old cold lizard eggs."

"Is something wrong?" thundered Father from the head of the table.

4

"No," said Tendai, Rita and Kuda all together.

"Everything's delicious," added Rita. "Especially the eggs."

"Is it too much to ask," shouted Father, "when I'm trying to protect ten million citizens from packs of hyenas that want to tear down our civilization, *is it too much to ask for a little peace and quiet at the breakfast table?*" He slammed the receiver down. The holophone whimpered and cowered against a wall.

Everyone ate in silence. Tendai had a mental picture of his father lining up everyone in the city. "Ten push-ups for you, twenty for you," he would growl as he inspected a line of ten million people. Tendai had to clench his jaws to keep from laughing.

"What's this?" said Father as the butler robot placed a rack of dry toast by his plate.

"No butter until your blood pressure goes down. Doctor's orders," the butler said.

"I hate dry toast." But Father piled it with blackberry jam and ate it anyway.

Tendai listened to the birdsong in the garden. He couldn't ask about the Scout trip now. They were going to spend another long, boring day locked up in the house. All because Father was afraid they would get kidnapped.

"It's time for the Mellower," said Mother in her gentle voice. Everyone looked up, even Father, although he pretended he was only checking the time. The butler robot cleared away the dishes. They sat expectantly, watching the door.

"He's late," said Mother.

"He's always late," said Father.

Tendai felt a disloyal twinge of pleasure. The Mellower was the one person Father couldn't organize. The Mellower had smudges on his shoes. Buttons dropped off his shirt and were forgotten. His lunches lasted three hours, and he made paper airplanes of the homework he was supposed to supervise. Tendai, Rita and Kuda often covered up for him.

"I'll send the butler after him," sighed Mother.

"If he were one of my soldiers, I'd order him to do fifty push-ups," Father said. "No, a hundred."

The sprinklers in the garden switched on; the odor of wet dust drifted through the window. It made Tendai think of the storms that blew out of the Indian Ocean. He thought of the faces of his ancestors turned toward the sky. They smiled as the rain opened the earth. They sang praises to *Mwari*, whose voice is thunder, and to *mhondoro*, the spirit of the land—

"Wake up," whispered Rita, kicking him under the table. Tendai straightened just as Father looked at his end of the table.

"It *can't* be seven-thirty," came the Mellower's voice from down the hall. "I'm sure I set the alarm. Oh, dear, I'm such a bad boy." He hurried through the door and brushed a mop of blond hair from his pale forehead.

"What wonderful, patient people you are!" he cried. "I'm *so* lucky to be here. When I tell the other Praise Singers I work for the great General Amadeus Matsika, they're so jealous they could *spit*!" And before Father could react, the Mellower launched into his Praise.

Tendai had heard Praise Singing described many ways. It was an ancient custom meant to call forth the powers of the seen and unseen worlds. It was music. It was poetry. But most of all, it was medicine for the soul. Some Mellowers were public and had offices. Many worked for hospitals, but a few were attached to great houses like the Matsikas'. They stood at the breakfast table and recounted the glories and strengths of each family member.

"Today this place is full of noise and happiness.
The guiding spirit of the General stands over us
Like a great tree: let all who are afraid
Take shelter under his mighty shadow!"

6

Tendai noticed he was starting out with traditional poetry. The Mellower compared Father to a victorious bull in a green field, to the lion that represented Father's totem.

Then he changed to modern speech and described some of Father's actual victories. He recounted how Father rescued the President when Gondwannan terrorists attacked her house, how she made him Chief of Security for the Land of Zimbabwe. He pictured the long, bitter struggle against the gangs. As the Mellower talked, the lines on Father's face relaxed. His eyes became distant and dreamy.

Tendai thought the change was amazing. As the cares and irritations dropped away, General Matsika became the father Tendai wished he really had.

Then the Mellower spoke of Mother's chemistry discoveries and her position as a professor at the University. Mother's eyes shone with pleasure. He praised Rita for winning a National Science Prize. He expressed happiness over her plumpness, which showed promise of great beauty. The peevishness in Rita's face melted away.

Kuda, said the Praise Singer, spoke as clearly as a child twice his age. Nor did he have childish fears. Kuda was brave, a little elephant whose tusks were itching for battle, like the great General himself. Kuda scowled fearsomely, as though enemies were present right in the room.

Now a struggle began as the Mellower turned to Tendai. The man always saved him for last because, Tendai suspected, he sensed the resistance. Tendai didn't like the power Praise had over him. Of course he trusted the Mellower. No one else paid him as much attention. If the truth were known, he liked the man as much as his own father, but sometimes— often, actually—he had trouble remembering exactly *what* the Mellower had said. Afterward there was a period when he felt sleepy and a little foolish. And so he fought to keep from being entranced.

Most of the time he won.

Tendai listened coldly to a description of his swimming prizes and the badges he won in the Scouts. He wavered a little when the Mellower talked about how he rescued Rita from a boating accident. Then the man reverted to the traditional style of Praise Singing:

"He goes forth to explore, as his ancestors once
Followed rivers to new lands, as they stood on hills,
Their spirits bold as lightning—"

Tendai was lost. Or perhaps it was a lingering effect of the dream he had that morning. He was surrounded by the scent of wood smoke mixed with distant honeyed flowers. He was following a trail. The pugmarks of a lion preceded him like flowers printed in the dust. It waited for him on a rise not far away and shook its glorious mane. *Follow me*, it whispered.

Tendai woke up. He couldn't tell how long he'd been hypnotized. Everyone sat around the table with contented smiles. Microchip birds sang sweetly from the garden.

"Mmm," sighed Mother, stretching her arms before her. Rita yawned and prodded Kuda.

"No push-ups for you," rumbled Father. The Mellower bowed politely and withdrew. Very slowly, the room came back to life. To Tendai, it was like walking underwater.

Father lounged in his great chair with his large feet stuck out before him. He nodded benevolently at the family. *Now* was the time to ask about the trip, but the same torpor that had overtaken Father also affected Tendai. He knew he ought to speak, but it was so comfortable to go back to the beautiful vision he had seen during Praise.

The holophone rang. "Library," ordered Father, rising from his chair. The holophone skittered in front of him as he strode down a passage. The library door closed, and Tendai's opportunity was lost.

"Where does the time go?" cried Mother as the ancestor clock in the hall announced that it was eight-thirty. She gathered up her lecture notes and, somewhat distractedly, called the children together. "Do your lessons well—remember, the martial arts instructor is coming at nine. Tell the Mellower I've programmed the pantry to provide a nutritious lunch, and this time he is to see that you actually eat it." She looked sharply at Rita. "Kuda, you may not tease the automatic Doberman. Its chain is almost worn through—bad boy! Tendai, I expect you to be responsible for the others." Then, because the stretch limo was already humming on the anti-grav pad, she patted them fondly and ran out the door.

Tendai, Rita and Kuda waved as the limo flew off toward the University. "Oh, bore," said Rita. "The martial arts instructor's already here."

aturally, because of the differences in their ages, the children didn't study the same things, but the warm-up at the beginning was for all. They moved through t'ai chi to more ordinary exercises, such as running in place and toe touching. Rita never, ever, managed to touch her toes. They ended with martial shouting, which Kuda greatly enjoyed.

"Very good," said the instructor as the little boy roared. The instructor was small and extremely tough. Rita said he was like a buffalo that had been boiled down until only the gristle was left.

After the warm-up, Kuda was allowed to play while Rita and Tendai studied strategy. Tendai was reading Sun Tzu's *Art of War*, and Rita had the writings of Julius Caesar. "Who cares how the Romans built their roads?" she grumbled. "They should all have stayed home and had orgies."

"Knowledge is a house that must be built from the ground up," said the instructor. "We know how to make the roof. The information is useless if we don't understand the foundations on which it is to be placed."

The man had absolutely no sense of humor. Still, Tendai thought the *Art of War* was more fun than weapons practice.

They learned to use bows and arrows, spears and nunchucks. Once a month, Father let them fly to the police rifle range to study more modern weapons.

Tendai liked the skill involved, but his imagination was a little too active. As he sent a spear into a bag of sand in the garden, he thought, What does it feel like to drive a spear into a *person*? And he thought of it happening to him.

"Stop *dwaal*ing!" shouted the instructor. "If you let your mind wander, your enemy will be right on top of you!"

Tendai felt hot with shame. This would be reported to Father. After the lessons, the children had a half-hour break. They snacked on milk and cookies on the lawn while the martial arts instructor reported on their progress.

"I'm glad this only happens once a week," said Rita.

"Me, too," agreed Tendai.

"I hate exercise!"

"You're both wimps," Kuda said as he threw a pebble at the automatic Doberman's kennel.

Most mornings Tendai and Rita were instructed via the holoscreen, with Kuda occasionally being included. They learned biology, African history, math, physics and a foreign language. Tendai did Chinese, and Rita French. They all studied Shona, the official language of Zimbabwe. Most afternoons were spent on homework, which the computer sent to the teachers. The corrections arrived after dinner.

And this was the way it had been as far back as Tendai could remember. He had never entered a noisy school yard. He had never played a team sport or shared a lunch with other children at a crowded table. Father was too worried about his enemies. Of course they visited acquaintances of Father and Mother, who sometimes had children. These meetings were awkward. Tendai found it difficult to make friends with people he might not see again for months.

"Are you going to ask him about the Scout trip?" said Rita as she fed cookie crumbs to a line of ants.

"I'm waiting for the right moment." Tendai looked up at the defenses on the garden wall: electrified wire, alarms, even machine guns. The gate was opened by a Pass Card. Now and then Father gave one to the Mellower to allow supplies to be delivered. It could only be used once.

"He's scared," Kuda said, pinging another pebble at the kennel. The Doberman charged out the opening with its metal hackles raised. It was brought up so sharply by the chain that it flipped over on its back. It scrabbled to its feet, barking hysterically. Kuda laughed.

"Someday that chain's going to break. Then you'll be sorry," said Rita.

"It won't bite. It knows my smell." The Doberman retreated to the kennel, where it growled a few moments before switching off.

Even Scout meetings were held via holoscreen, Tendai thought glumly. The merit badges were sent by mail. He had earned them all in the garden or at specially fortified places Father trusted. But Tendai needed an explorer's badge to become an Eagle Scout.

Exactly how much exploring could you do in a garden?

"I'll see what Father's up to," said Tendai, getting to his feet.

"He'll chicken out," Kuda told Rita.

Tendai walked along the hall that led to the library. It was Father's favorite workplace, fitted with holoscreens so he could stay in contact with the outside world. But it was also beautiful. Shelves reaching to the ceiling were filled with old books that gave a leathery, dusty scent to the air. Persian carpets covered the floor. Lamps with stained-glass shades cast a warm glow quite unlike the light in the rest of the house. Tendai was always surprised by this artistic streak in Father. He usually seemed interested only in machines.

Few people were allowed into the library. Perhaps, Tendai realized now, because it was one of the only places Father felt safe. It was at the very center of the house.

Now the door was open, which meant the martial arts instructor was still there. Tendai stopped. "His mind keeps wandering," the instructor said from inside. "I've been working with him for years and, honestly, I don't think he'll change. He seems to go into a trance."

"A sharp rap on the head ought to cure that," rumbled Father.

"Believe me, I've tried it. He thinks too much. Thinking has its place, but not during battle."

"What are you telling me?"

"That he isn't cut out for a military career," said the instructor. "I'm sorry. I know you don't want to hear this. Your other son has the right spirit. He's a real little lion."

"Are you"—Tendai could hear Father looming out of his chair—"are you saying my son's a *coward?*"

The instructor paused. Tendai held his breath. "Not exactly. He feels the other person's pain. That's a bad trait in a soldier."

Tendai leaned against the wall. He had thought the man too stupid to notice.

Father settled back with a heavy sigh. "I'll have to think about this."

"I wish you would. There's a problem in a completely different area."

"I would welcome a completely different area."

"A lot of people are worried about the trade agreement with Gondwanna," the instructor said. "It gives them entry into too many parts of the country."

Tendai stopped listening. The Gondwannans were everybody's bogeymen. They were blamed for everything from locusts to headaches. Zimbabwe had signed a peace treaty with them years before, but it seemed no one could let by-gones be bygones. Tendai was bored with Gondwannans, who lived far to the north and probably carried on their boring lives in exactly the same way as Zimbabweans.

What was he going to do about Father? It's not fair, he thought, clenching his fists. I hate that instructor. I'll stick *him* with a spear if he wants a good report. But even as he imagined this, Tendai *felt* the blade he had just—mentally—driven into the instructor's chest. The sensation made him sick. Does that make me a coward? he thought.

"I won't ever accept the Gondwannan ideas on sacrifice," came the instructor's voice from the library.

"We sacrifice animals," Father said, "and we aren't vegetarians."

"It's the *way* they do it. We kill mercifully. To them, the whole point is pain. They believe their gods are asleep and can only be roused if they send a messenger—a sacrifice, that is. The more pain the messenger has endured, the more brightly it burns with anger when it reaches the spirit world. Their gods are so used to messengers, it takes a lot to get their attention."

"Strange," said Father.

"Strange and terrible. The problem is, they've been doing it in Zimbabwe."

"I'll put a stop to that," growled Father.

"Here's just one example. In Bulawayo, a Gondwannan bought a goat. . . ." The instructor explained how the goat followed its buyer to a courtyard, where other Gondwannans waited. There, it ate the grass left out for it as the men sharpened their knives. Tendai didn't want to listen, but at the same time he was drawn into the story. It was the image of the trusting goat that impressed him.

The instructor began to describe what was done to the animal, leaving nothing out. It was as clear as the surgeon's report, but Tendai's mind added other details. He smelled the blood, he heard the bleating—

"What was that?" said Father. The men came to the door at once. Tendai looked at them from the floor, where he had slid when his knees turned to rubber. "Why are you sitting here?" thundered Father.

"I—didn't want to disturb you." Tendai scrambled to his feet.

"Were you eavesdropping?"

"I—yes. I didn't mean to—"

"It would be interesting to know how long he was there," the instructor said dryly.

"I will not be spied on in my own house!" shouted Father. "You of all people should know only cowards listen at doors. If you're curious, ask a question. Don't skulk! *Maiwee!*" He turned abruptly and strode back into the library with the instructor. The door slammed.

Tendai felt bathed in heat. His ears rang with Father's powerful voice. For a minute he couldn't do anything. Then he went to his room, where he sat with his eyes closed and tears running down his face. But he didn't make a sound. No way would he let Rita and Kuda find out he was crying. Presently, the tears dried up, leaving a heavy residue of despair behind. If he wasn't fit for a military career, what *was* he good for? And was being a coward something you were born with, like ears that stuck out?

The stretch limo whirred as it left the antigrav pad. Tendai squinted at the bright sky. He saw the chauffeur, the martial arts instructor and Father. They were probably going to meet Mother for lunch. Rita and Kuda waved at the limo from the garden.

A flutter caught Tendai's attention: the mynah was battering the force screen in an attempt to get out the window. "You're trapped, too," said Tendai, gently removing the bird to his table. He gave it the remains of a cookie from his pocket. The bird kept glancing at the window. Tendai examined its wings and saw that the leading pen feathers had grown back. The Mellower plucked them out of the right wing when he remembered. That unbalanced the mynah so it couldn't fly.

But of course the Mellower often forgot, as he forgot most things. The mynah was perfectly capable of flight now. Tendai switched off the force screen and waited. The bird, casting a quick look in his direction, flew at the window again, but this time it encountered no barrier. It gave a loud squawk of surprise as it sailed out. Then, realizing its good fortune, it rose up, up, up, following the path of the stretch limo.

The mynah lifted on a rise of warm air as it coasted over the garden wall, over the snapping electric wires and broken glass and machine guns. It was a black dot in a hot blue sky, going swiftly, and then it was gone.

Tendai, somewhat regretfully, closed the bird cage and put it into a closet. Well, the mynah was free now, and it hadn't even looked back.

endai went out to the garden, where he found Rita and Kuda trying to rouse the Mellower. The man was lying on a couch under a jacaranda tree. From the layer of purple petals that had drifted over him, it was clear he had been there awhile.

"Come on, Mellower," urged Rita. "Unlock the pantry so I can reprogram it."

"Let's tip over the couch," suggested Kuda. The little boy tried to lift the legs, but the couch was too heavy.

"Father's gone," Tendai said, who had an idea about what motivated the Mellower. The man opened one eye. "And Mother, too," he added.

The Praise Singer sat up and stretched. "What a wonderful day!" he cried. "Just look at that blue sky! Don't the jacaranda flowers make a magnificent carpet on the green grass?"

"Come on. I have to reprogram the pantry before it starts cooking." Rita grasped one of the Mellower's hands and Kuda took the other. Together, they pulled him to the kitchen, where a large control panel sat behind a locked glass door. The Mellower pressed his thumb to the lock, which hummed as it considered his print. It chimed, and the door slid into the wall.

"Hurrah!" yelled Kuda as Rita began to access the pantry. Tendai knew, as eldest brother, that he ought to object, but he was still in a grim mood about what he had heard in the library. It wasn't often they were left alone. As long as either Father or Mother were home—no matter how inaccessible—the Mellower wouldn't dare interfere with the day's activities. Of course, being the Mellower, he often did so by accident.

"What's for lunch?" inquired Kuda.

Rita called up the memory. "Soy burgers, stewed parsnips and brown rice."

"Ewww!"

"Any suggestions?"

"Sausages and potato chips!" cried Kuda. "Scones, jam and whipped cream!"

"Ice cream and chocolate sauce!" cried the Mellower.

"Chicken with that crispy batter—and fried shrimp!—and that cheesecake Aunt Farai made." Rita typed busily.

"Shouldn't we have vegetables?" said Tendai.

"A tomato for Tendai," finished Rita. "There!" She stood back watching the pantry whir and click. In a few minutes a delicious smell wafted out of the food compartment as plates were filled.

The Mellower threw open the kitchen windows. The air conditioner began to whine in protest. Rita turned it off. A warm breeze laden with the scent of freshly cut grass replaced the house air—not that anything was wrong with the house air. All the pollen, dust and pollution was filtered out, with artificial perfume added to cover up a rather flat smell. The house air was okay, but wild air was more interesting. Whenever Mother and Father were away, the children opened the windows.

Kuda tossed his chicken bones onto the floor, which sent the butler and maid robots scurrying to retrieve them. The Mellower talked so much, ice cream melted off his spoon and ran down his shirt. He told them about Great Zimbabwe, the ancient ruined city to the south, and of Monomatapa, who founded the Shona Empire.

As the man talked, Tendai imagined the ancient king. When Monomatapa traveled, his royal guard went before him with battle-axes and heavy-bladed hunting spears. Then came a ceremonial drum carried on a pole between two men. It was beaten continuously as they walked. The king rode on a litter, surrounded by Praise Singers, musicians and dancers. "Here comes the Lord of the Sun and Moon, the Lion that prowls by Night!" they sang to the sounds of hand pianos, iron bells and the shell anklets of the dancers. Red dust rose up around them, sending a plume into the air to alert people the king was approaching.

Behind the musicians walked women bearing Monomatapa's household needs, courtiers who carried his furniture and more soldiers.

Whenever the sound of the king's drum was heard, villagers threw down their tools and ran out to salute him. When he desired to eat, a ceremonial stool was placed in a clearing. His women approached him on their knees with food, and all the others waited in a ring to hear his good words and repeat them to the waiting crowds behind.

"I wish I were a king," sighed Kuda.

"Well, I wouldn't have liked to live then," Rita snapped. "Imagine creeping up to someone on your knees."

"How can you tell it so well? It's like we were really there." Tendai, for a moment, had actually been in the clearing, listening to the shrill, welcoming cries of the women.

"I have a *shave* for storytelling," the Mellower explained. Tendai nodded. A *shave* was a wandering spirit who entered you and taught you a special skill. It didn't matter that the Mellower was of the English tribe and the *shave* was obviously Shona. You didn't have a choice about who possessed you: when a spirit wanted you, he or she generally got his or her way. If you resisted, the spirit made you sick.

Rita, now, clearly showed that her great-grandmother, a gifted mathematician, had decided to pass on her skills.

Great-grandmother was a *mudzimu*, or family spirit. It wasn't surprising when a departed family member bestowed her blessing on a descendant. *Shaves* were more unusual but by no means rare. When someone died without a descendant or proper burial rites, he or she turned into a *shave* and wandered until a willing host was found.

Kuda was too young to be possessed. Tendai was certain some warlike ancestor would be delighted with his little brother when he was older. But what about me? he thought. He didn't have any special skills. Quite a lot of dull, ordinary people weren't ever possessed by anybody. They weren't worth it. Tendai sighed.

"You forgot to eat your tomato," said Rita.

"I don't want it."

"I do!" Kuda cried, and he hurled the tomato straight at the butler robot. It burst across the machine's dark blue uniform.

"Kuda!" yelled Rita.

"Food fight! Food fight!" Kuda shouted. He threw a fistful of potato chips at her. Rita immediately slopped ice cream onto his hair. Kuda armed himself with the remaining chicken bones.

"Not fair! I don't have any ammunition," cried Rita. The Mellower handed her the sugar bowl. The sugar did very well because it stuck to the ice cream. Next came raspberry jam, a cup of tea and the milk jug. The Mellower joined in, throwing chocolate sauce and dodging chicken bones. The floor and walls of the kitchen were splattered. Rita, Kuda and the Mellower dashed around, knocking over chairs, skidding on the wet floor and banging into the distraught robots, who were trying to clean up.

"Come on!" shouted Kuda to Tendai.

"No thanks!"

"You're a wimp!"

Tendai withdrew to a corner. He watched with irritation as the others turned the room upside down. Finally, they collapsed into a heap, panting with exhaustion. "Oh!" gasped Rita. "That was fun!" The automatic mop came out of its cubbyhole to repair the damage.

"One plate broken. Not too bad," said Kuda.

"I'll tell Mother it was too hot. It slipped out of my hands." Rita lay in a puddle of milk, which the automatic mop tried to reach.

"You'll have to change your clothes," Tendai said.

"Who cares? That's what washing machines are for."

"Wasting food is bad. Think of all the poor people in Harare."

"Oh, I give up!" cried Rita. "We never have any fun, and you have to sit there like an old vulture and preach. Go croak somewhere else!"

"Croak! Croak!" said Kuda.

"Tendai's right," the Mellower said mournfully. "I'm supposed to set an example. Your father will throw me into the street when he finds out. I'll starve! Oh, woe is me!"

"There now, you made him cry." Rita brought the Praise Singer a paper towel to blow his nose on. "Don't worry. We'll protect you. I'll program the pantry to say we ate those ghastly parsnips. The house robots won't tell on you. They don't know how."

The Mellower sniffed his thanks and immediately cheered up. They all went to change clothes, except Tendai, who didn't need to. Later, they played Monopoly, climbed trees, swam in the pool and took turns tormenting the automatic Doberman.

"I'm so *bored,*" said Rita, lying in the shade of the wall. Tendai, Kuda and the Mellower lounged nearby. The afternoon heat was great, and the air vibrated around the electrified razor wire overhead. "Did you ask Father about the Scout trip?"

"No," said Tendai.

"Told you so," Kuda said.

"Well, maybe you wouldn't be so sarcastic if you had to do it yourself," cried Tendai, suddenly angry. "Maybe you don't know what it's like being yelled at every time you open your mouth. He's nice to you—you're just a baby! Wait'll *you* have to stick your neck out!"

"I am not a baby!" yelled Kuda.

"You are so! You still take *naps!*"

"I'm not! I'm not! I'm not!" Kuda landed on Tendai and pounded him with his little fists.

"Oh, stop it," said Rita wearily. Tendai held Kuda at arm's length—it wasn't difficult—and let him swing his fists uselessly until he burst into tears of frustration.

"I understand," said the Mellower quietly.

"What?" Tendai turned his attention to the Praise Singer. Kuda sat on the ground with tears streaking his dusty face.

"I know what it's like to be yelled at very time I open my mouth. It's horrible."

Tendai felt uncomfortable. Adults weren't supposed to tell you their problems.

"What is this trip you keep talking about?" asked the Mellower.

"I need an explorer's badge to become an Eagle Scout," Tendai explained. "Some people walk through a game park—that's best, but Father would never agree to it. I can get one by traveling across the city, though."

"So can I," said Rita.

"And they said I could come," Kuda put in quickly.

"Wait, wait. Does this mean you'd walk across Harare? That's over fifty miles." The Mellower sat up and brushed grass clippings from his hair. They settled on his shirt again and were forgotten.

"We can take buses. We go to the terminal at Mbare Musika, catch a shuttle to the Mile-High MacIlwaine Hotel and go on to Beatrice at the far end of the city. Then we come back," explained Tendai.

"We've been saving our allowances for months," Rita said.

"Tendai has a pocketknife to kill enemies," said Kuda.

"Be quiet!" Rita smacked him.

"Let me think." The children watched anxiously as the Mellower idly chewed a grass stem and stared into the distance. "You'd leave in the morning and be back before dinner?"

"Yes, yes!" said Rita.

"You wouldn't talk to strangers or go on side trips?"

"Of course not," Tendai said.

"Well . . ." The man lay back with his head pillowed on a heap of cut grass. The automatic lawn mower whirred unhappily from where Rita had tied it to a tree. "I happen to know both your parents are leaving early tomorrow and won't be back till dark."

"Really?" said Rita.

"But we have to have permission," Tendai put in. "I'm not going behind Father's back."

Rita started to argue, but the Mellower held up his hand. "If I ask him, he'll give permission."

"I don't understand," said Tendai, who had never seen the Praise Singer do anything except cower in front of Father.

"If I did it during Praise," the man added.

Then Tendai understood. He remembered the sleepy, foolish feeling he had had after Praise. The Mellower intended to hypnotize Father! "That's dishonest."

"No, it isn't!" cried Rita. "He'll give his permission. Who cares how it's done? Oh, don't you see this is the only way we'll ever get out? Do you want to grow a *beard* before you learn how to ride a bus?"

"Please! Please!" Kuda said, looking up at his big brother.

It was Tendai's turn to stare into the distance and think. What would it be like to go outside the way everyone else did and fly—all alone, without bodyguards or the police or Father—to a magical place none of them had seen before? As he thought, the warm, excited feeling he had had that morning returned. His ancestors waited in the shadows of the walled garden. One of them raised the hollowed horn of a kudu bull to his lips and blew, to give courage to the hunters.

"Wake up. You're *dwaal*ing again," said Rita.

Tendai shook himself. "Let's do it," he said.

The rest of the day passed rapidly. Rita wanted to program the computer to say they'd already done the homework, and Tendai firmly told her no. Grumbling, she applied herself to memorizing the anatomy of a frog. Kuda practiced his writing. Tendai studied algebra, a subject he found soothing. You always knew when you had the right answer in math.

Tendai, Rita and Kuda were as perfect as they could manage the next morning. Rita even held in her stomach for the time it took Father to inspect them. Breakfast passed without mishaps.

"I'm afraid you're on your own today," Mother said as the dishes were cleared away. "I've promised to entertain a delegation from China. Your father has a meeting with the President, and we'll have dinner with her tonight. I'm sorry you can't come."

"That's all right," Rita said cheerfully.

"Let's see. I programmed the pantry—the floor was sticky next to the door. Do you know anything about that?"

"The automatic mop must be running out of soap. I'll check it." Rita gave Mother a wide-eyed, innocent look.

"Well, I don't have time to check it myself. Should we skip the Mellower this morning, Amadeus?"

Father glanced at the ancestor clock. Tendai, Rita and Kuda sat with their hands clasped tightly below the tablecloth. "We have forty-five minutes," he rumbled. He nodded at the butler robot, who wheeled down the hall to find the Praise Singer.

Isn't that typical? thought Tendai. The one morning when it matters, he's late as usual. The ancestor clock chimed the quarter hour. After a time—it was probably only five minutes—the Mellower appeared at the door, bowing, apologizing and calling himself a bad boy.

If he forgot the time, he probably forgot about the permission, too, Tendai thought. And indeed, the first part of the Praise was no different from the way it was any other morning. It changed, however, after Father and Mother had fallen under its spell. Tendai felt guilty. We wouldn't have to do this if they weren't so hard to reason with, he thought.

Gradually, subtly, the Mellower drew Father's attention to his duty to pass courage on to his children. And how better than an exercise in self-reliance? Father nodded with his eyes half-closed. Tendai watched the Praise Singer produce a letter giving them permission to go on the Scout trip. Father signed it. The Mellower obtained two Pass Cards for the gate, one for the departure and another for when they returned. He even talked Father out of money for bus fare. All this happened without a break in rhythm. The poetry flowed on; the Praise threw its shining coils around both parents. Tendai was amazed.

Finally, it wound down and seemed to fade away into that magic realm from which it came. Mother stretched her arms and said, "Mmm."

The ancestor clock chimed the hour.

"*Maiwee!* We're late!" cried Father. The stretch limo hummed on the antigrav pad. How long had it been ready? Tendai wondered. Father and Mother both ran out the door, with Mother pausing an instant to give them a quick smile. The limo took off at once. The house was theirs—and the Pass Cards, permission slip and money lay on the table! The Mellower sat in Father's chair, with his feet on the tablecloth. Tendai was vaguely shocked.

"No push-ups for you!" shouted Kuda, dancing around.

"I'm glad you're on *our* side," Rita said, folding her napkin and placing it neatly on the table. "Well, don't sit there *dwaal*ing, Tendai. Let's make a break for it."

"Do you want me to pin the money inside your pocket?" said the Mellower.

"No!" Tendai said.

"Silly me! Of course you're too old for that. All of you are too old, even Kuda."

Tendai looked at his little brother, who was dressed in his best shorts and shirt. He had had a steak knife stuck in his belt until Rita took it away.

"I don't think Kuda should come," Tendai said slowly.

"You promised!" shouted Kuda.

"I know, but parts of the city aren't safe."

"A Scout keeps his word! You promised."

"You can't go on a Scout trip if you haven't joined," Tendai said.

"I'll be a Cub next year. I'm just as brave as you. Tell him, Mellower."

"You're a little lion!" The Mellower picked up Kuda and swung him around. Kuda roared fiercely. Around and around they went, with Rita shrieking encouragement. The Praise Singer collapsed on the rug with Kuda and Rita on top.

"More! More!" yelled the little boy. Tendai felt his heart sink. It was hopeless to expect the Mellower to back him up. He always said what people wanted to hear.

"You'll have to do everything I say," Tendai told his brother.

"Yes, *sir*!" said Kuda, in perfect imitation of one of Father's soldiers. The Mellower puffed with exhaustion as he picked himself up from the rug.

"All present and accounted for, *sir*!" Rita shouted, standing at attention. "Kit bag inspected! Map, compass, rations all in order! *Fall in, troops!*" She marched around the room, swinging her arms.

Tendai knew the situation had gotten out of control. "All right," he sighed. "The route's marked on the map. We'll go to Mbare Musika first. Rita, keep an eye on Kuda. I think he should stay home, but it's only for a few hours." He shouldered his backpack.

Sunlight filled the orderly garden with its trimmed walks and hedges. Tendai found himself looking at each detail as they left. I hope Father doesn't remember what he did during Praise, he thought. The Mellower says he won't—but who knows?

The Praise Singer slid the Pass Card into the gate slot. He pressed the hold button on the weapons detector, so Tendai could take his Scout knife out with him. It was a wonderful knife with a gold-washed blade and red dragons curled around the handle. Father had brought it to him from China. "You're going to have a wonderful time!" called the Mellower.

Tendai looked back at him, framed in the gate. For one second he wanted to run back to the safety of the walled garden, but then the Praise Singer closed the opening. They were alone. The wind ruffled the shadow of trees on the sidewalk.

"We're on our own," said Tendai as he led Rita and Kuda up the steps to the bus stop.

4

Mother lightened the window of the stretch limo and looked down on the city beneath. Mount Hampden passed on their right, glittering with solar panels to catch the energy of the sun. That's a nice place to live, she thought. Still, it was hard to find fault with Mazoe, and the crime rate was certainly low. Not that anyone with half a brain would bother General Matsika. She smiled fondly at her husband.

What was it the Mellower said? The General was a great tree whose branches protected them—or something like that. The Mellower certainly knew how to put things. She was lucky to have a live-in Praise Singer. Amadeus was suspicious at first. He thought compliments were for sissies, but he changed his mind after the first few sessions.

The limo changed direction and headed for the University. The Chinese delegation was suffering from rocket lag and wouldn't show up for another hour. She had time for a leisurely cup of tea. Mother sighed with contentment.

Now they were passing over the gray ruin of Dead Man's Vlei. Mother looked regretfully at the ancient mountains of garbage. What a shame so much land went to waste in the middle of the city, but what could one do? It had been contaminated with toxic chemicals over a century ago.

They said people lived in Dead Man's Vlei. Not nice people. Not people she'd invite for tea in Mazoe. Mother wondered idly what the children were up to. They were so restless in the hot weather. Tendai kept nagging about a Scout trip.

Wait a minute, thought Mother. Something happened during the Mellower's session this morning. It was odd how difficult it was to remember what the man said. It was pleasant, of course. She could listen all day, but often she couldn't remember *why* she felt happy.

The Scout trip. Something about the Scout trip. She looked over at Amadeus and saw him frown as though he, too, were trying to remember. In her mind's eye, Mother saw two cards on the dining room table. Amadeus had placed them there. They were—oh *Mwari*!—Pass Cards.

Mother and Father looked up at each other at the same time. "Curse that Mellower!" shouted Father. "Turn this limo at once!"

The chauffeur flew a figure eight as he reacted to the General's furious voice. Then he straightened out and made a beeline for Mazoe. The General sent a message on the limo's computer to seal the gates of his house.

Tendai, Rita and Kuda fought their way down the steps of the bus stop. "Hold on!" shouted Tendai over the noise of the crowd. Kuda clung to Rita, and she grabbed Tendai's hand so hard he winced.

"I never saw so many people!" Rita cried. "Ow! That woman just stepped on my foot!"

Tendai grimly led them through the mob. People struggled past them with bags of groceries balanced on their heads. A trussed-up chicken stuck its head out of a sack and watched them mournfully as it was carried past. "It's like being squeezed in a toothpaste tube," gasped Rita.

At last they reached the bottom and made their way to an empty area under a platform. It was shady, but foul with rotting vegetables and debris from the meat market. A huge rat considered them with its flat black eyes before bending again to gnaw on a bone.

"A *rat!*" cried Rita in delight. "I've never seen one outside a book. Do you think it's tame?"

"Don't touch it!" yelled Tendai, slapping her hand.

"You bully! How dare you hit me?"

"That's not a tame animal. Look at the marks it's making on that bone."

The rat continued scrunching bits of sinew and meat. It lifted its muzzle and chittered at them.

"He thinks you want his dinner," said Tendai.

"Very funny." Rita threw a chunk of bread from her backpack at the animal. It gobbled it up and waited for more. "See. It *is* tame." She threw it another chunk. The rat finished this and waited. When no more food came, it walked deliberately toward her. Tendai tried to pull her back, but Rita stubbornly held her ground. The rat suddenly leaped for her shoe and scrabbled its paws on her leg as it squealed with rage.

"Help!" shrieked Rita, kicking wildly. Tendai swung his backpack and caught the animal by surprise. It spun around on the cement and bumped into a pillar. At once it sprang up and hurled itself at Rita, but Tendai struck it again. The rat clung to the backpack. He swung it against a wall, knocking the animal senseless. It flopped onto a mass of cabbage leaves.

He didn't know whether it was dead or merely stunned, and he didn't care. He dragged Rita and Kuda back to the noisy crowd before anything worse happened. They found another pocket of calm behind a chili-bite stall. Rita was trembling with shock.

"Animals aren't supposed to do that," she wailed. "It was tame. I fed it."

"We aren't used to wild creatures," said Tendai.

"Rita's a wimp," said Kuda.

"Don't you start. If you had a big rat on your foot, you'd wet your pants."

"I'd kill it with a Scout knife."

Tendai ignored him. Kuda, in spite of his brave words, hung on to Rita's hand as though he were welded to her. "Look, you can get a badge for observing wild animals," Tendai told his sister.

Rita lifted her tear-streaked face.

"We've only been gone a few minutes and already you have a badge. Think how many you'll have at the end of the day. Would you like a chili-bite?"

She wiped her eyes. The heavy smell of fried dough filled the space behind the stall. "Mmm," she murmured.

"Ugh! Look at your pack," said Kuda.

Tendai saw with horror that a chunk had been ripped out by the rat's teeth. A damp patch had to be urine. "I'll wash it in the public rest room." He sighed. "Come on. We all need to cheer up." They went to the front of the stall, where a man tended a pot of boiling oil. Trays of greasy chili-bites cooled on mats of newspaper.

"Could we watch you make some?" asked Tendai.

"Sure," the man said. "How many do you want?"

"Lots," said Rita.

So Tendai ordered two dozen. The vendor spooned blobs of batter into the pot of oil, where they hissed and bubbled with a satisfying roar. He turned them with a slotted spoon. The chili-bites were filled with onions and shreds of hot peppers. The smell was maddening. The man dumped them on a newspaper-covered tray. "That's my table under the tree," he said as he accepted Tendai's money. "Bring the tray back when you're finished."

They sat in the shade, devouring the hot fried dough. Their faces gleamed with oil, and the chilies brought tears to their eyes. "This is *living*," said Rita. "Let's get something to drink."

Tendai brought them cups of freshly squeezed pineapple juice. They lazed under the tree, feeling slightly sick but satisfied. Tendai rinsed his pack under the chili-bite vendor's faucet. The huge market of Mbare Musika no longer seemed threatening. It hummed with laughter and shouts like a big party. Buses took off from the Central Depot, going to all points of the city, going farther to Mozambique and Kenya and even Gondwanna, in the north.

Long sunshades covered the various markets. Each street was devoted to a different product: fruit, vegetables, clothes, crockery and soap. Meat sellers slapped sides of beef to dislodge flies and show off their wares. *Ngangas* squatted before heaps of roots and herbs. They wore feathered caps banded with wildcat fur and smoked long pipes as they dozed in the heat. There were even a few public Mellowers.

Each Praise Singer had his own booth with a comfortable couch. When someone felt depressed and needed a quick Praise, he gave the Mellower a brief rundown of his best points. The person would lie down on the couch while the Praise Singer created a poem about him.

Tendai, Rita and Kuda watched as closely as they dared. The poems started out in the standard way, but once the Mellower got going, he added the desired compliments. It didn't matter, Tendai thought, whether the Praise was true or not. Once the listener fell under the spell, he accepted it all as his due. Potbellied men were praised for their lean, hard muscles. Skinny, bitter-looking women were told how plump and kind they were.

And the extraordinary thing was that people began to *look* like their descriptions—for a few minutes, at least.

"This is boring," said Rita. "Can't we do something else?"

"He's not as good as *our* Mellower," Kuda said.

Tendai led them along the rows of fruit and vegetables. The sun was climbing—they had been at the Mbare Musika at least an hour. They would have to leave soon if they were to get to Beatrice and back before dark. But Tendai found he didn't want to go. Mbare Musika was so full of life.

He realized he was happy, and he hadn't known he was sad before. He liked the noise and the smells, both good and bad, and the faces, both innocent and crafty. He liked being surrounded by people. He liked them in all their shapes and dispositions simply because they were people and not machines.

"Look," cried Kuda. They were walking along the animal pens. Vendors haggled over goats and chickens. Fancy show cats yawned contemptuously at the crowds that milled around them. But on a table at the end, all by itself, sat a most amazing creature.

It was blue. Its fur stood out in a handsome ruff around its face, and its tail hung down almost to the ground. It wore a leather collar attached to a chain. Its owner, who had a surprising number of bandages on various parts of his body, sat glumly in a chair and smoked a cigarette.

"That's a genetically engineered monkey," said Tendai in wonder.

"I thought they were illegal," Rita said.

"They are."

The Blue Monkey reached out a long arm and snatched the cigarette from its owner's mouth. The man tried to retrieve it, but the monkey bared its teeth at him. It calmly began to puff on the cigarette itself. "What are *you* staring at, roach face?" it snarled.

"It talks!" Rita cried.

"Of course I do, when I have someone worth talking to. Not him." The Blue Monkey spat in the direction of its owner. Two other men had stopped at the table. One of them flicked a peanut at the animal.

"When I want a peanut, I'll go to the market and buy one!" shouted the monkey in a rage. "Get me a hamburger, you tightwads!" The men laughed.

Tendai noticed, out of the corner of his eye, that one was burly like a prizefighter while the other was slender and somehow unpleasant. But he was far too interested in the animal to pay much attention. "I thought genetically engineered monkeys were illegal," he said.

"They are now," said the owner, "but you can hardly kill off the ones already made."

"Not that you haven't tried," the monkey said bitterly. "Look at the swill he feeds me: black bananas they can't sell in the market."

"Go on! You eat better than I do."

"Lies! Lies!" shrieked the monkey. "I earn all the money, and he drinks it away. He passes out in the gutter every night, and I have to fight the rats off him!"

"You poor thing," cried Rita.

"You said it, sweetheart. I'm the unhappiest creature alive. Too bright for my cousins in the bush. Too bright for this lump of donkey doodoo. Why don't *you* buy me, sugar? You look like a nice kid."

"Oh, Tendai, could we?" said Rita.

Tendai thought about how Father would react to the foul-mouthed animal—or, for that matter, Mother, with her tasteful tea parties. It was almost worth it.

"Please!" Kuda said excitedly. "He can stay in the garden."

"Yeah, the garden," said the monkey, fixing Tendai with its bright, intelligent eyes.

If they got the monkey, they would have to go straight home. Tendai couldn't see their taking it all over the city.

"I'm housebroken. I play the harmonica. I'm a barrel of laughs. Come into the back so we can talk business." The animal tugged at Tendai's sleeve.

He allowed himself to be pulled behind a wall, while the owner followed with a hangdog look. Rita and Kuda danced along with the Blue Monkey. They found themselves in a dimly lit area like the place Rita encountered the rat.

"Wait. Why can't we talk about this outside?" said Tendai, but instantly the monkey sank its teeth into his hand. Rita and Kuda screamed as the two men—who had silently followed behind—pounced on them and stuffed rags into their faces. Tendai struggled with the monkey, but the owner threw his arm around Tendai's throat and plastered a rag to his face, too. His lungs burned and his legs turned to jelly.

Chloroform, he thought as the pain faded and he fell to the garbage on the ground.

5

The Blue Monkey sat on the table and scratched itself. Its owner slumped in a chair at the side. The prizefighter carried two grain bags while the smaller, weasel-like man only had one. "I get ten percent," said the monkey.

"When the She Elephant sells them," said the small man.

"Don't make me wait too long. Remember, I can't go to jail if I squeal. I'm only a dumb animal."

"You can go to a laboratory," the small man said pleasantly.

"Ha, ha. Give me an advance so I can keep him in beer." The monkey jabbed a toe at its owner. The small man fished a fifty-dollar bill from his pocket.

"Let's get out before the chloroform wears off," urged the prizefighter. The monkey quickly tucked the money into its collar and snapped its teeth when the owner tried to take it. The two men shouldered their loads and headed for the nearest bus stop. They were on the last bus to take off before the police surrounded Mbare Musika.

Mother was sitting with a damp handkerchief twisted in her fingers. The dining room table had been cleared to make space for a computer. The police chief frowned as he clicked in information. "I can't keep my men away from their duties much longer," he said to Father.

"My children are missing!" Father shouted.

"Please understand me, General. Millions of people take public transport every day. No harm comes to them. I know you're worried, and I'm certainly checking all the buses, but isn't it too soon to panic?"

"You don't understand! These aren't just any children. The Masks would fall all over themselves to get them. Besides"—Father looked embarrassed—"they've never been on a bus."

The police chief stared at him in amazement. "The oldest one's thirteen!"

"I know. I know. I meant to give them freedom. You understand how it is. First they're babies. Then, when they walk, you worry about them falling into swimming pools and so forth. It was so easy to keep them here, hire tutors—don't look at me like that! I have lots of enemies."

"I wasn't criticizing," the police chief said mildly.

"When I was a boy, gangs were everywhere. I saw my brothers gunned down in the yard. I swore I would never expose my children to danger like that."

"Surely you, of all people, know gangs are almost extinct."

Father got up and paced around the room. Mother saw he was remembering the long war against crime when he was a young officer. The trouble with Amadeus, she thought, was that he had to be *doing* something. Waiting for the children to come home was completely foreign to his nature.

"I made Tendai weak," Father said.

"He's probably a lot stronger than you imagine," said the police chief.

Mother looked out the window. A group of policemen were clustered around a guava tree. The branches quivered. The policemen had shouted themselves hoarse and were clearly losing their tempers. They formed a circle around the tree and began to shake it violently. Ripe guavas plopped onto the lawn.

"It's that damn Mellower's fault," Father said. "He gave the children everything they wanted. He tricked me!"

The policemen were shaking the trunk so hard, Mother could hear it crack. All at once she heard a shriek, and the Mellower dropped out of the branches.

"Were you able to get any sense out of your Praise Singer before he, er, took to the trees?" asked the police chief.

Father looked sheepish. Mother glanced at the smashed glass on the rug, the bits of shattered chair near the wall. No, she thought, Amadeus hadn't handled that well at all. It took an hour to get more than a frightened squeak out of the man.

"What do you plan to do with him?" the police chief said.

"Drop him in the Lion Park. I'm sure they like poetry."

Mother looked up to see the police dragging in the disheveled Mellower. She was shocked to see his shirt was torn and his hands scratched. His lower lip puffed out, giving him a sulky expression.

"Amadeus, they didn't—" she began.

"Don't waste your pity on him!" Father yelled at her. "This isn't one of your tea parties! Do you want me to feed him cookies? Poor Mellower," he said in a wheedling tone. "Is he feeling out of sorts? Is he anxious? *Does he want to be the main course at the crocodile farm?* Find my children if you want to see the sun rise!" Father lifted the Mellower right off the ground and shook him. The Praise Singer began to whimper.

"Fah!" said Father, dropping him. "I can't keep it up. It's like kicking a puppy."

And indeed, Mother thought, the Mellower looked just like a little dog that had been scolded for making a mess on the carpet. "He can't think if he's frightened," she said gently. "Let me talk to him. Alone."

"You always stick up for people," said Father, making it sound like a vice. But he took the police chief and his men out to the front lawn.

Mother waited patiently until the man stopped sniffling. She sent the butler robot for tea with cream and sugar. The Praise Singer's cup rattled against the saucer as he drank.

"Now," said Mother, "take a deep breath. No one's going to hurt you. When we're finished, you can go off to your room for a nap. I'm sure this is just as upsetting to you as to us."

"You're so kind," said the Mellower. "You're the kindest person I know—like a refreshing breeze drifting in the window when it's hot or a sparkling fountain in a garden—"

"*Please!* No Praise! This isn't the time. I want you to tell me everything that happened before the children left."

"I—I tried."

"I know you did," Mother said encouragingly. "We were all a little excited. Now that you're relaxed, it will be easy to remember. Tell me everything, even if you think it isn't important."

So the Mellower described how he swung Kuda around and how Rita danced with glee. Mother had to swallow hard as she listened. She didn't believe—yet—that the children were in danger, but it was very worrying not to know where they were.

"They argued about taking Kuda," the man said. "Tendai thought he was too young, but the others shouted him down. Then—then he said they were going to Mbare Musika. Yes! That was it! They went to Mbare Musika! And they were going on to Beatrice."

"Wonderful!" Mother cried. "What else?"

But the Praise Singer couldn't recall anything else. "I have a suggestion," he said shyly as Mother rose to go.

She thought now he looked like a puppy that had successfully retrieved a ball. He almost wagged his tail.

"In stories, if someone gets lost, people hire a detective."

"A what?" said Mother.

"A sleuth, a gumshoe, a private eye."

"I never heard those words."

"They're used in children's books. I read a lot of children's books."

Yes, thought Mother, I'll bet you do.

"Anyhow, one day when I had nothing better to do, I checked the holophone directory for detectives. There's only one agency in Harare. It's called the Ear, the Eye and the Arm. It's in the Cow's Guts." Having delivered the ball, the Mellower sat back expectantly.

"Thank you. You're very clever," Mother said. "That's a brilliant idea." The Mellower sat up proudly and grinned. Really, he's almost a child himself, she thought. And he needs Praise just as much as the rest of us. Somehow she never thought of his having needs.

Mother told Amadeus about Mbare Musika and then, in her study, contacted the Ear, the Eye and the Arm Detective Agency.

Tendai was having a nightmare. He was sick and dizzy, crammed into a small space. He was surrounded by a hot, scratchy material. He thought he was going to vomit, and realized to his horror he had already done so.

A voice came from somewhere outside. "I don't take this bus any farther."

"Here's fifty dollars that says you do," said another voice.

"Sure. Get me onto Dead Man's Vlei, and I might as well give you the bus. Get out of here before I press the panic button."

Tendai felt himself swing into the air. That made him ill again. By the time he had recovered, he was on the ground and jouncing along at a great rate.

"I should have cut his throat," said a third voice from outside.

"Stuff it, Knife," said the person who was carrying Tendai. "We'd have cops on us like flies on your granny."

"Don't you insult my granny!" shouted Knife. "She's the best woman in the world."

"How come she keeps trying to turn us in?"

"That proves how good she is, Fist. She doesn't like low-down crooks."

"I'll never understand you," said Fist.

Tendai went over the last moments at Mbare Musika. These must be the men who threw peanuts at the Blue Monkey. That rotten monkey! Tendai understood how betrayed Rita felt when the rat attacked her. Rita, he thought. Where is she? And Kuda?

He felt gently around the bag and found a Rita-sized lump pressing against the cloth. Tendai still had his Scout knife, so he carefully cut a small opening and looked out. To the right, also bouncing along on Fist's back, was a second bag. Farther away, Knife carried a third one.

So they were all together. Tendai could rip through the cloth and yell for help—except that he didn't see people or buildings through the hole. They were being carried through a vast wasteland. Greasy gray hills rose on either side. The ground squelched under Fist's heavy feet, and his footprints filled with sludge. Everything looked impossibly used and discouraged.

This must be Dead Man's Vlei, thought Tendai. He didn't know anything about it, except that the bus driver refused to land there. What do I do now? he thought. I can't abandon Rita and Kuda. It struck Tendai that Father had been right all along: the minute they got outside, they *had* been kidnapped. Father will be furious when he finds out, thought Tendai with a lump in his throat. He'll blame me. I wonder *why* Fist and Knife want to carry us off.

So far, neither man had mentioned where they were going. Will they hold us for ransom? wondered Tendai.

Maybe we're going to be *slaves*! The Mellower had told them about such things in bedtime stories.

The slave trade once flourished in Africa, the Praise Singer said. It still existed in Gondwanna. Children sent out to herd goats were snapped up by evil traders, loaded onto camels and taken to far cities where they suffered horribly. In the Mellower's stories, these children always escaped and wound up rich and happy. It sounded exciting, but right now, in the first part of the story—the suffering part—Tendai thought he would rather be home and bored.

Still, the idea of a real adventure lifted his spirits. He made another opening in the bag, next to Fist's belt. The belt was a crude twist of sisal. Tendai cut through it except for a few strands.

"I don't see the She Elephant," said Knife, startling Tendai so much he almost severed the belt completely.

"She's in the *shebeen*. Smell the pineapples?" Fist said. Even through the bag Tendai picked up the reek of overripe fruit.

"Come forth, my beauty!" shouted Fist. "Your glances stick to my heart like peanut butter to the gums!"

Knife cried, "See what gifts we bring, oh, generously shaped one, whose neck a louse may not climb without a rest—"

"Hold your noise!" said a cross voice that seemed to come out of the earth. "Nag, nag, nag! The minute I sit down. Never a moment's peace. Wait up, you *tsotsis*."

Knife and Fist laughed and shook out their bags. Tendai, Rita and Kuda fell onto the ground. Tendai pretended to be unconscious, but Rita scrambled to her feet and shrieked, "You booboo heads! Wait'll my father gets his hands on you! You'll need a rocket ship to stay ahead of him!"

"Squeaks loudly, doesn't she?" remarked Fist.

"If I'm a mouse, you're a dirty old rat in a pile of rotten meat bones! Take us home at once!" screamed Rita.

Tendai saw, through half-closed eyes, that Kuda was sitting up and holding his head. The little boy seemed too dazed to speak.

"Look what you did to him!" Rita yelled, hauling Kuda to his feet. "You're going to prison *forever*!"

"Sounds like Granny," said Fist.

"Yes, she does," replied Knife with grudging admiration.

Tendai flopped over to bring himself near Rita and Kuda, but he pretended to be too weak to stand. "What did you do to *him*?" demanded Rita. "He'd better be okay. If you so much as chipped a *toenail*, Father'll chew you up like a lion's dinner!"

"Who is this Father you keep squeaking about?" said Knife in a bored voice.

"No, don't tell him," whispered Tendai, grasping Rita by the ankle.

But she stamped her foot angrily. "General Matsika, that's who. You don't think you're so clever now."

The two men did seem stunned by this news. "Oh, mother," said Fist.

"Oh, Granny," murmured Knife.

Tendai lunged at Fist and yanked his pant leg. The belt parted; the pants fell down. Fist struggled to grab them, and Tendai pulled his leg out from under him. "Run!" he shouted at Rita and Kuda. Rita reacted at once. She bounded over the *vlei* with a speed surprising for her plumpness. Knife started after her.

Kuda tried to run, but he couldn't keep up on his short legs. As Tendai went by, he scooped the little boy into his arms. The added weight slowed him terribly.

Fist tripped over his pants again and fell with a splat on the ground. He hit his head on a rock and lay still. Knife, a much smaller and more fit man, zigzagged after Rita as she darted around hillocks and bushes. He roared at her to stop, and she yelled insults back. Tendai thought, as he struggled with Kuda, that Rita never knew when to leave well enough alone. Every time she turned to scream, she lost some of the distance between herself and Knife.

Then Tendai lost sight of them behind a hill. He swung down a valley and up again. His side stabbed with pain. His lungs couldn't get enough air. His legs threatened to collapse. He rounded another hill and threw himself into a hollow in the ground. Kuda, bug-eyed with terror, seemed about to scream.

"Don't," gasped Tendai, covering his brother's mouth with his hand. "Hide."

Kuda seemed to understand. He clamped his mouth shut and stared solemnly at Tendai. They listened to the wind rustling the heaps of trash—because now that Tendai had time to rest, he saw that the hills, the ground and everything was a mass of packed garbage. The springiness of the earth was caused by thousands and thousands of plastic bags. Tendai was awed.

Plastic hadn't been used for a hundred years, not since the energy famine of the twenty-first century. He had seen plastic bowls and cups in museums, but the raw material lay all around them here. It was torn and greasy and caked with mud, but it was still *plastic*.

After he had caught his breath, Tendai stood up and pulled Kuda to his feet. "Let's go," he whispered, but froze at once. Up from the lonely hills, drifting on the wind, came a woman's voice.

"Catch children," it boomed, deep down from the earth itself. "Catch children. Bring them to meeeee." The wind blew it away. Tendai hoisted Kuda to his back, and the little boy clasped his arms around his big brother's neck.

"Bring them to meeeee," called the far deep voice. Tendai stumbled on, trying to ignore the ache in his legs.

Kuda screamed. "The ground is moving!"

Tendai saw—and almost fell, so great was his terror—that chunks of the ground that he took for trash *stood up*. They moved toward him from all sides. Even down in the hollow where they had just hidden, a lump detached itself and crept up the side.

"Mama! Mama!" Kuda screamed. Tendai turned desperately, trying to find an opening, but the creatures were all around. They moved toward him with a shambling gait. They had eyes—

They were people. Tendai watched them slowly turn from nameless horrors to human beings like himself. "It's all right, Kuda," he whispered. "They're like us."

"They're *tokoloshes*! Demons!" sobbed Kuda.

"No, it's all right," murmured Tendai, lowering his brother to the ground. "Look at them. They're just very muddy." Kuda clung to his brother, but he seemed less panic-stricken. Tendai took out his knife and pointed it toward the nearest person, an old man with a floppy hat the same color and texture as the ground. "Don't touch us," he said quietly. "We'll go back with you. Just don't touch us."

hen the holophone rang at the Ear, the Eye and the Arm Detective Agency, all three men sprang to answer it. Arm won, as he always did. His long black snaky arm far outreached anyone else's. Besides, the tips of his fingers were slightly sticky.

"Hello! Detective agency. You lose 'em, we find 'em. Sneaky husbands our specialty," he cried. Ear folded his sensitive ears, and a look of pain crossed his face.

"Sorry," said Arm, lowering his voice.

"I—I need your help," said Mother on the holoscreen.

"You came to the right place," Arm said. "Nobody else can do what we do. We can hear a bat burp in the basement. We can see a gnat's navel on a foggy night. Hunches stick to us like gum to your shoe. Got a sneaky husband?"

"Of course not," Mother said with surprise. "I'm married to General Amadeus Matsika."

"Ouch," murmured Ear with his ears folded in like morning glories. Eye blinked, a longer process with him than with most people.

"I can't explain on the phone," said Mother. "If you're not busy, could I send the stretch limo to pick you up? Please don't be busy," she added with a tremor Arm picked up at once.

"At your service. We'll rearrange our appointments," the detective said graciously.

"Oh, thank you," Mother cried. She hung up.

The men smiled at one another. The area in front of the holophone showed a desk neatly piled with papers, a swivel chair and what appeared to be a diploma on the wall. Close up, the diploma turned out to be a gift certificate from Mr. Thirsty's Beer Hall. Just out of holoscreen range were a sink full of dirty dishes, a muddle of food containers and a sagging couch. Hanging on the wall were the only things of value in the whole office: three Nirvana guns, obtained at great expense when the detectives opened their office. They had been fired only once at the police training range.

"Do you want me to rearrange the appointments?" said Eye. Arm nodded, so Eye took down the calendar and erased *Take clothes to laundry* and wrote in *Important case for General Matsika* instead.

"She didn't ask how much we charged. That's always a good sign," remarked Ear.

"But what can Matsika want that he can't get?" Arm said. "He can call in the police, the army and the secret service. If he says 'boo,' a mugger at the other end of the city drops a wallet."

Eye fitted on dark glasses in preparation for going outside. "Perhaps it's a question of being too powerful."

"What do you mean?" Ear settled muffs over his ears to protect them from the noisy streets.

"What happens if an ant bites a lion on the toe?" said Eye. "The lion roars, but the ant scurries into a hole. The lion can't find it. He's too big."

"So you're saying there's a whole world running around under General Matsika's feet that he can't reach," said Ear as he looked into the cracked mirror over the dirty dishes. His muffs were getting bald in spots.

"We know that's true," said Eye soberly. "You have only to look at the Cow's Guts."

"Come on. We don't want to miss the limo," Arm said.

The three men strapped on the Nirvana guns and triple-checked the locks on the office. Arm braced himself for the assault of sensations from the street. He was the only one who couldn't protect himself, although the thick adobe walls of the office made life somewhat bearable. The others walked on either side as if to shelter him, but there was nothing they could really do. Arm almost cried out as the door opened and the tangle of emotions rushed in.

Ear, his ears safely nestled in the ragged muffs, could listen to the outside world without pain. Eye was able to look around confidently: ninety-five percent of his eyesight was blocked out. Arm had to suffer the hate, greed and anger boiling around the suburb known as the Cow's Guts. Only an occasional whiff of kindness, like a pale flower wilting in an alley, softened his pain. Ear and Eye half carried him. Gradually, Arm adjusted, as one adjusts to the sound of a jackhammer, but he was never really comfortable.

They stood on the limo landing pad and looked out at the Cow's Guts. The streets rioted in all directions, twisting around in a confusing way. Newcomers always got lost, to the delight of the muggers. Stolen goods were sold openly here. Drugs were bought as easily as bananas. Beer halls blasted music that made everyone's ribs rattle, but here and there, among the pickpockets and dealers, a family struggled to survive. These were people from the villages who couldn't afford anything better. Children sailed boats down the fetid gutters and flew kites between the beer hall signs.

Here, too, came the beggars after their day's work in the wealthy suburbs. Legless men pushed themselves on little carts. Women with milky eyes led children whose hands stuck out like wings from their shoulders. After dark, these people settled in alleys, where they built cook fires and where they sang and danced.

Ear, Eye and Arm often looked down on these fires and imagined they were back in the distant village of their childhood.

Suddenly, the streets of the Cow's Guts began to empty all around the pad. People disappeared into doorways with magical speed. Eye laughed as he pointed to General Matsika's limo settling down toward the antigrav units. The government symbol, a black Zimbabwe bird on a green-and-red background, was clearly marked on the side.

"They think it's a raid. What wonderful quiet," Ear said.

"Are you the detectives? Yes, you'd have to be," said the chauffeur after the door sprang open. "Do you have a permit for those guns?"

Arm produced the license, but he still had to hand the weapons to the chauffeur for safekeeping. "No weapons allowed at the Matsikas," the chauffeur explained. "Say, would you mind sitting in the back? No offense, but you guys give me the creeps."

Ear, Eye and Arm didn't take offense—or not much. They were used to startling people, except in the Cow's Guts. In the Cow's Guts a person could have green wings and purple horns: no one would be the least surprised.

Mother had seen the detectives on the holoscreen, but she couldn't help jumping when they appeared close up. "I—I'm sorry," she stammered. "I haven't seen anyone like you before."

"There isn't anyone like us," said Arm. He extended his hand, and Mother, with only a tiny pause, shook it. She felt the strangest sensation as she grasped the fingers—and not only because they were slightly sticky. It was like touching an electric dynamo. Somewhere inside, energy hummed and might leap out at her. She was relieved when Arm let go.

Eye removed his dark glasses, and Ear took off his muffs. The three men stood in front of Mother and let her take a long look. Ear, who was white, unfolded his ears. They opened out like huge flowers, pink and almost transparent. Eye, who was brown, blinked his huge eyes, which were all pupil inside and no white. Arm, who could just as well have been called Leg, stretched out his long black limbs. He reminded Mother of a wall spider.

"How—how did you happen?" she asked.

Arm replied, "We all come from the village of Hwange, near the nuclear power plant."

"Oh yes," said Mother. "That's where the plutonium got into the drinking water."

"Our mothers drank it."

Mother stared at them. She knew about the accident, of course, in a distant sort of way. A few people died. Others got sick, but it had happened long ago. What must it have been like to have such babies? Hers had been so beautiful.

"Our parents were delighted when they found out what we could do," said Eye, blinking in a slow, unnerving way. "I could see a flea clinging to a hawk's feathers. My mother never lost anything."

"I could hear an ant creeping up on the sugar bowl," boasted Ear.

"And what could you do?" said Mother, bewildered by these strange creatures.

"I got hunches," Arm said. "I used to know when the baboons were planning to raid the fields. So you see, we were ideally suited to become detectives."

"Who are these people?" growled Father from the doorway. Ear closed his ears at once. Arm staggered back as though struck.

"Detectives," Mother replied. "They're going to look for the children."

"Humph." Father stalked around Ear, Eye and Arm, looking them over. "They wouldn't get into the army," he concluded.

"They have special abilities." Mother hastily explained what these were.

"Humph," said Father. Only Mother could tell the difference between the two humphs. The second meant he was actively interested in the men and was considering using their services. "You're hired," he said abruptly. Then he quickly produced pictures of the children, credit cards, maps of the city with phone numbers of the police stations, his own private number to be used day or night and a great deal of advice.

Almost before they knew it, Ear, Eye and Arm were handed their Nirvana guns and herded back to the limo. "Use the bus for business," Father said. "You'd scare witnesses away with the limo. Report to me six times a day. Good luck." He shook hands with each detective but paused and raised his eyebrows when he touched Arm.

The limo took off. He turned back to Mother. "It's bad news, I'm afraid. We traced them to a chili-bite stall, where they were charged three times the going price. No one else remembers them. They're like babies out there! Why, why didn't I let them grow up?" Father rubbed his eyes; he looked around sharply to be sure none of his officers saw him with his guard down.

"They're probably all right," Mother said, but she was beginning to be affected by Amadeus's gloom. The sun was settling toward the west. Shadows grew along the garden. If the children didn't come soon . . .

"That Arm has the funniest handshake," said Father, watching the shadows creep across the grass. "He's stronger than he looks, too."

endai kept Kuda close to him as they were herded back to the person known as the She Elephant. All around them, the mournful shapes of men and women rose from the ground or emerged from holes. Dead Man's Vlei wasn't empty at all.

They're like moths, Tendai thought. They've camouflaged themselves to fit their background.

And he wondered at their silence. They didn't laugh or talk. They didn't even make much noise as they shuffled across the ground. It's not surprising this place is called *dead*, he thought with a shudder.

They came down to a large flat field surrounded by hills. In the middle was a cooking area with a fireplace and stew pots. There were a few trestle tables and four or five old armchairs. An ancient woman sat in a rocking chair and sipped a mug of tea. Knife stood by her, his hand clamped on Rita's arm. Fist scowled at Tendai as he went by. "Little rats," hissed the old woman as she rocked monotonously.

"Tendai!" shouted Rita. "Tell these old squashy banana faces to let us go!" She shook her arm, but Knife grimly held on. Tendai suddenly noticed the woman who was sitting in one of the armchairs. She was so large, he had thought she *was* an armchair. The woman stood up and planted her ham-like hands on her hips.

"So here are the other little squealers," she said in a deep, hearty voice. "Bring 'em up and let's see if they're big enough to eat!"

Tendai and Kuda were urged forward by the silent *vlei* people. "Don't you hurt my brother. He's only a baby," Tendai said.

"I am not!" yelled Kuda.

"My father'll lock you up for a thousand years!" Rita screamed.

The She Elephant roared with laughter. "They're Matsika's brats all right. Well, listen up, little squealers. This is my country. Your father comes snooping around, I'll run a train over him. You do what I say, and we'll get along fine. Now get down that hole and change your clothes."

She picked up Rita, who pounded vigorously on the big woman's back, and disappeared down a burrow. Tendai and Kuda were carried down another by Fist and Knife. They were dumped on the floor of a gloomy chamber, shucked out of their clothes and left a pile of rags to put on. Knife held the Scout knife up to admire the dragons before shoving it into his belt.

Tendai was trembling with shock and anger, but he tried to appear calm for Kuda's sake. "Let me help you get dressed," he said. "Ugh! These clothes are filthy!"

Kuda rummaged through the rags until he found a man's shirt with the sleeves torn off. "Nice," he commented. He smiled as Tendai buttoned it and tied a rag around him for a belt.

"It's like one of the Mellower's stories," Tendai said, smiling back, but he instantly regretted mentioning the Praise Singer.

"I want the Mellower," said Kuda with his face screwed up. "I don't like these other people."

"This is like a story, remember. We'll have lots of adventures and then go home."

"We will go home, won't we?"

"Of course. We're going to have fun." Tendai hoped his face didn't show how worried he was. Kuda seemed to accept his big brother's promise, because he immediately began to explore the chamber. It was hollowed out of the ground with tunnels leading out on all sides. A single candle trembled in a slight breeze. The walls and floor were a mishmash of plastic bags, dirt, grass roots and stones.

"Get up here!" shouted Fist down the tunnel that led to the surface. Tendai helped Kuda up the steep slope. He felt inexpressibly dirty in the rags. They had a dank smell that reminded him of an old refrigerator.

Rita was weeping on the ground by the She Elephant's chair. She wore a shapeless brown-gray dress with many patches. One side of her face was swollen, and her hair and hands were caked with dirt.

On the other hand, Rita had given nearly as good as she got: there were several deep scratches on the She Elephant's arms.

"Here. Sell these in the Cow's Guts." The She Elephant tossed the children's good clothes to Fist. She then washed Tendai's monkey bite with boiled water and applied disinfectant. "Someone should give that beast a teething ring," she said, shaking her head. "Sit down at the table, brats. You can eat something before you work."

Tendai and Kuda climbed onto a bench at the side of a trestle table. Rita, still sniffling, sat across from them. The She Elephant busied herself at the cooking pots. From one, filled with boiling water, she fished out three metal plates with a pair of tongs and clanged them onto the table. They steamed and dried in the afternoon sun. She plopped a ladle of *sadza* onto each plate and drenched it with sauce from a third pot.

Tendai had planned to reject food, the way heroes did in stories when they were captured by enemies, but the sauce smelled delicious. It was richly red with tomatoes, spicy with onions and garlic and laced with enough chilies to make his nose prickle. It won't do any good to get weak, he thought. Besides, Kuda won't eat unless I do, and it isn't good for little children to starve. So Tendai, not seeing any spoons or forks, broke off a piece of *sadza* with his fingers and popped it into his mouth. Kuda immediately copied him.

"It's *good*," said the little boy with his mouth full. "More!" The She Elephant filled his plate again when he was finished.

Tendai found himself eating as though he hadn't had anything for days. The tomatoes were more tomato-y, the onions stronger, even the salt more saltlike. And mixed with them was a hint of smoke from the She Elephant's fire. Maybe it's because we're eating outdoors, thought Tendai. Whatever it was, he found himself holding out his plate like Kuda and asking for more.

It was only when he finished the second helping that he looked up and saw that Rita hadn't touched her food. "Go on," he whispered. "It's delicious."

"I don't eat with my hands," sneered Rita. "And I don't eat without washing my hands. I'm not an animal."

"We're not at home. Please, Rita. Eat. You'll feel better."

"I don't lower *my* standards because I'm surrounded with riffraff."

"Riffraff, huh?" said the She Elephant, hugely amused. "You should see yourself in the mirror."

"I can't help what's on the outside, but inside I know what I'm worth. Not like some."

"Be quiet, Rita," whispered Tendai. He saw, with a sinking heart, where the argument was going. Rita was an incurable *shooper*er. A *shooper*er always said the one thing guaranteed to tip a friendly discussion into a quarrel. When everyone was tired of fighting and wanted to make peace, a *shooper*er said the one thing calculated to start the argument again.

"Rotten to the core," said Rita.

"You mean me, you little squealer?" snarled the She Elephant.

"I wouldn't know. I can't see past all that blubber."

The She Elephant snatched away Rita's plate and dumped the contents into the *sadza* pot. "You can eat rats for all I care!" she roared. "Now get off that bench. Around here, people work for a living." She plucked Rita from her seat and tucked her under one enormous arm. Tendai put his arm around Kuda. He didn't know what they were in for now.

Suddenly, he noticed that the *vlei* people had silently crept up to them while they were eating. They pressed in, almost like a tide in the ground. "Nice children," one of them said in a whispery voice.

"Poor babies," sighed an old woman, timidly reaching out her hand to touch Kuda.

"Back! Back!" shouted the She Elephant as Kuda screamed. "The afternoon shift isn't over. Get to work or you'll get no dinner!" Regretfully, the *vlei* people moved away as silently as they had come. They melted into the landscape on either side. Soon the *vlei* looked as deserted as a valley on the moon. The wind mournfully riffled the hills of garbage.

T
he She Elephant hustled them into a tunnel. Down, down they went, much farther than the chamber in which Tendai and Kuda had changed their clothes. The ground became muddy, and by the time the trail leveled out, they had to wade through water. The She Elephant put Rita down and switched on a flashlight. "Go on," she said.

Tendai hoisted Kuda to his back and followed. Tunnels branched and rebranched in a bewildering way. Water dripped from the ceiling. Knotted grass roots hung down and brushed them as they passed.

"We don't use this area in the rainy season," said the She Elephant. "You'd need fins to get around. Go up here." She indicated an upward tunnel with the flashlight. Tendai was relieved to find dry ground under his feet again. He put Kuda down. His legs still ached from his flight over the *vlei*.

They came to a large round chamber. The She Elephant took three lamps from a shelf in the wall. Tendai was intrigued. He had seen ones like them in history books. They were called kerosene lamps. The woman pumped and adjusted the fuel gauge on one until it hissed. She lit it, taking care not to set the screen surrounding the fuel outlet on fire. It gave a surprisingly cheerful light.

"That's right," said the She Elephant when she noticed Tendai's interest. "Learn how it works. You can help me set them up." She demonstrated the procedure with the next lamp, turned it off and let Tendai do it himself. "They run out of kerosene after a while. When that happens, let them cool, fill the fuel chamber and turn them on again." She indicated a fuel drum by the wall and a box of matches.

Tendai felt—very slightly—that the She Elephant might not be as bad as she seemed, but her next action drove that idea out of his head. She led them down a tunnel that ended abruptly in a wall of trash. "Get to work," she said, handing out picks and shovels. "Put the extra dirt in a cart and pull it back to that chamber. Someone will get rid of it for you."

"You want us to dig?" asked Tendai.

"*Mine*, stupid. This is a plastic mine. You pull out the trash and sift through it. Anything interesting—a bowl or a cup—put to one side. Old glassware's okay, too. Everything else goes on the cart. Oh, and don't get fancy with the digging. Holes can collapse. And be sure the lamp's burning brightly. If it starts to turn red, the air's going bad."

She clamped a chain around Tendai's ankle and fastened it with a padlock. The chain was attached to a chunk of cement. Rita was fettered the same way. "I don't think you can find your way out, but this'll slow you down. Especially in the deep water."

"We're not going to do anything!" Rita said shrilly.

"Loaf if you like." The big woman shrugged. "The workers trap rats when they don't satisfy me enough to get fed. Some of the grass roots are said to be tasty. I wouldn't know." The She Elephant lumbered back to the round chamber.

Tendai tried to follow, but the cement block stopped him. He yanked on it. It moved forward a few inches. He sat down on the ground and tried to think.

"It's so dirty and horrible!" cried Rita. "How are we ever going to get away?"

"I want Mama," Kuda whimpered.

"It's okay. This is a game," Tendai told his little brother.

"We'll never see Mother or Father again. We'll die down here with the rats and mud." Rita burst into tears. Kuda began to wail.

"Rita!" shouted Tendai, shaking her. "If they were going to hurt us, they would have done so already. This is a *game*! You're scaring Kuda."

She hugged herself and rocked back and forth. Presently, her sobs died down to sniffles. "You're right. I'm being stupid. It's a treasure hunt, Kuda. We're going to dig up toys from the ground."

"You can have a shovel all to yourself." Tendai folded the little boy's fingers around the handle.

Kuda's eyes grew round. "It's big!"

"It's the same size as mine. Look, we'll start on that patch over there."

Rita wiped her eyes. "Maybe we'll find something valuable. I've always admired the plastic dishes people had in their living rooms. I never knew where they came from."

"That's the spirit! We're Scouts, after all. We're prepared for everything."

"We could get badges for this," said Rita.

"Of course. For geology and nature study."

"For exploring," Rita said bitterly. "I'm sure even the Scoutmaster doesn't know about *this* place."

Tendai began working on a mass of ancient shopping bags. They disintegrated as he pulled them from the wall. He found pieces of old glass, mottled with rainbow swirls, and fragments of pottery. A strange feeling came over him. The ancestors had been here, might be here even now, watching him pull out the remnants of their lives. Did they mind?

"Here's an unbroken bottle," said Rita. It was a flask about three inches tall.

"The surface is lumpy," Tendai said, feeling the glass. He held it close to the lamp. "It's writing—English!" He searched his mind for the correct translation. His English was limited. "Pink Pills for Pale People."

Rita laughed. "It must be old. There aren't many pale people around now. This must be from colonial days, when—what was the name of that tribe?"

"The British."

"Yes, when the British ruled Zimbabwe. This is exciting! It must be worth a lot—and look! Here's a plastic duck." Rita gave the red plastic duck to Kuda, who ran it around the ground, quacking.

"Here's part of an old quilt." Tendai tried to work it loose, but dampness and rot made it crumble. He chipped out a clump of earth, with a bright square of cloth still attached, and took it to the light. It was beautifully done. Someone had spent hours fitting together jewel-like bits of material with tiny stitches. Any attempt to free it made the cloth disintegrate into mold no different from the earth.

Once again, Tendai felt uneasy. "I'm sorry," he apologized to the unknown ancestor who had patiently made the quilt. He dug a little hole in the side of the tunnel and buried the cloth there, to honor his or her memory.

"There are lots of valuable things down here. We could become millionaires," said Rita cheerfully. She seemed to have no qualms about disturbing the ancestors. Tendai didn't say that if they found anything valuable, the She Elephant would certainly take it from them.

When the cart was filled with refuse, Rita and Tendai pulled it down the tunnel to the main chamber. They had to drag their chunks of cement behind them. Kuda, who wasn't chained, helped them as best he could. They found a new, empty cart each time they visited the chamber and rolled it slowly back.

Once, Tendai looked behind to see one of the *vlei* people detach himself from the wall and shamble over to the cart. He did not tell the others.

It was impossible to say how long they had been working, but they were exhausted by the time the She Elephant fetched them. "Not bad for spoiled brats," she said, looking over the pile of treasures. Kuda cried when she took the red duck.

"It's a toy! He needs it!" cried Rita.

"He can make one out of mud." The She Elephant slapped Kuda's hands away and bent to unchain the others.

"Mean old hog," muttered Rita, and yelped when the She Elephant pinched her.

They followed the woman through a different tangle of tunnels, going down until they came to an underground pool that was fed by a spring. "Wash your hands here, princess," she told Rita.

All three children knelt to wash their faces and hands. The water was cold and almost black with vegetable material. It looked like tea. Tendai tasted it: the cold liquid seemed to sink into his tongue. "It's okay to drink," observed the She Elephant. "It's better where it comes out." So Tendai sat where the dark stream spilled from the rock, filled his hands and drank deeply.

"You'll get a disease," said Rita with a shudder. "All pond water should be boiled for five minutes to remove germs. It's in the Scout handbook."

But Tendai didn't care. The cold dark water put strength into him. It came from the same place as the whisper that had awakened him in Mazoe. It came from the ancestors.

"Don't fall asleep there!" The She Elephant yanked him to his feet. She led them to the surface. Tendai was amazed to find the sky black and spangled with stars. The cooking pots bubbled on crackling red fires. Lamps were lit on every table. They reflected on the ghostly faces of the *vlei* people.

The big woman ladled out dinner. When anyone asked for more, she gave it to him. She wasn't stingy. Knife sat beside the old woman's rocking chair. He rolled up balls of *sadʐa* and fed them into her toothless mouth. "You're all crooks," she muttered. "Jail rats."

"That's right, Granny," said the She Elephant. "We're lower than snakes' bellies. Want some tea?" Granny rattled her mug on the arm of her chair, and the She Elephant filled it.

Fist sat with a few of the more alert *vlei* people and applied himself to a mountain of food. Most of the others preferred to hide in the shadows on the ground. From the smacking noises, they appeared to be enjoying the meal as much as anyone else.

And the food was excellent. Even Rita gave in and asked for more. It might have been the hard work. It might have been the breeze making the fires dance or the bright stars frosting the sky, but Tendai thought he had never eaten a better meal.

Afterward, he staggered to the entrance of a mine and flopped down. The She Elephant took Rita and Kuda to an underground chamber, but she contented herself with chaining Tendai to another chunk of cement. He fell asleep at once. Later, he woke briefly to find himself covered with a rough blanket. He looked up at the sky. Never had he seen anything so awe-inspiring. At home, the big security lights washed out the stars, but here they stared down at him with an intensity that was almost frightening.

He listened to Knife and Fist kick dirt over the coals. "We're in it up to our necks," said Knife in a low voice.

"I don't like dealing with gangs, especially the Masks. I've heard stories . . . ," Fist said.

"Who hasn't? Help me shift this pot." Tendai heard water slosh and scatter a few hissing drops over the coals. Then he began drifting off again.

He tried to remember Mazoe and couldn't. All his life seemed pale and distant compared to what he was experiencing now. Tendai was frightened by this sudden lack of memory, but his exhaustion would not let him dwell on it long. He fell into a deep dream that he would not remember when he awoke.

n the Cow's Guts, Eye fed General Matsika's credit card into the computer. He almost fainted when he saw how big their expense account was.

"Beautiful, beautiful money," sang Ear, looking over his shoulder.

"We'll have to work for it. I wouldn't like to have the General after me if I made him angry," Arm said, which sobered up the other detectives at once.

Eye withdrew a hundred dollars from the expense account. The computer hummed and clicked. A hundred dollars slowly creaked out the money slot at the side. It had been so long since it had been used, the slot was clogged with dust. "Let's think about this logically," said Eye, sniffing the green ink on the dollars. "The children went to Mbare Musika and were headed for Beatrice, in the south."

"Maybe they took a subway," Ear said.

"Surely they wouldn't be that foolish."

"They don't know that much about the outside world," said Arm. "However, the police have checked all the obvious possibilities. Our job is to think of something unusual. If you were a child and had just escaped from a boring, oppressive house—"

"It was a beautiful house," Eye objected.

"It *looked* beautiful. Excuse me, my friend. I know seeing is your specialty, but I could feel the unhappiness. It was a home full of machines rather than people, with parents who are always busy and a father who wants everything so perfect no one can relax."

"You could tell all that?" asked Eye.

"That's *my* specialty." Arm unfolded a map of Harare and studied it carefully. "If I were one of those children, I'd want some fun. I'd eat all the food I wasn't allowed at home—chilibites, for example. I wouldn't go straight to Beatrice either. I'd take a side trip to the Bird Garden or the Lion Park or the Mile-High MacIlwaine to ride the elevators."

The detectives spent the afternoon calling all the places that looked like fun, with no results. Finally, as night fell, it was clear to everyone the General's fears had been correct. He called to report that the children had not come home.

"They might have been kidnapped at Mbare Musika. It's an excellent place for it," said Arm, draping his long limbs over the threadbare sofa. He watched Ear feed synth-food into the microwave. A moment later, a sickly smell floated through the office. "I hate bacteria burgers."

"Be thankful your special abilities don't include taste," said Ear, fanning the hot plates with his ears. They sat around a rickety card table and ate, with many helpings of ketchup and mustard.

"We'll have to visit Mbare Musika," Arm said as he jammed the plates into the overloaded sink. "We don't know what we're looking for, but maybe something will come looking for us."

A few minutes later, the detectives were seated at the back of a bus. The other passengers had moved to the front, but Ear, Eye and Arm were so used to this reaction, they didn't notice. Eye sat between the other two with his eyes closed because he was afraid of heights.

The bus took the long way around, stopping at the Mile-High MacIlwaine—once at the two hundredth floor and once two floors below the Starlight Room Restaurant. A pair of dishwashers got off. The bus had to veer sharply to avoid a collection of diplomatic limos. They flew the Gondwannan flag and blared noisy sirens. The windows were tinted so no one could look in.

It was ten o'clock at night. The vast city of Harare was spread out like a jeweled sea. Traffic lights blinked at the tops of buildings. Buses, taxis and limos swarmed through the skyways, patrolled by cops in night-black cars that reflected no light. They were like patches of moving darkness in the rowdy, noisy traffic.

The bus finally settled at Mbare Musika. Ear, Eye and Arm wandered around, waiting for something to happen. "Sometimes children are stolen by women who can't have babies," remarked Ear, overhearing a woman complain that she had too many.

"They don't take the ones old enough to remember their parents," said Eye.

"Maybe they're being trained as beggars or pickpockets." Arm looked down the street of the animal markets. It was mostly deserted, but a few persistent salesmen waited for customers. Something—he didn't know what—sent out a tremor of emotion unlike anything he had ever felt. It wasn't the animals. The goats dozed in their pens, dreaming dull, goatlike dreams. A pedigreed cat brooded with resentment. The salesmen emitted sleepy impressions of hunger. No, it was something else, painfully alert and malicious.

Intrigued, Arm started down the street. At the end, a man slept on a chair with a leash looped around his wrist. On a table next to him squatted a blue monkey. It watched the detectives with bright, unkind eyes. Others might think it was cute. Arm knew differently.

"Don't," he began, but it was too late. Ear tried to pat the monkey. It sprang and buried its teeth in the detective's ear.

"Help!" Ear screamed. Eye tried to pry the animal's jaws open, but it was much stronger than it looked. Arm circled its neck with his long fingers and squeezed. The monkey opened its mouth and shrieked, causing both detectives to loosen their hold. It sprang to the other end of the table and danced back and forth with its fur erect. The owner hunched in his chair, pretending not to notice.

"He ought to be in a cage!" shouted Arm, stanching the blood on Ear's ear with a handkerchief.

"Yaa! Push off, rope arms!" screamed the monkey.

"It talks!" the detective said in surprise.

"Of course I talk, you booboo brain. Hey, elephant ears! What cesspool did you crawl out of? Can you beat time with those?"

"Shut up! You hurt him badly!"

"Ask me if I care," said the monkey, presenting its backside insultingly.

"Shall I grab him?" Eye said.

"He'll only bite you." Arm held up the now fainting Ear.

"I've tasted better things," the Blue Monkey jeered. "I bit a kid this morning who tasted like strawberries compared to him!"

"Kid? What kid?" Arm said.

"Shut up," hissed the owner, pulling the animal's tail.

"Do that again and I'll turn your mouth inside out," the monkey snarled. "There were three of them. Ugly, like all humans. The She Elephant got them. Ow!" The Blue Monkey and its owner fell to the ground in a furious fight.

Arm was seriously worried by Ear, who had passed out cold. "Call a paramedic," he whispered to Eye. "Then contact General Matsika."

He thought his voice was too low to be overheard, but the Blue Monkey raised its head in midsnap and shrieked, "Matsika! Cops! Run for it!" Instantly, the street emptied. The animal sellers disappeared into the shadows. The monkey and its owner made up their quarrel at once and streaked off into the night.

"My big mouth," groaned Arm. He dragged Ear to a table and laid him out. The wound wasn't bad, but Ear was more sensitive than most people. He was falling into a state of shock. Eye returned with a paramedic and a squad of policemen. The latter fanned through the market, searching for the Blue Monkey. The paramedic disinfected Ear's wound and fed plasma into his arm to counteract the shock.

"I ruined things," said Ear after Arm and Eye had settled him on the office sofa. "I should never have patted a wild animal. Was it my imagination, or did it talk?"

"It talked," said Arm, who had received a report from General Matsika. "Blue monkeys are genetically engineered creatures—someone's Ph.D. project. They have a basic monkey structure with genes spliced from pit bulls and humans. They were supposed to be the ideal guard dog, but you can see why they didn't work out."

"Tell me, is there—is there permanent damage?"

"You'll be good as new in a day or two."

Ear sighed with relief.

"They can't find anything specific on the She Elephant," said Eye, looking over the police records the General had sent. "Ten million people live in Harare, and 'She Elephant' is a more common nickname than you might think."

"It was one of the titles of the ancient Swazi queens," Arm said. "She's probably a small-time crook, because there isn't a record on her."

Arm looked out the window of the office. It was three in the morning, but that was the middle of the working day in the Cow's Guts. Behind the big front windows of the dance halls, people gyrated to pounding music as though they were struck with some serious disease. The double-glass windows of the office kept out most of the noise. At Mr. Thirsty's across the way, a bouncer dragged a patron to a Dumpster and fed him in. In the alleys, a few beggars sat around a fire and listened to a man without arms or legs tell a story.

"What could the She Elephant want with General Matsika's children?" Arm wondered aloud.

68

endai wondered about the same thing, but he thought about it less as the weeks went by. Once, soon after arriving, he tried to escape. By that time, it seemed the She Elephant and her cronies did not intend to harm them. If I can make it to those lights, he thought at night as he watched the nearest suburb five miles away, I can call the police. They'll rescue Rita and Kuda.

When he was unchained in the morning, he bolted past Fist. The man didn't even attempt to follow him. That's strange, Tendai thought, but he soon found out why. The She Elephant's deep voice boomed out from under the hills. The *vlei* people roused themselves and overwhelmed him before he got half a mile.

Later, he was shown a large round chamber at the hub of a network of tunnels. Battery-operated cables ran from a loudspeaker at the center. "I call in here, see," said the She Elephant. "It goes all over the *vlei*, so you can forget about running away. Save your breath for digging."

Tendai also saw, in the larger tunnels, a system of rails going off into the dark. An ancient handcar allowed Fist and Knife to move quickly through the system. Clearly, Dead Man's Vlei had been inhabited a long time. He considered using the car to escape but decided he knew too little about the system. There must be *miles* of tunnels down there, he thought with a thrill of fear.

It occurred to him that if he did—by some miracle—manage to escape, the She Elephant could hide Rita and Kuda so deeply no one would ever find them.

Slowly, insidiously, he fell into the routine of life on the *vlei*. He awoke before dawn with the cold dew soaking his blanket. He toiled in the mines, with occasional tea breaks in the fresh air. At night, he ate ravenously and slept as though drugged.

Sometimes he woke at night with a longing so sharp, it felt like a knife. He missed Mother and Father, and the Mellower, too. But as time went on, his memories of Mazoe became less distinct, and this frightened him most of all. Kuda was worse.

Rita conducted memory drills. "You have to remember home," she told the little boy. "Mother often wore a hand-dyed caftan—brown and blue—and her hair was braided with ribbons. Father had a uniform with medals and jingled when he walked."

"I know," said Kuda. Tendai suspected he said this to shut Rita up. He himself was finding it difficult to put faces with the caftan and uniform. But Rita didn't give up on the drills, and she didn't give up needling the She Elephant.

Her ability to *shooper* was great. Often the She Elephant picked fights with Fist and Knife without knowing the cause of her irritation. The only person Rita got along with was Granny.

Granny sat in her rocking chair day after day, seething with resentment. "If my family could see me now, they'd shoot me. Yes, they would. They were decent people. Except my grandson, God rot his bones."

Tendai thought her life wasn't that bad. Knife waited on her slavishly. He brought her treats, read her stories and listened to her monotonous complaints. "She's used to better things. She's a real lady," he explained to Tendai.

Tendai didn't think so. She reminded him of a snake coiled up with no one to bite. She and Knife were members of the Portuguese tribe, who once ruled Mozambique and Angola. Granny never stopped reminding Knife of this: "They were aristocrats who would rather cut their throats than consort with criminals. You're merely spoiled goods."

"She's right. I am a crook," Knife said. Tendai was disgusted by his lack of pride.

But Rita liked the old woman, and Granny, grudgingly, accepted her. It was partly because Rita had a Portuguese name and partly because the two of them could be so much more insulting when they worked together.

"Look at the She Elephant," sneered Granny. "Drunk as a civet cat."

"Her mouth's open. She's *drooling*," said Rita, pointing at the big woman who sprawled in an easy chair.

"She stinks like a goat!"

"She eats like a hog!"

"She laughs like a hyena!"

None of this was true, except the drunk part. The She Elephant had a large underground brewery, where she made pineapple wine, millet beer and a fiery alcoholic drink called *kachasu*. Some of this was sold to beer halls in the Cow's Guts, and some was given to the *vlei* people, many of whom were untreated alcoholics.

Every afternoon at about three, the She Elephant and the others took a siesta. They lounged in the sun like so many lizards. Granny dozed in her chair, and Rita curled up on the ground beside her. Tendai saw, with growing concern, that Rita was beginning to blend in with her surroundings.

During the siesta, Tendai and Kuda worked in the vegetable gardens spread higgledy-piggledy among the trash hills. Tendai wasn't chained for this, but Fist accompanied them. The man hadn't forgotten his humiliation when Tendai cut through his belt. He didn't relax for a second.

71

They removed insects from the tomatoes, mealies, squash and pumpkins and fed them to bantam chickens penned at the mouths of the tunnels. Tendai liked this part of the day. If Fist could have been persuaded to nap, he would have liked it even more.

One morning something unusual happened. Tendai, Rita and Kuda were seated on a hill, drinking tea with milk and sugar. It was the first break of the day, and the camp was bustling. *Vlei* people carried buckets of water. Knife and Fist peeled potatoes. Granny worried a plug of tobacco with her gums. The She Elephant chopped the heads off chickens and doused them in boiling water to loosen the feathers.

It was because of this last activity that the children were on top of a hill, facing the other way. They were enjoying the morning breeze when they heard an odd noise.

First it was a humming, then a muttered conversation as though several people were talking at once. They heard a cackle of laughter and a fragment of song. Along the trail at the bottom of the hill came a man.

He was dressed in an old grain bag, and his feet were bare. He could have been one of the *vlei* people except there was nothing tired or defeated about him. He was about twenty years old. As he walked, he carried on a conversation with someone Tendai couldn't see.

The talking sounded like words but wasn't. It reminded Tendai of a parakeet they once had. When it was alone, the bird would try to imitate the things it had heard. It could do men's, women's and children's voices, yet nothing was clear enough to understand. That was how this man sounded.

He climbed the hill and sat down. He pointed to the cup Rita had, and she gave it to him without hesitation. This was very surprising because Rita hated to let anyone drink out of her cup. The man gulped down the tea and babbled at them.

"He says he's on his way to lunch," Kuda translated.

"You can't understand that," said Tendai.

"I can so." Kuda held out his arms, and the man picked him up. Man and boy smiled at each other. "He says the sun is shining," said Kuda after the man spoke again.

"You're making it up," Rita said scornfully.

"I am not. Bye-bye." The man put Kuda down and walked off without looking back. He went down to one of the trestle tables. The She Elephant grunted and swept aside a heap of chicken heads to make room for him. Fist gave him a raw potato, which he crunched up with strong white teeth. Even Granny stopped gumming her tobacco and looked interested.

Intrigued, the children climbed down the hill. "Who's that?" asked Tendai, trying not to notice the chicken heads.

"Trashman," the She Elephant said. "He's strong as an ox, but he has the mind of a four-year-old. He can't remember anything for more than a minute." She ladled out a bowl of stew Tendai knew she had planned for her midmorning snack and gave it to Trashman. He ate it noisily and patted his stomach. Knife gave him one of the chocolates he was saving for Granny.

Granny smiled benevolently, an expression almost as repellent as her usual scowl. "Good boy," she purred. "Come to Granny." Trashman sat by the rocking chair and let her rumple his hair. "Good boy. Honest boy," she crooned. "*You* don't pick pockets. *You* don't sell whiskey to eat out people's brains. You're my sweet, innocent child." Trashman smiled and let her pet him as though he were a big dog.

Knife sullenly peeled potatoes while Fist watched the scene uneasily. Suddenly Knife hurled his knife—*thok!*—into the back of Granny's chair. Tendai shouted. Rita screamed. But the weapon was well aimed and merely lodged in the wood. Knife stalked off, trembling with rage, with Fist anxiously following behind.

Granny calmly patted Trashman's hair. "*You* don't try to kill a poor old woman whose only crime is decency. *You* don't drag her off to live in a moral sewer."

"Moral sewage, that's us," said the She Elephant, stuffing a bag with chicken feathers. "I'm surprised you don't choke on all the food us sewer rats give you." Granny glared at her and continued to praise Trashman. Tendai turned away in disgust.

And yet it was impossible to dislike Trashman. He accepted affection as easily as a kitten accepts its mother's licks—and forgot it as quickly. At mealtimes he stood by the cooking pots and rubbed his stomach. The She Elephant fed him. He followed the *vlei* people as they worked. They, who were normally reclusive, welcomed him. In the evenings, they started up a soccer game with crude wooden goalposts and a flabby ball. Trashman watched with delight. He slapped his hands on his knees when someone scored a goal. Tendai realized the whole point of the game was to amuse Trashman.

Knife, in spite of his jealousy, brought extra treats for him. Fist smeared honey on Trashman's fingers and stuck a chicken feather to them. Trashman spent many happy hours gluing the feather first to one hand, then the other. It was awful to watch but somehow endearing.

The young man greeted Tendai, Rita and Kuda enthusiastically every time he saw them, but each time was like the first. He simply had no memory of the other meetings.

The most amazing thing, though, was how he and Kuda talked. Trashman babbled in his strange mix of almost-words, and the little boy translated: "He says the ground is cold" or "He says the *sadza* tastes good." It was impossible to tell if Kuda was making it up. It drove Rita wild. In the evenings, man and boy watched the soccer match with equal delight. Tendai could have sworn they were commenting on the game. But they might only have been chirping at each other like the birds that nested on the *vlei*.

"Where did he come from?" Tendai asked one evening, as he watched the She Elephant dump dirty plates into the pot of boiling water. She never used soap. The metal plates bumped around in the pot, and grease and bits of food floated off. After a while she pulled them out with tongs to let them steam dry on a table.

"Who cares?" she snapped. "One day he showed up, stayed awhile and pushed off. He wanders through every few months."

"Where does he go?"

"I don't know and I don't care. Stop yapping. You're giving me a headache."

Tendai knew the She Elephant had a headache because she had tried out a new batch of *kachasu* that afternoon. He left her and wandered through the darkening camp, dragging the heavy block of cement behind him. Rita was no longer shackled, but Fist hadn't forgiven Tendai for trying to escape. Some nights he could hardly bear to be chained up. He wanted to be free to run and run and run—it didn't matter where, only to have the feeling of freedom again.

He looked for company. Rita and Granny were gloating together. Granny was planning her birthday luncheon in the city. "You wait," she told Rita. "Knife will take me to a bar and feed me pork rinds. He doesn't know decent places exist."

"Shocking," said Rita.

Kuda and Trashman watched the soccer match. Tendai wondered how they could see anything. The *vlei* people melted into the shadows, and all he could detect were their melancholy cries and the squelch of their feet.

He slowly climbed a hill and looked out over the *vlei*. Far away, he saw lights. He didn't know what suburb it was: his map had gone with the Scout knife. The knife gave him a real pang. It was the one thing that connected him to Father. He could remember Father's hand holding it out long ago. He forced his memory to move beyond the hand to the arm: it was clad in olive drab, army cloth. The arm was attached to a chest decorated with many medals, and above floated a general's cap. But between . . . ?

Tendai put his face in his hands and wept silently above the camp where no one could see him.

The trail was cold. It had ended with the Blue Monkey, which the police were unable to find. Three children had walked out one morning and simply vanished. They might never have existed, except for the pictures Arm held in his long fingers. He traced a line of spilled Coke on a table in Mr. Thirsty's. A fly crept up to drink.

"Shall I catch it?" said Eye. He amused himself by trapping flies under a glass. He had ten at the moment. The trick was to get the next one in without releasing the others.

"Oh, let them go," said Arm wearily. Eye upended the glass, and the ten flies zapped out to circle in the center of the room.

Someone put a coin in the boom box. "Oh, no!" cried Ear as a heavy rhythm began to vibrate the floor. He clasped his hands over his muffs. Behind the bar Mr. Thirsty, a skinny man with a large Adam's apple, polished a glass. It was eleven in the morning, but business was already brisk. Soon Ear, Eye and Arm would have to leave. They didn't drink alcohol and were known to approve of law and order. Mr. Thirsty said they lowered the tone of the place.

"Fine detectives we turned out to be!" Arm said. "What are we doing in here? We're supposed to be hunting those children."

"You're the one who gets hunches," said Ear sullenly.

"*I* wasn't the one who tangled with the Blue Monkey."

"You scared him off with your big mouth."

"Stop it! It doesn't do any good to fight." Eye blinked in the dim light. He automatically checked the inhabitants of the room, a habit that had saved the detectives from more than one barroom brawl. In a corner booth, an old woman yammered endlessly about how disgusting everything was. A pair of *tsotsis*, street hoodlums, listened politely. Eye nudged Ear, who shifted his muffs to listen over the boom box.

"I don't know why I let you take me out," said the old woman. "I might have known we'd wind up here. You could have taken me to an art gallery, but no. We have to wallow in this pigsty. I suppose this is where you sell your brain poison."

"Would you like something to eat, Granny?" said the smaller of the two *tsotsis*.

"Oh, sure. Take me to a beer hall for lunch. Some birthday party this is! Look at these people. Steeped in sin. Brains the size of walnuts."

"I can get you *caldo verde*. Real Portuguese soup," said the smaller *tsotsi*.

"What do you know about real anything, Knife? A bowl of toxic waste is more likely. Well, go ahead. You devote your life to shortening mine, but why should I care? I'm better off dead."

"Would you go, Fist?" said Knife.

"It's nice to see a family outing," remarked Ear after he repeated what he had heard. The other sniggered. Presently, the big *tsotsi* returned with a carton and a spoon. By now the boom box had finished. A man staggered out of a booth to add more money, and Arm tripped him with his long leg. The man lay on the floor, complaining feebly. All the detectives could hear the conversation now.

"It's greasy," said Granny. "You call that soup? I've seen better things dug out of the *vlei*." But she ate greedily, smacking her lips over the *caldo verde*. Arm could smell hot cabbage and garlic.

Suddenly, Granny flung the spoon against a wall. "Filth!" she screamed. "I might have known! *There's a fly in this soup!*"

"One of yours," murmured Arm to Eye.

"You put it there! Don't deny it! You thought, Let's take Granny out to lunch. Let's play a trick on her. Oh, you worthless hooligans! Even the She Elephant isn't this bad!"

The detectives rose at once. This time Arm didn't speak. He ran for the public holophone. The man he tripped earlier grabbed his ankle. Ear sprang for the door, but Fist was already out of his chair. He shoved Ear against a table and gestured wildly to Knife and Granny. They scrambled out of the booth.

Eye tackled Knife, but Granny banged him over the head with her handbag. "Leave my grandson alone, you bully!" she shrieked. Eye lost his grip, and Knife wriggled free. Granny hit Eye one last time before she was dragged away. He staggered against the bar, where Mr. Thirsty was calmly polishing glasses.

The *tsotsis* had reached the door. Fist slung Granny over his shoulder, but Knife turned abruptly and—quick as a mamba—hurled his knife at Eye. The detective was leaning over the bar with his back exposed. It happened so fast, no one even had time to yell. The knife sped straight for the man's heart—and clanged into a brass tray held out by Mr. Thirsty. Eye slumped to the floor.

"General Matsika!" cried Arm, who had finally reached the phone. "Cordon off the Cow's Guts! We found the She Elephant!" At the word *Matsika*, the beer hall emptied out. Panic spread in all directions. As fast as the police reacted, the crooks reacted even faster. In no time, the place was a ghost town with only a few scrawny dogs riffling through garbage and crows watching from the rooftops.

"You really are bad for business," remarked Mr. Thirsty as he went back to polishing.

"Thanks—thanks for saving his life," stammered Ear as he checked Eye for wounds.

"It was the least I could do. You paid your bill last month," said Mr. Thirsty.

The knife had gone through the brass tray. The tip went out the other side and lodged in Eye's shirt, but beyond that was only a shallow cut. Eye, however, being supersensitive, had passed out. Ear laid him on the floor, and Arm wiped his face with a wet towel provided by the bartender.

"Do you know the people who did this?" Arm asked.

"Of course. Knife and Fist provide me with *kachasu*. I never saw the old woman before, though," said Mr. Thirsty.

"Have you heard of the She Elephant?"

"Naturally. She brews the stuff."

Arm gritted his teeth with exasperation. "Why didn't you tell me?"

"You never asked." Mr. Thirsty lined up the sparkling glasses on a shelf and arranged the brass trays behind them. He stepped back to admire the effect. "I don't usually get a chance to see everything tidy like this. It gives the place a touch of class, don't you think?"

"Where does the She Elephant live?"

"Sorry. The dealers don't give me their addresses. These won't be back either, which is a pity. The She Elephant made excellent *kachasu*, although the latest batch was a little rough."

By now, a paramedic had arrived. He came warily into the beer hall but relaxed when he saw it was nearly empty. "You!" he called cheerfully. "How's that ear?" Ear extended his to show that the Blue Monkey's bite had healed. "A mere scratch," the paramedic announced after he examined Eye. "I'll slap a bandage on it, and he'll be ready to party in no time. You guys go in for rough stuff, don't you?" He looked around at the overturned chairs and spilled beer.

"Please hurry," said Arm. Something was happening outside. His extrasense fluttered with anxiety. The police might not be able to see the dwellers in the Cow's Guts, but Arm could feel them. Someone had just arrived who sent a current of dismay through the concealed hoodlums. "Matsika," he whispered. Mr. Thirsty stopped wiping a table, and the paramedic spilled the disinfectant he was applying to Eye's back.

General Matsika stood in the doorway. With the light behind him, Arm thought, he looked like a uniform with a hat floating over it. The face was lost in the gloom. The detective was almost knocked over by the force of the man's personality. This was power. This was the energy that directed the armies of the law in Harare. This was the image that haunted the guilty dreams of the wicked. The paramedic stared at the door with a face gone pale. The bottle of disinfectant made a dark puddle on the floor. Mr. Thirsty's Adam's apple bobbed up and down. It would have been funny if they hadn't been so frightened.

The General switched on the lights, and his face suddenly appeared. "Who were those *tsotsis*?" he demanded in a deep voice.

Arm shook himself loose from the spell. "They called themselves Fist and Knife. They were with an old woman called Granny."

"Where did they come from?"

"I don't know."

"Speak up, man!"

Arm cleared his throat. "People come and go through this suburb without leaving traces. They say everyone eventually passes through the Cow's Guts."

"Don't try to be funny. You!" General Matsika advanced on Mr. Thirsty, who dropped his dishcloth. The General grabbed him by the shirt and lifted him right off the floor. "You own this place. Tell me what you know if you don't want me to rip out the walls to see what you're hiding!" The bartender opened and shut his mouth, but no sounds came out.

"He's never seen them before either," said Arm. He was astounded at himself. Why was he lying? He didn't like to tell lies. The General let Mr. Thirsty slide to the floor and turned his attention to the rest of the room.

"Ah!" he cried, as though he had been struck. He dropped to his knees, and Arm hurried over to see what had been so startling. On the floor lay the knife the *tsotsi* had hurled at Eye. It was most unusual, with a gold-washed blade and red dragons curled around the handle. The blade was tipped with blood. Arm felt sick.

"Tendai's knife," said the General in a low voice. Arm looked sidelong at him and was amazed. All the power that had emanated from him in the doorway was gone. He looked like any other father who was desperately worried about his children. His eyes were filled with tears. Arm stepped back, but the General had sensed he was there and turned away. When he faced Arm again, his expression was again powerful and confident. His eyes seemed to have drunk up the tears.

"Go over this room with a microscope," he ordered the policemen clustered in the doorway. "Lift the fingerprints off this knife. Hold and question anyone you can catch—oh, and pour out the vat of *kachasu* in the back. I want to see how many dead dogs are at the bottom of it." Mr. Thirsty, moaning, was dragged out the door between two officers.

Arm looked out the window at the alleyway across the street. The beggars' camp fire had died down to embers. Bundles of rags huddled around it. Even the beer halls were unusually quiet, and Mr. Thirsty's was completely dark.

"Let's go over the clues again," he said. Ear drooped over a bowl of soybean stew on the table, and Eye lay on the sofa with his lids at half-mast. "It's Granny's birthday. She's about eighty years old and belongs to the Portuguese tribe. How many people are there like that on the city's computer?"

"A hundred and six." Ear yawned. "The police contacted all of them." Ear's head dipped so far, the lobe of one of his ears fell into the stew. He jerked himself awake.

"These *tsotsis* make their living selling illegal alcohol," Arm went on. "How many people do that?"

"More than you want to know," Eye said from the sofa.

"What about the *vlei*?"

"There are hundreds of *vleis* around Harare."

Someone tapped at the door. The detectives immediately became alert. Arm reached for a Nirvana gun. "What do you hear?" he said in a low voice.

Ear extended his ear over the keyhole. "The door's in the way, but I think it's only one person." Arm undid the eight locks and left on the chain. He opened the door a crack.

Someone swallowed outside. "It's Mr. Thirsty," Ear whispered. Arm threw open the door to show the disheveled bartender with his Adam's apple bobbing up and down. He pulled the man inside with his long arm and slammed the door shut.

"Don't shoot!" cried Mr. Thirsty.

"As if we would harm you," Arm said as he hung the Nirvana gun on a hook. "You saved Eye's life."

"Yes, well"—the bartender swallowed nervously—"you saved *mine*. The General—ah—the General is a most forceful character. Most forceful. But he believed me because you backed me up."

"You don't have any information, do you?" said Arm.

"Well, ah, you see I *might*—only you mustn't tell anyone. My life wouldn't be worth a flattened flea. But I did hear—I won't say where—that the Masks are looking for children to adopt."

"I don't understand," Arm said.

"Oh, it's so complicated! They lost one of their members in a street fight. They want to train a new Mask, and it's better to start young, don't you think?"

"Go on."

"One of the She Elephant's little services is to provide children for people who can't have them."

"She's a filthy kidnapper!" shouted Ear, raising his fist. Mr. Thirsty backed away, and Arm placed himself between them.

"It's only a service," the bartender said. "What's a child or two? Anyhow, the Masks wanted two or three to round out their gang. A couple of backups in case the first one doesn't work out—don't hit me!" he cried as Ear raised his fist again.

"Who is the head of the Masks?" said Arm quietly.

Mr. Thirsty shivered. "No one asks that kind of question. Believe me, if they have the children, you can forget about them. But Matsika's kids might—I'm not promising any-thing—still be with the She Elephant."

"And you know where she lives," said Arm, trying not to look disgusted at the little man.

"Well, yes and no. I hear—this might be false—that she lives in Dead Man's Vlei."

"That's a toxic-waste dump!"

"It *was*." Mr. Thirsty looked around nervously, checking the door, the window, the holophone. "A hundred years ago it was. But time has healed it. Hundreds of people live there now, mining the old trash, and the She Elephant is their queen. Don't think it will be easy to find her, though. The *vlei* is honeycombed with tunnels. People say you can walk two hundred miles, going up and down and round about. The She Elephant has ways of telling when danger's near. If Matsika went there, she'd take his kids down so far they'd never see the sun again."

Mr. Thirsty looked up at Arm, and his Adam's apple bobbed. The detective knew he was a crook who saw nothing wrong with stealing children or selling whiskey brewed in a toxic-waste dump, but a decent impulse had put out a feeble shoot in the man's heart.

He put his hands on Mr. Thirsty's shoulders. The man winced, but just as quickly a pleased expression crossed his face. Arm felt a kind of energy flow from him to the ratlike bartender. He glimpsed, briefly, a home far from the Cow's Guts where three daughters waited for their father to return from work.

"I feel *happy*," Mr. Thirsty said in wonder. "Oh, my, so this is what goodness feels like. Who would have known? Oh, my." Arm removed his hands. Mr. Thirsty stood there with a bemused smile as the detective unlocked the door. The bartender scurried out into the night, turning once to wave before the door was closed.

"That never happened before," murmured Arm. "I saw into his mind."

"Ugh," said Ear.

"And somehow I woke up something decent in him."

"It'll wear off," said Eye.

"Maybe. Anyhow, we have work to do. The She Elephant will certainly know if General Matsika's coming—he can't seem to go anywhere without sirens—but she isn't expecting *us*."

"Us? Go to Dead Man's Vlei? At night?" Eye sat back down on the sofa and looked faint.

"I'm scared," Ear said.

"So am I." Arm strapped on his Nirvana gun. "Unfortunately, that doesn't change a thing."

uch earlier that day, before Granny discovered the fly in her *caldo verde*, Tendai was slaving away in the She Elephant's *shebeen*. Of all the jobs he was given, this was the worst. The stench of fermenting fruit made him dizzy. The fire under the *kachasu* vat devoured oxygen and raised the temperature unbearably. If the chamber hadn't been close to the surface, he would have passed out from lack of air. The only consolation was that he wasn't chained.

Not that this gave him an opportunity to escape. Unlike the other rooms underground, *this* chamber was connected to only two tunnels: one leading down to a pool of water and another going up to the air. The She Elephant sat in a chair blocking this exit.

Tendai raked out a load of pineapple peels from under the wine vat. He grimaced as a tide of cockroaches swarmed over his hands. It isn't fair, he thought. I should be outside at this time of day, but Fist and Knife aren't around to watch me. I hope Granny has a rotten time.

And she would, he thought. Knife could take her to the Starlight Room in the Mile-High MacIlwaine, and Granny would still find something to grumble about. "Why couldn't she stay here? She'd be just as miserable," he muttered.

The She Elephant wasn't all that watchful at the moment. She sprawled over the chair with a bottle of *kachasu* cradled in her arms. Her eyes were glazed, but they hadn't closed yet. Now and then they twitched in Tendai's direction. "Fetch water," said the big woman in a slurred voice. She rolled a bucket toward him with her foot.

Tendai took it gratefully and started down the tunnel to the water. The air became much fresher. He shone a flashlight on the dark path. It went down and down until he passed the level of packed garbage and came to natural earth and rock. The trail stopped descending, and astonishingly, the light began to grow. Soon he was able to switch off the flashlight. He arrived at a deep dark pool. It lay at the bottom of a grotto, like a bubble in the earth. In the low ceiling was a shaft that led up to the sky.

Tendai guessed it was an old well. The sides of the shaft were lined with stone, and the light fell from the distant sky to fill the chamber with a ghostly radiance. Tendai often wondered whether he could use it to escape, but the water was very deep. If he swam out, his hands would only reach a third of the way to the opening.

He filled the bucket and sat down to rest. If he waited too long, the She Elephant would beat him. On the other hand, she might fall asleep. And then, oh, then . . .

The rage for freedom struck him most forcefully when he was deep underground. It was almost as though a voice called to him: *Run! Run now!* He rubbed his hands against the walls of the chamber to quiet his nerves. He felt something hard under the soil. A rock, he thought, and almost passed on, but a patch of white caught his attention.

He shone the flashlight on it. It had an unusual luster, so he worked it loose. It was a flat ridged disk perhaps two inches in diameter, and it was thick, like the bottom of a drinking glass. Tendai's heart began to race with excitement.

He washed it in the pool. The dirt came off, although the ridges were stained with vegetable matter.

It was an *ndoro*. *Ndoros* were still worn by spirit mediums, but they were made of porcelain. The really old ones came from the shell of a sea mollusk. They had always been extremely rare. This one was formed of a heavy spiral of white shell and had a hole bored at the center to allow it to be hung around the neck. Tendai had seen one in a painting of Monomatapa.

He cupped it in his hands, feeling it the way its original owner had done. He saw the unknown ancestor standing in a forest clearing, smelting red ore in a beehive oven. The man hammered out metal on a rock, making a ringing sound through the trees. He fashioned a spear shaft from a young tree and fastened the leaf-shaped blade to it with a neat coil of copper wire. The ancestor balanced his weapon, feeling how it became part of his arm, and he touched the *ndoro* to send a prayer to the spirit world—

"You fool!" roared the She Elephant down the tunnel. Tendai jumped up so fast, he knocked over the bucket. He hastily buried the *ndoro* in the mud at the edge of the pool and plunged the bucket into the dark water. He dragged it up the tunnel as fast as he could manage. But as he got nearer, it became clear the She Elephant was not shouting at him. He stopped near the *shebeen* and listened.

"You idiot! You ball of hyena dung! How could you leave that knife behind!"

"He attacked Granny," began Knife.

"The best thing that could happen is for you to lose Granny! She's a poisonous old hag!" the She Elephant shouted. "Now Matsika knows we have his brats!"

"Don't you insult my granny!" Knife shouted back.

"*Shut up!* Matsika will roast everyone in the Cow's Guts until he gets what he wants. Then he'll come down here with a hundred *bulldozers*!"

Fist jumped into the argument. "We can clear out. We've done it before. And the *vlei* people are as hard to spot as chameleons."

"We're going to get rid of those brats before it's too late," snarled the She Elephant.

"What do you mean?" Knife said.

"I mean, *sell* them as we meant to do all along. To the Masks."

"Oh, no. I don't like that," said Fist in a shocked voice.

"Why not? They need recruits."

"Are you sure of that?"

"Listen," the She Elephant said. "Nothing would give the head of the Masks more pleasure than to take Matsika's son and turn him into a criminal. To tell the truth, it would cheer me up, too."

"That takes care of Tendai. What about the others?" said Fist.

"The man has four wives and no children. He'd be willing to pay fifty thousand dollars for Kuda."

"And Rita?" Knife said.

"Who cares about her? She'll grow up like Granny—you can hear it in her nasty little voice. I understand the slave trade is doing well in Gondwanna."

"I don't like it!" cried Knife.

"You should have thought of that before you threw the knife. Now pour me a drink. I'll drug the little squealers tonight. No! Not another word!"

Tendai heard the sound of pouring liquid. The *tsotsis* and the She Elephant settled down for some serious drinking, interrupted only when the jug gurgled or someone belched. He leaned against the wall and tried to sort out his jumbled thoughts.

Everybody knew about the Masks, even inside the walled garden in Mazoe. They moved like smoke through the subways, springing out to terrorize a train. They tore necklaces from women's necks and cut off their fingers to get the rings. Father paid informers to hunt them. The informers disappeared, and others refused to take their places.

One reason the Masks were so difficult to trace was because their motives were unclear: they weren't interested in drugs, and they stole for sport rather than greed. They might kill a dozen men and leave their wallets piled insultingly on top. When they did steal, none of the loot ever showed up on the black market. It simply vanished.

Father said they wanted power, and the easiest way to feel you had power over someone was to terrify him. Father hated them and they hated him. It was perfectly believable that the Masks would want to turn their enemy's son to evil.

"But I won't give in," Tendai said to himself. Kuda, now, was too young to resist in spite of his tough spirit. And what of Rita? How could he protect her?

Tendai went back to the dark pool and sat there. He didn't know what to do. He stared at the well opening over the water. Even if he swam out there, he could never raise his hands high enough to reach it. He thought of a dozen desperate plans. He could burst into the *shebeen* and knock out all three adults with the bucket. He could creep along the ceiling like a fly and reach the well opening. Nothing would work.

Finally, all he could think of was to retrieve the *ndoro* from the mud.

The cool shell rested in his palms and grew warm from his body's heat. "Help me," said Tendai to the unknown ancestor who had owned it. "I am your child. I'm alone in a dark place, and I don't know what to do. Please, please help me."

He held the ancient *ndoro* and prayed. And gradually, he became aware that the light was strengthening. The hair stood up on his neck, but still he held the *ndoro* and prayed. The light crept down the well shaft until it flooded straight into the dark water. It was the sun! Perhaps once a year, the sun passed over the well in exactly the right way and shone into this deep chamber. The brilliant light fell into the water, and *under* the water—

—was a flat stone. Tendai gasped in wonder. He would never have guessed it was there! Only the sunlight, falling down the well on this single day of the year, marked it out. Then the radiance moved on, fading, retreating, but Tendai knew what he had to do.

"Thank you," he whispered to the unknown ancestor. He tore off a strip of shirt and tied the *ndoro* around his neck. Then he stepped into the water and swam confidently to the rock. Standing on it, he reached into the shaft. His hands felt a metal rung.

When Tendai first came to Dead Man's Vlei, he wouldn't have had the strength to pull himself up, but hard labor had toughened him. Tendai raised himself into the well until his head knocked against another rung. He let go with one hand and grasped the second rung before he fell out of the shaft. His back knocked against the rough stones, bringing tears to his eyes.

He wedged his foot against the side of the well. He edged himself farther up, feeling the cloth of his shirt tear. The stones scraped his skin. Finally, he was able to place both feet on the first rung and grasp the second one with his hands. He rested with his back pressed against the opposite wall. He was almost sobbing for breath.

When his heart had settled back to normal, he inched farther up. Rungs existed at regular intervals, but some of them had broken, and one even broke under his foot, sending him slamming against the wall. He had to move on with his back pressed to one side and his feet and hands on the other. It was terribly tiring. He thought that if more than one rung was broken in a row, he might never make it to the top.

Finally, the light became brighter, and the scent of the She Elephant's camp fire reached him. The next rung was missing—and the next! Tendai looked up at the blue sky and despaired. He couldn't do it.

A shadow passed over the mouth of the well as a *vlei* person walked past. It startled Tendai so much, he almost let go, but the fright charged him with enough energy to try again. He wedged himself in the shaft and crept upward. His shirt tore away, the stones cut his skin. He gritted his teeth and kept going.

At last his fingers found the rim. He pulled himself the rest of the way out. He lay on the ground in a half-faint, panting and unable to move for several minutes.

13

The *vlei* people moved around him as they went about their dreary work. They paid him not the slightest attention—and perhaps they didn't see him. Tendai had noticed that both Kuda and Rita blended into the background now. Probably he did, too.

But he couldn't rest long. Sooner or later, the She Elephant would remember to look for him. He got up and fell. His legs were still shaking. Grimly, he tried again. Once he began walking, his strength came back.

He found Rita and Kuda in a vegetable patch, sitting next to Granny's chair. What rotten luck, Tendai thought.

"You should have seen them," said Granny. "One had big ears like an elephant; one had bulging eyes like a frog. The third was like a wall spider. Oh! I almost died of fright! Wouldn't you know my grandson would pick a place full of monsters? *I* wanted to go to an art gallery."

Tendai beckoned to Rita and Kuda. "Come here. I've got something important to tell you."

"She's telling us the most exciting story," said Rita. "Go on, Granny. What did you do when the froggy grabbed Knife?"

"I hit him with my purse—and let me tell you, it wasn't light. I carry nails in it, yes I do. I have to, in the kind of dives my grandson likes."

"Come *on*," Tendai said, yanking Rita by the hand.

"Let go, you bully!"

"You stupid girl!"

Rita clung to Granny's chair, but the old woman pushed her away. "You listen to him," she said in a low voice. "Don't think I'm senile. That's the mistake everyone makes. They think old Granny's wandering in her wits, but she hears a thing or two. You were going to tell her about the Masks, weren't you?"

Tendai gaped at her, and Granny laughed so hard her rocking chair almost tipped over.

"The—Masks?" said Rita.

"Yes, you silly sausage," cackled Granny. "Why do you think Knife and Fist brought you here? Not to work in the mines—they have *vlei* people for that. They wanted to sell you to the Masks. Now"—Granny leaned forward, and her white hair tumbled over her face—"Knife has done a stupid thing. As usual. He threw *your* knife at the froggy, and he left it behind. What do you think your father's going to make of that?" The old woman sat back and grinned, showing her naked gums.

"They're going to sell us to the *Masks?*" wailed Rita.

"Keep your voice down," hissed Tendai.

"Who are the Masks?" Kuda said from his seat on the ground.

"Horrible, horrible gangsters! They cut off people's ears and things!" Rita twisted her hair around her finger so hard she almost pulled it out.

"Shut up! You're frightening him," said Tendai.

"He *should* be frightened. They'll chop us into little bits—"

"I want Mama!" cried Kuda.

"Now look what you've done!" Tendai picked up the little boy, but Kuda flung himself down and screamed at the top of his voice.

"I want Mama!"

"If the She Elephant hears him, we're lost," said Tendai.

"Shut up or I'll really give you something to cry about!" Rita shook Kuda. He only howled louder. Footsteps pounded from around a hill.

"Now he's done it," Tendai groaned. But along a path came not the She Elephant but Trashman. His face was screwed up with worry, and he babbled anxiously.

"I want my mama!" screamed Kuda. Trashman straightened up as though he had been given an order. He scooped up the little boy and ran.

"Wait! Wait!" shouted Rita, but the man and boy were off as though a pride of lions were after them.

"What can I do?" Tendai cried.

"I'd go with them," Granny said calmly. "The She Elephant's going to burst a blood vessel when she finds you gone. Won't that be fun to watch, nasty cow that she is. And she won't ask Granny because poor old Granny's wandering in her wits." The old woman rocked back and forth with malicious glee.

Tendai didn't know whether she would really cover up for them, but it hardly mattered. He grabbed Rita by the hand and pulled her along. She woke up from her surprise and took off like a deer. The *vlei* people gazed at them as they passed, but without the She Elephant's orders, they had no interest in the fleeing children.

On they ran but stopped to rest when the pace became unbearable. They saw Trashman in the distance. He was striding along purposefully with Kuda perched on his shoulders. Tendai and Rita began walking, too. And still, no one had alerted the She Elephant.

"I don't understand it," whispered Tendai as they rested in a hollow. "I thought Granny hated everyone. Why hasn't she given the alarm?" Rita blended in so well, he couldn't see her unless she moved.

"You don't understand," Rita said. "More than anything, she hates criminals. She was raised in a convent, you see. She told awfully interesting stories about her childhood."

Tendai looked over to where he thought his sister lay. This was a side of the old woman he hadn't known, but he hadn't gone near her if he could help it.

"Granny's dearest wish is to reenter a convent and pray for Knife's soul before it's too late. She really loves him."

Tendai stifled a snort of laughter. "You know, I can't see you when you don't move."

"I can't see you either. We're turning into *vlei* people. After a while, we'll start shuffling around and moaning like them, too."

Tendai had a cold feeling she was right. "We'd better go before our luck runs out."

Now the edge of the *vlei* was very near. They could see tall buildings and streets. A supermarket bore a sign that said VAINONA GROCERY in bright red letters. The world they were approaching was like a dream. Tendai heard music, traffic, lawn mowers. Even a jackhammer trilled like a distant woodpecker. It was all so beautiful! He was dangerously close to tears.

"Listen!" cried Rita, clutching his arm.

Out over the *vlei* came a distant cry. They couldn't hear the words yet, but Tendai knew what they said.

"Run!" he shouted. They stumbled on. The cry approached them, speeding under the earth, echoing out of the mine shafts.

"Find! . . . Bring! . . . Meeee!" Rita fell and Tendai hauled her to her feet. The streets of Vainona were only a few yards away. The She Elephant's commands burst out of the ground. Bits of the hills began to detach and creep after them. "Find children! Bring them to meeee!"

They reached the cement walk surrounding the suburb. Tendai dragged Rita over it. They fell to their hands and knees and continued crawling on all fours. Rita was sobbing with terror. Tendai urged her on until they collapsed onto a neat green lawn bordered with daisies. He couldn't move anymore. If the She Elephant herself charged after them, he couldn't react. He watched the *vlei* with a kind of numb despair.

The edge of the wasteland humped up. The *vlei* people gathered, shifted, turned. They were unwilling to pass beyond their domain. They hovered in a gray tide, watching the children. Then they simply melted away. Tendai didn't know whether they were waiting or had gone back to their burrows. He could see Rita clearly now. She was a horrid patch of mud on the beautiful lawn.

"You! Tramps! Get off my property!" a woman shouted. The children sat up. The woman stood in the doorway of her house and shook a broom at them. She was neatly dressed, with a flowered *doek,* or scarf, tied around her hair. She was so tidy, both Tendai and Rita laughed for pure joy.

"Go away before I set the dogs on you! Crazy," the woman muttered to herself as they left the lawn. "Laughing like little maniacs."

"Look, there's Kuda," Rita said, pointing at a bus platform. A border of zinnias surrounded an oval parking area. At one end were several benches shaded by a sprawling rose tree. At the other was a drinking fountain. Kuda and Trashman were taking turns squirting each other. Trashman babbled excitedly as Tendai and Rita ran up.

"He says the bus is coming," translated Kuda, and so it was. A silver gray dot in the sky settled down toward the landing pad. The bus let off two men, who frowned at the collection of tramps in their suburb. Then the bus was empty.

"Hey, Trashman," called the driver. "Where did you get those kids? You're not old enough to be their daddy."

"We were kidnapped by the She Elephant," Tendai said. "Please. We want to get away, but we don't have any money."

"I heard the She Elephant was into nasty stuff—*and there she is!*"

Tendai saw the big woman charge out of the *vlei* with Knife and Fist behind. They must have followed on one of the handcars. She was roaring drunk. She staggered down the street, brandishing an ax. "You filthy brats!" she screamed.

Tendai, Rita, Kuda and Trashman jumped into the bus. The ax clanged onto the front window and cracked it in two. The driver took off. The She Elephant lunged for the door and fell heavily to the cement.

"You poor kids!" panted the driver as he maneuvered between the buildings. "I pressed the panic button. The cops'll be on her in no time."

But Tendai doubted very much that the police would find anyone when they arrived.

"Well. So you're kidnapped. What are your names?" the driver asked.

A few weeks before, Tendai would have given him the information without thinking. Now he no longer trusted the outside world. Fuzzy blue monkeys turned into vicious brutes. Sweet old ladies turned out to be Grannies. And the Masks would soon be hunting them. Who knew who their allies might be? "I'm Jiri Ndlovu," he said, giving a common name. "That's my sister, Rose, and my brother, Jabu. You already know Trashman."

"I see him all the time," said the bus driver, smiling. "Listen, why don't I drop you where he always goes? The people there take care of him, so they'll certainly be nice to you. I'll make a special stop outside Resthaven."

Tendai looked at Trashman, who was holding Kuda as though he were a large teddy bear. Trashman smiled and said, "Mama." It was the first word Tendai had been able to understand.

14

The driver brought his bus to a landing outside a high gray wall. "I'm not really allowed to stop here," he explained. "See, this is a taxi stand, but it's as close as I can get to Resthaven."

"Thank you," said Tendai. "I hope the She Elephant doesn't hurt you."

"Don't worry. My vacation is due to start tomorrow. I'll find someone to cover my route the rest of today." The driver closed the door, and they watched him maneuver out of the narrow taxi landing.

It was an impressive wall, higher than Tendai could see. It curved away without a window or opening except for a single gate directly in front of them. "Who lives here?" Tendai asked.

"Mama," replied Trashman. He yanked on a chain hanging by the gate, and a bell rang somewhere inside. It wasn't a mechanical sound like the ring of a holophone but a real bell with a metal clapper. It rang deeply, sweetly, dying away like far music.

"Oh!" said Rita. "Do it again." So Trashman rang it several times until Tendai caught his arm.

"He might make them angry," he said.

And indeed, the face that showed up at the peephole did look angry. "What do you want? Go away!" it said, but then it recognized Trashman. "Chedu!" it cried in a pleased voice.

"Mama," said Trashman. The gate opened after many locks and bolts had been undone, and an enormous woman stood before them. She was fully as large as the She Elephant, but where the queen of the *vlei* people had been coarse, this woman was dignified. She was wrapped in a rough bark cloth and wore no shoes; yet she did not look poor. She had a handsome, intelligent face.

"Oh, Chedu, what have you done?" she said. Trashman held out Kuda and babbled happily. "I can see he's cute, but he's not one of us. You can't bring him in."

"Please, *mai*," Tendai said politely. "We were kidnapped and Trashman rescued us. We're awfully tired. Can't we come in for a while?"

"Chedu is always welcome, of course, but we don't like strangers. They bring contamination."

"I know we're dirty, but we can wash," said Rita desperately.

The gatekeeper looked at her. "I wasn't thinking of the kind of dirt that can be washed off. You bring with you evil city ways."

"Oh, please," cried Rita, bursting into tears. Kuda, catching her misery, began to cry, too. Trashman's face screwed up when he saw Kuda's distress. He sat down on the cement and howled.

"Stop! Stop!" cried the large woman, covering her ears. "Very well, Chedu! They can come in—but only for a while." Trashman's tears dried up at once, and he beamed happily as though nothing had ever been wrong.

Grumbling and complaining, the woman led them inside and slammed the gate. She began to fasten the many locks and bolts, but Tendai had no eyes for this. He was far too surprised by the scene inside.

They had just left a tangle of apartment buildings in the year 2194. They had stepped into a vanished world from the distant past. A trail led down a hillside past *msasa* trees to a small village. Down the middle of the valley ran a stream with marshy paddocks on either side. Goats and cattle cropped the grass, while small boys guarded them with switches. Someone played a drum in the distance. Nearby, a woman sang a lullaby to a baby.

Tendai thought he had never seen anything so peaceful. "What happened to the city?" he whispered. All traces of the world as he knew it had vanished. Even the wall seemed to disappear, and he saw it was a giant curving mirror on the inside. The effect of this was that the land seemed to go on forever.

"We do not speak of the city here," said the gatekeeper, "and I warn you not to do so either. I am the only one who deals with the outside. Forget your robots and traffic, your crime and drugs. This is Resthaven, the Heart of Africa." She led them down the path. Trashman bounced along, chattering happily and holding out Kuda as though he were a trophy.

"Very nice, Chedu," the woman said.

"Is that his name? I thought he was called Trashman," said Rita.

"That is what we call him."

"Are you his mother?"

The woman laughed. "He calls everyone here Mother. He has belonged to the whole village ever since we found him abandoned outside the gate. At first, no one wanted him."

"Why not?" asked Rita.

"He was a *muramwiwa*, a child whose mother had thrown him away. His ancestral spirits might have brought us trouble."

"You mean, you might have left him to die?" Rita cried.

"It's very foolish to neglect the ancestral spirits," said the gatekeeper. "Just look at the world you come from: gang warfare, drugs, crime, broken families. Your people have forgotten about the ancestors, and the spirits are angry with you. But as you can see"—she led them past a group of children who clapped politely to greet them—"we *didn't* leave Chedu to die."

The children stood respectfully to one side as the visitors walked down the trail. Tendai was struck by their good manners. In Mazoe, a stranger would have been greeted with suspicion, if not fear.

"We decided that no one should adopt him," the woman went on, "but that all of us would feed him if he came to the door. He has a wandering spirit, though." She sighed. "He can't stay anywhere more than a few days. I suppose it's because his mother threw him away."

"I think it's because he had to wander from house to house here," said Rita.

They came to a collection of huts set around a neat courtyard. Tendai saw with delight that it was exactly like the villages in his history books. Separating the huts from the trees was a wide stretch of bare ground, which he knew would be inspected each morning for the footprints of rodents or the looping trails of snakes. The grass roofs of the houses extended out from the walls to be supported by a circle of poles. This provided an attractive area of shade.

All the entrances faced west, and each door consisted of a wooden panel hung on ox-hide loops. These panels were propped open in the heat of the day. The walls of the huts were decorated with black, red and ocher designs, while the doors were carved with crosshatched decorations.

The finest building was, he knew, the kitchen hut, but the cook fire had been moved outside for the summer. Beside the fire rested a drying rack for wooden bowls. But the thing that struck Tendai most was the smell.

The She Elephant's cook fires always had something vaguely unpleasant about them. It might have been the mixture of twisted *vlei* bushes and peat she used for fuel. Or it might have been the plastic-filled soil of the *vlei* itself under the fires.

This fire was of natural wood. It called to something deeply buried in Tendai, an ancestral memory of sitting by such a hearth and letting the smoke wash over him. Rita noticed it, too. "Ohhh," she sighed. "Just smell that. It's so *right*." And that was it, of course. There was a feeling of righteousness about the cook fire. It must come from paying attention to the ancestors, Tendai thought.

A small, heavily pregnant woman came out of one of the huts. "Greeting, *vakoma*, elder sister," she called.

"Greeting, *mun)nguna*, younger sister," replied the gate-keeper. "Behold, Chipo! We have visitors from afar."

Tendai noticed she didn't mention the city outside the wall.

"They are welcome," said Chipo, clapping her hands in greeting. She approached them, smiling, and then wrinkled her nose. "Do you suppose, Myanda, that our guests would enjoy a refreshing bath?"

Myanda laughed. "A bath is an excellent idea, younger sister, and they need fresh clothes, too. Those rags can be fed to the metal worker's furnace. I wouldn't dare use them in a cook fire."

"Are they going to *stay*?" Chipo asked, with a funny emphasis on *stay*. Myanda only raised her eyebrows and said nothing.

The big woman led Rita off to the women's bathing area, while Chipo took Tendai to a part of the stream sheltered by reeds. She handed him a strip of cloth and a loofah pod to scrape off the dirt.

It felt wonderful to throw off the evil-smelling rags and plunge into the stream. Tendai swam along the bottom, over waterweeds that bent in the current, and splashed to the surface beside a flat rock. Thousands of black tadpoles scattered before him as he clambered through the shallows. He scrubbed and scrubbed with the loofah pod until the top layer of skin seemed worn away. He was washing off the despair of Dead Man's Vlei. He was removing the feel of the chain around his ankle. He untied the *ndoro* and carefully rinsed it.

"These are your people," he told the unknown ancestor. "Thank you for bringing me here." He fastened it around his neck again and wrapped the cloth around his hips the best way he could figure. His old rags were already gone.

With a sigh of pure happiness, Tendai lay back on the flat rock and let the dappled sunlight play over his face.

So much of the Valley of Resthaven was familiar to him. He hadn't learned it from books, or even from Father and Mother. Tendai felt a pang of guilt when he thought about his parents. He should have asked Myanda for the holophone straightaway, but it was so tempting, after the exhausting escape from Dead Man's Vlei, to rest awhile.

Yes, thought Tendai. That's all we're doing: catching our breath. After all, we've been missing so long, a few more hours won't matter. I'll ask for the phone after dinner.

Meanwhile, it was extremely pleasant to lie on the warm stone and let the breeze dry his skin. Somewhere, not far away, he heard a drum beat. It had an earthy sound, not like the metal drum at home, of something burrowed out of a tree trunk with an animal skin stretched over the top.

Now how had he known what it looked like? The Mellower, of course.

Night after night, the Mellower had told them stories of faraway times. He had told them how the houses were made and the weapons were forged, how the pots were laid in hot coals for many days to season them. It was all part of the unending wandering story he wove about them. Sometimes it was Praise, sometimes history, and a lot of the time it was pure fantasy, but told with such authority that they all believed it. And the Mellower believed it, too. They could see it in his eyes. That was the best kind of story: when the teller was as much under its spell as the listener.

The incredible thing was that the Mellower was *white*. He belonged to the English tribe. His ancestors had lived in a completely different way, so how could he speak so convincingly of Tendai's ancestors?

The answer's simple, thought Tendai, feeling a pleasant ache in his legs as he rested from the long climb up the well and the flight across Dead Man's Vlei. The Mellower has a Shona *shave*. Aren't we lucky a spirit decided to possess him? I wish someone would take an interest in me. But he was too contented to worry long. With his hands folded on the *ndoro*, he drifted off into a dreamless sleep.

ar, Eye and Arm had trouble finding a taxi that would take them to Dead Man's Vlei after dark. Finally, they located an old broken-down pirate taxi whose owner charged them four times the going rate.

"I'll give you eight if you wait for us," said Arm.

"Nuts to you. I can't spend it when I'm dead," the driver replied.

The detectives checked their Nirvana guns as they sailed over the city. "How much getaway time do these give us?" asked Ear.

"Fifteen minutes. Then whoever we shoot wakes up. And remember, we have a limited number of rounds." Arm sighted along his weapon and tried to remember the police drill.

Eye sat stiffly between the other men and refused to enjoy the view. "I'll get airsick, and then you'll be sorry," he said when Ear tried to interest him. They flew over apartment buildings fifty stories high and as long as city blocks. People were having parties on the roofs of some of them. Ear could hear the music. Arm wished he was down there rather than flying to Dead Man's Vlei.

The lights below grew sparser, and presently they came to a great dark gash in the city. "That's Vainona." Arm pointed at the edge of the wilderness. The taxi driver went down at once and opened the door.

"You said you were taking us *into* the *vlei*," Eye cried. "We could have taken a bus!"

"Take it or leave it."

"At least wait," Arm said, counting out the money.

"Waste of time. You bozos aren't coming out." The driver ran a flashlight over the money to be sure it wasn't counterfeit. Then he took off, and they watched his taillights fade into the distance.

"Vainona's deserted at this time of night," said Eye.

Arm noted that the houses were shuttered and bolted, the lawns empty. Even the doghouses had locks on them.

"Maybe we should wait till morning," Ear said.

"Sooner or later, Matsika's going to find out what we know and come down here. Then I very much doubt the children will survive. The man's incapable of doing anything quietly. No, comrades," Arm sighed, "I'm afraid it's up to us."

The detectives walked carefully into the wasteland. The cement gave way to springy earth, stones, stunted bushes, gullies and hills. The comforting lights of Vainona retreated, and the watchful dark of Dead Man's Vlei surrounded them.

"I get the feeling—I don't know why—this place is *full*," remarked Arm.

"Don't. I'm nervous enough," said Eye.

"It's not like anything I've experienced before. It's not a thousand thoughts scurrying in all directions like the Cow's Guts, but one mind. The closest I can describe it is the feeling I get from an ant nest. The queen is at the center, and all the workers mirror and feed on her thoughts."

"You're giving me the heebie-jeebies," Ear said.

"I thought you'd be interested. *This* mind doesn't like us at all, by the way. *It* would like to see us buried under ten feet of sludge."

"Shut up, Arm," said Eye.

The detectives sat down on a hill and waited. Ear spread his ears until they fluttered in the breeze. Eye opened his lids wide and scanned the hills and hollows. Arm pressed his fingers to the earth and felt the vibrations. They sat like this for a long time.

"There *are* people here. I hear snoring," Ear said.

"I see a little camp fire. There's an old woman in a rocking chair," said Eye.

"Granny," murmured Arm. "Anyone else?"

"Too many bushes in the way." Eye moved his head from side to side, a motion that always reminded Arm of an alert cobra.

"I can feel several voices, but I can't make out the words," said Arm with his long fingers splayed out on the soil. "We'll have to go closer."

The detectives picked their way down the hill. First came Eye, moving his head from side to side; then Ear, whose ears bellied out like radar disks; then Arm. Owls hooted and left their perches, spreading pale wings over the black ground. Rats scurried into holes. Moths fluttered from under the men's feet, and a few ticks brushed off the bushes to quest for food.

The detectives felt as conspicuous as one of Matsika's police cars with its siren blaring, but to normal people they would have passed like shadows in the gloom. They stopped just outside the firelight and watched the four people sitting there.

"We'll get those brats and—*zzt!*" The She Elephant made a cutting motion across her throat. "I'm going to kill Trashman when I catch him."

"It's not his fault. He probably thought he was playing soccer with Kuda," said Fist.

"You're soft in the head. You deserve to spend the rest of your life in prison."

"Prison, yesss," Granny hissed. "That's where you belong. Criminals! Sinners! You're all going straight to hell!"

"Oh, shut up," said the She Elephant wearily.

"When's the last bus to Vainona?" Knife asked.

"In about twenty minutes. That's when the afternoon driver passes through again. I'm going to squeeze him until his eyes pop out—hey! What was that?"

Arm, in shifting to a more comfortable position, had put his foot squarely on one of the *vlei* people. The person sank his teeth into the detective's ankle. Arm screamed. Eye fired his Nirvana gun at the creature.

"Intruders! Stop them!" roared the She Elephant. All around, piles of trash came alive. Ear and Eye fired in all directions as they pulled Arm with them.

It was a nightmare trip. Arm stumbled along, trying to keep his mind off the pain. They tripped over bushes and slid down hollows as they struggled to reach the lights of Vainona. Sometimes they came down on something soft that went "Oof!" and tried to bite them. Eye, remembering Mr. Thirsty's Beer Hall, shot Knife before he could throw anything. Ear knocked down Fist, but they fired again and again at the She Elephant.

"She's made of steel!" gasped Eye.

She came after them, snarling with rage, and her black dress and skin melted perfectly into the night. They could hear her heavy footsteps as she pursued them. Finally, after ten direct hits, she fell with a groan. "She'll recover fast," panted Ear. Meanwhile, the *vlei* people boiled out of their tunnels and tried to cling to the men. They couldn't move as rapidly as the detectives, but there were many more of them, and more still came up from the lower depths.

"Don't lose your heads, comrades!" shouted Arm. He was really telling himself not to panic. The malevolence he had felt when the *vlei* was asleep was nothing to what it was producing now. It burned his mind like fire. All the insults and humiliation the *vlei* people had endured from normal folk bubbled up like hot acid. It was hate, rather than the pain in his ankle, that threatened to overwhelm him.

Ear and Eye dragged him the last few feet across the cement strip that surrounded Vainona. Then they lifted him and ran toward the bus platform not far away. "Help! Help! Call the police!" shouted Eye, but the houses were as silent as craters on the moon.

"There's got to be a phone! Something!" Ear cried. Arm's leg was bleeding badly. They put him down on a lawn, and Ear wrapped an emergency bandage around his ankle. "My gun's gone flat," said Eye in a low voice.

"Mine, too. We'll use his." Ear unstrapped the Nirvana gun from Arm. Arm was too weak to speak. He watched helplessly as Ear and Eye dragged a bus-stop bench in front of him for protection. A trash can whistled past them and crashed into a wall with a shockingly loud sound. The *vlei* people gathered at the border of Vainona. Some of them, emboldened by the dark, actually spilled across the cement walk. They made smudgy shadows on the street. More piled up behind, pushing the ones in front across the boundary.

The detectives stood back-to-back over Arm, but only Ear had ammunition. A chunk of cement thudded on the street not far away.

"Mwari! They're tearing it up!" cried Eye. The *vlei* people reached under the cement walk and lifted it right out of the ground. It crumbled under their hands. They tore chunks loose and hurled them at the detectives. A roar echoed out over the *vlei*.

"The She Elephant," said Ear.

"Good-bye, comrade." Eye squeezed his friend's shoulder. "I'm saying it now because I might not have time later. I forgive you for not washing the dishes when it was your turn."

"I forgive you for not taking out the trash—listen!" Ear turned his face to the sky. "The bus!"

The bus purred to a stop and dropped onto the landing pad. Instantly, Ear and Eye tore the door open and dragged Arm inside.

"Don't shoot! I don't carry money!" shouted the driver.

"We're detectives!" yelled Eye, slamming the door. "Get out of here if you value your life!" The driver took off at once as the She Elephant lunged out of the *vlei*. She shook her fist at them.

"We aren't thieves. See, here are our identity cards from the police," Eye said as Ear tried to make Arm comfortable. Arm's mind had cleared somewhat now that the emotions of the *vlei* people faded into the distance.

"I've read about detectives in books." The driver studied the card, with interest. "I didn't know they still existed. Listen, this is my last run. Can I take you to Paririnyatwa Hospital?"

"Yes, please! Tell me, have you seen any lost children today?" asked Ear.

"I swapped routes with another driver. He didn't mention children, but he said the She Elephant was after him. I assumed he meant an old girlfriend."

"That was the woman who shook her fist at you when we took off."

"You don't say! There's no accounting for taste."

The bus landed at Paririnyatwa Hospital, and paramedics raced out to care for Arm. "You again!" cried one of them, and Ear and Eye recognized the man who had treated them before. "I don't mean to nag, but couldn't you people stay home and watch holovision some nights?" He strapped Arm onto a stretcher and wheeled him off to the emergency ward. Ear and Eye waved at the bus as it flew away.

t was night when Chipo fetched Tendai to come and eat. "You looked so comfortable, I let you sleep," she said. Tendai followed her as she waddled ahead of him on the trail. She seemed extremely young to be pregnant, but he wasn't good at judging women's ages. They came to the village, where several fires now bloomed.

Rita was dressed in a bark sarong and couldn't stop grinning. "Isn't it wonderful? We're free! And we're *clean*."

"Not without work," remarked Myanda, who was kneeling on a grass mat beside a pot of bubbling *rapoko*.

"You should have heard Kuda yell when she scrubbed him," said Rita. Kuda sat next to several other boys of similar age. He glared resentfully at Myanda.

"He won't attract the vultures now," said the big woman, stirring the *rapoko* vigorously. "Oh!" She almost dropped the wooden spoon. "What's that around your neck?"

Tendai felt his chest. "That's an *ndoro* I found in a mine." Chipo and several other women gathered around him. Their stares made him uneasy.

"It's *old*," said one woman.

"Real shell. Not like the pottery one our Spirit Medium wears," said another. One of them timidly put out her hand but drew back before she could touch it.

"Is he going to *stay*?" the first woman asked.

"I don't know. I was going to feed him with the boys, but I suppose I'd better seat him with the men. He'll have his own bowl," Myanda said.

Tendai felt a little insulted. He knew the reason he would not eat from the communal bowl was because he might come from a family of witches. Modern people didn't believe in them. But since the Resthaven people did and, after all, knew nothing of his background, he forgave them.

He was led to the *dare,* the men's meeting place, which was surrounded by a sketchy fence. Myanda bowed and withdrew. Tendai looked around at the solemn villagers. They all sat on low stools, and they were all older than he. Some were ancient. They waited to be greeted. Tendai suddenly felt he was in over his head. What did you say to elders three hundred years ago? Their rules of etiquette were strict and inflexible. *That* much he remembered.

The silence grew. Tendai broke out in a sweat, although the evening was cool. He touched the *ndoro* and imagined the Mellower standing in his place. The Mellower had—many times—described the exact way a stranger entered a village. Tendai took a deep breath, bent forward and czlapped his hands in the masculine way. That is, his palms were flat and held vertically above the ground, not cupped and horizontal to it, after the manner of women. This was done softly, to alert the men to his presence. "Please excuse me, grandfathers. May I be allowed to clap hands?"

No one forbade him, so he clapped again, loudly, four or five times and greeted each man politely. Since he didn't know their totems, he wasn't able to do it perfectly. They seemed to accept this, because they addressed him in turn. They, too, clapped in greeting. They indicated that he should sit on the ground, as was correct for a mere boy.

Tendai sat with his knees flexed, almost in a lotus position, with his hands on his ankles. This, he remembered, was a position of humility. He couldn't remember whether it was the posture of a son-in-law approaching his father-in-law or a servant his master or just anybody approaching a chief. Again, no one corrected him, but no one smiled either. Tendai felt sweat break out again.

He didn't know what to do next, so he stared down at his ankles and waited. "It would be good to know how we may greet this stranger," said an old man with a stern face. "It would be a mark of politeness to know his family."

Then Tendai understood that they wanted to know his totems, the *mutupo* of his father and *chidao* of his mother. This was a custom that had almost entirely died out in modern Harare. It was rather like the English custom of shaking hands: the original use was to find out whether your visitor was armed. The purpose of knowing totems was to work out a relationship, if possible.

He ceremoniously announced Father's *mutupo*—the lion—and Mother's *chidao*—the heart.

"Our *mutupo* is also the lion," said the old man with slightly more friendliness.

"And my third wife is of the heart clan," said another man.

Third wife? thought Tendai.

The men went back to conversing among themselves. Eventually they let Tendai know their names. The old man was called Garikayi, and most of the others were his younger brothers. They didn't reveal too much about their totems, because such information could be used by witches. Slowly, tediously, the conversation wound on.

Most of it involved cattle. Tendai didn't know how much you *could* say about such boring animals until the men got going. Then he learned that each creature had a personality. They had bad habits, silly cravings and just about every weakness a person might have. Since he didn't know the cattle personally, Tendai's head began to nod.

He jolted awake when the water was brought. The women arrived with pots that they set before the men. Rita appeared, her face wet with tears. She slammed a pot down in front of Tendai, causing several of the men to raise their eyebrows. Everyone washed hands as the women went back to fetch dinner.

Each wife came in with a communal bowl, knelt and presented it to her husband. The women retired immediately. Tendai noted that both Myanda and Chipo presented bowls to Garikayi. Then Rita came in. She knelt and practically flung two small bowls—*sadza* and relish—at his feet. "Thank you," whispered Tendai. He noticed the men did not thank their wives.

"Don't expect me to do this when we get home," Rita whispered back. She disappeared before he could say more.

The men solemnly clapped their hands and said *pamusoro,* "Excuse me," as was polite when preparing to dine.

They ate from the communal bowls, going methodically from one to the next—except for Tendai, who was expected to keep separate. No one spoke now. They attended to the serious business of eating. Tendai saw that while each large bowl contained *sadza,* not all the relishes were the same. Most were a mix of tomatoes, onions and chilies, like the relish Rita had brought him, but one was composed of toasted termites, another of small dried fish, and a third was a platter of fried mice. Tendai was just as happy not to be included in the communal dinner.

The men didn't seem that fond of fried mice either. They left half of them on the platter.

At the end of the meal, everyone washed hands again. A troop of boys arrived to carry off the bowls. After a few moments, the boys returned and greeted their elders before sitting on the ground. A few older women entered the *dare* to listen, and Chipo squeezed herself in by the boys. Garikayi told them to bring her a stool. Tendai could see he was very proud of her pregnancy.

A mutter of anticipation went around the gathering. A few men lit clay pipes with hot coals and puffed out a rank smoke. Garikayi cleared his throat. "What is the small pot that feeds the whole family?" he asked a child of about five.

"The cook fire, honored grandfather," replied the boy.

"Who is the toddler who topples even the chief?" Garikayi inquired of a youth about Tendai's age.

"Sleep, o *sekuru*," he answered.

Around the fire went the riddles until each child had answered. They were traditional, and Tendai had heard most of them. When his turn came, Garikayi asked, "My mother's house has no door. What am I?"

"An egg," answered Tendai promptly. The men nodded, and he knew he had passed a test.

Then the elders asked each child to recite a proverb. The old sayings had a purpose in village life, but they were completely meaningless in modern Harare. Tendai had trouble remembering them.

"Don't touch the back of your head while walking, or someone in your family will die," said a boy.

"A boy who peeks into the cooking pot will beat his wife when he grows up."

"If you squat on a path, you'll get boils on your backside." Tendai saw a kind of logic to this one: it was the adults' way of keeping the little children from using a public walkway as a toilet.

"If you sing while eating, you'll get mumps," said a child who looked as though he might sing a lot when his mother wanted quiet.

"If you eat while lying down, you'll grow two navels." Weird, definitely weird, thought Tendai. Then they came to him.

"If a black cat crosses your path, you'll have bad luck," hazarded Tendai.

"Never heard that one," said a man.

"I've never seen a black cat. Are you sure that's a Shona proverb?" said another. Garikayi pointed to the next boy, and Tendai knew he had failed that test, whatever it was.

Why should I care? he thought. I'm going home tomorrow. But he found himself wanting to please them.

Garikayi started a chant that turned into a story. It was clear everyone knew it, but the people settled themselves down happily just as Kuda did when the Mellower recited *Peter Rabbit* for the twentieth time.

Garikayi said: *Once there was a man.*

The audience responded: *Go on.*

Garikayi: *That man was a king.*

Audience: *Go on.*

Garikayi: *He had a daughter.*

Audience: *Go on.*

Garikayi: *As beautiful as the sun.*

Audience: *Go on.*

The story continued in this way, half music, half poetry, as Garikayi told them of a king who placed his daughter on a platform over a big nest of bees in a tree. Anyone who wanted to marry her had to climb over the bees' nest. All the young men got stung so badly, they fell to the ground. At this point, the audience's response changed to: "Oh! Oh! The bees sting! Oh, my mother!"

Tendai thought it was a pleasant way to tell a story. It involved everyone and made them part of the unfolding adventure. In fact, as Tendai joined in with the responses, clapped his hands and swayed with the others, he felt a wonderful sense of belonging. These were his people. He was part of them. It was like being held in many, many arms.

Garikayi told them that one day a man arrived who had a bad skin disease. He was covered with scabs. He was disgusting to look at, and the other men laughed at him. The ugly man climbed the tree, but when the bees came out to sting him, they couldn't get through the scabs.

Garikayi: *His skin was like a rock.*

Audience: *Oh! Oh! A rock!*

Garikayi: *The bees stung him.*

Audience: *Go on.*

Garikayi: *They broke their stingers.*

Audience: *Go on.*

Garikayi: *They fell all over the ground.*

Audience: *Go on.*

The ugly man reached the princess and carried her down. The king married his beautiful daughter to him, and the other suitors were sent home in disgrace.

Garikayi said, "This is where Sarungano the storyteller died," which was the traditional way of ending a tale. The Mellower sometimes said that, but more often he ended with "and they lived happily ever after."

Everyone sighed with satisfaction. Tendai thought it was hard luck for the princess to marry someone covered with scabs. The Mellower would have cured the man of his skin problem.

An elder with gray hair and a beard began a fable about a baboon. The animal was tired of getting hungry, and he asked a rabbit to sew up his bottom so no food could get out. Later, he couldn't get the stitches out. The poor baboon swelled up until his paws stuck straight out. Everyone roared with laughter when the stitches finally broke. Tendai was embarrassed. Of course he had heard such stories, but not from dignified old men. He was glad Rita wasn't present.

"We would be honored," said Garikayi, breaking in on Tendai's thoughts, "if our visitor from afar would recount something from his people."

Tendai felt as though a big spotlight had suddenly switched on. Everyone fell silent and turned toward him. He could hear the fire rustle and the distant clunk of dishes being washed. He stood up on rubbery legs. His mouth opened, but no sound came out.

Tendai laid his hands on the *ndoro*. What could make a better story than his own kidnapping? He took a deep breath, remembering that the Mellower always did that before starting a Praise.

"I come from a far land," he began.

"Go on," said a few people in the audience.

"My father is a chief." Well, he is, thought Tendai. He's Chief of Security.

"Go on," said the audience.

"My brother and sister and I went on a trip."

"Go on," said all the people sitting around. Slowly, Tendai wove the events of their enslavement, the finding of the *ndoro* and the shaft of light sent by the ancestors into a magnificent tale. Even he could tell it was well done. The shining eyes of the listeners told him he had utterly captured their attention. All those nights listening to the Mellower had given him the skills he needed now. Tendai changed the tale to remove all mention of modern things. At the end, he substituted a magic cooking pot for the bus that carried them to Resthaven.

"This is where Sarungano the storyteller died," he finished.

"Ahhh! What a good tale!" a young man murmured.

"Wonderful! He has a *shave* for storytelling," agreed another.

"But that was why the *ndoro* was sent to him!" exclaimed Garikayi, and everyone nodded. "It's perfectly clear an ancestor waited in that mine for many years until he found a willing person to possess."

"He might even be a spirit medium when he gets older," said the first young man. Everyone brightened up at this idea. Tendai began to feel uneasy.

"I would never criticize our Spirit Medium," said the elder who had told the baboon story, "but he has never been good at poetry."

"He can't keep a beat—although he's an *excellent* witch finder," said the young man, looking nervously around.

"Well, that's settled," Garikayi said. "I was a little worried when this boy didn't know the proverbs, but it's clear the ancestors have sent him. I vote he stays."

"Yes! Yes!" everyone cried. A hubbub of voices drowned out Tendai's objections. The people rose to go. The women appeared from the shadows to whisk the smaller boys off to bed. The young men helped the elderly to rise. Laughing and talking, they left the *dare*.

"Wait! What's going on?" Tendai called.

Garikayi turned back briefly. "You can *stay*, provided the Spirit Medium agrees to it."

"But I don't want to! I need to call my parents on the holophone!"

Garikayi stumped on up the path, leaning on a twisted cane, until he was met by his two wives. It was Myanda who finally came for Tendai and led him to the boys' hut. "Don't mention holophones if you know what's good for you," she said in a low voice.

"I have to. I can't stay."

"It's out of my hands. They all think the ancestors sent you, and Garikayi has forbidden me to open the gate."

"For how long?" Tendai felt as though the ground had dropped out from under his feet.

"Don't you know, you poor fool?" said Myanda. "Once Resthaven has accepted you, you can never go home again."

17

The house in Mazoe was quiet, terribly quiet, without its children, but for the first time in several weeks Mother was able to listen to the silence without crying.

The children were alive.

She didn't know where they were, but they were following someone called Trashman. The name filled her with dismay. How could any reliable adult be called Trashman? Still, Tendai, Rita and Kuda had trusted him, so he must be all right.

Amadeus hadn't been able to trace him. How could he? The people her children had fallen among didn't have normal names: Fist, Knife, Granny. These creatures drifted around without families, totems or tribes, although Knife and Granny seemed to be Portuguese. Was Trashman Shona, Matabele or Batonka? No one knew. Mother wrung her hands in frustration.

Amadeus, naturally, had hunted for the bus driver, but he was hiding—no one knew where—from the She Elephant. If Mother's thoughts could have taken form, they would have looked like a big fireball falling out of the sky, aimed straight at the She Elephant. She hated her more intensely than she believed possible. That greedy monster had stolen her children!

Worst of all, Mother couldn't even look for them. In a village, she could have hunted for footprints. She could have stood on a hill and called for them. Not here.

The only person who suffered more than she did was Amadeus. He might look the same to outsiders—the very image of a powerful Chief of Security—but Mother knew otherwise. He was eaten up with worry. "I'm to blame," he said over and over when they were alone. "I didn't let them grow up. I taught them useless things like ancient military strategy. They didn't even know how to go to the store and buy rice!" No matter how often Mother tried to reassure him, he came back to the same lament.

The Mellower could have helped him. At the mere mention of the Praise Singer, however, Amadeus threatened to feed him, an inch at a time, to the crocodiles at the zoo. Well, thought Mother with a rueful smile, at least Amadeus looked like his old self then.

The Mellower was another problem. He hid in his room. His skin had begun to sag, and his face turned gray. Mother suspected he was drinking. Amadeus despised alcohol. He refused to allow it in the house, except for the millet beer that was necessary for religious ceremonies. But the Mellower got around the ban, as he got around so many things.

Mother stood up and took a deep breath. She was not going to let herself fall apart. She went to the Mellower's door and knocked. When he didn't answer, she went in.

The scene was worse than she had imagined! The windows were closed, and the curtains were drawn. The air stank of cheap sherry. "How dare you!" she shouted, yanking open the curtains. "You ought to be ashamed of yourself!"

"Oh, I am," moaned the Mellower from the bed. "I'm the awfulest, most despicable creature that ever existed. I ought to be fed to the crocodiles at the zoo."

"At least you and Amadeus agree about something," Mother snapped. She threw open the windows to let in the clean air of the garden.

"Get off that bed at once. Faugh! How can you drink this trash?" She gathered up the sherry bottles and hurled them through a window; they crashed and broke on the walk.

She called the butler and maid robots and instructed them to douse the Mellower in a cold bath. "When you're finished, make him run around the house ten times. Pinch him if he doesn't obey."

"We aren't allowed to pinch humans," said the butler robot.

"Well, then, unlock the automatic Doberman and tell it he's an intruder. I'll wait for you in the sitting room."

Mother drank tea while she listened to the mechanical yapping of the Doberman. The Mellower huffed and puffed past the window until he had done his ten laps. The butler robot dragged him inside and dropped him at Mother's feet. "Would you care for tea?" she inquired.

She poured him several cups with lots of milk and sugar. It was probably the only nourishment he had taken for days.

"Now," she said, "the time has come to stop wallowing in self-pity."

B-but I *miss* them," whimpered the Mellower.

"So do I," said Mother, fighting to keep back the tears.

"You don't understand. My whole d-day centered on them. We had picnics on the lawn. We gardened. I told them s-stories. Without them I'm nothing!" The Mellower buried his face in his hands and burst into loud sobs.

Mother felt exasperated and hysterical at the same time. "Crying won't do any good. The children are alive, and we have to keep trying. Right now, I think we should help the only people who have had any success in tracking them."

"The detectives?" said the Mellower, sniffing.

"Yes. Apparently, one of them was badly hurt. The medical report says he didn't lose much blood, but he seems to be suffering in his mind. He has special abilities, you see, and *there* was where he was wounded."

"That's interesting," said the Mellower, lifting a tear-streaked face to look at her. "You don't suppose—he might—like a little Praise?"

"That's exactly what he needs," Mother said.

The change that came over the Mellower was astonishing. The hangdog look left his eyes, and the hunch went out of his shoulders. Even his skin seemed to firm up. He jumped out of his chair and paced around the room. "I'd be *delighted* to do it. Let me wash my face and comb my hair. I'll change into fresh clothes. Let me see, the new brown shoes should do. No, no. Too formal. The beige sandals. And the pink shirt—pink is so cheerful—just the thing. Oh, my. The first Praise in weeks. I can hardly wait!"

He strode off as enthusiastically as Amadeus did when he was going to review troops. Mother was so amazed, she put her teacup down a full inch away from the table.

Half an hour later, Ear opened the door for a flustered, damp-looking man. He was tall with lank blond hair that fell over his face when he bobbed his head. "Where's that fine man? Where's the hero of Dead Man's Vlei?" he cried.

"Someone to see you, Arm," said Ear, who had been warned of the visit by Mother.

Arm lay on the sofa. He was even thinner than usual and hardly made a lump under the threadbare sheet. He opened one eye and studied the Mellower.

"What a marvelous apartment!" gushed the Praise Singer. "I love the exciting compromise between order and chaos. And who bought those exquisite curtains? I'll bet it was you." He playfully punched Eye on the shoulder.

"They keep people from looking in," said Eye, moving out of range.

"You must be the hero!" The Mellower plumped down on the end of the sofa. Arm opened both eyes and looked thoroughly alarmed. "Poor soldier! Wounded on the battlefield of life. I hope they give you the People's Medal."

"Would you like something to drink?" said Ear, throwing a towel over the heap of dirty dishes in the sink.

"You don't need to hide that from me," the Mellower said. "True creativity *thrives* on disorder, simply tucks in its roots and grows on chaos. I wouldn't say no to a sweet sherry."

So Ear rummaged around until he found a bottle sent over by Mr. Thirsty. It was a genuine bottle with a real cork, not the stuff the bartender usually ladled out of a washtub. The detectives didn't drink alcohol, but Arm said they had to encourage Mr. Thirsty's kind impulses, however misguided. The Mellower rolled the sherry around in his mouth and pronounced it quite the best he had tasted since an unfortunate accident overtook his wine cellar.

Arm hadn't been able to get out of bed since the terrible events on Dead Man's Vlei, but he found himself sitting up after only a few moments of Praise. Ear and Eye bent toward the Mellower like flowers to the sunlight. This was the first time any of them had been exposed to top-quality, state-of-the-art Mellowing, and it went straight to their heads.

The Praise Singer told them how kind, how brave and how intelligent they were. Arm, whose mind had been seared by the hatred of the *vlei* people, felt the scars drop off like so many bloated ticks. He was a wonderful creation, unique in all the city of Harare. He was one with his comrades, Ear and Eye. Together they saw into the heart of things. They were the true spirit mediums of the city. They did not, as spirit mediums usually did, take messages from the upper world to common humanity. Rather, they took the voices of the lowly and let them be heard on high.

Oh, it was heady stuff! It was almost too much sympathy for Arm after the bleak malice of Dead Man's Vlei, but it healed him.

At the same time, Arm saw into the mind of the Mellower. He didn't mean to, and he backed away at once. For only an instant he glimpsed, at the center of the man's weak-willed soul, a great kindness.

One thing disturbed him in spite of the wonderful healing: as long as the Mellower talked, Arm couldn't worry. He knew the She Elephant planned to sell the children to the Masks. He knew Tendai, Rita and Kuda were in deadly peril, but he didn't care. That was the effect Mellowers had on people. And perhaps, Arm thought, it was one of the reasons places like Dead Man's Vlei still existed.

When it was over, Eye sighed and Ear shook himself as though he had awakened from a lovely dream. Arm stretched out his long arms (which the Mellower had said were handsome) and murmured, "Why doesn't General Matsika offer a reward for the return of his children?"

"How clever of you to think of it," said the Praise Singer, holding his glass out for a refill. "Our General is a man of the law. He has to put the good of the city before his own needs. Children used to be snatched off the streets every day before he became Chief of Security, just for the ransom. He put a stop to that when he broke up the gangs. Now no one is allowed to pay money for the return of a kidnapped person. It's very hard for him to obey his own rules, but in the long run it's the right thing."

"And Matsika always does the right thing," said Arm. "An extraordinary man."

"Oh, he is. Now I simply must fly. Good-bye, you marvelous, courageous people. I hope I can Praise you again soon." And with that, the Mellower flitted out the door to the waiting limo.

18

It's all right for you," said Rita tearfully. "You're a *boy*. You get to lie around listening to stories. I have to scrub the floor, wash clothes, sweep the courtyard and—and—air out the babies' bedding. It's so horrible! Why don't you ask for the holophone? Nobody listens to me."

Rita was hiding in a tiny clearing surrounded by thick bushes. She had a heap of appallingly dirty mats that Tendai assumed was the babies' bedding.

"They don't listen to me either. I've been trying for days," he whispered. By all the rules, he wasn't supposed to be with Rita. Boys his age didn't play with girls—or not until they began the housekeeping games that led up to marriage.

"They will *so*. I hear them talking: 'Oh, the new boy's so clever. Oh, he's a wonderful storyteller.' They think you're the greatest thing since fried mice. Did you *see* those poor little creatures that first night?"

"Our ancestors ate them, and we're not vegetarians," Tendai reminded her.

"Our ancestors ate them, but our ancestors' *wives* had to kill them. You should have heard their little squeaks."

"Don't," Tendai said.

"And speaking of wives, do you know how old Chipo is? *Fourteen!* And she's eight months' pregnant!"

"Keep your voice down."

"I'll keep my voice down if you keep your ears open. Myanda was Garikayi's first wife, but she couldn't have any children. The Spirit Medium said she might be a secret witch. He said witches eat their babies on the sly. Have you ever heard of anything so stupid?"

Tendai put his hand over Rita's mouth because her anger was making her reckless. The reek of the babies' bedding was overpowering in the airless thicket. He wanted to help her with the dirty mats, but that would certainly not be allowed. Tribal law was perfectly clear on that point: boys and girls had different duties, and unfortunately, the nastiest ones fell on the girls.

"All right, I'll keep my voice down," Rita whispered. "Garikayi married Chipo when she was only twelve, but she didn't get pregnant till now. You can bet he's anxious about it. He doesn't have any children. It's considered a disgrace."

And it was, in old tribal law. The Mellower had told them.

"Don't you wonder where Kuda and Trashman are?" asked Rita.

Tendai felt guilty. He had been so wrapped up in his own affairs, he had forgotten about them. He had assumed Kuda was with Myanda.

"They're at the opposite end of Resthaven," Rita said. "Chipo isn't allowed to look at Trashman, because it might affect her baby, and he won't go anywhere without Kuda."

"Trashman can't hurt her baby," said Tendai.

"Of course not, but you wouldn't believe the fuss they're making over her. She's loaded down with charms and rubbed with ointments. If she so much as opens her mouth, someone puts food in it. It's lucky Chipo's so good-natured or she'd be spoiled rotten."

"So what's the problem?" Tendai could hear the other boys in the distance, calling his name. He was supposed to be helping with the cattle.

"Who do you think they'll blame if something goes wrong with the birth?"

Tendai stared at her. The sun cast harsh bands of black shadow and bright light over Rita's face. He couldn't read her expression, but her voice told him she was deeply worried.

"This is a village," she said urgently. "No antibiotics. No doctors."

"Women survived for thousands of years without them."

"*Some* of the women, you stupid boy. Oh, why do I even bother to explain? Chipo's too young! You may be in love with traditional life, but women and babies used to die in those wonderful old-fashioned villages."

The boys' voices were nearer now. Tendai would have to go soon if he wanted to keep Rita out of trouble.

"And think about *this*: I'm loaded with all kinds of work except one. They won't let me near the food. And you have to eat out of special bowls that no one else will touch. Do you understand?"

"Witchcraft," breathed Tendai.

"You said it. Witches put things in people's food. None of them will really trust us until the Spirit Medium says we don't have witch blood in the family. And he won't do that until Chipo has her baby."

The boys passed by the thicket, calling for Tendai. He let them go on. "I'll make a plan," he whispered, although he had not the slightest idea what to do.

"Get us out of here," began Rita, but Tendai stepped quickly out of the thicket and ran after the boys.

"There you are," said Hodza, a handsome boy of Tendai's age but of a frailer build. He was one of Garikayi's nephews, as was everyone Tendai met in the boys' hut.

"You may be new, but you can't get out of work," called another youth, named Banga. He was the largest and brawniest of the boys and seemed to be their leader. The group joked and chattered as they went toward the meadow where the cattle grazed. The boys were greatly awed by Tendai's storytelling ability as well as the possibility that he might be a spirit medium someday.

At night, in the boys' hut, they begged him for tales. "You'd be a better medium than the one we have," whispered Hodza, as they all sat around on mats. The mats smelled faintly of ammonia for reasons Tendai didn't care to imagine.

"Quiet," said Banga. "*He* might hear you."

"He's not a witch. The owls don't carry him messages." But Hodza didn't mention the Spirit Medium again.

"Speaking of witches," another boy said, and proceeded to tell a gruesome story about someone who wrapped herself in other people's skins.

After a while, the big boys had to wake up the little ones and march them outside to urinate. Hodza imitated an owl and the little boys screamed. Myanda yelled at them to be quiet.

Tendai remembered the boys' hut as they walked down to the meadow. He had never been surrounded by friends of his own age, and he thoroughly enjoyed it. So what if Rita was having a hard time? "She's like Granny," he told himself. "She'll complain no matter where she is." But a picture of her sitting in the hot thicket surrounded by the babies' bedding spoiled his pleasure.

"Do you know where the holophone is?" he asked Hodza.

"The what?"

"You know. It's a screen with a three-dimensional picture in it. You say the number, and the operator dials it for you." But Tendai might have been talking Tibetan for all Hodza understood. "Well, what about the police? How do you call them?"

"What are police?" said Hodza.

"They keep law and order. They arrest criminals."

"When anything goes wrong, we have a village council," Hodza said. "The elders discuss the problem, and if they can't work it out, they ask the Spirit Medium. He's in direct contact with the ancestors."

Great, thought Tendai. Dial-an-ancestor. A service provided by your friendly holophone company. "Maybe you don't have things like that here," he went on, "but surely you know they exist outside the wall?"

"What wall?" said Hodza.

"He means the edge of the world," Banga explained. "Outside is *Mwari*'s country."

"What do you think is in *Mwari*'s country?" said Tendai, who was beginning to lose patience with the whole argument.

The boys looked at one another as though the question had never occurred to them. "Who cares?" Banga said. "When we need more people, *Mwari* sends them to us. Sometimes they work out and sometimes not. Myanda did fine, except she doesn't have any children."

"That's because she's a witch," remarked a boy.

"That's ridiculous," said Hodza.

"We don't know anything about her family."

The argument went on about whether Myanda was a witch or merely unlucky, and Tendai realized it was useless to expect help from the boys. Not only were they ignorant about what lay outside, they weren't even curious.

The cows raised their heads and watched the boys come down to the meadow. A gang of seven- to nine-year-olds threw down their switches and greeted them. "About time," grumbled the leader of the smaller boys. They trooped off, and the older children took their places on the rocks.

19

The cattle went about the business of feeding, while a few goats milled among them. A pair of young billies butted each other with their horns, but most of the time the animals were perfectly orderly. And boring, Tendai decided. He was given a switch to drive the animals from vegetable gardens, should they be tempted. They never were.

The meadow was full of foxtail and whisk and couch and many other kinds of grass Tendai didn't recognize. Up the sides of the valley grew thick stands of thatching grass. It was woody and not attractive to the cattle. Tendai knew it would be harvested to mend the roofs of the huts.

The boys sat on rocks. They chewed tender new stems of foxtail, almost as placidly as the animals below. *Mopani* flies hovered around their eyes. They brushed them away. The shadows under the trees shrank as the sun moved toward noon.

What must it be like to sit here month after month? thought Tendai. You listened to the monotonous chewing of cattle, the tepid rustle of water as it fingered its way through the reeds. You brushed away thousands of *mopani* flies through the years. No wonder you brooded a lot about the personalities of your cattle.

A cow bawled from the middle of the stream. "That's Clay Belly," said Banga. "She always wants the grass on the other side, and she always gets stuck in the mud." Tendai welcomed the diversion. He followed Banga into the water. "Stay on the rocks. The bottom is sticky around here."

Tendai got behind Clay Belly and pushed her rump, while Banga hauled on her horns. Clay Belly complained but eventually worked herself loose. She lolloped up the bank, spraying mud and water on all sides. Everyone laughed.

Then it was back to the rocks, to chewing on grass stems, listening to the *sluck* of water and brushing away *mopani* flies. Tendai had a lot of sympathy for Clay Belly. She at least had the imagination to try for something beyond her reach.

The sun crawled to noon and past.

"Let's play a game," suggested Hodza. Tendai brightened. The boys went to a flat hollow in a stone. The hollow formed a tiny arena. Each boy produced a fat peanut that had been marked with charcoal to show the owner. Two boys would set their peanuts twirling like little tops in the arena. The object was to knock your opponent's piece out of the hollow. Tendai didn't do well at the game. Time after time, his peanut was sent flying, to the delight of the others. After a while, the game became as deadly as sitting on the rocks. No one, except Tendai, noticed.

Finally, when he was ready to scream with impatience, a girl showed up with lunch. The boys fell upon roasted mealies and boiled pumpkins. They drank a sweetish slightly alcoholic liquid called *maheu* made of *sadza* and water left to ferment from the night before. Tendai, as usual, had a separate bowl and a calabash full of *maheu*.

The food disappeared very quickly, and still the boys were hungry. To quiet their stomach pangs, they set about coaxing termites from nests. They poked grass stems down holes. The soldier termites fastened onto these and were pulled up and eaten.

132

Banga produced a leather sling. They all collected smooth pebbles from the stream and took turns slinging them at targets. Tendai did very well at this.

On the plants growing out of the water, a colony of weaverbirds had built their nests. These were cleverly constructed baskets attached to the tips of reeds. They swayed in the breeze as the bright yellow birds zipped in and out with food for their young. Banga suddenly hurled a rock and struck a weaverbird just as it perched on its nest. The bird dropped straight into the stream.

Everyone cheered as Banga waded out to claim his prize. He proudly displayed the little heap of bloodstained yellow feathers. Tendai thought about the baby birds waiting inside the nest for food that would never come. I'm a fool, he thought. This is a traditional village. These people can't go to a restaurant for lunch. They have to hunt. But he couldn't help feeling sorry.

The boys killed several *quelea* birds, which was all right. They flocked by the hundreds in the reeds and were a serious pest. Banga built a fire and roasted the tiny creatures on a spit.

"Here comes the Kamba clan," said Hodza, just as they finished picking the bones.

"They don't graze this meadow until tomorrow," Banga said, but he didn't seem surprised. Along the ridge at the top of the meadow came a gang of strange boys and another herd of cattle. The boys halted, but the animals kept on coming.

"Shouldn't we stop them?" Tendai said.

"Not yet." Banga's eyes shone with excitement. The others of Garikayi's clan were suddenly wide awake.

"Won't the cattle get mixed up?"

Banga looked at Tendai as though he were crazy. "How could they? You don't get your brother mixed up when he's playing with other children." But to Tendai, all the animals looked the same, except for Clay Belly, who was covered with mud.

The Kambas began constructing something on a small hill. Tendai couldn't see what until they stepped back to reveal two mounds of dirt the size of small anthills. Things were getting stranger by the minute.

"You be our bull," said Banga, pushing Tendai to the front.

"He's a visitor," objected Hodza.

"Grandfather says he's going to be one of us, so he has to prove himself." Banga yelled a perfectly filthy insult at the Kambas, and they answered back in the same way. A big mean-looking boy shouldered his way to the front of the rival gang. He had a horribly scarred face. He made hand signals Tendai didn't understand.

"Ooo," said the Garikayi clan. "You aren't going to let him get away with *that*?"

Tendai didn't know what to do. He didn't understand the situation. "What's wrong with his face?" he whispered to Hodza.

"He fell into a cook fire when he was a baby," Hodza answered. Tendai was horrified. In the city, such an injury could have been corrected.

"What's his name?"

"Why are you asking all these questions? He's the Kamba's bull. That's all you need to know. However, we call him Head Buster."

Great, thought Tendai. He watched with a sinking heart as the mean-looking boy swaggered up and down in front of the mounds of dirt. Boys on both sides hurled insults. Suddenly, Head Buster spun around and kicked one of the mounds to smithereens.

"Ooo!" cried the Garikayi clan.

"Get him! Get him now!" yelled Banga.

"I don't understand," Tendai said.

"You idiot! He just insulted your *mother*! Those mounds are your mother's breasts. He just *kicked* one of them!"

Then Tendai understood. It was a ritual fight, one gang against another, him against Head Buster. He hated fighting unless it had a purpose. The ritual of building his mother's breasts and insulting them simply had no meaning. He would have fought to the death to protect Mother if she were really there, but this was a stupid game.

Banga and Hodza and the others yelled themselves hoarse, trying to goad him into battle. No one needed to push Head Buster. He looked as if he wrestled hyenas for sport. "This isn't fair," Tendai murmured.

"Fair? Fair? You're our bull, you coward! Go get him!" shouted Banga.

Finally, reluctantly, Tendai sprang into action. He ran up the hill, circling around to get the advantage of the slope between him and his opponent. The other boys scattered. Head Buster swayed back and forth with his arms out like the pincers of a scorpion. Tendai let him get close. Head Buster lunged, head down, and Tendai stepped aside and threw him down the slope.

The crowd went wild. Head Buster roared and charged up the hill again. Tendai threw him back. Every time the bigger boy tried to butt him, Tendai used his momentum to throw him off balance. Finally, he rolled the big boy all the way down the hill to bang against a rock. Blood poured from Head Buster's face. He howled with rage and pain.

And that seemed to be it. The fight was automatically stopped. The Kambas helped their bull stagger off along the ridge. They rounded up their cattle and drove them away. The Garikayi clan danced around Tendai.

"I thought you were afraid," said Banga. "That was a good trick, brother. You really caught him off guard."

"You're the best bull we ever had!" cried the others.

Tendai laughed along with everyone else, but inside he felt dishonest. The fight hadn't been fair, and not for reasons the Garikayi clan could imagine. All those years of practicing with the martial arts instructor had paid off. Tendai might not like jujitsu, but he knew a lot more about it than Head Buster.

And for an instant, when the ugly, scarred boy lay at the bottom of the hill, Tendai had been right down there with him. He knew what it was to be overcome with terror. He felt the dull, oxlike panic as blood dripped down his face. Then the instant was gone as he was surrounded by the ecstatic Garikayi clan.

The martial arts instructor said that was what made me a bad warrior, Tendai thought as he was carried in triumph around the meadow. I didn't do too badly, though. It felt good when Banga called me "brother."

At the end of the day, the boys herded the cattle and goats into a *kraal* surrounded by thornbushes. Tendai understood that the fight was to be kept secret. The elders forbade such goings-on—while at the same time expecting them. It was one of those confusing village rules.

If Tendai had run away from the fight, everyone from the smallest child to Garikayi would have been ashamed of him. The old man wasn't supposed to know, but from the smile he gave Tendai at the *dare* it was clear he had been informed about the victory.

Tendai was completely happy that night as he took his place in the *dare*. Everyone included him in the conversation. This time there were no riddles but much lighthearted banter about bulls. It was only when Rita entered with his dinner that Tendai became uneasy.

She looked so tired! Her face was pinched as though she hadn't been eating enough. She even had little *burns* on her upper chest. What on earth was going on? Rita stumbled with weariness as she left the *dare*.

Tendai knew then he would have to confront Garikayi about leaving Resthaven. Rita was suffering, and he didn't even know what was happening to Kuda. He took a few deep breaths to get his courage up—

—and an ancient woman he had not seen before hobbled into the men's meeting place. She whispered something to Garikayi. Immediately, the atmosphere of the *dare* changed. The boys were sent out while their elders stayed to confer.

Tendai branched off from the others to hunt for Rita. He found her cleaning pots with sand and ashes. "Want me to help you?" he whispered.

She moved aside, and he took over the work. A cry sounded in the distance. "Something's happening," he said.

"Poor Chipo. She's having her baby," said Rita.

Tendai worked silently. Childbirth was something he didn't like to discuss.

"It's too early. She was supposed to travel to her own family at the other end of the valley. Women do that with their first child. Now she can't. Myanda sent people scurrying in all directions to find midwives."

"More than one?"

"Garikayi insists on at least three." Another cry sounded in the night.

Tendai shivered. "How are *you*? You have burns on your chest."

"Oh, that," Rita said dully. "I ran afoul of one of the rules in this charming place. I ate one of the mealies meant for your lunch."

"I wouldn't have minded."

"Even the She Elephant didn't care if I ate something extra. She always gave us enough." Rita was crying silently, hopelessly. "Myanda said I was stealing. I don't steal. I was hungry. I didn't know I had to ask."

"I'll save you my food," promised Tendai. Why hadn't he thought of that before?

"The women heated peanuts on the coals. They held me down and put them on my chest."

Tendai was so shocked he couldn't speak. He found Rita's hand and held it tightly.

"I suppose it will scar. A doctor might be able to fix it. If we ever see a doctor again."

"Of course we will," Tendai said. "Oh, Rita, I'm so sorry. I'll make it up to you." They sat together, holding hands in the dark.

The moon rose over the wall of Resthaven, painting the quiet *msasa* trees with silver and trailing a bright shimmer on the stream at the valley's heart.

20

"**D**inner with the Matsikas. We've come up in the world," said Eye, admiring his new *dashiki* in the mirror over the sink.

"Hurry up," Ear complained. "You've been standing there for fifteen minutes." The dirty dishes had, for once, been washed and put away. The mirror had been polished, but nothing could be done about the crack. When Eye looked in it, half his face appeared to be lower than the other half.

Arm lounged in an easy chair. He wiggled his freshly polished shoes to catch the light. "Mrs. Matsika insisted we take these *dashikis* because they were a gift to the General. 'He never takes gifts,' she said. 'People might think they were bribes. He always gives things away.' Hah!"

"You don't believe anyone gave the General a skinny six-and-a-half-foot-long *dashiki*?" Ear said, watching Arm uncurl from the chair.

"No more than they gave him earmuffs."

Ear smiled into the mirror over Eye's shoulder and patted the new muffs. They exactly matched his *dashiki*. "I wonder how she knew we didn't have suitable clothes."

Arm looked around at the sagging furniture and peeling paint. "It must have been a lucky guess."

The doorbell rang. Arm peered through the peephole and saw General Matsika's chauffeur glancing around anxiously. Shortly afterward, they were sailing off over the Cow's Guts on their way to the Mile-High MacIlwaine. The detectives sat in the back so they wouldn't make the chauffeur nervous.

As they approached, they could see tier upon tier of lights festooning the Mile-High MacIlwaine. Everything a human could want was there, from the grand lobby on the ground floor to the elegant Starlight Room one mile up. It was the kind of place the detectives could only afford in dreams. At the moment the Starlight Room was obscured by a small cloud.

"You have time to visit the lobby. I have to pick up the General and his wife at the University," the chauffeur told them. So Ear, Eye and Arm walked through the magnificent entranceway and tried not to look like tourists.

The lobby was built over a lake. Guests could catch bream or tiger fish for dinner, if they liked. Giant glass walls separated a wilderness area from the walkways, which had glass floors over the water. The sun was near setting, and day animals were changing places with those of the night.

Lily-trotters stepped delicately from lotus pad to lotus pad; kingfishers darted among the reeds; flocks of *queleas* flew in formation. They turned, dipped and landed in a twittering bunch. Under the glass floor, a crocodile gazed up at them with slitted, calculating eyes.

Eye grasped Arm. "I can't help it. I used to watch them on the river where my mother washed clothes."

"So did we all," said Arm, steering him past the spot. The crocodile rose gently until its eyes poked out of the water. It floated along under them, keeping pace with their feet. At last, it sank down again.

"To wait for another tourist," Ear said with a shudder.

They came to a large enclosed island where hippos grazed. A family of giraffes was silhouetted against a bank of picture windows. "Beautiful," murmured Arm as he watched the scene.

But by now the sun had set, and they would have to get to the Starlight Room. Arm rang a bell at the desk. A clerk bustled over and only blinked once when he saw such unusual guests. "The Starlight Room?" he said. "Do you have reservations? Ah! The General. Let me escort you to the elevator." He led them to a wall of doors, pressed a button and bowed slightly to show them in.

"Wait a minute. This is *glass*," said Eye.

"But of course," the clerk replied. "What would a trip to the Starlight Room be without a ride in our famous glass elevators? They go up like rockets."

"I—I'm terrified of heights."

"Let me assure you, terror is half the fun. You should hear the ladies squeal! But don't worry. After the first quarter mile, the ground becomes a blur."

"Not to me," Eye said.

"Isn't there another way?" Arm asked.

"There *is* a service elevator for bananas and so forth," said the clerk in a frosty voice. "It's completely off-limits to, um, humans. Perhaps you would prefer dining in the basement. You'll find sandwich machines there."

"Cover your face, Eye," Arm said gently. "Surely you'll be all right if you don't look."

"I'll know," moaned Eye, but he let himself be led onto the glass floor. He crouched with the neck of the *dashiki* pulled up over his head and screamed as the elevator shot up. It was a little scream, as screams go, but it felt like a blow to Arm. He had forgotten he was vulnerable to Eye's fear.

The elevator of the Mile-High MacIlwaine whizzed up past apartments, schools, clinics, supermarkets and sports clubs. It passed churches, meditation halls, mosques, drop-in clinics for Mellowers and an entire floor devoted to the Lion Spirit Medium, who relayed messages from *mhondoro*, the spirit of the land. Ordinary mediums had offices every fifty floors. The Mile-High MacIlwaine wasn't a building so much as a vertical town within the great city of Harare.

Ear, Eye and Arm passed health spas, vegetable markets, a junior college, beauty salons and libraries, although only Ear appreciated the view. Eye was curled up in a ball; Arm was trying to block out his fear. Once, Arm had heard, the system had broken down, and food could not be sent to the top one hundred floors. Then there was a very small famine.

It was like rushing up in a bubble released from the bottom of the sea. By the quarter-mile mark, Eye had fainted, and Arm shook himself free of his friend's thoughts. He didn't believe he could have taken another minute of terror.

And still the elevator rose, above all the other buildings in Harare. It plunged into a shallow cloud bank and popped out the other side. Now all Arm could see was an ocean of cloud, glowing with the last rays of sunset.

The door slid open at last. Ear and Arm dragged out Eye and laid him on the carpet. The waiters, who were delivering snacks, stepped around them with expressions of distaste.

The detectives fed Eye Earl Grey tea until he recovered. By then, General Matsika and his wife had arrived, and the waiters gathered by the door to greet them. Arm asked that they be seated away from the window.

"It's all right with me, but it's a waste of a good view," said the General. "Being sensitive is a handicap, isn't it?"

"And a great gift as well," Mrs. Matsika added, laying her hand on the General's arm.

They had the restaurant to themselves. The General's bodyguards formed a cordon by the door. They checked the waiters with metal detectors as they left the kitchen.

The food was fantastic. They began with chilled avocado soup and prawns in aspic. They moved on to grilled guinea fowl, baby carrots in herb butter and red Mangalore rice from India. Dessert was mango parfait dotted with toasted macadamia nuts.

Of course Arm wondered why the General was entertaining them. Matsika talked of seemingly innocent topics, but the detective had the impression he was studying them. He asked questions about their work, their lives. He seemed interested in every detail.

At the end of the meal, a group of men appeared at the door and demanded to be let in. "I'm sorry. The Starlight Room is reserved," the maître d' began.

"Totally unacceptable!" grated a voice that fluttered Arm's nerves. "We always eat here. I shall complain to the President!"

The General stood up. "Of course let them in," he called. "I had no idea the honored Gondwannan Ambassador wished to dine at the Starlight Room. Please accept my apology."

A large man with the shoulders of a prizefighter strode into the room. "Amadeus!" he cried. "Such a pleasure to see you!"

Arm felt a wave of hostility so intense, he almost fainted.

"My dear Ambassador! We were about to leave or we would certainly have treasured your company. Consider the place yours." The General indicated the restaurant with a sweep of his arm.

He paid his bill, adding a generous tip, and bowed to the diplomats as he left. The Gondwannans drew tables together and yelled for brandy. Arm noticed every one of them had set off metal detectors when they passed General Matsika's bodyguards.

As they walked to the elevator, Arm looked back. He had an impression of dark shadows hovering over the Starlight Room. And this was odd because the men themselves were perfectly ordinary. They were brutish, with too much money and power, but Arm had met characters like that before. Something else flitted around and behind them. He had never seen anything like it.

They went down only two floors to the nearest limo landing. Arm expected to be dropped off in the Cow's Guts, but to his surprise the limo sailed toward Mazoe. "Too early to go to bed," rumbled the General. "From what I hear, you fellows are out all night anyway."

Arm nodded. Of course the General knew about the visit to Dead Man's Vlei, and perhaps a good deal more than they had reported. He looked out at Mount Hampden, a largely English suburb. It wasn't long until Christmas, a popular English holiday. Some of the houses were decked out in colored lights, and one had a wooden model of a bearded man in a cart pulled by eight antelope.

They passed over the Iron Mask Mountains and came in low over Mazoe Reservoir. They landed at the Matsika estate, with searchlights trained on them from all sides.

"Don't get out until I've deactivated the weapons system," said the General. Arm saw, with a tightening of his throat muscles, machine guns slide back into the walls.

The automatic Doberman fawned at the General's feet but raised metal hackles at the sight of the detectives. "Friend," said Matsika, placing his hand on each detective in turn. The Doberman retreated, growling, to its kennel.

They went inside, and Mrs. Matsika sent the maid robot off for fruit juice. A sewing basket offered her a selection of knitting. She waved it away. The butler robot hung up the General's cap. The holophone danced around eagerly until it was ordered to stand in a corner. Machines were everywhere.

Could I get used to this? thought Arm as he lazed on a sofa with his long arms resting along the top. No metal springs dug into his back. No suspicious ratty odors wafted out of the stuffing. I could, he decided—and yet where are the people?

Ear and Eye happily dug into a plate of cookies provided by Mrs. Matsika as she asked them about their childhood in Hwange.

"Come on. We have something to discuss," General Matsika told Arm. He began to put his glass on a table, and the maid robot managed to slide a coaster under it before it touched the wood. They went down a hall to a library. The General sat on one side of a large desk and indicated that Arm should take an easy chair on the other. They sat for a moment, studying each other, before the General cleared his throat.

"I know where the children are," he said.

"They're in Resthaven."

Arm stared at General Matsika. He had heard vague tales of the place.

"I located the bus driver at once." The General got up and prowled the walls of the library. Surprisingly, because he didn't seem like a scholar, the shelves were loaded from floor to ceiling with books. A sliding ladder allowed one to reach the upper levels. "He was visiting his parents in Mtoko. He was perfectly cooperative—had no idea of the harm he had done." The man climbed the ladder and removed a weighty old-fashioned book with a leather cover. The rungs of the ladder creaked as he descended.

"I don't understand. Why don't you bring the children home?" Arm said.

"Resthaven isn't part of Harare," said Matsika, opening the book on the desk. He blew dust off the pages. "Strictly speaking, it isn't even part of the world. Look here."

Arm leaned over the picture the General had found. It was a painting of a tall thin man. He wore a painted bark apron that reached to his knees and a short sword at his hip. The scabbard was richly wound with gold filigree. The man's hair was elaborately decorated. Hanging on his chest, which was otherwise bare, was a white disk with a spiral pattern on it.

The man stared directly out of the page. Arm had seen that look before on one of the lions at the Lion Park. The animals were overweight and placid, but for an instant one of them had gazed at him with the same expression. It meant *If you and I were alone on a jungle path, I wouldn't give a bent pin for your chance of survival.*

"Who's that?" Arm asked.

"An artist's idea of Monomatapa. Of course no one knows what he really looked like, but there's a lot of information about his time. Two hundred years ago, a group of traditionalists decided to go back to the world of Monomatapa."

"Resthaven," said Arm.

"They were financed by a multimillionaire and backed by many influential politicians. It was a compelling idea, to return to the past. It also appealed to a desire to preserve the spirit of Africa." General Matsika turned the pages. Arm saw paintings of huts, fields and people.

"Much of Africa was being overlaid by European customs. It seemed—then—that our culture would be destroyed by the outside world. And so Resthaven was created." More pictures: women carrying pots of water or grinding millet in giant mortars. The paintings displayed beautiful women cheerfully going about their tasks, but a few old photographs pictured gaunt crones with backs bowed by years of heavy labor.

"The founders didn't want Resthaven to be a tourist resort," Matsika went on. "They made it a separate country, recognized by all the nations of the world. Resthaven is independent, as much as Mozambique or Gondwanna. Its sovereignty is protected by international law.

"When someone is tired of modern life, he or she can apply for citizenship. Very, very few are admitted. They are subjected to tests. If they pass, they become part of Monomatapa's country. Forever."

"We have to get the children out of there at once!" cried Arm.

The General sat down again and stared at the old book. "I can't invade Resthaven any more than I can go into Gondwanna. It would be an act of war. And you have to understand the emotional appeal the place has for Africans: it's Jerusalem, it's Mecca, it's the Hindu city of Ayodhya. Every culture has one place it will not allow to be touched. This is ours. As long as Resthaven exists, the Heart of Africa is safe. If I invaded, every country on the African continent would rise up against Zimbabwe."

"But—surely, the children didn't ask to be taken in."

"I don't know. I've gone there every morning. I've asked them to return my children. I've *begged* them. They refuse." The General closed his eyes, and his face became as still and remote as a stone carving in a museum.

Time passed. The silence grew. Arm heard Ear telling a joke in the living room and Mrs. Matsika's polite laughter. Arm put his hands on the General's shoulders.

He saw into his mind. This time he did not flinch away as he had with Mr. Thirsty and the Mellower. He felt the cold bleakness of the General's childhood underlying the man's personality. He felt the hot hate of the years spent battling gangs. He saw, through the General's eyes, the vast, sprawling city of Harare, which no one could completely control.

It was like walking into a dark house with many rooms. He didn't want to find out what was hidden in some of those rooms. Arm felt a deep pity for this man who had so much power and yet was utterly helpless to get back the one thing that had meaning for him.

Carefully, cautiously, Arm walked through the dark house that was General Matsika's mind. And then he seemed to turn a corner and come into a sunlit garden. The children were playing on a broad green lawn. Rita tickled Kuda. They shrieked with laughter and rolled over and over on the grass. Tendai stood beside them. He was too old to join in such childish games and too young not to want to. He glanced up and gazed directly at Arm. His face was serious beyond his years. Arm could see the man hovering inside the boy.

It was an actual memory! Arm let go of the General's shoulders at once, and his face burned with embarrassment. It was an unforgivable invasion of privacy!

Matsika still sat with his eyes closed, but his face had relaxed. He was smiling faintly. After a long moment he opened his eyes and said, "Thank you. I sometimes forget there is any goodness in the world."

Then, as Arm was leaving, he added, "I haven't told Beauty about Resthaven yet. She wouldn't understand. Please keep the secret."

"Beauty?" said Arm.

"My wife."

Arm went out.

"What a party!" cried Eye. "What a wonderful, fabulous, marvelous party! I wish I were rich!" He unbolted the many locks of the office and grimaced as he looked around the room.

"I'm not going to eat for three days," Ear said. "I'm going to lie in bed and relive all the courses in the Starlight Room. You should try that, Arm. You have the best imagination. Arm?"

But Arm lay down on the sofa and stared at a blot on the ceiling. The other detectives ignored him. Ear and Eye fought over the tiny shower. "Why don't you ever clean this out?" yelled Eye. "There's green slime everywhere!"

"Only you can see it," Ear said tranquilly. He shook out his sleeping bag and grit pattered over the floor.

"Listen," said Arm. He told them about the meeting in Matsika's study, including the eerie moment when he had looked into the General's mind.

"I've heard of Resthaven. Even thought of going there once, but it's almost, you know, a myth," Eye remarked.

"I've seen the wall," said Ear.

They all lay in bed and stared up at the ceiling. Ear and Eye had sleeping bags, but Arm, in deference to his recent illness, was given the sofa. A roach crept across the ceiling, nearly reached the center and fell off.

"Poor creature. I wonder if he had a wife and family," said Eye.

"He has *lots* of family," Ear said.

They continued to think. Even with the heavy curtain, it was impossible to block out the lights of the Cow's Guts. BEER! BEER! BEER! shouted a pink neon sign across the street.

"The Mellower says Matsika always does the right thing," said Ear. "Now if it were *my* children and I had the whole army at my disposal, I'd knock down that wall. They can't have anything more dangerous than spears in Resthaven."

"What's in there," Arm said slowly, "is a dream everyone has agreed to preserve. No buses or rockets are allowed to fly over it. No city noises can be permitted to interfere with the natural sounds." Arm got up, making a spidery silhouette against the pink curtain. "If Matsika broke into Resthaven, he'd destroy it."

"Looks like we've come to a dead end. I wonder why the General bothered to tell us anything?" Ear yawned. When he did this, not only did his mouth open, but his ears rustled out and back again.

"I wonder, too." Arm went over to the sink. An unpleasant scurrying told him the roach's family was searching for the dishes that were usually stacked there. He rinsed out a cup and filled it with cold water from the tiny fridge. It tasted of the cabbage Eye had allowed to spoil at the back. "I believe the General wants *us* to break into Resthaven."

"Oh, sure! Nice of him! Then we get tied to a not-so-mythical anthill in Monomatapa's country," said Eye.

"If anyone else tried it, he'd do irreparable harm, but look at us."

"I think we're pretty nice," Eye said.

"Be honest. What's most people's reaction?"

Ear and Eye sat up. They didn't answer.

"What would a traditional villager think if he came across us on a dark path?"

"He'd think we were bogeymen. Witches' monsters," said Eye reluctantly.

"Exactly. We'd fit right in."

"You sure know how to spoil a beautiful mood." Eye sighed and lay back down on his lumpy sleeping bag.

endai didn't intend to go to sleep. Events were moving rapidly, and he would have to find a way out of Resthaven before the Spirit Medium judged them. Rita had been called to the girls' hut long ago. He lay sleepless on a grass mat wedged in with the other boys.

He went over the possible outcomes. If Chipo's baby died, they would be sent away as witches. He couldn't wish for that, even though it would solve their problems. If the baby lived, they would probably be accepted as members of the tribe. They could never go home again.

In the distance he heard a murmur of voices and a drum. Perhaps the Spirit Medium was sitting with Garikayi right now. Tendai wondered about the medium. People seemed afraid of him. He wasn't like the man Father visited in the Mile-High MacIlwaine. That person wore a suit. He told jokes when he wasn't in a trance and pretended to find pennies in Kuda's ears. In the middle of this memory, Tendai fell asleep.

A high ululating cry brought him instantly awake. He sat up, groping for a weapon. Another cry tore through the sleeping village. Voices were raised. Footsteps pattered by the hut.

"What is it? What happened?" Tendai cried, as the other boys gathered at the door. The first glimmer of dawn shone on their faces.

"Chipo's baby. It's a boy," said Hodza.

"How do you know that?"

"Two cries. One for girls and two for boys."

"That's because boys are more important," added Banga. Tendai got up and followed the others to a big camp fire. Garikayi sat on a stool next to a man Tendai had not seen before. He had a hard, bitter face, and his eyes were so bloodshot they were almost red. His clawlike hand grasped a walking stick carved into the shape of a serpent. He wore many charms, among which was an *ndoro*.

Even from where he stood, Tendai could see the *ndoro* was a cheap pottery imitation. The man's eyes restlessly searched the crowd that had gathered. When they found Tendai, the eyes stopped. They flicked down to the true *ndoro* and back up to send a message of pure hate.

It had to be the Spirit Medium.

People talked in low voices. They hugged themselves against the chilly dew that had settled everywhere. The flames crackled and sent sparks high into the brightening air. Finally, the Spirit Medium turned his eyes away. Tendai relaxed. He hadn't even been aware he was tense.

He searched the crowd for Rita, but she wasn't there. He hoped she had taken the opportunity to sleep late. The villagers waited patiently as the sun painted the dawn clouds over Resthaven, and gradually Tendai became aware that all was *not* right with the situation. Surely, if the chief had just had an heir after years of waiting, people would be rejoicing. They weren't.

They talked in quiet voices, but they didn't mention the baby. Their mood, as far as Tendai could tell, was anxious. Was the baby deformed? Was Chipo dead?

An old woman emerged from a hut, and the crowd parted before her. She slowly approached the stools where Garikayi and the Spirit Medium sat. The old woman unwrapped the blanket.

An outraged yowl arose as the infant was exposed to air. A murmur of surprise rippled around the gathering. "Taking a baby out before its umbilical cord has dropped off? What can they be thinking of?" whispered a woman.

"Shhh!" said her companion. "The Spirit Medium has to make up his mind."

"He's strong," Garikayi announced, as the baby squalled and kicked. The old man obviously wanted to hold it, but Tendai knew that would go against custom. No one but the mother and midwives could touch it for several days.

The Spirit Medium inspected the infant. It was clear he was not fond of children, or at least this one. He frowned as he studied the wrinkled little face. The moments passed.

"He's one of us," the man said at last. A collective sigh went around the crowd.

"I have a son," cried Garikayi over the howls of the infant. "Now take it to the safety of the hut!" The old woman, smiling toothlessly, began to hobble back through the villagers. They smiled in return. The anxious feeling Tendai had noticed earlier was gone.

Suddenly a pot crashed. Someone screamed. Everyone froze. Above the rustling fire, Tendai heard a baby—*another baby*—wailing. A girl emerged from the same hut as the old woman had. She, too, carried a bundle. She resolutely approached Garikayi, who looked as though the sky had fallen on his head. His mouth dropped open. The girl drew near and held out the second bundle.

It was Rita!

"No," said Garikayi, waving her away.

"It's your daughter," Rita said.

"I do not accept her. She is an accursed twin."

"She's perfectly healthy," said Rita, whose voice was beginning to get shrill. "The midwife was going to *kill* her."

"It is a weak, unnatural child. It will die."

"Listen to her! She's not weak! Oh, I won't let you kill a tiny baby!" Rita began to cry. Her sobs resounded through the village clearing.

154

"Twins are evil," came the thin voice of the Spirit Medium. "They are against *Mwari*'s order."

"No baby is evil," sobbed Rita.

"One must die and be buried under the floor of the hut where it was born."

"So of course it's the *girl* who has to go," cried Rita. "Let's throw the *girl* away. She's no good! She's worthless! You're all a bunch of *vicious!—rotten!—ignorant!—pigs!*" She was screaming now. Myanda pushed through the crowd and snatched the infant from Rita's arms. The Spirit Medium raised his walking stick, but Tendai wrenched it away before he could strike his sister. The medium was so startled, he let go without a struggle. Tendai flung the stick into the heart of the fire. It burst into flames at once.

The villagers gasped in horror. They pounced on the children and stretched them out on the ground. Someone handed Garikayi a club. Oh, *Mwari*, he's going to kill us, thought Tendai. Garikayi stood over them a long, long moment. Tendai gritted his teeth as he waited for the first blow. But the old man's face suddenly contorted with anguish. He threw the club away and tottered back to his stool. His face was etched with deep lines, and he seemed to have aged ten years.

"Take these little hyenas to the punishment hut," hissed the Spirit Medium. Tendai and Rita were carried off by many hands—it was as if the whole village had risen against them with one thought and one purpose. The last thing Tendai saw before they were flung through a door was Myanda holding the girl baby against her breast.

"Thank you for sticking up for me," said Rita after she had recovered from being thrown down. She shivered violently, and Tendai hugged her. She burst into sobs. He rocked her back and forth as she wept. He knew this wasn't how a traditional brother treated his sister, but he was thoroughly sick of village ways.

Rita cried until she was exhausted. Then she lay down and sucked the knuckles of her right hand, as she had done when she was a small child.

"What happened?" said Tendai gently.

"I wasn't supposed to be there." Rita sighed and snuggled next to the wall, fitting her body into its curve. "But I just had to watch. I've never seen a newborn baby. I sneaked up to the door, and there it was. There *he* was, all wet like a fish. Then *she* was born.

"The midwives began to argue, and Chipo started to cry. Myanda sat against a wall and didn't say anything. After a while, she went out to tell Garikayi."

"So he knew," Tendai said.

"They all did, except they pretended not to. They don't like to kill babies."

"Who would?"

"They think twins are caused by witchcraft. There's a good twin and an evil one they have to get rid of. The midwives decided to take the boy out to Garikayi and leave the girl alone with a midwife. You understand?"

Tendai did.

"I heard them say it was important for the baby to be quiet. If she cried, everyone would know she existed. They couldn't pretend she was stillborn."

"But everyone knew," said Tendai.

"Of course." Rita shivered again. Tendai looked around for something to cover her with, but there was nothing. Her eyes began to close from sheer weariness. She jerked and forced them open again. Tendai wondered whether she had slept at all the night before. "It's like the hamburgers we eat at home," she explained. "We know a cow died to provide them, but we don't like to think about it. We pretend they came out of the pantry. Well, the villagers pretend the evil baby was born dead." She yawned. Her speech was getting slurred.

"How did you save it?" urged Tendai.

"They all went out except Chipo, who was too weak to stand, and one old woman. She got a handful of ashes to fill the baby's mouth."

"*Maiwee!*"

"I bopped her on the head with a pot, grabbed the baby and pinched her. She howled then all right. They couldn't pretend she wasn't alive." Rita couldn't keep her eyes open anymore. Her hand dropped to the floor. Her breathing became deep and regular.

Tendai sat in the dark hut and watched his sister. She had always seemed foolish to him, and often irritated him by picking silly quarrels. Now he saw this trait was really a form of courage. Father would have been proud of her.

The day dragged on. No one brought them any food, although Tendai found a pot of stagnant water. He drank sparingly, saving the rest for Rita. She slept on and on, without even turning over. Finally, in the late afternoon, the door opened and Myanda came in. She inspected Rita before sitting down.

"We have to talk," she said in a low voice. "I don't know why I'm bothering to do this. You certainly don't deserve any help."

Tendai didn't say he was sorry. He wasn't.

"It's my fault for letting you in at all, but I thought you couldn't do much harm."

Tendai looked at her steadily, the way Father did when he wanted to make someone perspire.

"You don't know what a serious mistake Rita made."

"In the city we think killing babies is a mistake," Tendai said.

"In the city they kill babies all the time with poverty and crime. You're so stupid! You haven't been here two weeks and already you dare to judge us. Resthaven is a living culture. You can't pick out the bits you like and throw away the rest. It all works together."

Tendai turned his back. He didn't even try to be polite. Myanda spun him around with her big hands. "Listen to me, you fool! I know what it's like outside the wall. I was born there."

"So I heard," Tendai said coldly.

"I belonged to a gang. It was when your father was breaking them up."

"You know about Father?"

"Of course I do. He hunted down the gangs one by one, making the nights safe for decent people. We thought that was pretty funny. Me and my friends used to raid old people's homes for drugs. We rode on robocycles to make a fast getaway. One night, General Matsika's men ambushed us. I was shot off my cycle and ended up in a prison hospital. Guess who visited me?"

Tendai shook his head. He was trying to picture Myanda on a robocycle without success.

"General Matsika."

"Father?"

"He scared the hell out of me. I mean he has quite a reputation, but the funny thing was, he was *nice*."

Tendai tried to imagine it. He didn't really know much about Father's work.

"I was only fourteen. He talked to me like the parent I never had. He said I could go to school or learn a trade, but I would have to be absolutely perfect. If I wasn't, he would drop me off the Mile-High MacIlwaine. He was joking. I think. Anyhow, he also told me about Resthaven."

Tendai gaped at her. So Myanda knew Father. Why didn't she contact him? Rita sighed and turned over. Her eyelids fluttered, but she wasn't ready to wake up yet. A drum began to throb not far away.

"Almost no one is allowed into Resthaven, but I made it because I understood what it meant. It's whole in a way the city never is."

Tendai nodded, remembering the storytelling at the *dare* and the feeling of righteousness about the wood smoke. He remembered being carried home in triumph after the fight with Head Buster.

"You can't yank out part of the pattern and not damage the rest," said Myanda.

"Even the part about killing babies?"

"Even that."

Tendai remembered the girl twin cuddled up to Myanda's breast. He shivered.

"In a few hours the Spirit Medium is going to hold a witch-finding ceremony," the woman went on. "Now you're really in trouble."

"I don't know," said Tendai. "If he finds us guilty, we'll be thrown out of Resthaven."

"Wrong! Before Rita rescued Sekai—"

"Who?"

Myanda seemed embarrassed. "The girl twin. I, uh, once had a friend with that name. Anyhow, before Rita meddled with things, the Spirit Medium intended to send you home. He doesn't like you, and he doesn't like *that*." Myanda pointed at the *ndoro*, but Tendai noticed she didn't touch it. "Now he wants revenge. He'll keep you here to make you suffer."

"They—they don't kill witches, do they?" said Tendai, who remembered some horrible stories.

"Traditional Africans didn't kill witches unless they'd murdered someone. But you'll wish you died. You'll get food the goats wouldn't touch and the nastiest chores. But worst of all, people will hate you. They'll look at you with loathing for the rest of your days. It's a terrible fate."

On the whole, Tendai thought it was better than being burned alive or buried in an anthill.

"I'm going to help you," whispered Myanda. She handed him two small bags. "Tonight the Spirit Medium will make some of the people drink witch-finding *muteyo*. It's full of nasty herbs he grows in a special garden. The stuff is so horrible, people vomit it right back up. That's what you're supposed to do."

"Great," said Tendai.

"I suspect—I don't know—that your *muteyo* won't taste so bad."

The drumming went on and on. Tendai smelled a cook fire and a sauce of tomatoes and onions. His empty stomach rumbled almost as loudly as the drum.

"If you don't expel the *muteyo*, everyone will think you're witches. I think that will please the Spirit Medium very much."

"So what do we do?"

"Chew this." Myanda pointed at the little bags. "Hide it in your clothes and eat it after you take the *muteyo*. Don't let anyone see you."

"What is it?"

"Chicken droppings."

Tendai almost dropped the bags.

"Do it if you want to escape Resthaven. I took a vow never to contact the outside world, but I owe your father this one. If you ever get home, tell him he was the best thing that ever happened to me." Myanda got up quickly and left the hut. The door was locked behind her.

Rita drifted in and out of sleep for another hour. Tendai put his ear to the clay wall to pick up sounds from outside. Garikayi and his relatives were conducting ceremonies for the baby boy. He was told about his ancestors and his family line. He was protected with amulets to ensure he would be fertile when he arrived at manhood.

The girl, Sekai, was not introduced to her ancestors. There was no need. She was not being given food or water and would not live long.

Tendai slid to the floor and sat next to the half-conscious Rita. He wouldn't tell her about Sekai.

23

After Rita had woken up enough to listen, Tendai told her about Myanda's visit. Rita made a face and hid the little bag of chicken droppings inside her dress. "You say Myanda knows Father? Why doesn't she call him?"

"She took a vow of silence."

"It's all stupid. This whole village is stupid. If Myanda wants to turn herself into a slave, that's fine by me. But *I* don't have to hold out my wrists and ask someone to snap chains on them." Rita found the pot of stagnant water and began drinking.

"Try to make it last," said Tendai.

"Boys are stupid, too." Rita drank as much of the water as she could manage.

She reminded him of Granny on one of her bad days. But she's been through a lot, he reminded himself. I can be patient a little longer. How much longer? he thought. Tonight would decide their fate. They might find themselves trapped in this village forever.

The drum went on incessantly. Father's spirit medium needed a drum to go into a trance. When Father had to make a difficult decision, the whole family took the limo to the Mile-High MacIlwaine. They went to the one hundred fortieth floor, where the spirit medium's secretary made them all comfortable with cups of tea. After a few minutes, the man came out to discuss the problem with Father and to name a fee. A drummer settled himself in the corner and got to work.

Very quickly, the medium went into a trance. His eyes glazed. Sometimes he fell out of his chair. The secretary helped him back and dusted off his suit. The *mudzimu* of the Matsika clan would possess him and give Father advice from the ancestors. After a while the *mudzimu* would go back to his world, and the spirit medium would become his old, cheerful self. Tendai noticed the visit took about fifty minutes, neither more nor less.

If Father had a really big problem, involving state matters, he went to an entirely different person, the Lion Spirit Medium, who was able to contact the *mhondoro*, the spirit of the land. Only two people in the country were qualified to do this, and Tendai was never taken to one of these possessions. Lion Spirit Mediums looked down on ordinary mediums, the way great concert musicians looked down on people who played the harmonica.

"I feel sick. The water was dirty," moaned Rita.

"You can't vomit now," Tendai told her. "You have to, you know, save it for later."

"Oh, leave me alone!" cried Rita. She curled up by the wall with her back to him.

Then it got dark. The hut had no windows, but a few glimmers of light had shone through the gaps between the thatch and the top of the wall. Now it was totally black. A stealthy rustling told Tendai they were not alone. He began to feel things walking across his body. The rapid ones were probably roaches. The ones that tickled were ants, and the one that took a long time to cross his hand (which he held perfectly still) could have been a centipede.

"Get off! Get them off me!" shrieked Rita, slapping at something.

"Don't hit them. You'll only make them angry."

"Help me!" Rita wailed, so Tendai groped his way to her side. He brushed off her skin. The creatures seemed no more dangerous than sugar ants, but something worried him far more. Her skin was too warm.

Rita was sick. It hadn't occurred to him that her irritable mood might have a cause. What do I do now? he thought desperately. People almost never got diseases anymore, but Resthaven was different.

What kind of germs would they allow here? he thought. In a place that accepted infanticide and witch trials, anything was possible. He felt Rita's skin again. She was *hot*. He poured a little of the remaining water into his hand and rubbed it over her face.

"Stop it!" she cried.

"I'm trying to cool you down." He tried to blow on her skin—it was the only thing he could think of—but Rita struck him, knocked over the pot and spilled the rest of the water. In spite of his good resolutions, Tendai slapped her back.

"Crazy girl," he muttered as he crawled to the other side of the hut. Rita didn't respond. That was even more worrying: she never missed an opportunity to get even. After a while, he crawled back in an effort to make up.

They were sitting together when the villagers came for them. The men burst in and dragged them out to a cook fire. Tendai's stomach reacted to the smell of popcorn someone was preparing in a large pot.

"The lion wants his dinner," a man said as Tendai's belly grumbled, but no one offered any food.

They were pushed along a forest path. Men went before and behind with torches; the bushes seemed to press in on all sides. Once, an owl hooted and they all ducked. "It's looking for its witch master," someone whispered. The others laughed nervously. On they went, gradually moving up from the stream. Not far away, Tendai could see the wall. It rose, massive and dark, against the stars.

They came through a tangle of thornbushes to a large clearing. A fire burned in the middle, and all around stood the villagers. Behind the fire, set into the side of a cliff, was a cave. The Spirit Medium sat in the opening. His skinniness made him seem even more like a messenger from the world of the ancestors. He was dressed in a bark loincloth and wore the pottery *ndoro* around his neck. Clustered at the mouth of the cave were clay pots that probably contained the *muteyo*. The drums beat hypnotically.

On another stool at the edge of the crowd sat Garikayi. He looked like any other old man. All the authority of being a chief had gone to the Spirit Medium. Myanda stood behind Garikayi and at his feet lay Chipo.

"She's still weak from childbirth. They're so cruel," said Rita. The men shoved her and Tendai into the clearing, and Tendai was alarmed to see Trashman with Kuda perched on his broad shoulders. Surely they won't have to go through the ordeal, he thought.

Now the drumming grew more frenzied. The people began to clap. A man played a monotonous tune on an *mbira*. His thumbnail twanged the flat iron keys of the instrument, and the sound resonated inside the calabash on his knees. Women shook rattles with river pebbles in them. A man played a reed flute. The music was wild and infectious. Tendai's body began to move to it in spite of himself. Rita began to tremble. All around, the music vibrated through the assembled villagers, making them sway like a wind driving through a wheat field.

"Eh!" shouted the Spirit Medium. "Eh! Eh! Eh!" He sprang to his feet and began to dance. His arms jerked back and forth, and his feet smacked the ground, raising puffs of dust. "Eh! Eh! Eh!" He seemed to be on puppet strings. He lunged forward in grotesque spurts around the clearing. His head wobbled on his skinny neck, and his eyes rolled up until only the whites were showing. The music went faster and faster.

"Eeeeaugh!" The Spirit Medium fell on the ground and shook as though a huge lion had him in its jaws. Several men rushed from the sidelines to hold him down. The medium threw back his head and bared his teeth. Even four men had trouble restraining him. "Augh! Augh! Augh!" He suddenly went limp.

The men hauled him back to his stool and propped him up. A woman knelt before him with a bowl of millet beer. The Spirit Medium didn't move. He *couldn't* move: his face was knotted with anguish, and the muscles of his neck stood out like cords. Very gently, the men bent the medium's body forward until his lips touched the beer. He began to lap it like a dog.

All at once an astonishing change came over the Spirit Medium. He drew himself up without any help, and the men backed away hurriedly. He seemed to grow right before Tendai's eyes. His face was painted with firelight, but his back was hidden in shadow.

"My people," he said in a deep, deep voice. If Tendai hadn't heard it, he wouldn't have believed it came from the same man. The voice sounded as though it rose out of the earth. "I am *mudzimu*. A dirty spirit has invaded this clan, and we must seek it out." The medium began to stalk around the clearing, skewering the villagers with his gaze. They flinched when he looked at them.

"This one must take the *muteyo*," he cried suddenly, pointing at an old woman Tendai recognized as one of the midwives. She moaned and sank to her knees. "This one . . . and this one," the Spirit Medium went on in his deep voice. He pointed out Myanda and Chipo. He passed by Kuda and Trashman; Tendai breathed a sigh of relief. Then he came around the circle. "This one," he said, pointing at

Rita. He stared a long time at Tendai, his eyes fixed on the true *ndoro*.

Tendai forced himself to look directly at the man's face. He would not desert Rita. Not this time.

The Spirit Medium turned his attention from the *ndoro* to Tendai's face. Tendai expected to see hatred, but what he detected was far more surprising: it wasn't the Spirit Medium at all! The shape was the same, but the *presence* hovering inside the man's body was completely different. It gazed at him from a vast distance, full of deep knowledge he couldn't begin to understand. It neither approved nor disapproved of him, but it *knew* him right down to the soles of his feet.

"This one," said the Spirit Medium.

He strode back to the ceremonial stool and motioned for the assistants to administer the *muteyo*. They brought pots to the old midwife, to Myanda and Chipo. A woman removed two more from a special shelf in the wall of the cave. Wouldn't you know it, Tendai thought bitterly. He has it all set up for us.

"Come back," commanded the Spirit Medium. Instantly, the woman turned, and he smashed the pots out of her hand. The crowd moaned with terror. Tendai realized the man who was the Spirit Medium might have petty hatreds, but *mudzimu* inside his body had no patience with such things. "Take those," ordered *mudzimu*. Trembling, the woman fetched two more pots from the cluster at the cave entrance. She presented one to Rita, who stuck her tongue out.

Please don't do anything stupid, Tendai silently prayed, but Rita obediently gulped the *muteyo* down. At once, she doubled up and vomited right at his feet. Several people moved away with expressions of dismay. Lucky Rita, thought Tendai. She's already so sick, she doesn't need chicken droppings.

Then it was his turn. Tendai drank the *muteyo*. It was sweetish and not at all unpleasant. It reminded him slightly of the *rooibos* tea Mother gave them on cold mornings. He felt for the bag of chicken droppings hidden in his loincloth. How was he ever going to take it out with this crowd watching him? But he needn't have worried. When the *muteyo* hit his stomach, it turned on him like a rabid hyena. Pain wrenched his throat. He dropped to his hands and knees, retching up the poison like a dog that had eaten rotten meat.

Tendai was so sick, he didn't even have time to feel ashamed. He vomited until it felt like the two sides of his stomach were pressed together. And still he heaved until he fell over on his side from sheer weakness. "Drink some water," a man said kindly, holding a calabash to his lips. A woman bent and washed Rita's face with a cloth.

Tendai's head was thudding with pain. The man gave him more water and patted his shoulder. "You're okay now." Suddenly, the villagers were all smiles. Tendai and Rita had proved they weren't witches. Everyone could like them again.

"Oooh," wailed Rita, rocking back and forth and holding onto her stomach. Across the way, Tendai saw the old midwife writhing in a pool of vomit. Her face was an alarming shade of gray. Chipo, too, was gasping and coughing, while anxious women held her shoulders and murmured encouragement. But Myanda?

Myanda stood like a sturdy tree behind Garikayi. Her face was shiny with sweat and she seemed to be concentrating deeply, but she wasn't sick. Please, Tendai prayed to the unknown ancestor whose *ndoro* he wore. Please make her sick. But Myanda was too strong. Her body refused to give in.

The minutes passed. People drew away from the gatekeeper, and even the drummer stopped his incessant tattoo. The old midwife was lifted and carried off into the dark. Tendai hoped she would recover. Chipo was tenderly laid next to the fire. Her face was sponged and her feet massaged. And still Myanda stood with the sweat dripping off her body. Garikayi wrung his hands as he watched.

He loves her, thought Tendai in amazement. She was the old wife, the outsider who could not give him children. By all the laws of the tribe, Garikayi should have rejected her, but he didn't.

"Confess or die," said *mudzimu* from inside the Spirit Medium's body.

"Please," said Garikayi, clenching his hands until the bones stood out. Myanda held her stomach, and the sides of her mouth curved down with despair. She was in severe pain, Tendai realized. And still she was unable to expel the *muteyo*.

"Confess!" cried several voices from the crowd. "Confess, witch!" Everyone began to shout at her. For years the villagers had lived with her, eaten her food and allowed her to stand between them and the outside world. Now all that was forgotten. Even Chipo shrank from her. Only Garikayi watched her with compassion.

"Quiet!" he shouted at the villagers. The hubbub died away. "My senior wife," he addressed Myanda. "You came to us from *Mwari*'s country. We accepted you. We still do." He looked around, daring the others to object. "Witchcraft has entered you, but it can be driven out. I will provide the sacrifices, as many as are needed. You know this can be done!" His fierce eyes challenged the villagers. The Spirit Medium watched quietly from the shadows.

"But you must confess. Otherwise you will die." *Please. It's the only way I can save you,* the eyes of the old chief said.

Myanda writhed in agony. The pain brought her to her knees. Suddenly, she threw back her head and screamed, "Yes! Yes! I am a witch!" Rita grabbed Tendai's arm in terror. "I rode hyenas after dark! I made *chidoma*, bogeymen, out of dead bodies! I caused Chipo to have twins! Augh! Augh!" Myanda scurried on hands and knees into the bushes. The villagers followed her eagerly.

Tendai was shaking as though he had a fever. Rita clung to his arm so tightly she cut off the circulation to his hand.

The sounds of Myanda crashing through bushes died away, along with the excited voices of the people who had followed her.

"Now what?" said Tendai to no one in particular.

"Now she will get rid of the *muteyo*," said the man who had given him water. "This was a very good ceremony. It's nice to have the village clean again."

"What do you mean, 'get rid of the *muteyo*'?" said Tendai.

"What doesn't go out one way will go out the other," the man said tranquilly.

"How horrible!" cried Rita.

"They're checking for baby bones." The man indicated the absent villagers with a sweep of his hands. "That will prove she ate her own babies."

"Or turned them into bogeymen. Then they'd still be around," remarked a woman.

"Yes. That's always possible."

Tendai noticed the man didn't look so relaxed anymore.

The Spirit Medium sank to the ground with a sigh. He stretched out on the dirt, jerked once or twice and lay still. His assistants quickly poured water over him.

"*Mudzimu* has left him," the man explained. Everyone watched as the assistants cooled down the Spirit Medium's body. Garikayi sat on the chief's stool, and his face seemed carved out of stone.

After a while, the medium recovered enough to sit up, point at the children and shout, "Those ones! They do not belong. Throw all three out!"

At last, thought Tendai. The man's voice—thin and suspicious—had returned to normal, and his old, envious personality was back. Tendai, Rita and Kuda were herded onto a path leading upward. Trashman immediately caught up with them.

"You don't have to go, Chedu," said one of the guards.

"Oh, you know him," said another. "Here one day, gone the next."

They climbed until they reached the gate. The torchlight gleamed on its mirrorlike surface and picked out the many locks and bolts. The guards were unsure what to do next. "Myanda always opened it," one of them said nervously.

"Filthy witch!" another spat out.

They stood before the locks, trying to look purposeful, until Tendai offered to do the job. They had to lift him to reach the upper bolts. But when he tried to pull the handle, the gate proved too heavy to move.

"Help me," he asked the guards. They were afraid to touch it. Rita was too sick, and Trashman merely gabbled at him.

"He says he's waiting for Mama," translated Kuda.

"Tell him Mama's busy," snapped Tendai. He pulled on the handle with all his might. The gate barely responded. Kuda knelt down and tried to work his fingers into the narrow opening. He only managed to fall over backward with his legs kicking in the air. Trashman laughed and slapped his knees.

"He thinks it's a game," Tendai said wearily. But Trashman suddenly grabbed the handle and pulled the great gate of Resthaven ajar.

"Hurrah!" shouted Kuda. Trashman grinned, scooped him up and strode out. The guards shielded their eyes from the dreaded sight of *Mwari*'s country. Tendai took Rita's hand—it was so hot it made his heart turn over—and gently led her to freedom.

"Aren't we going to close it?" she asked.

"That's their problem." Personally, Tendai didn't care if a gang of robocycles thundered through the opening, but the guards had apparently worked up enough courage to close the rift in their wall. The gate swung to with a *whump*. They were shut out of Resthaven forever.

"Lovely, lovely cement," said Rita, lying down to press her cheek on the cool sidewalk.

"We have to find a policeman," Tendai said.

"Just want to rest," muttered Rita. She spread-eagled herself on the walk. Tendai left her alone for a few minutes. She turned over to cool her back and to look up at the apartment buildings. The street was deserted. A clock stood at 2:00 A.M. over the entrance to a subway. Trashman chattered and pointed.

"He says the moon is shining," Kuda said. And so it was, at the end of the street. It looked dull and shrunken from what it had been in Resthaven.

"I wonder why they let him in and out," said Rita, looking up at Trashman's cheerful face.

"I suppose Myanda would say he wasn't corrupt," Tendai said.

"I suppose he isn't. Poor Myanda. Poor baby girl." Tendai pulled Rita to her feet before she could dwell on that distressing topic. She groaned when her feet touched the ground. "I ache all over. Even my skin hurts!"

"Come on. We only have a little farther to go," Tendai urged. But the truth was, he hadn't the slightest idea what to do next.

24

Tendai pulled Rita along. He went to the security door on the nearest apartment building and tried to ring the bell. "I'm-sorry," said a robot voice from behind the metal grille. "All-our-tenants-are-sleeping. If-you-would-like-to-leave-a-message, please-speak-into-the-microphone-after the-beep."

Tendai waited and said, "Please call the police and tell them General Matsika's children are waiting outside Resthaven Gate." He would rather have been more cautious, but Rita's illness worried him. He had barely finished speaking when the microphone clicked off.

"Thank-you-for-visiting. Have-a-nice-night," said the robot.

Tendai kicked the grille. "Maybe if I make enough noise, I can set off a burglar alarm." He rattled and banged as hard as he could, but it made no difference. He couldn't even find rocks to throw. "We may have to sit in a doorway till morning," he told Rita.

"What doorway?" she said dully. And Tendai saw that up and down the street all the doors were fitted with grilles. A cool breeze blew down the walk between the apartments and the wall.

"Hey! Where's Kuda?" said Tendai. "Wait, Trashman! Stop!" But the man had already reached the dark stairway to the subway. He disappeared down the steps with Kuda. Tendai pulled Rita along with him as he set off in pursuit. "Now what?" he groaned. "Doesn't he know the subway's dangerous?" The clock over the entrance read 2:15 as they went down.

The place was every bit as dangerous-looking as Tendai had feared. They went along a tunnel with a row of dim lights at the top. Stale air drifted from black openings at the ends of the platform. Rails lay on either side.

"At least it's warmer," said Rita. They had trouble keeping up with Trashman, who seemed to know exactly where he was going. The benches lining the platform were gouged with knives. Gang slogans covered the gray walls. Most of them were faded, but a few seemed painted yesterday. DON'T LOOK BEHIND A MASK, they said.

"This is where the Masks *live*. Come on, Trashman. Go find Mama," whispered Tendai. The man stopped before a candy machine. Behind smudgy glass hung chocolate bars, licorice whips and lemon drops.

"We don't have money," Tendai said.

"I want chocolate!" cried Kuda, suddenly waking up. Trashman searched the litter on the platform until he found a bottle cap. He straightened out the edge with his big strong teeth.

"Stop it! Don't you know that's bad for you?" Rita tried to take the cap from him, but he dodged her and kept chewing.

"Keep your voice down, Rita," Tendai said. Trashman inserted the flattened cap into the candy machine. It was exactly the size of a two-dollar coin. Kuda pressed a button, and four chocolate bars fell out. The man and boy laughed with glee.

"That's stealing," said Tendai.

"He can't understand. Money means nothing to him," sighed Rita as Trashman tore off the paper covering and began to eat. She helped Kuda peel his bar and perched him on a bench. Tendai frowned at her. "*I* didn't steal it," she said. "You can't even say Trashman stole it. He doesn't know the meaning of the word." Trashman had two chocolate bars and Kuda had one. Rita tried to eat, but her stomach was too queasy. Tendai refused to take part in what he considered a crime, so she gave hers to Kuda.

"More," said the little boy, fishing another bottle cap from the litter.

"No," Tendai said. Kuda clenched his little fist around the cap, and Tendai despaired of trying to explain why they couldn't use it as money. Father was absolutely against stealing, but Kuda was hungry. And so, of course, was he.

"Look!" cried Rita. Deep in the tunnel, so much in shadow Tendai couldn't be sure whether it was real or not, something large slunk along the wall. It flowed along as rapidly as a running man. As it approached, he saw a nightmare face suddenly shine as it caught the light. Then it disappeared as though someone had thrown a bottle of ink over it. At the same time, the wind in the tunnel increased, and the tracks began to hum.

The shadow reached the mouth of the tunnel and poured out. It had just reached the edge of the platform when a train shot from the tunnel at the opposite end of the station. The cars thundered to a halt. Tendai, Rita, Kuda and Trashman bounded in through the nearest door. The shadow at the end of the platform heaved up and threw itself at the train.

"The Masks! The Masks!" cried the train guards. They snapped the doors shut, and the passengers dove for cover. The train jerked away, gathering speed. A wild undulating cry broke out as the train sped for safety. The shadow broke up into a mass of black-cloaked men swarming over the outside of the cars. But that was not the most terrifying thing.

None of the men had proper faces. Some were swollen, with slobbering mouths. Some were long and cruel and had eyes that glittered red. The creatures tried to glue themselves to the sides of the train with suckers attached to their hands and knees. The cars whizzed past, the suckers failed to con-

174

nect, the faces fell back. And then the men were gone as the train plunged into the tunnel.

"That was a close one!" breathed a guard.

"It's a disgrace!" an old man exclaimed. He was accompanied by his personal robot, a model Tendai hadn't seen in years.

"It's-a-disgrace!" the robot echoed in a cheap, tinny voice.

Tendai helped Rita climb onto a seat as he looked around the car. Some people, like the old man, seemed harmless. Others were not. A woman casually cleaned her nails with a switchblade. Her companion grinned, showing filed teeth. Tendai remembered that Father had broken up the Filed Teeth gang, but what happened to old gang members? Did they get jobs at the bank and move to the suburbs? Tendai suspected not. It was probably a bad idea to let someone with filed teeth find out General Matsika's children were lost and alone on the subway.

"The police will be too late," grumbled a train guard as he punched in the alarm. "They always are. The Masks travel around the subways like smoke."

"I had a boyfriend who joined the Masks," said the woman with filed teeth. "He had to kill ten people to pass the entrance exam." The other passengers became interested in watching the dark tunnel flash by outside.

"She's only bragging," the woman with the switchblade told the others.

"Tickets, please," called the conductor as he worked his way down the car.

"We don't have any," Tendai said.

"That will be a dollar for you, sir, and fifty cents for each of the children."

Maiwee, he thinks Trashman's our father, thought Tendai. "We don't have money," he said aloud.

"No money! That will never do!" the conductor said. Kuda handed Trashman a bottle cap, and he began to flatten it with his teeth. "Stop that! You'll hurt yourself," cried the conductor, but Trashman held him away with one hand while he turned the bottle cap in his jaws with the other. When it was flat, he handed it over.

"He says that's enough to pay for the train," translated Kuda.

"Don't be ridiculous!"

"We don't have another bottle cap," Kuda said crossly.

"Open your eyes," said the old man with the robot. "The big one's simple. They're a family of beggars. Where do you want to go, children?"

"Want-to-go," echoed the robot.

"Mazoe," Tendai said.

"We aren't going that way. See the map on the wall?" The conductor ran his finger along the stops. Tendai saw, with a sinking heart, that they were getting farther from Mazoe by the minute.

"Wait. We know someone in Borrowdale. That's the next stop," Rita said.

"Who?" asked Tendai.

"The Mellower's mother. I saw a letter once. I think I remember the address."

"You still need tickets," the conductor said.

"I'll get them." The old man dug in his pockets. "The whole system's gone to pot. Masks everywhere, grown men threatening children—"

"I'm only doing my job," said the conductor.

"Where's my money?" The old man patted his jacket and pants.

"You-told-me-to-carry-it," said the robot.

"Well, pay him, you bag of bolts! The whole system's crazy!"

"Thank you, *vababa*," Tendai said politely.

"Thank you, honored father." Rita poked Kuda, who added his response. The train rattled to a halt, and Tendai saw the word BORROWDALE. He quickly led the others to the platform.

"The subway's a disgrace," he heard the old man say as the door started to close.

"Disgrace," echoed the robot. The train disappeared down the tunnel.

"I don't want to spend a second down here," said Rita, but she only went a few steps before she collapsed. "Ohhh! I feel awful!" She fell to her knees and began to shake violently.

Tendai put his arm around her. "Please try to get up the stairs. I'll find help. I promise."

"Something smells nasty."

"Do you still have that bag of chicken droppings?"

"Oh, *no!*" shrieked Rita. She found the bag in the top of her dress and flung it over the side of the platform. In a way, this heartened Tendai. It showed that the old Rita was still there under the sickness.

"Now climb the stairs," he said, "even if you have to go on hands and knees. You're too big for me to carry." Rita tried, but she was too ill. Tendai pulled Trashman by the hand and pointed at his sister. The man watched her with interest. After a moment, he got down on his hands and knees and began to shake, too. "No! No!" yelled Tendai.

In the end, Kuda got the point across. Tendai couldn't understand what the little boy said, but Trashman did. He hoisted Rita to his shoulders and trotted up the stairs.

The digital clock over the subway read 2:20 when the taxi landed outside Resthaven Gate. Arm was the first one out, followed by Ear and Eye.

"Quiet, isn't it?" Eye remarked. Arm paid the driver, who took off at once.

"I hear footsteps," Ear said, extending his ears to full range. "Several people are walking along the subway platform down below. Now they've stopped."

"The subway doesn't concern us. We have to get through this gate." Arm leaned back to study the giant wall.

Eye whistled. "That thing goes up half a mile. Does anyone have a half-mile ladder?"

"I've got something better." Arm put on heavy gloves. He unpacked a coil of metal that twanged and glittered from a steel box in his backpack. "Triple-hardened titanium-molybdenum razor wire."

"I thought that stuff was illegal." Ear bent down to examine the coil. He was careful not to touch it.

"Mr. Thirsty just happened to have some in his cupboard," said Arm.

"Next to the can opener, I suppose."

Arm threaded the razor wire into a long curved needle like the ones furniture makers used to sew upholstery. He inserted it into the crack of Resthaven Gate, worked it around until the tip emerged a few inches up and pulled the needle out. The razor wire was threaded around a lock. Arm sawed it back and forth. It made a high rasping sound like a cricket and sent a shower of metal fragments to glitter in the light Eye trained on the gate.

"I hear someone operating a candy machine in the subway," said Ear. "If you'd stop a minute, I could make out the voices."

"Will you stop nagging me?" cried Arm. "We're breaking the most sacred law in Harare. *Mwari* knows what will happen on the other side—and you keep going on about the subway. Pay attention!"

"Sorry!" Ear folded his ears until they looked like tightly closed rosebuds.

After a few moments, Arm apologized. "I didn't mean to hurt your feelings. I'm just worried. I'm only guessing Matsika wants us to do this."

"I hear they have a good job-training program in Waa Waa Prison," Eye said brightly.

Ear opened his ears a little to show he wasn't sulking. Arm quickly worked his way up the gate until he couldn't find any more locks. "I think that's it," he said, stowing the razor wire back in its box. Eye pushed on the gate. It hardly budged. In the end, all three of them had to struggle to force it open.

"I hear a train coming into the subway—sorry!" said Ear. He slipped through the opening after the other detectives and helped them close the gate.

They all stood for a long, long moment, lost in the beauty of Resthaven. "I never knew," began Eye, and fell silent because his voice seemed to boom in the quiet air. A path descended right at their feet to disappear under *msasa* trees.

Arm lacked the abilities of his comrades, but even he could hear and see the differences between the city and Monomatapa's country. The moon, suddenly large and impressive, dusted the shoal of trees covering the hillside below with a serene fire. The darkness beneath was that much more profound, and yet it wasn't threatening, as shadows were in the city. Far away, a stream pattered through reeds, while near at hand bush babies shrilled at the unwelcome presence of Ear, Eye and Arm. Nightjars, cousins to the owl, called from their sandy perches on the earth. A fruit bat gave a high pinging cry as it left the branches of a wild fig.

Here and there came impressions that Arm could not ever remember having and yet were printed on his being. His ancestors had walked in just such a valley. They had smelled the distant wood smoke and the pattering stream, the hint of *mutara*, the wild gardenia, on the breeze. Arm realized his face was wet with tears. He was glad it was too dark for the others to see them.

"It's so *right*," whispered Eye in a suspiciously husky voice.

Arm heard Ear's ears rustle out to their full extent. For once he envied his ability to pick up the slightest sounds. Far away, a hum rose and fell in the darkness. It died away for a moment, then rose with more urgency.

"It's voices," Ear said.

"Villagers don't go out in the middle of the night," said Arm.

"Hell of an *ndaba* going on over there."

"Arguments?"

"I'll say. They seem to have discovered a witch."

"*Maiwee*. Do you think it's the children?" Arm said.

Ear turned his head from side to side with that disturbing snakelike movement. "Everyone's yelling. I can't make anything out."

Eye led the way along the path. They had to depend on him because Arm said a flashlight was too big a disruption for Resthaven. They stumbled and slid on loose stones. Once even Eye stubbed his toe on a rock. They came to a fork in the path, and Ear selected the one to the right.

"I can hear a fire," he said. "They're talking about burning the witch."

"What a time to be a bogeyman," muttered Arm. As they got closer, gleams of light shot between the trees and lit the path. When they were almost at the clearing, Ear, Eye and Arm glided into the shadows at the side to listen.

"*She* let in those children," shrieked a gaunt man dressed in a bark loincloth. Arm noticed that he wore an *ndoro*. The spirit mediums in the villages did that, although the ones in the city had dropped the custom. "*She* was the gatekeeper. It was up to her to keep out evil, but she welcomed it in!"

"They have been expelled," said an old man who was as agitated as the other. Between them stood a large—Arm would have said *majestic*—woman clutching a tiny baby.

"As you say, Garikayi," said the Spirit Medium. "They have been expelled, but this witch has been carrying on her crimes for years. She devoured your children! Or turned them into bogeymen. For all we know, her misshapen zombies are creeping around the forest right now!"

If you only knew, thought Arm.

"Witchcraft is like an illness," said Garikayi wearily. "It can be cured."

"She polluted your junior wife!" The thin man strode over to a young woman crouched on the ground. She was weeping bitterly. He pulled her head back by the hair. "This one has given birth to twins. Your only heir is threatened. Think! You can't allow Myanda to live!"

"You can cast witchcraft out into a goat—or as many goats as you need. I want you to cure my elder wife." Garikayi stared at the thin man, and a message flashed between them. It didn't take special powers to read it: *if you want to keep your position as Spirit Medium, I believe we should come to an understanding.*

As Arm looked around the clearing at the many villagers gathered there, he realized the outcome of the argument wasn't at all certain. Some people nodded in agreement with Garikayi, but just as many supported the Spirit Medium.

Myanda stood, tall and dignified, at the center of the controversy. The infant whimpered faintly.

Myanda's courage impressed the detective, but the deciding factor was the baby. He didn't know what happened to unwanted twins, but it couldn't be good. Without allowing himself to think of the danger, Arm stepped into the clearing. Eye tried to grab him; Ear stifled a cry.

The effect on the villagers was instantaneous. Women screamed and fled into the shadows. The men tried to look brave, but first one and then another was overcome with panic and bolted from the firelight. Of the few left, several had wet loincloths. Arm smiled bitterly.

He knew what he looked like. He was six and a half feet tall and skinny as a rail. His arms and legs were much too long for a normal human. If he crooked his elbows and knees, he reminded people of one of the wall spiders that lurked in dark closets.

Arm crooked his elbows and knees. The Spirit Medium's eyes almost popped out of his head. Garikayi took a step backward, but he didn't run. He was utterly terrified and utterly courageous. Such a man might stare into the eyes of a lion that was about to devour him.

The young woman who had been weeping fled on hands and knees from the awful sight. When she reached the bushes, many hands reached out to help her on to safety.

Only Myanda gazed at Arm without a trace of fear. "Mother," said Arm. Myanda blinked, startled. "We have come, my brothers and I." He gestured back at the path. From the moan that escaped the Spirit Medium, he knew that Ear and Eye had entered the clearing. "We do not like it here. This man's courage is too strong." Arm pointed at Garikayi. Damned if he was going to give credit to the Spirit Medium. "We want to go outside, to find another village where people are easier to frighten. We don't want this man's spirit to chase us anymore."

"When we want to hurt someone, he makes us afraid," said Eye, joining in.

"Yeah, he's a real pest," Ear said.

"Don't overdo it," hissed Eye.

"We want to leave and take all the witchcraft away." Arm hunched down like a spider about to spring. The Spirit Medium flinched. "Come with us, Myanda!"

She suddenly woke up and looked at him in a most knowing way. "Me? Come with you? I hate witchcraft! Go away, you dirty zombies! Get out of Resthaven—and take this with you!" Myanda thrust the infant at Arm.

He backed away. "I don't want it!"

"Take it!" yelled the woman. She advanced, and Ear, Eye and Arm retreated until they were out of the clearing. "Take her, you fool," she whispered.

"Are you sure?" Arm said.

"I can't protect her." Myanda firmly placed the baby in Arm's hands and touched her cheek softly. "Her name's Sekai. I don't know how Matsika did this, but tell him thank you. His kids are outside. They can't have gone far."

The woman ran back to the clearing before Arm could react. "Augh! Augh!" she screamed. "The spirit of witchcraft is leaving me! Protect me! Don't let it come back!" She threw herself on the ground and rolled around in a most alarming way. She kicked her heels and bared her teeth. She pulled out clumps of hair.

Garikayi grabbed a burning branch from the fire and stepped between her and Arm, who still watched from the shadows. "Leave my senior wife alone!" he roared. "You!" he ordered the Spirit Medium. "Cast out those monsters!" The Spirit Medium grasped his *ndoro* and began to chant a spell. The few men who remained reached down for stones.

Borrowdale wasn't full of apartments like the area outside Resthaven, nor was it bustling like Mbare Musika. It wasn't open country like Dead Man's Vlei, although the streets were wide and the air fresh. Each house had a high wall, over which peeped jacarandas, wisteria and Kenya coffee trees, which towered over the other plants. Everything seemed a little run-down. A dog barked from behind an iron gate. Another answered.

They were *real* dogs, not automatic Dobermans. Suddenly, Tendai became aware of a whole range of noises from near and far. A kitten mewed outside someone's door. A rooster crowed. A horse blew noisily through its nostrils. A dog snuffled along a gate as they passed.

People in Mazoe had pets, of course, but it was far more fashionable to own robots. Robots didn't have fleas or dig up flower beds, except when their circuits were old. Most important, they didn't present their owners with a litter of new robots every six months.

"It's so alive," Tendai whispered. The dawn breeze brought him hints of the world hidden behind the walls: flowers, dogs, cut grass. It was different from the air of Resthaven. Resthaven smelled of the remote past, but Borrowdale was close to the world Tendai knew. It was, almost, home.

"What was the address of the Mellower's mother?" he asked. He had to shake Rita to get her attention.

"Twenty-five Horsepool Lane," she muttered.

"And her name?"

"I don't know. Don't bother me." Which was like Rita, of course. She had a remarkable memory for numbers but forgot names as soon as she heard them.

Tendai was afraid they would have to wait until the Borrowdale people woke up when he saw a newspaper robot purring down the street. It paused at intervals and shot papers over the walls.

"Excuse me, do you know where Horsepool Lane is?" Tendai asked.

"Have-you-missed-a-newspaper?" it said.

"No, I—"

"I-cannot-help-you." The robot pivoted around him and rolled down the street. Tendai followed it. Trashman came behind with Rita draped over one shoulder and Kuda over the other. The man didn't seem to mind the extra weight. *Whir,* pause, *kachung,* went the robot as it delivered another paper. *Whir,* pause, *kachung.*

"Yes, we have missed a paper!" shouted Tendai. The machine turned abruptly and came back to him. "We live at Twenty-five Horsepool Lane, and our paper hasn't come. The whole system's a disgrace!" he added.

The robot riffled through the papers stored inside its tummy. "That-is-not-true. I-have-not-gotten-to-Horsepool-Lane-yet."

"Very good. Carry on." Tendai followed as the machine continued its rounds. It was tiring to stop and start—*whir,* pause, *kachung*—but at last they came to a short street with frangipani trees on either side. At the end was Twenty-five Horsepool Lane, THE PADDOCK.

By now the air was a deep, damp blue. Roosters crowed from a dozen places. A hoopoe called from a Kenya coffee tree and was answered by another. All at once, hundreds of birds woke up and began to chirrup loudly. Tendai rang the bell of number twenty-five. After a few moments, a robot voice called out, "Who-is-there?"

"Friends of the Mellower," called Tendai.

He heard the robot go down steps and along a walk. It creaked badly. It undid the bolts of the gate but left the chain on. "Do-you-have-an-appointment?"

"Yes!" said Tendai before it could close the opening.

"Very-well. Please-wait-inside." It let them in and creaked back to the house. Once, it caught a wheel in a pothole and almost tumbled over. Tendai looked around at their new surroundings.

He saw a dry fountain with a headless mermaid perched on a pillar. A long porch was almost pulled down by an ancient wisteria vine. Weeds grew out of the tennis court; the tile roof of the house was patched with sheets of tin. And yet it once had been a great estate. It was still impressive.

"You miserable rust bucket!" shrieked a voice from the house. "How dare you wake me at this hour! Get out before I take a can opener to you!"

"Visitors-madam. They-have-an-appointment," came the mournful voice of the robot.

"Burglars, more likely. Where's my Nirvana gun? Where's the remote control for the Doberman cage?"

Tendai watched anxiously, but after a few moments the front door opened and a small woman came out. She was dressed in a threadbare bathrobe and wore fuzzy bunny slippers on her feet. She carried a large Nirvana gun. "Don't move an inch till I look at you," she commanded.

"We're children—and he's just like one," said Tendai, pointing at Trashman. "Our father is General Matsika. We were kidnapped."

At the mention of General Matsika, the woman lowered the gun. "Why, so you are," she murmured.

"Please. We're awfully tired, and my sister is sick. Couldn't we come in?"

"Of course. Poor little puppies, you must have had a terrible time—but who's that tramp with you?" She raised the gun again.

"He's not really a tramp," began Tendai.

Kuda woke up and stared owlishly at the woman. "He's my friend," he announced.

"I know a hobo when I see one! You children may come inside, but he has to stay in the garden. I wouldn't feel safe." Tendai was afraid they would have trouble with Trashman, but he didn't seem at all surprised to be rejected. He wandered over to a pile of grass clippings and lay down.

The woman led them to the kitchen. Rita staggered into a chair and slumped over the table. "She certainly looks sick," observed the woman. "Sit up, miss. Let me have a look at you." Rita moaned and obeyed. Tendai was alarmed to see small bumps on her skin.

"My, my, my. You're hot as a mug of tea." The woman brought a lamp close to Rita's face. "Well, I never! I haven't seen this in years. She's got chicken pox."

"*What?*" Tendai cried.

"Everyone caught it when I was a girl. Oh, it's nothing serious. Toughens you up, I'd say. Of course," she paused, and went on more softly, "you'll have to go into quarantine."

"We can't," gasped Tendai.

"Fiddle-dee-dee. Of course you can. You *have* to. Doctors don't let diseases gallivant all over the city. I'll make up cots in the den. If she's sick, the rest of you will certainly come down with it."

Tendai's heart sank. "How long is a quarantine?"

"Three or four weeks. Depends on when the scabs drop off. Don't worry, I'll call your parents and put their minds at rest. You wouldn't want to make *them* sick. Much worse for adults. Land them in the hospital, I should say." Tendai was horribly disappointed, but he helped the woman make cocoa and toast. The cocoa was watery and the toast covered by only a thin layer of margarine, but he and Kuda were too hungry to care. Rita was unable to eat.

Afterward, he helped the woman make up cots. He wished he knew her name, but the moment had passed to ask. He realized he didn't even know the Mellower's name. The man had cared for them as long as he could remember. After Mother and Father, he was the most important person in their lives, and yet no one ever used his real name. Tendai felt vaguely guilty about this.

When the cots were made up—they were sturdy wooden ones with metal hinges and canvas coverings—Rita was allowed to lie down. Tendai and Kuda were expected to take baths. "You're whiffy. Distinctly whiffy," announced the woman. She trickled two inches of lukewarm water into an old claw-footed bathtub and handed them a slab of laundry soap. "Do the necessary," she instructed Tendai. "I've put some of Anthony's old clothes on the hamper. And drop those—whatever they are—into the laundry basket."

"They're bark cloth from Resthaven," said Tendai.

"You went to *Resthaven?* That makes them museum pieces. Quite valuable, I should say."

Tendai didn't exactly like the way she said *valuable*. I've become too suspicious, he told himself. After all, she is the Mellower's mother. No one could be kinder than he is. But he kept the *ndoro* and his bag of chicken droppings—probably what the woman found "whiffy"—secret. He didn't know why he kept the bag, except that it was made from a scrap of bark cloth and had come from Myanda.

He scrubbed Kuda with a bath brush and washed his hair as well.

"Who's Anthony?" asked the little boy.

"The Mellower, I think."

"No, it isn't. The Mellower doesn't have a name," Kuda said with his usual bulldog tenacity. Tendai didn't bother to argue. He dressed him in a long T-shirt.

The cots were hard and dusty, but Tendai was so exhausted he barely noticed. His head ached. He fell into a confused dream in which monsters pursued him through a dark forest. One had ears like radar disks and another stared at him with the large eyes of a praying mantis. A third had skinny black arms that stretched longer and longer until he awoke, sweating and shivering.

Great, Tendai thought as he stared at the unfamiliar clutter of the den. *Now I'm sick, too.*

Time to go," cried Ear. The detectives ran as fast as they could. They slipped and slid on rocks and banged into trees. Only fear kept them ahead of the villagers. "Turn here!" gasped Ear as they reached the fork in the path. A rock thudded past him to smack into a tree.

"That came from a sling," panted Eye.

"Ow!" A stone hit him in the back. Darkness and the speed they were traveling made most of the stones miss their target, but not all. One struck Arm on the shoulder, sending such a shock of pain that he almost dropped Sekai. She began to wail rhythmically, in time to his pounding feet.

"Open the gate!" Arm shouted. "I'll try to hold them off!" Ear and Eye yanked on the handle, but the gate was so heavy, it moved with excruciating slowness. Stones zinged past their heads.

"Owooo!" wailed Arm, crooking his legs and advancing on the villagers like a giant spider. "Aaaahhhh," he hissed, weaving back and forth. He covered Sekai as best he could with his arms. The villagers halted and crowded back. "Woowoowoowoooo!" shrieked Arm, dancing up and down.

The villagers tripped one another in their eagerness to hide behind trees. *"I'm going to get you!"* yelled Arm. *"And you! And you! And you!"*

"Come on! The gate's open!" called Ear. Arm gave a heart-stopping scream as he turned and fled out of Resthaven. He ran straight into a group of policemen, who were watching from outside. They collared him and marched him over to Ear and Eye, who were already standing by a squad car.

Behind, the great gate of Resthaven slammed closed. They could hear boulders being rolled against it. The sound boomed even through the thick wall.

"First time I've seen anyone thrown out of Resthaven," said a policeman. "It's too bad, my friends," he told the detectives. "A lot of people would like to live there, but they're as fussy as cats." Arm realized he didn't know they entered illegally.

"A baby!" cried the police captain as Sekai began to cry again. "Oh! It's so tiny. Is it yours?"

"Why—yes, she is," replied Arm.

"Poor thing, she's hungry," crooned the captain. "Is your wife . . . ?" The woman nodded at the gate.

"I'm afraid so," Arm said.

"That's so cruel. Here, Officer Moyo." The captain tossed him some keys. "Get the formula from the medical kit."

Arm was delighted to find that the police carried baby bottles, in case they found an abandoned child. Officer Moyo quickly warmed the food, and soon Sekai was working busily on the first meal of her life. Arm felt a strange sensation as he held her.

It was how his foot felt when it had fallen asleep and sensation was returning. It was a tickling, wriggling, gurgling feeling as life trickled back. Arm realized he had claimed her without thinking, and whatever spirits listened to such things had made it true. He had bonded to her in exactly the same way a parent did when presented with his or her newborn child. Except that Arm, whose psychic abilities were developed far beyond those of ordinary folk, could feel the exact instant when it happened.

He belonged to her, and as she nestled in his arms and her stomach rejoiced over the meal, he knew that Sekai thought she belonged to him, too.

"Why are you here? Did you find General Matsika's children?" came Eye's voice.

"Why, no," said the captain. "The Masks attacked a subway train. No one hurt, for a change. But tell me. How do you know about the children?"

Arm explained that Tendai, Rita and Kuda had been expelled from Resthaven earlier. To avoid trouble, he pretended to have met them inside.

"Call in reserves," commanded the captain. "We'll go over these streets with a microscope, and check the trains, too." She insisted that Ear, Eye and Arm go home, especially after examining the lumps and bruises caused by the stones.

Arm had to agree with her. He didn't think they would have more luck than hundreds of policemen, and his shoulder throbbed painfully. He and the other detectives sat in the squad car—in the back, where they wouldn't make the driver nervous.

"I can see why they were thrown out of Resthaven," whispered one of the policewomen in front. "Maybe there's something wrong with the baby, too." Her companion told her to be quiet.

"Don't feel bad," Ear told Arm. "You made a great bogeyman."

"Where did you learn to moan like that?" asked Eye.

"Late-night holovision. *I Was a Teenage Werewolf.*" Arm cuddled Sekai and felt her memory of floating on a dark sea and of listening to the boom of her mother's heart in the distance.

"He's been like this ever since we got home," said Ear as he let the doctor in. This time it wasn't a paramedic but a real medical specialist with degrees in psychology and abnormal spirit possession. Mother had sent him over as soon as she heard of Arm's strange state.

"We all took some thumps—*tsotsis* pelted us with rocks— but nothing we haven't experienced before." Ear was careful not to mention Resthaven. "Arm seemed all right then, but this morning . . ."

Arm lay on the sofa with his eyes closed. He didn't react when the doctor clapped his hands by his ear. He didn't flinch when he was pricked with a pin. Sekai stirred in her bed—a beer crate donated by Mr. Thirsty—and made sucking noises.

Arm pursed his lips.

Sekai began to complain, softly at first, then more insistently. Arm blinked and looked up at the doctor. "Who are you?" he asked.

"He's awake!" cried Eye.

"Of course I'm awake—and very hungry. I think—I think I'd like a glass of warm milk."

"Extraordinary," said the doctor.

"Good morning, Sekai," Arm said as he got up. "You sound hungry, too. Where are those bottles the police gave us? I'll get the formula out of the fridge." He warmed it in a pot of hot water. "Mmm! That smells good!"

"Arm, that's baby formula," said Ear.

"And very good, too. You like it, don't you, Sekai?" He popped the bottle into her mouth, and she began sucking greedily. "I can almost taste it. In fact . . . *I can.*"

"Just what I was afraid of," said the doctor. "I've always been interested in your cases. I studied them in medical school. Only one in a million such mutations prove beneficial. You're remarkable people."

"We know that. What's wrong with Arm?" Eye asked.

The doctor refused to be hurried. "You have remarkable eyesight: you can see a drop of rain in a thundercloud. *You* have amazing ears: a whisper in the next room sounds like a shout."

"Perfectly true," Ear said, patting his muffs.

"Tell me. Do your abilities get better as you get older?"

Ear and Eye looked at each other and shook their heads.

"How about you, Arm?"

Arm went to the window and pulled the curtain aside slightly. Eye reached for his dark glasses. Outside, the late-afternoon sun gilded the roofs of the Cow's Guts. It was too early for the beggars to return and too soon for the drunks to get rowdy. "A few weeks ago, I looked into Mr. Thirsty's mind," Arm said. "It was only for a minute. I had never focused on one person before. It was like seeing into the man's soul."

"Ugh!" said Eye.

"Strangely enough, underneath—deep down—I found something decent."

"Go on," the doctor said. Arm described his glimpse inside the Mellower and how, after the dinner party, he had walked through General Matsika's thoughts, opened a door and stepped into an actual memory. Suddenly, his knees buckled. Ear and Eye had to catch him. The doctor went to Sekai's crib and took the bottle out of her mouth. Her eyes popped open.

Arm woke up.

"You bonded with the baby, didn't you?" said the doctor. Arm nodded. "Bonding happens between parents and their children during the first few hours of life. It's the strongest emotion anyone can feel, but you aren't just anyone. Your mind is too sensitive for ordinary emotions." The doctor shook the baby gently, and Arm's head jerked up from the doze he was falling into. "You and the infant are one," he said urgently.

Arm rested his head on his hands while he thought. He could feel Sekai's irritability at not being allowed to nap. A gas bubble worked its way through her stomach. "What am I to do?"

"You need distance. No"—the doctor held up his hand—"I'm not telling you to give her away. That would be cruel to both of you. But her attention has to be diverted, or we're going to have to buy you the large size in diapers."

"Don't even *think* of it," said Arm with a grimace. Then he fell into a deep sleep, and this time no one could rouse him.

The Mellower arrived the next morning. Arm and Sekai were awake and enjoying their breakfasts. Sekai had milk; Arm had scrambled eggs, but he kept looking hungrily at her bottle.

"A baby!" cried the Mellower. "I adore babies! Wuggie-wuggie-woo. Oh, the sweet-ums, the little darling!" He picked up Sekai. Arm felt unreasonably jealous.

"She likes you," he accused.

"Well, of course. Who's the cleverest baby in Africa? Who's got the cutest little button nose?"

"Come on, Arm. Let's go for a walk," said Ear. He and Eye pulled him across the street to Mr. Thirsty's.

"I'm sure he'll drop her. He's so scatterbrained," Arm said.

"He's going to be fine. Now we've got to discuss the other children." Eye signaled to the bartender, who threw down his dish towel immediately. He scurried over with three glasses of fruit juice before bustling off to wrench a broken beer bottle out of someone's hand.

"Tendai, Rita and Kuda got on the train that was attacked by the Masks. They were with a big man who was probably Trashman," said Eye.

"You mean they were in the *subway* while we were breaking into Resthaven?"

"I'm afraid so."

Morosely, Arm looked across the beer hall. The light was dim and the air musty. In deference to Christmas, which a few people celebrated even in the Cow's Guts, Mr. Thirsty had decorated the bar with a stuffed antelope on a platter garnished with holly. Its head was topped with a pair of fake reindeer antlers, and it had an apple in its mouth.

"Somehow, I don't think Mr. Thirsty has quite captured the spirit of Christmas," remarked Ear.

"I owe you an apology, Ear," said Arm. "You wanted to listen to the subway, and I wouldn't let you."

"That's all right."

"No, it isn't. I was a bully. I was overbearing. I'm the worst detective in history." Tears ran down Arm's face.

"Arm, is Sekai crying?"

"Why, yes, she is."

Ear and Eye looked at each other in consternation. "You're picking up her unhappiness. She probably only has colic," said Ear.

Arm sat still a minute, then burped loudly. "You're right."

Eye went on: "The conductor says the General's children got off at Borrowdale, but one of the passengers—an ex-member of the Filed Teeth gang—swears they caught the next train to Mazoe."

"Volunteering information to the police isn't like an old Filed Teeth member," Arm said.

"She said she had been possessed by a *shave* for stealing, but a spirit medium drove it out."

"Oh, sure," said Arm.

"At any rate, it makes sense. Why stay in Borrowdale? The conductor said an old man gave them the money to travel." Eye signaled to Mr. Thirsty. He brought them more fruit juice. Arm's glass was decorated with a sprig of mint and a little umbrella. "The police located the old man, but his short-term memory is poor. He *did* give them money. He can't remember how much."

Ear shook Arm. "What's the matter? Is Sekai going to sleep again?"

Arm stretched his long, long arms, an activity that caused the drinkers at the next table to move their chairs. "I can hardly keep my eyes open. Keep shaking me."

"The children never got to Mazoe," said Eye.

The beer hall's bouncer removed a customer who had passed out. He expertly dragged the man in and out of the tables. One of the man's shoes came off, and someone picked it up. A moment later, the thief went outside to get the other one.

"You know, this isn't a good environment for raising a child," said Arm.

"Let's worry about that later," Ear said in exasperation, but Arm had nodded off again. The detectives carried their comrade back to the apartment. Outside, the man who had passed out was being used for third base by a gang of street urchins. Once inside the office, Arm could only be kept awake by having ice cubes poured down his neck.

"This isn't working," he said in a thick voice. "Mellower, could you take Sekai with you for a while?"

"Do you mean it?" cried the Praise Singer. "I'll get Kuda's old cradle from the basement—and the lullaby robot—and the stuffed elephant. Tendai used to sleep on it for hours. Let's see, I'll need formula. . . ."

Arm was dismayed by how quickly the Mellower organized his life around the baby. "She's only yours for a few hours."

"And what a wonderful few hours they're going to be!" The Praise Singer lifted Sekai from her beer crate, and she smiled at him.

It wasn't actually a smile, that is, it wasn't on the outside. But Arm knew as soon as she figured out how her face worked, she would produce a real one—*for the Mellower!* He silently took the infant away and held her. Yes, there it was: the niggling, tickling feeling of belonging. Their spirits were together in a way no one else could ever duplicate. Satisfied, Arm handed the baby back. "Have you heard anything about the other children?" he asked suddenly.

"Who? Me?" The Mellower was so startled, he almost tripped over Eye's sleeping bag.

"Is the General going to offer a reward? I know it's against his principles, but it might work."

The Praise Singer turned so pale Arm thought he was going to faint. "Why are you asking *me*? The General doesn't tell *me* anything. Oh, my! I can hear the limo now. I simply must fly." He gathered up a baby bottle and a towel to cover Sekai. "Be back this evening. Good-bye, you wonderfully talented people!" And with that he was out the door.

"Strange man," murmured Arm. As the limo receded into the distance, he felt the heavy, drugged sleepiness go away.

"He acted as though he were hiding something," Ear said.

"Yes. Why should he care about a reward?" And why did I think to ask about it? thought Arm. He pushed the Praise Singer out of his mind and gave his attention to the General's children, who needed his help far more. "I wish they weren't in the subway," he said aloud. "That's the Masks' favorite hunting ground."

Ear adjusted his muffs, and Eye put on his sunglasses. Arm braced himself for the barrage of emotions from the Cow's Guts. It was beginning to reach him even before the door opened these days.

I *am* getting more sensitive, Arm thought. Soon I won't be able to rest at all.

"What's the Mellower's real name?" asked Tendai. He was lying on a hard canvas cot, and Rita was across the room near a window. She seemed better this morning, although her skin was covered with little blisters from the chicken pox.

"I never thought about it," she said.

"He doesn't have a name," said Kuda, who was busily exploring the den. It was a large dark overcrowded room. Old chairs with sagging backs sat next to crooked lamps. Every shelf and table were covered with knickknacks. All the vases and baskets were stuffed with broken pens, dried-up gumdrops, sprung paper clips and smudgy erasers.

Tendai noticed a number of animal statuettes. These, too, were old. Three-legged dogs leaned against tailless cats. Pictures of animals decorated the walls. Dusty trophies lined the top of a mantelpiece. But most startling of all was a stuffed horse's head over the fireplace. A brass plaque underneath read:

SON OF STEEL
WE SHALL NOT LOOK UPON HIS LIKE AGAIN

"That's certainly going to give me nightmares," said Rita when she first noticed it.

"Don't you think it's strange she doesn't have pictures of people?" Tendai said.

"I don't know. I've never been in an English house before."

Which was true, of course. Father and Mother hardly knew anyone from the English tribe. The Mellower was so much a part of the family, it was difficult to think of him as an outsider.

"Oh, look!" Rita pointed out the window.

A shrill voice cried, "Stop that at once, you fiend!" Trashman loped past with a T-bone steak in his teeth.

"It's *raw*," said Rita in disgust. She opened the window. Kuda wrestled himself over the sill and dropped to the grass. Tendai's head hurt so much he had to rest a moment before he could get up.

The Mellower's mother huffed past with a broom in her hands. "Slasher! Fang! Attack that monster!" She was answered by a miserable whine. Tendai saw two Doberman dogs high in a jacaranda tree, where Trashman must have perched them. They were clinging to a branch.

Trashman danced around, dodging the broom. He seemed in a fine mood. He removed the steak from his teeth to babble.

"He says he took the doggies' dinner," translated Kuda.

"I can *see* that! Tell him to get them down before they do themselves an injury. Ha!" She swung the broom at Trashman, who hooted with delight.

Kuda explained what the woman wanted. Trashman, clenching the meat again in his jaws, grasped each dog by the scruff of the neck. They snarled, and he shook them until they howled. Then he dropped them on a pile of grass clippings. They backed away with their tails between their legs.

"I hope you have more meat," called Rita from the window. "Trashman didn't know he wasn't supposed to take it. He isn't very bright."

"I think he's too clever by half," said the Mellower's mother. "And you, miss, if you're well enough to chatter, you're well enough to work. Get back through the window, little boy." She stalked off after the dogs.

"I don't feel right yet," observed Rita. "Just think! We have *chicken pox*! It's like something out of a history book."

Tendai crawled back into bed and pulled up the blanket. If this was history, he wanted no part of it. Rita talked brightly about germs, while Kuda continued to explore the den. He found an enormous cat in one of the chairs. It had long hair and a flat, stupid face. He tried to pick it up, and it hissed at him.

"Leave Pasha's Favorite alone. He might bite you," said the Mellower's mother as she came into the room. Kuda let go of the cat, which had roused itself enough to twitch the tip of its tail.

The woman carried a tray with beef broth and dry crackers. She felt everyone's head before giving them food. "Now you've got it," she informed Tendai. "Don't scratch, miss, unless you want big ugly scars. That's rule one with chicken pox: break a blister and leave a pit. You'll resemble Swiss cheese in no time." Rita looked with dismay at the blisters she had already broken.

"Who was Son of Steel?" asked Tendai.

"Finest show-jumper in Harare. His father was Heather Pride out of Malagasy. He won me all those trophies." She gestured at the mantelpiece.

"You ride horses?" said Rita.

"Of course. I'm a smashing horsewoman. If you *will* open Pasha's mouth, little boy, I can't be responsible for the outcome." Kuda let go of the cat's head. It glared at him sullenly with one fang over its lower lip.

"Pasha's Favorite won the Harare cat show three years running," the woman went on. "His father was Satin Streak out of Midnight Madness."

"What does that mean? Out of—whatever?" From the way Rita was eating, it was clear her illness was on the mend. Tendai's throat was so sore, he could barely swallow the broth.

"It's a way of saying who the animal's father is."

"You know its *parents*?" said Rita with great interest.

"Its parents and grandparents and great-grandparents," said the Mellower's mother. "The dog Slasher, for example, is really named Slash von Hare Hunter the Third. His mother was Delfina Handchopper out of Gnash von Hare Hunter the *Second*. Gnash was Delfina's father."

Tendai was impatient with all this talk about animals. When the woman paused for breath, he quickly interrupted with: "Have you called our parents?"

"Of course," she replied. "But I'm afraid they weren't at home. They had to go to an important meeting in Beijing. Very hush-hush. Something to do with defense contracts. I'm sure the message will be relayed to them."

"Did you tell the Mellower?"

"Mellower!" exploded the woman. "Is that what you call him? He may be a Mellower in your house, but in this one he is called by his right name."

"Please. I don't know what it is."

"Isn't that just typical! Have someone around for donkey's years and don't bother to find out what he's called. I suppose you think he's one of the robots. Well! His name is Anthony Horsepool-Worthingham, and a very fine one it is."

"I'm sorry. It was rude," said Tendai.

"You don't know *my* name either, of course. Beryl Horsepool-Worthingham. *My* mother was a member of parliament—Vera Bloodworthy—and my father was High Court Justice Stilton Horsepool."

"Beryl Horsepool-Worthingham out of Stilton Horsepool," said Rita with satisfaction.

The Mellower's mother flared her nostrils. "That description of one's family is *only* used with animals—as I suspect you realize, Miss Impertinence. If I didn't know better, I would guess *you* were discovered in a basket at Mbare Musika. Now since your tongue is so very active, the rest of you can hop out of bed. Run along to the bathroom—you're decidedly whiffy. You may clear the dishes later. No, *don't* scratch. You'll look like the craters of the moon."

Mrs. Horsepool-Worthingham's voice died away as she ferried Rita down the hall. Tendai lay back on the hard cot and shivered. He was too wretched to sleep. Even the blanket hurt his skin. He watched Kuda roll Pasha's Favorite on its back. The cat waved its paws in the air and slowly rolled back. Kuda turned it over again.

Rita returned in an old shirt and shorts that had belonged to the Mellower. She gathered up the dishes and cups.

"What's that smell?" said Tendai.

"Olive oil." Rita grimaced. "Mrs. Horsepool-Worthingham says it will keep my skin from scarring. I smell like a pizza."

It made Tendai sick. He was glad when she left. He drifted off to sleep and awoke to find a lunch of tea and cream crackers covered with a thin layer of marmalade.

"They're stale," said Rita, wrinkling her nose. Tendai thought she was definitely recovering. Kuda squatted by the cat's bowl as Mrs. Horsepool-Worthingham cut up raw liver with a pair of silver scissors. He tried to take a piece, and she slapped his hands.

"Raw liver is stuffed with tapeworms, little boy. Once they're inside, they grow in a bunch until they're as big as a soccer ball."

"That's why the cat's so fat," said Kuda, nodding with understanding.

"Children should come with zippers on their mouths and a sign saying *Not to be opened until age eighteen*," snapped Mrs. Horsepool-Worthingham.

In the afternoon, Tendai heard her screaming at Trashman to keep out of the mango trees. Rita came in for a nap, but

Kuda wouldn't stay in bed. He climbed out the window and found Trashman. Together, they sat under a tree and ate fruit.

Dinner was skim milk, boiled carrots and toast spread with fish paste. It was served in the den because Tendai was too sick to move. "Don't waste food," said the Mellower's mother as Rita tried to scrape the fish paste off. "In my day we ate what was put before us or went without. Clean your plate, and you may have a graham cracker for dessert."

"Why can't we have steak like the dogs?" complained Rita.

"Those are *show* dogs. They have to be kept in peak condition to win prizes. Plain food is good for children anyway. It builds character. You have only yourself to blame for a bellyache, Kuda. Green mangoes will do it every time."

Tendai drifted in and out of sleep as he listened. Sometimes the bed seemed to be floating on a dark sea with little sunlit islands that resolved into the crooked lamps when he focused on them. He was unable to eat. Once he saw Rita squinting at a mending job Mrs. Horsepool-Worthingham had given her. Once he saw Kuda defiantly kicking as he was lifted into bed. The little sunlit islands floated away, and it was dark.

In a shaft of moonlight he saw the horse's head with one of its glass eyes shining. Outside, the Dobermans loped through the garden. Tendai got up. He saw Trashman sprawled on a pile of dry leaves. The dogs rushed past. Their eyes flashed red, and their long teeth gleamed. He held his breath.

They swerved over to the heap of leaves. Then, with a melancholy howl, they backed away. They ran on in the darkness, patrolling the house.

They didn't hurt Trashman, but Tendai was not at all sure they would be as kind to him. He sighed and went back to bed.

It was three days before he was able to come to the breakfast table in the kitchen. By that time, Kuda had come down with the sickness. Rita bustled importantly around the stove, adjusting the temperature, moving a teakettle, flicking toast over with a long fork. The mournful robot creaked after her.

The table was laid with a starched cloth and good, if chipped, dishes. The robot placed a small egg in a china cup by each plate. It filled crystal glasses with orange juice. Tendai was cheered by the sight.

Mrs. Horsepool-Worthingham sat in a captain's chair at the head of the table. She expertly tapped off a little crown of shell from her egg. "What's this? It's hard! I ordered three-minute eggs."

"My-timer-is-broken," said the robot gloomily.

"A likely excuse! You've been at the machine oil again. Don't lie to me! I checked the level yesterday." Mrs. Horsepool-Worthingham poked at her egg with a spoon. "All you robots do is lie about and drink machine oil. I ought to send you to the dump."

"Yes-madam," said the robot.

Rita dished up bowls of oatmeal. She filled a large jug with skim milk, but the Mellower's mother measured out the sugar. She said, "When I was a girl, we only had sugar on Sundays." Rita made a face behind her back, and Tendai frowned at his sister. After all, Mrs. Horsepool-Worthingham was taking care of them. She could have left them outside the gate, chicken pox and all.

"When can we go home?" he asked.

"Not yet! Good heavens, you're shedding germs all over the place. If the health department caught you, they'd put you in quarantine for a month. There's too much margarine on that toast, Rita. You may have the next piece dry to make up for it."

"Couldn't we talk to Mother and Father on the holo-phone?" The thought of actually seeing his parents' faces after so long made Tendai's throat feel tight. He took a deep breath to keep from crying in front of Rita.

"They're still in Beijing. I understand they took the opportunity to enjoy a cruise on the Yellow River—*very* luxurious, with thirty-course dinners." Mrs. Horsepool-Worthingham's face became wistful.

"You mean—you mean they went off on a *vacation?* With us missing?" gasped Rita.

"You mustn't be selfish," said the woman, sipping her tea. "Adults need their time off, indeed they do. Why, Anthony would have had me at his beck and call if I hadn't put my foot down."

Kuda began to wail from a back room. Rita jumped up.

"That's exactly the kind of thing I mean! Sit down. He won't get well any faster if you coddle him." Rita looked anxiously at the door. Kuda's cries sounded angry rather than frightened. Rita finally returned to the table. "He's only whining for attention, you see," explained Mrs. Horsepool-Worthingham. "Anthony used to do that, but I soon put him right."

Anthony, Tendai reminded himself, was the Mellower. Tendai remembered the time he broke his arm during one of the martial arts classes. The Mellower waited on him day and night. He told him stories; he fed him treats; he even brought him a chameleon from Mbare Musika. It was hard to believe this was his mother.

A crash sounded from the back of the house. Mrs. Horsepool-Worthingham jumped up. She, Rita and Tendai hurried toward the noise. Glass tinkled; pieces of wood were ripped, groaning, from a wall. Kuda wasn't yelling anymore.

The Dobermans, thought Tendai, with his heart pounding. But when they all crowded into the back room, the dogs were nowhere in sight. Instead, Trashman beamed happily as he perched Kuda on his wide shoulders. The window had been too small for him to enter through, so he had ripped out part of the wall. Mrs. Horsepool-Worthingham was so outraged, she was unable to speak. She opened and shut her mouth like a fish.

"Strong, isn't he?" remarked Rita.

The woman at last got back her voice. "You *juggernaut*! You *dinosaur*! Look what you've done! Oh, my poor, poor house!" She knelt in the bits of plaster and glass. "I'm a poor old woman with no money. How can I afford the repairs? Oh, why did I take you little fiends off the streets?"

"What's a juggernaut?" asked Rita.

"Not *now*," Tendai hissed. He knelt beside the Mellower's mother and tentatively patted her arm. She pushed him away. "I'm sure Father will pay for the repairs," he began. "Father always does the right thing. He might even give you a reward."

Mrs. Horsepool-Worthingham looked up with an expression Tendai didn't exactly like.

"He won't do that. He says rewards only encourage gang members to hold people for ransom," said Rita.

Tendai pinched her leg, and she kicked him. "This is different. We aren't being held for ransom. It's more like paying rent. Yes, that's it. Rent for use of the house and for food."

"And baby-sitting," added Rita. "How much *do* nannies get paid?"

"Nannies!" exploded Mrs. Horsepool-Worthingham. "I'll thank you to remember who I am! My mother was a member of parliament, and my father was a high court justice. Nanny, indeed! Mr. Worthingham, my late husband, ran for city council ten times."

"Did he catch it?" said Rita before Tendai could stop her.

Mrs. Horsepool-Worthingham's nostrils flared so widely, they turned white. "I'm going to put the lot of you outside. I have never been so insulted in my life! I shall give you a quarter for the pay phone—there's one at the public library. You may call the city health department and ask them to prepare beds at the infectious-diseases hospital!"

"No. Please," said Tendai. "We don't think you're a nanny at all, do we, Rita?"

And to his relief, Rita apologized. She did so with charm and apparent sincerity. Mrs. Horsepool-Worthingham relaxed. "Very well, you may stay. But only if that creature remains in the garden. One more incident—*one more*—and out you go. Now! You may sweep up that mess, Tendai. Rita, take care of your little brother. It's clear I shall have to take steps to avoid having the house pulled down about my ears."

It wasn't easy persuading Trashman to give up Kuda, but at last Tendai got the man to climb back through the hole in the wall. The robot was sent to fetch tools; Tendai hammered plywood over the hole and broken window. The room was dark, but it would have to stay that way until Father paid for the repairs. And Father would certainly do that. Whether he also gave Mrs. Horsepool-Worthingham a reward remained to be seen.

We can't travel now, Tendai told himself. Kuda's still sick. But deep down, he knew he himself was afraid to leave. He still felt weak, and his skin was covered with itchy chicken-pox blisters. The Mellower's mother rubbed them with olive oil.

"Two dollars a bottle," she said crossly as she examined Tendai's chest. "Still, we can't send you home looking like a cheese grater, can we?"

Quarantine, to Mrs. Horsepool-Worthingham, did not mean sitting idle. As soon as Rita's and Tendai's fevers were down, she had them weeding, polishing, sweeping and painting. Tendai wondered what she did when only the robot was around.

The garden had been allowed to go wild, except for the area on each side of the front walk. Now the children were set to cutting grass and digging flower beds. They toiled until the sweat ran down into their eyes.

Still, Tendai found it pleasant to get his hands into the good red soil. He was becoming an expert on such things. The ground in Dead Man's Vlei was gray and sickly. The earth of Resthaven was heavy with clay: it baked hard in the sun. Mrs. Horsepool-Worthingham's garden had been lovingly worked with compost for many years until it crumbled like a rich cake in his fingers.

"The red color is due to iron," she told him. "Good for blood, good for sap." And it must have been, because the weeds rioted everywhere. Now and then, in the tall grass, they came across statues of little men. Rita screamed when she encountered the first one.

"I thought it was one of the Dobermans," she explained. Tendai studied it curiously. It was about two feet high with a stocking cap and white beard.

"That's a garden gnome," said the Mellower's mother. "He watches over the plants."

Tendai and Rita nodded in appreciation. "It's a fetish," Rita whispered. "I didn't know the English tribe had them." They carefully trimmed the lawn around the gnomes, of which they eventually found fifteen. When they planted the marigolds, they put a flowered border around each statue.

Inside the house, they sanded and polished the scratches out of the furniture. They waxed the floor, took down curtains to wash and arranged books on the shelves. Rita polished the eyes of Son of Steel until they shone like jewels.

"This is fun," said Rita as she dumped an armload of twigs from a roof gutter to the yard below. Tendai had his legs hooked around an old chimney as he cut away the wisteria vine that threatened to topple it. He smiled in agreement as he wiped the sweat from his face.

Down below, Mrs. Horsepool-Worthingham threw a rock at Trashman, who was working his way through a mango tree. It bounced off his broad back. "She ought to leave well enough alone," Rita whispered. When Trashman was driven away from the fruit trees, he ripped open the Doberman cage to get at the steaks. This upset the Mellower's mother so much, she retired to a far wing of the house.

Tendai wondered what she did there. The property was so large, he hadn't explored all of it yet. And he wasn't welcome in all of it either. That wasn't surprising. Father had never invited him to play in the library. Elders had their mysteries, which children disturbed at their peril. But still he wondered, when she took down the sherry bottle and withdrew down a vine-shadowed walkway, what she was up to.

Where, for example, was the holophone? She must have had one to call the Mellower. Why wasn't he allowed to use it? No one could catch chicken pox over the phone. The more Tendai thought about it, the more he came to the same conclusion: Mrs. Horsepool-Worthingham didn't want them to contact home. But why would she not want them to?

"Tendai! Rita! Come prepare dinner," the woman called from a window. Rita dropped a last load of twigs and dusted off her hands. Tendai watched a blue-and-yellow-striped lizard scurry out of the wisteria and wriggle across the roof tiles before he followed Rita down the ladder.

"Guess what we're having for dinner," Rita said brightly as they washed their hands at a sprinkler.

"Don't start," said Tendai.

"Yummy canned peas. Lovely boiled squash and cream crackers with—are you ready?—*fish paste à la margarine.* The best kind, with the little bones inside."

"We've eaten worse."

"And for dessert, an *entire* graham cracker with stewed guavas from which most of the grubs have been removed."

"Are you complaining about my food?" said Mrs. Horse-pool-Worthingham from the window.

"No, indeed. I look forward to it," Rita said, bowing.

"I'm not made out of money like your father. If you want larks' tongues on toast, you'll have to whistle for it!" The woman slammed the window.

"Why do you do that?" said Tendai wearily.

"Because there's perfectly good food in this house. Steaks for the dogs, cream for Pasha's Favorite, cakes for those awful visitors." The awful visitors were the women who belonged to the Animal Fanciers' Society. They came in ones and twos, sipped expensive tea and ate little almond tarts.

Rita and Tendai were banished to a far room when the women arrived, but they always crept back. It was a game. They moved silently between the hedge and window to watch the tea parties from deep shade. They were greatly curious about English customs, and Rita pointed out that they could get Scout badges in anthropology if they took notes.

The visitors paid as much attention to their animals as Garikayi's clan did to cattle. Each dog or horse was lovingly described. The ladies ate from a communal bowl of snacks, although they transferred the food to personal plates. To be polite, each always left a half-eaten almond tart behind, a habit that drove Rita wild. These were later fed to Slasher and Fang.

"It's her house. We can't tell her how to run it," Tendai said. Rita squared her jaw exactly as Granny did when the She Elephant needled her.

Now Rita and Tendai fired up the old coal stove in the kitchen, cut grubs out of the guavas and boiled the squash. The late-afternoon sun slanted over the wall, highlighting blood-red petals from the rose tree that framed the window. Swallows darted in and out of clay nests built under the eaves.

Tendai sighed with contentment. Of course he would rather be home, but they had been gone so long, home had grown somewhat hazy in his mind. In the meantime, it was extremely pleasant to laze in Mrs. Horsepool-Worthingham's kitchen after a vigorous day's work. The teakettle purred on the stove. The squash bubbled. Pasha's Favorite burped as his stomach worked on the sardines he had had for lunch.

"I shall retire for a few moments' peace," Mrs. Horsepool-Worthingham announced as she removed the sherry bottle from the pantry. "Ring the bell when dinner is served." She went off to the wing Tendai hadn't explored. He rose to follow, but Rita put her hand on his arm.

"Kuda," she said. And of course she was right. Kuda's welfare was more important than satisfying his curiosity.

If it hadn't been for his little brother, Tendai would have been completely happy. The little boy had a far worse case of chicken pox than he or Rita. Furthermore, he had no patience with it. "I hate being sick!" he screamed. "I want Mama! Make me better now! Now! Now! Now!" And so, to keep Trashman from ripping out another wall, Kuda had been moved to a tiny room at the center of the house.

It was called the Invalid's Room.

It had been a mistake, the Mellower's mother explained as she led Tendai and Rita into the dark little chamber. "Long ago, my great-great-grandfather—Vice-president Dashwell Horsepool—you *must* have heard of him—built this house with his own hands. Somehow he left a space at the center. Perhaps it was where he rested his teacup when he was working out the plans. At any rate, when all was done, this space was left. It was too big for a closet and too small for a proper bedroom.

"This chamber"—she lowered her voice—"is where all my relatives have died."

"No!" cried Rita.

"It makes an excellent Invalid's Room—warm and quiet—cozy, you might say. Anyhow, no one else cared to be without windows."

"Sick people wouldn't like it either," Tendai said.

"Fiddle-dee-dee. It's just the thing. No nasty germs drifting about. For a reasonably bright boy, you show a distressing lack of intelligence. Quite a few of my relatives *recovered* here."

"You sound disappointed," observed Rita.

"For that bit of impertinence you may polish the coal stove tomorrow. This room is the perfect place for a noisy, I might say badly spoiled, little tyrant to have his sulks in private."

The worst part, however, was not the room but the cot. The normal, adult bed—"in which my late husband breathed his last," said Mrs. Horsepool-Worthingham—was moved out. Rita and Tendai could hardly bring themselves to touch it. A new, sinister child's cot was rolled in. It was like a cage on wheels. The sides were steel mesh, and a lid with a padlock fitted over the top. It was called a Kiddie Koop.

"Anthony used to get the sulks, too," said the Mellower's mother. "This soon put him right. Why, after a while all I had to say was 'Kiddie Koop,' and he stopped fussing at once."

Tendai could believe it. The sight of Kuda in a cage in a dark airless room made him sick. Rita wept and threatened, but nothing could change Mrs. Horsepool-Worthingham's resolve. She unlocked the Kiddie Koop several times a day, to allow Kuda to go to the bathroom. She certainly fed and bathed him, rubbed him with olive oil and gave him medicine. His physical needs were met, but Tendai believed his brother's illness was worse because he was so unhappy.

Rita and Tendai were banned from the Invalid's Room after Kuda was moved in. They went there anyway, whenever the Mellower's mother was busy. Right now, Tendai could count on her to retire for half an hour. Kuda was sitting up in the Kiddie Koop. His face was shiny with sweat and his eyes glittered with fever, but he was still General Matsika's son. He had kicked at the steel mesh until it was covered with dents. "Get me out!" he screamed when Tendai entered.

Tendai pressed his hands against the mesh, and his little brother pressed his hands on the other side. "I want Mama!" he yelled. "I hate you! I hate everybody!" Tendai wasn't hurt by Kuda's outburst. He knew it was a righteous anger at being caged and not really directed at him. He began to sing a lullaby he learned in Resthaven:

> *"Shiri yakanaka unoendepi?*
> *Uya, uya, uya kuneni,*
> *Ndiri kuenda kumakore*
> *Kuti ndifanane nemakore."*

> Beautiful bird, where are you off to?
> Come on, come to me.
> I am going right into the clouds
> So that I can be part of them.

He sang it again and again, as he had seen Myanda do with Garikayi's small nephews. The thought of Myanda made him heavy and sad. Kuda lay down on the mattress and watched him. He sucked his thumb. Presently, his eyes closed, and he went to sleep.

The thing that worried Tendai most was the almost certain presence of dead spirits in the room. The souls of Mrs. Horsepool-Worthingham's relatives might be looking for someone to possess. It wasn't bad—usually—to be possessed: the Mellower had a *shave* for storytelling. A *shave* was a friendly spirit with a skill to bestow. But sometimes people died full of anger. They had unfinished business with the world. Their spirits became *ngozi,* and they did terrible things to their hosts.

Tendai took off the *ndoro* and laid it on the Kiddie Koop. He spoke to the unknown ancestor, explaining that this was one of his children. "Please tell the *ngozi* to stay away. This is a Shona child. Please ask them to wait for an English person." Such as Mrs. Horsepool-Worthingham, he thought. He stood with his hands on the *ndoro,* and it seemed to grow warm beneath his fingers. Kuda sighed and turned over on his back. It might have been his imagination, but Tendai thought his brother looked a little less feverish.

Finally, he had to go. He wanted to leave the *ndoro,* but Mrs. Horsepool-Worthingham would take it if she thought it had any value.

rm stood in front of Resthaven Gate. It was as silent and immovable as the stones in the rest of the wall. No one answered its bell. No news, for good or ill, passed out of Monomatapa's country. "Can you hear anything?" he asked Ear.

Ear listened at the door crack. He shook his head.

"It could mean anything," Eye said. "We heard them piling boulders up on the other side. They've decided to ignore the outside world for a while."

"Or they could be sick or starving or killing one another off." Arm laid his sensitive fingers on the gate, but even he could detect nothing.

"Mrs. Matsika said it happened before. Once, about a century ago, they remained silent for fifteen years."

"I just wanted to tell Myanda that Sekai is all right."

"I think we could only do her harm," Eye said gently.

They went down into the subway. Each time they came—and this would be the eleventh or twelfth visit—they found more disturbing evidence of the Masks. DON'T LOOK BEHIND A MASK was freshly sprayed on the gray walls. A train had recently plowed into the platform, after which the driver was discovered with his throat cut. The far end of the walkway had crumbled away, but still people crowded into the remaining area.

Ear, Eye and Arm had little trouble walking because people edged away from them. Arm could see over their heads, but unfortunately his eyes were no keener than the next man's. He thought he detected an unusually large woman shouldering her way through the crowd.

"It's her! It's her!" Eye suddenly cried out, clutching Arm's sleeve.

"Who?"

"The She Elephant!"

Arm drew his Nirvana gun, and an immediate hole formed around him. "They've got guns!" someone yelled.

"It's the Masks!" someone else shouted. People dove for cover behind benches. Men skidded along the cement; women screamed. They threw themselves on top of children to protect them. The children yelled even louder as they were suddenly squashed by falling mothers, grandmothers, aunts and older sisters. At the same instant, two trains thundered in, one on either side of the platform. People whisked into the cars like flies disappearing into the mouths of frogs. The doors clanged shut. The trains lurched off with the guards watching anxiously from the windows. In a moment, the platform was deserted.

"Well, that was clever," said Eye.

"You're the one who yelled about the She Elephant." Arm stuffed the Nirvana gun back into his shoulder holster.

"Don't blame me. I didn't charge down the platform like Shaka Zulu and his troops."

"Oh, sure! You shout, 'Fire!' in a crowded theater and wonder why people get hurt!"

"Comrades! Comrades!" cried Ear. "It doesn't do any good to fight. The point is, what was the She Elephant doing here?"

Arm and Eye stopped squabbling at once. They looked up and down the tracks. A few people were descending to catch the next train.

216

"The General caught Knife, Fist and Granny, but there's an all-points bulletin out on her. You'd expect her to lie low." Ear folded his ears as a small boy began to throw a temper tantrum by the candy machine.

"Look at that. She's buying him candy," said Arm disapprovingly as the boy's mother fed money into the machine. "I'm not going to let Sekai get away with things like that."

"Go on. She wraps you around her finger like wet spaghetti," Eye said.

"Pay attention," said Ear in exasperation. "The She Elephant was down here. Do you suppose *she's* looking for the children?"

"I never did trust the report that ex–gang member gave the police. She was lying through her filed teeth." Arm frowned as the boy screeched and tipped over a garbage can. "Sekai would never do that. She's too refined."

"She's only three weeks old," said Eye.

"Keep your mind on business! The gang member might be working for the She Elephant—or the Masks. I think the She Elephant might have some idea about where the children went. At the moment, it's our only clue. I wish we knew which train she took." Ear opened his ears to their full extent and waved them at the little boy. He squealed in terror and buried his head in his mother's skirt. "That hurt, but it was worth it."

"We do know where she went," said Eye. He, of course, was able to read the subway schedule in the shadows at the far end of the platform. "It's rush hour, and practically everyone is heading out. At 4:51 both trains were going to Borrowdale, so it doesn't matter which one she took."

"Well, well," murmured Arm. At 5:02 they squeezed into another car loaded with glum passengers. They rattled and swayed in unison until they reached Borrowdale. Then they walked up and down the platform, as they had done on almost a dozen other occasions, and waited for something to happen.

"Borrowdale is mostly English," said Ear, who was mostly English himself. "Does the General know anyone here?"

"We went over that. There are members of the English tribe in the army, of course, but none of them is a close friend of the Matsikas," Arm said.

"We're overlooking something," Eye muttered. He went to the end of the platform, kicking aside the litter the cleaning robots hadn't got to yet. "Hello! What's that?" He knelt at the edge.

"Be careful! The rails can kill you!" Ear held on to his friend. The air around the magnetic rails shivered with lethal coldness.

"I can see a little bag—"

A train rumbled out of the tunnel. It glided to a stop a few inches over the supercooled track. Ear, Eye and Arm waited for it to depart. The commuters glanced uneasily at them before scurrying up the steps.

"I can't reach it," said Eye when the cars had moved on. So Arm lay on his stomach and stretched his long arm toward the little bag. He felt a mist of ice crystals settle on his fingers. If he touched the rail, his hand would freeze and shatter. He inched forward a fraction, touched the cloth and felt the cold bite into his fingers.

"Careful," whispered Eye.

Arm found the loop of string with which the bag was tied. He hooked it around a finger and jerked it up. A second later, he was rocking back and forth on the platform. "It hurts!" he cried.

Ear quickly fed a coin into a machine and plunged Arm's fingers into a steaming cup of coffee. Arm groaned as the heat fought with the extreme cold. "Ahhh. That's good," he sighed at last.

"I learned to do that from a City Scout manual," said Ear proudly. Then they set about examining the little bag. It had been frozen solid, but the ice crystals were already melting.

"It smells, you know, *ripe*," Eye remarked. "It reminds me of the village where we grew up."

"Chickens," said Ear.

Arm turned the bag over in his hand. The contents were surprising, but the cloth was even more so. It was a scrap of ancient bark material tied with a twist of sisal. Arm had never seen anything like it outside a museum. "This came from Resthaven, I think."

"At last!" Eye cried.

"The police can double-check it, but I'm convinced. It proves the children were here."

"Let's get to a computer terminal and go over the Matsika list of acquaintances again," said Ear.

Arm looked up at the darkening sky at the top of the subway stairs. "I just don't like the idea of the She Elephant out there hunting." And in his mind, Arm saw her tramping along the quiet tree-lined streets of Borrowdale. She was dressed in black, and when night fell, she would blend very well into the shadows. She reached into a pocket for a flask of *kachasu*. Arm felt her teeth grip the cork and pull it from the mouth of the flask. His eyes filled with tears as the fiery drink sloshed down her throat—

"Watch your step," said Ear, leading him onto a train.

Now where did that come from? thought Arm.

"I phoned the General to tell him to keep an eye on Borrowdale," Eye told him.

Where did the time go? thought Arm. I don't remember Eye making a call. I really was with the She Elephant! I could find her! But the train started off toward the Cow's Guts, and Arm remembered that Sekai would be coming home soon.

At the thought of the baby, Arm forgot about his search for the other children. All he could think of was how wonderful it would be to get home again. "I'll bet the Mellower forgot to warm her bottle," he said aloud. "She told me he gave it to her ice-cold yesterday."

Eye shook his head. Ear pretended to be interested in the dark tunnel flying past outside.

The Mellower had not forgotten to warm the formula. Sekai radiated contentment when the Praise Singer brought her in, nestled in a baby pouch strapped to his chest. She was singing a song inside her head:

> Milk, milk, beautiful milk.
> Warm, warm, wonderful warm.
> Happy, happy, happy, happy.

Arm was enchanted. He lifted her from the pouch. She gasped and stiffened. The song changed:

> Big booming things,
> Big awful things!
> No, no, no, *no!*

She screamed and clenched her little fists. It was like a physical blow. Sekai was pushing him away! The Mellower immediately scooped her back into his arms. "There, there. Did the awful man scare you? Oh, foo! We can't have that. Princess is safe now, yes, she is." He tucked her back inside the baby pouch.

"You—stole—her—love. You *thief*!" Arm was so outraged he could hardly speak.

"Can I help it if Princess prefers me? Don't hurt me!" The Praise Singer backed away from Arm's long reach.

Eye stepped between them. "You can't hit a man with a baby."

"Bully!" said the Mellower from behind Eye's back.

Arm collapsed on the sofa. He began to cry, not like an adult but with the all-out, stormy, the-world-is-coming-to-an-end sobs of a baby. Sekai answered him with equally desperate howls. Eye quickly lifted her from the carrier and presented her to Arm.

"Are you sure that's a good idea?" said Ear.

"Trust me."

Arm held the infant, and both of them, at exactly the same time, stopped howling. He felt the baby song again:

They fell into a kind of bliss together. "It's okay," Arm whispered.

"No, it is not," said Eye. "Don't you see what's happening? You're projecting your thoughts into her, just as you did with Mr. Thirsty. What were you thinking about when you came into the room?"

"Trains," said Arm. Sekai's mind immediately filled with alarm. He changed the image of the rattling subway car into that of a rocking horse. She stopped being frightened and became curious. He rocked it back and forth. Sekai cooed with appreciation.

"We have a problem," Eye said.

Then Arm understood. How long could he keep his mind on childlike images? How long before an intrusion from the adult world terrified Sekai? She was too young for such things.

Swallowing hard, he handed her back to the Mellower. The baby settled into the familiar pouch with a nagging sensation that something was missing.

"I'll take good care of her," promised the Mellower. For the first time, Arm noticed that the man's face was drawn with worry. He had lost weight. Deep lines were etched beside his mouth.

Later, the three detectives silently drank papaya juice as they sat in Mr. Thirsty's. Arm shredded the little umbrella the bartender had perched on his glass and let the savage emotions of the Cow's Guts wash through him. I'm glad the Mellower is suffering, he thought bitterly. I hope whatever's eating him has a good, hearty appetite.

"Eeee!" shrieked Mrs. Horsepool-Worthingham early one morning. "You parasite! You vandal! All my strawberries gone! You greedy guts!" Trashman hooted as he galloped past the window.

"He's done it this time." Rita yawned. "She was saving them for cream tarts this afternoon."

Then Tendai remembered that the entire Borrowdale Animal Fanciers' Society was meeting this afternoon. He and Rita were supposed to bake the cakes. "We'll have to use guavas."

"There aren't many of those left either." Rita smiled wickedly. Trashman not only liked guavas, he seemed to enjoy the nutty taste of the grubs.

While Rita visited Kuda, Tendai distracted Mrs. Horsepool-Worthingham in the kitchen. "He has to go," she said, blowing on the hot coffee Tendai brought her. "I shouldn't have put up with him so long. It's my kind heart, you see. People have always told me, 'Beryl, you're too good for this world. So trusting and generous to a fault.' No! No! Put *two* tablespoons of oats in the water, not three!"

Tendai stirred the thin porridge and tried to keep dismay from showing on his face. Trashman might be annoying, but somehow, through the weeks, he had become part of the family.

When Rita returned, the Mellower's mother sent her out to collect fruit. "I shall find it difficult to hold up my head at the meeting," she mourned. "'Poor Beryl,' they'll say. 'Can't afford anything but guavas.' That horrible tramp!" Tendai hoped, as sometimes happened, that Mrs. Horsepool-Worthingham would use up all her anger in talking and not really do anything.

He offered her oatmeal, but she waved it away. "I'm too upset! Put it on the back burner for later." She strode off in the direction of the unexplored wing of the house.

Tendai waited a moment and followed. She went along a sunlit veranda and through a series of storage rooms. Evidence of the house's once-grand days was stacked everywhere: magnificent rugs, original paintings, statues, busts of gloomy Horsepools and Worthinghams, antique furniture and a real horse dipped in bronze that Tendai avoided touching. It was easy to hide.

Mrs. Horsepool-Worthingham went into a den and closed the door. At the top of the door was a stained-glass fanlight with a panel broken out. Tendai climbed on top of a grand piano—he shared the space with a stuffed pheasant and a hippopotamus foot hollowed out for umbrellas. He settled himself next to the broken glass.

The woman was sitting in front of a holophone.

At last, thought Tendai.

She asked for a number he recognized as his own. In a few moments, the harassed face of the Mellower appeared. "Oh! Hello, Mummy. How nice of you to call. How thoughtful."

"Don't give me that Mellowing nonsense. Listen, is anyone near?"

The Praise Singer didn't look well. His skin hung loosely, and deep lines had appeared beside his mouth. Tendai was shocked. "Mrs. Matsika is lying down. She had a bad night.

The General is meeting with the President over a national emergency. I think the Gondwannans shot down a Zimbabwean airplane."

"I don't care about airplanes! Have you planted the idea about offering a reward?"

Tendai turned cold. So his parents weren't in Beijing at all! He leaned against the fanlight. Mrs. Horsepool-Worthingham was yellow behind the stained glass, and the Mellower was blue. He certainly looked blue. His mouth turned down, and he dabbed at his eyes with a large cloth that looked suspiciously like a diaper.

"I—I did try. During Mrs. Matsika's therapy session."

"Therapy, hah! Unvarnished flattery is what you hand out—and they eat it up with a trowel. Disgusting! Why couldn't you have gone into law like your father?"

"Please, Mummy. Don't start. I haven't got the nerves for a law court." The Mellower ran his fingers through his lank blond hair. It was a lot thinner than Tendai remembered. "Anyhow, it *is* therapy. It makes people feel good."

"So does heroin," sneered Mrs. Horsepool-Worthingham. "I'm glad your father isn't alive to see you cringing and bowing like a whipped dog."

"Mummy, I have to work."

"You listen!" Mrs. Horsepool-Worthingham had several ways of talking, but she saved one tone of voice for special occasions. She used it when the dogs made a mess on the carpet. She used it when Rita broke a prized bone-china teacup. She used it now. Tendai winced.

"Yes, Mummy," said the Mellower.

"I want you to hypnotize the Matsikas into offering a large sum of money for the return of their brats."

"That's cruel!" said the Praise Singer with more spirit than Tendai had given him credit for. The man's face had gone white as chalk.

"Nonsense! I'm only redistributing the wealth. I need to repair the roof and fix the robot, have the tennis court put to rights and replace the pipe in the fountain. The stables are collapsing, too."

"It's cruel and it's a crime!"

"Be quiet, you lily-livered Mellower!" said Mrs. Horsepool-Worthingham, using her special voice. "I intend to keep the children until the General offers a reward. If you inform on me, I'll go to prison. How would you like that? Your poor old mother shivering in Waa Waa Prison because you were too selfish to keep your mouth shut. *That's* cruel for you, you ungrateful serpent's tooth!"

The Mellower clasped his hands until the joints cracked. Tendai saw that his fingernails were chewed down to the quick. "Why don't *you* call the General, Mummy? I'm sure he'll be grateful."

The woman laughed harshly. "What a ninny you are! Gratitude doesn't fill your pockets! The General doesn't pay you what *you're* worth, and that's not much. Mark my words, the only way you get by in this world is to grab the opportunity when it presents itself."

A baby cried in the background. The Mellower looked quickly toward the sound. "I have to go."

"Put a word in his ear, in that smarmy way of yours. Suggest delicately that a reward might do wonders."

"I have my professional ethics," said the Mellower, trying to outstare his mother with his watery blue eyes.

"Ethics, rubbish!" said Mrs. Horsepool-Worthingham, glaring back with her steel gray ones. "You wouldn't want anything to happen to your poor old mother, all alone in a hovel that is falling down around her ears. You wouldn't want her to end her days sewing mailbags in a cold gray cell."

"Don't talk like that! Of course not!" The baby's cries became more insistent. "Oh, I don't know what to do!" The

Mellower snapped off the holoscreen without even saying good-bye.

Tendai stayed perfectly still as the woman locked the door of the den and went back to the main part of the house. He might have been another stuffed animal. He hugged himself to get control of his rage. His first impulse was to denounce Mrs. Horsepool-Worthingham as a traitor. That is what Rita would have done. But first impulses weren't always wise.

I wish the Mellower weren't involved, he thought. It isn't really his fault. If my mother asked me to do something criminal, I'd probably agree, too. But Mother wouldn't do that.

Tendai's mind was whirling. What would Father do to Mrs. Horsepool-Worthingham? In spite of her dishonesty, she had taken them in and fed them. She was cruel to Kuda. But did she really know that? "I'm building character," she always said when they complained. Father made them do things they hated, too, in order to build character. And what would he do to the Mellower?

I have to keep my mind on getting home, he thought. He examined the fanlight: even if it were completely broken in, he was too large to crawl through to reach the holophone. The quickest way out, of course, was to confront Mrs. Horsepool-Worthingham. The thought dismayed him: she was so *old*. The one thing that had been drummed into all their heads from the moment they were able to understand was that you never seriously argued with elders. You could needle them or complain—Rita was an expert at this—but you didn't go too far. And the older an elder was, the more careful *you* were.

Mrs. Horsepool-Worthingham had *white hair*! She was the Mellower's mother, and he was almost like a third parent!

He decided to visit the Invalid's Room first, to check up on Kuda. Or perhaps, he thought unhappily, he was only putting off what would certainly be an ugly confrontation.

The little boy was still asleep when he arrived. His face was peaceful and unmarked by the sweat of fever. Tendai thanked the unknown ancestor who had owned the *ndoro*. Rita burst into the room. "Come quickly! She's getting rid of Trashman!"

"I didn't know what she was up to right away," Rita said as they hurried outside. By now they were in the garden, and Tendai took in the situation instantly.

Mrs. Horsepool-Worthingham stood at the top of a tall ladder. The robot waited by the front gate, which was open. The woman had a fishing rod trained over the wall, and dangling on the other side was a T-bone steak. Even as they arrived, Trashman loped through the opening and pounced on the steak. The robot slammed the gate. The locks snapped into place, and the burglar-alarm light went on. Mrs. Horsepool-Worthingham cut the fishing line and came down the ladder.

"Open it at once!" shouted Rita.

"Don't you give orders in my house," said the Mellower's mother.

"He's our friend!"

"Then I must say you have rotten taste. I can smell cream tarts burning from here, Rita. You are the most impossibly scatterbrained child I have ever seen."

"I hope they all burn to little balls of soot!" screamed Rita as Tendai dragged her away. "Why don't you do something? How can you let her get away with that?" she yelled as he pulled her to the other end of the garden.

"Listen. I have something very important to say," he said. He told her about the call to the Mellower. Rita's mouth formed an O, and her eyes got very big.

"So they didn't go on a cruise. Oh, Tendai, you don't know how worried I was. I thought they—I thought they were partying while we—" She began to cry. Tendai was amazed. He hadn't known she was upset. "Every night when

I went to bed, I imagined them having thirty-course dinners, like Mrs. Horsepool-Worthingham said." She hiccuped and wiped her eyes on the sleeve of her T-shirt. "I thought they were *happy* because we were gone."

Tendai took her hand. "Of course they wouldn't be," he said.

"It's been so long. I forgot."

He waited until she had calmed down. "Don't worry about Trashman. He got along fine before he met us. He's probably on his way to Resthaven now. When we get home, I'll ask Father to look for him," whispered Tendai.

"Poor Chedu. He probably doesn't remember we exist." Rita gave her brother a watery smile.

Tendai explained that he would have to confront Mrs. Horsepool-Worthingham.

"She'll only think of a way to excuse herself!" Rita said fiercely. "She'll tell Father she rescued us—and he'll believe her. He never believes us!"

"Maybe it doesn't matter, as long as we get home."

"It does *so* matter! She ought to be punished for the suffering she's caused."

"Do you really want her to go to Waa Waa Prison?"

Rita stared at a garden gnome. The fetish stood up to his knees in morning glories and marigolds. He smiled cheerfully at Rita as she brooded. "No," she answered at last. "There *is* a way she can be punished right here, and we can go home afterward."

It was a good plan. Tendai was impressed. It would inflict maximum humiliation without involving the police. The Mellower needn't be involved at all. The only problem was that they would have to wait a few more hours to make it work. But they had already waited so long, what difference could a few hours possibly make?

Rita apologized prettily to the Mellower's mother for shouting. Tendai mixed up a new batch of cream tarts. They raked the front garden, set out tea tables and folded napkins into decorative shapes. When Mrs. Horsepool-Worthingham fed them stale crackers and fish paste for lunch, they didn't even complain. She was so surprised, she gave them each a cream tart as a reward. They saved them to feed to Kuda, crumb by crumb, through the space between the lid and sides of the Kiddie Koop.

ar answered the holophone, although Arm was sitting right next to it. Arm didn't even blink when it rang. He was sunk in gloom, and the other detectives tiptoed around him.

"Ear, Eye and Arm Detective Agency. You lose 'em, we find 'em—oh, hello, Mrs. Matsika."

"H-have you got any news?" said Mother. In spite of his depression, Arm noticed the despair in her voice.

"I'm sorry," Ear said.

"It's just that . . ." Mother paused, unable to go on. All three men were alert now. They watched the screen as Mother struggled to find words. "It's almost Tendai's birthday. He would have been fourteen. *Will* be fourteen, I mean. I always took him to the Starlight Room . . . to ride the elevator . . . and have dinner. . . ."

Arm was ashamed of himself. He was sulking because the Mellower had Sekai. Sekai was fine. Mrs. Matsika had lost all her children.

"I need advice," she went on. "Amadeus is against it, but it's so easy to offer a reward—and it might work. That's what's important, isn't it? To get them back. You could offer it for me. I have my salary from the University. I know Amadeus would be angry, but if they came back it wouldn't matter. . . ." She stopped speaking again, and a tear rolled down her cheek.

Arm took the phone. "Mrs. Matsika, has anything new happened to upset you?"

"Why . . ." She hesitated. "Nothing I can think of. Only after this morning's Praise I felt so low. It usually makes me happy. I remembered about Tendai's birthday, and it suddenly seemed so *stupid* to be rich and not use that fact to get him back. I mean, the money has no meaning without the children."

"What, exactly, was the subject of the Praise?"

Mrs. Matsika seemed confused. She was not the brave, confident woman Arm had seen before. "I—don't quite remember. But that's not unusual. Praise is like beautiful music. It carries you away and makes you feel better."

"Listen to me," Arm said. "I'm convinced the children are okay. They've shown themselves to be surprisingly resourceful. I'm sure we'll get them back. Now please do me a favor. Don't listen to any more Praise. If you're depressed, see a doctor or a spirit medium."

"That's what Amadeus said, but it usually makes me so happy."

"Not anymore. Please don't listen to anything you can't remember later."

"Well . . . all right." She seemed dazed, so Arm repeated his words. When she had hung up, he went at once to the computer the General had installed in the office.

"That cursed Mellower," he said under his breath.

"Are you sure you aren't just angry because he has Sekai?" began Eye, but Arm gave him such a poisonous look, he closed his mouth at once.

"I'm angry at myself. All the clues have been right under my nose, and I was too wrapped up in the baby to notice. The Mellower has been wasting away before our eyes. Why? He's eaten up with worry. About what? *The reward.* Curse it all, what's that creature's name?" Arm slammed his fist on the table next to the computer.

"I don't know," said Eye.

"It's funny. I never thought of him as having a name," Ear remarked.

Arm called up the list of professional Praise Singers in Harare. He narrowed the search to those who worked for private families. This produced about fifty names. The only one operating in Mazoe was Anthony Horsepool-Worthingham.

"He was so close, he was like one of the family. We didn't look up Mrs. Matsika's sisters either, did we? We assumed they would send the children home if they found them. The Mellower's like a damned cobweb, always hanging around in the background with his oh-so-soft suggestions that no one can remember."

"Now, now," said Ear.

"There!" Arm stabbed a button to call up the Praise Singer's official residence, a place he hadn't lived for years. Mrs. Horsepool-Worthingham's address in Borrowdale flashed across the screen.

"I don't want children underfoot," said Mrs. Horsepool-Worthingham. "You will stay out of sight until evening. You may play with Pasha's Favorite if you're bored."

"It's like petting a bag of cement." Rita lifted one of the cat's forepaws and dropped it. The paw fell heavily, and Pasha's Favorite continued to snooze.

As soon as the guests began to arrive and the Mellower's mother was busy, Tendai and Rita crept up to the window to watch.

The guests were all older women and members of the English tribe. Some wore tight-fitting pants and boots, which Rita found fascinating. She had never seen Shona women dressed this way.

"I saw the most awful tramp outside," one of the women complained. "You really ought to call the police."

"I can't be bothered," said Mrs. Horsepool-Worthingham.

"Trashman," whispered Tendai.

"*We* know why she won't call the police," Rita said bitterly.

Soon all the women were seated around picnic tables and talking in shrill voices. The robot shuffled here and there with trays of refreshments.

"I bought the most marvelous pit bull," said one of the ladies. "Simply stacks of pedigree and so cheeky. Nipped a finger off the garden boy—*and* swallowed it."

Her companion shrieked with laughter.

"I have never recovered," sniffled another woman. "Poor High Hooves. Such a fine horse."

"He was over twenty," Mrs. Horsepool-Worthingham said gently.

"I sent a notice to the newspaper, and do you know, they put it under *pets* instead of in the obituaries."

"Shocking."

"Here! You spilled that tea on purpose!" cried the woman who had lost the horse.

"Sorry-sorry-sorry," said the robot.

"Have you been at the machine oil again?" Mrs. Horsepool-Worthingham said. "Come here and let me smell your joints."

Tendai and Rita watched the gathering in amazement. The women sounded like a flock of mynah birds as they recounted tales of dogs, cats, budgies and horses. Once, Mrs. Horsepool-Worthingham called, "Kitty, kitty! Come and get your cream." Pasha's Favorite woke up and moved with surprising speed toward the party.

"Don't they have children? Why don't they ever talk about them?" asked Rita.

"Mrs. Horsepool-Worthingham had the Mellower," Tendai said doubtfully.

"Humph! I don't believe she's his mother. She's a nasty old witch."

"It's time." Tendai looked at his sister, and they exchanged slightly malicious smiles. They went off to the Invalid's Room, where Kuda was methodically shredding his mattress. They wheeled the Kiddie Koop through the halls.

"I want out," said Kuda.

"Shhh. We're working on it." Tendai rolled him onto the porch while Rita held open the door. Down below, the members of the Animal Fanciers' Society sat around the dry fountain and sipped tea. They hadn't noticed the children yet.

The plan was to wheel Kuda straight into the middle of the gathering and announce that Mrs. Horsepool-Worthingham was holding them for ransom. Tendai and Rita had observed the English long enough to know they would close ranks. They wouldn't tell Father anything, and so neither the Mellower nor his mother would go to prison.

At the same time, their code of honor would insist that Mrs. Horsepool-Worthingham be forced to call Father herself. The English tribe would punish her in their own way later. Never again would they come for tea; never would they invite her to their houses. In many ways, they operated like Garikayi's clan in Resthaven. Mrs. Horsepool-Worthingham was about to be declared a witch.

Tendai hesitated on the porch as the memory of how the villagers turned on Myanda came back to him. "Maybe this isn't a good idea," he whispered.

"It's *fair*," Rita whispered back. "You can bet the She Elephant would be punished for her crimes. Why should the Mellower's mother be any different?"

"Look." Tendai pointed at the front gate, which was certainly behaving strangely. It was shivering. A wire looped around a hinge sawed steadily, but the women were talking so loudly they couldn't hear it. All the other hinges had been cut, and as Tendai watched, the last one divided in two.

The gate fell in with a *whump*. The burglar alarm began to whoop in panic. The ladies all dropped their cups and spilled tea and cream tarts over the lawn.

In the gateway, nearly filling the gateway, stood the big black shape of the She Elephant.

or an instant, everyone was petrified. Then the robot came forward, saying, "Do-you-have-an-appointment? Do-you-have-an-appointment?" The She Elephant smashed it to one side and charged into the garden.

"You!" she bellowed in a terrifying voice. Tendai pushed Rita behind him. Rita tried to wheel the Kiddie Koop inside, but in her panic only smashed it into the door frame. Kuda yelled, "Trashman!" The ladies of the Animal Fanciers' Society scrambled into the dry fountain, and all of them tried to climb the mermaid at once. Mrs. Horsepool-Worthingham grabbed a pitchfork that was leaning against the porch.

She placed herself between the children and the She Elephant and aimed the pitchfork. "*You* will leave this property at once," she said in a steely voice.

The She Elephant halted and stepped back. She tripped over a garden gnome and fell with a splat onto a freshly watered bed of marigolds. Roaring with fury, she clawed her way up and lunged at the Mellower's mother. Calmly, Mrs. Horsepool-Worthingham jabbed at her and tore a big hole in her black dress.

"Oooo," said the members of the Animal Fanciers' Society huddled in the fountain.

The She Elephant went berserk. She ranged around the garden, smashing tea tables, kicking garden gnomes and uttering the most terrible curses. Every time she broke something, the ladies in the fountain cried "Oooo!" like a covey of frightened doves.

And still Mrs. Horsepool-Worthingham attempted to drive her toward the gate. "Get inside and lock the door," she crisply ordered Tendai. Tendai tried to push the Kiddie Koop to safety, but Rita had managed to snap off a wheel. The broken spike dug into the porch. "Trashman!" wailed Kuda, and suddenly the man was there, yanking the Kiddie Koop in the opposite direction.

"Tell him to stop!" shouted Tendai. But Kuda was so frightened, he could only cry. Trashman wedged his fingers under the lid and pulled. The lock snapped; the lid tore off its hinges. Trashman lifted the little boy out and danced around with glee.

The She Elephant almost grabbed the pitchfork out of Mrs. Horsepool-Worthingham's hands. The small woman parried and ripped off another strip of cloth. Tendai knew the battle couldn't go on much longer. The Mellower's mother was panting for breath. The only reason she had lasted this long, as Tendai knew from evil experience, was because the She Elephant was drunk.

He dashed to the back garden, where Fang and Slasher were hurling themselves against the wire of their cage. Tendai took a deep breath. He was terrified of the dogs. They were so excited, they might well mistake *him* for the enemy. But it was Mrs. Horsepool-Worthingham's only chance.

With shaking hands he unbolted the lock. The dogs barreled out, knocking him over and scratching him with their toenails. They flew to the front garden. Fang fastened onto the She Elephant's left ankle and Slasher onto the right. She stamped furiously, shaking the dogs up and down. Mrs.

Horsepool-Worthingham leaned on the pitchfork to catch her breath.

The big woman lurched around until she was able to catch each dog by the scruff of the neck. Swearing loudly, she hurled them across the garden and into a gooseberry hedge.

"Oooo," moaned the members of the Animal Fanciers' Society.

Next, she tore the pitchfork from Mrs. Horsepool-Worthingham's hands and turned it around. The Mellower's mother stepped back—and tripped over Pasha's Favorite! The cat had gorged itself on cream and was lying like a side of bacon in the middle of the tea party. The small woman landed on him. The cat squawked. The pitchfork whizzed over them both to bury itself in a tree.

The She Elephant didn't bother to retrieve it. She launched herself at Rita. "Help!" Rita shrieked as she was stuffed under the big woman's arm.

"You, too!" snarled the She Elephant at Tendai, who had followed the dogs to the front garden. "Come here or I'll break her neck!"

Tendai knew she meant it. He approached the big woman and gasped as she snatched him up. She hoisted him to her hip, bending him double at the waist. The little bag from Resthaven—the one Myanda had given him—fell out of his pocket and landed at the feet of a toppled garden gnome. The ground bounced past as he was carried outside. Behind them, Trashman trotted with Kuda perched on his shoulders.

Tendai's head bobbed up and down as the heavy feet of the She Elephant struck the pavement. Rita tried to yell, but the big woman squeezed the breath out of her. Tendai was afraid she had been hurt. A moment later he heard his sister cough. "Fat cow—oof!" grunted Rita. She never knew when to keep quiet.

They arrived at a taxi stand just as one was landing. A dignified gentleman in a three-piece suit alighted. He raised his eyebrows at the She Elephant. "I say!" he cried as she kicked his feet out from under him. Using Tendai's head to push back the door, she forced her way inside.

"Do what you're told or I'll rip your throat out," she growled at the driver. She wedged Rita under a foot and clamped her big hand over the terrified man's windpipe.

"Please, madam. I can't breathe, madam," he squeaked. The She Elephant shifted to let Trashman and Kuda inside. She loosened her hold slightly on the driver's neck.

"Don't try any funny business. If I see you touch that panic button, you can kiss your tonsils good-bye!"

"You're most unmannerly," said the elegant gentleman outside. "No cause to grab a cab like that. It isn't rush hour. I say, my good man, what do I owe you?"

"This one's on the house." The She Elephant grinned. "Get out of here!"

"I have a wife and kids." The taxi driver moaned as he took off.

"Who cares? Take us to Mufakose and don't break any speed limits." The She Elephant settled back, and the driver felt his throat for bruises. Trashman and Kuda excitedly pressed their noses against the window and discussed the scene passing below.

"How did you find us?" asked Tendai.

"A little birdie told me you got off in Borrowdale." The She Elephant felt in one of her pockets. She frowned at the many holes torn out by Mrs. Horsepool-Worthingham. Finding a flask of *kachasu*, she uncorked it with her teeth and swigged it down. The sickly smell of raw alcohol filled the taxi. "A member of the old Filed Teeth gang was questioned by the police. She told them you went to Mazoe. She told *me* where you really went—for a price. You brats have cost me plenty, and I intend to get every penny back." The She Elephant finished the *kachasu* and tossed the bottle to the floor. "I looked off and on for days, until I saw *him*." She nodded at Trashman, who was waving at a passing bus.

"He was sitting outside the gate, looking like someone'd taken his last marble. 'What's wrong?' I asked. 'Kuda,' he answered, banging on the gate. Took me by surprise, all right. I didn't know he could talk."

"Kuda," said Trashman, turning from the window to beam at the little boy. Kuda beamed back.

"So why go to all the trouble to find us?" Tendai asked wearily. "You have everything you want in Dead Man's Vlei. You're practically a queen."

To his surprise, the She Elephant's face twisted with grief. "Your father took everyone away!"

"Good," said Rita.

The She Elephant put her foot down more firmly. "You spoiled little maggots don't know anything. We were happy."

"Sure. Running a slave ring—oof!" said Rita from the floor.

"Where do you think the *vlei* people are now? In a nasty hospital where they can't get fresh air or work how they please. They get drugs pumped into them to keep them quiet. *They're* never going to work in a bank or teach a class at the University."

Tendai had the uncomfortable feeling she was right. "Granny was unhappy."

"Don't you believe it! She had the time of her life whining about us. 'You're all going straight to hell, yesss,'" the She Elephant said in a perfect imitation.

"Well, you stole children."

"Why not?" The woman seemed honestly surprised anything was wrong with this. "People want brats. I supply them."

"By hurting their parents!"

"The way I look at it, I make one lot glum and the next happy. It balances out, see? And I make a profit. Now stop your squeaking. I want to rest." The She Elephant dug her fingers into the taxi driver's neck. He yelped. "Just a little reminder. Don't even *think* of dropping in on a police station."

The taxi descended when they got to Mufakose, and, under the She Elephant's directions, settled down on a deserted parking lot. She produced a glass vial and snapped it under the driver's nose. He slumped over the controls.

"You didn't—" began Tendai.

But the woman cracked a vial under his nose before he could ask the question "You didn't kill him, did you?"

Tendai awoke slung over someone's shoulder. His head ached and his mouth felt numb. For a moment it was like being carried across Dead Man's Vlei, but this time he wasn't in a bag. The sun was setting behind a cluster of small houses. It was evening, and people were coming home from work.

Mufakose thronged with a fascinating mix of food sellers and gamblers with playing cards and bottle tops. Peanuts roasted on charcoal braziers. Women sat behind bright cloths heaped with mangoes. Street musicians banged their drums while dancers jigged around the dusty road. It wasn't frantic, however, like Mbare Musika. These were ordinary folk relaxing after a hard day's work.

Tendai blinked to clear the cobwebs from his mind and saw a creature he never expected to encounter again. The Blue Monkey strode along with its leash dragging in the dust. It counted a roll of money clutched in one paw. The animal glanced up at him, bared its fangs and continued to count.

To the right, the She Elephant toted Rita, and behind came Trashman with Kuda. Kuda carried a paper cone full of roasted peanuts. He was feeding them into the man's mouth. Trashman chewed them up, shell and all.

"I get this much to boogie in the street," complained the Blue Monkey.

"Wait till I get paid," the She Elephant said.

"I want it *now*, or I'll pull the nearest fire alarm."

Grumbling, the She Elephant peeled off more notes from a wad she produced from a pocket.

"Nice dress," remarked the Blue Monkey. "Is that a new style with the air holes?"

Tendai thought they must look strange in Mufakose. All the other people were normal, law-abiding citizens. They arrived on buses and strolled along the walks to pass the time of day with friends. Children came out of the little houses to greet them.

The She Elephant swaggered among them like a gangster. The Blue Monkey drew stares, which he answered with rude hand signals. Tendai saw the people of Mufakose frown: these weren't the kind of visitors they wanted in their neighborhood.

But this was exactly the kind of neighborhood that would help him. "We're kidnapped! Call the police!" Tendai yelled. All that came out of his mouth was a hiss. His tongue would not respond! He tried again and again. A long string of drool came out and dripped into the dust. He pounded his fists on the man who was carrying him.

"Now you know what it feels like to be a dumb beast," said the Blue Monkey, laughing nastily, "like my little brothers and sisters at the zoo."

"Awake, eh?" the She Elephant said. "That's a little side effect of the stuff I gave the taxi driver. *He* won't be singing for a while."

Tendai tried to break the grip of whoever was carrying him. The man merely shifted him to the other shoulder. Tendai saw a swollen eye and a bandage over one ear: it was the owner of the Blue Monkey.

"They think you're a half-wit like Trashman," said the Blue Monkey.

Rita reached out to yank a woman's sleeve.

"Stop that!" shouted the woman. "They're pickpockets," she explained to a man who carried a basket of dried fish. "The big ones are training the little ones right now."

The She Elephant patted Rita's head. "It's the longest this brat's been quiet in her whole life." Rita kicked at her, and the big woman laughed.

The She Elephant bought loaves of hot bread and mugs of sweet milky tea from street vendors. They all sat by the dusty road to eat, although Tendai found it difficult. He choked on the bread and dribbled tea onto his shirt. The Blue Monkey thought this was a great joke.

Now the sun had set: the air was a deep pure blue. Charcoal smoke drifted over them, sinking into their clothes and hair. Tendai felt his mouth begin to stir with sensation. "When did you tell them to come?" the She Elephant asked suddenly.

"They're already here." The Blue Monkey pointed a hairy finger at the darkening sky. A cluster of stretch limos lowered over a distant building. They were black—or perhaps it was only the fading sunset behind them. They stirred something in Tendai's memory. He tried to speak, and an audible sound came out of his mouth.

"Not a moment too soon. That one's getting his voice back." The She Elephant picked up Rita and patted Trashman on the shoulder. He obediently lifted Kuda. They walked off briskly, leaving the crowds behind. Soon they came to deserted streets flanked by old factories and continued on until the She Elephant led them into a dark alley.

"Augh!" croaked Tendai.

"Yii!" shrilled Rita, but no words came out. The alley twisted in a confusing way, and presently they arrived at a dark doorway.

"Time to go," the Blue Monkey announced.

"Wait a minute. Aren't you going to help me?" said the She Elephant.

"I'm not going up *those* stairs."

"But I paid you—"

"You paid me to contact the buyers. No way am I getting near them. They'd love a blue monkey skin on their wall."

The She Elephant swore and threatened, but the animal ordered his owner to put Tendai down. She clamped Tendai in an iron grip before he could bolt. "Help! Help!" he shouted, his voice back at last. The deserted alley swallowed up the sound. He saw the Blue Monkey and his owner disappear into the shadows. The She Elephant dragged him through the door and kicked it shut. And then they were alone— Tendai, Rita, Kuda, the She Elephant and Trashman—at the foot of a long dark stair.

The steps went up and up and up, spiraling along the inside of the building. At intervals, a cold green light shone from a panel in the wall. It reminded Tendai of the glowworms that came out on rainy nights. The light was just enough to keep them from stumbling, but not enough to spread any cheer.

The air was dank and cool, the walls scored with alarming cracks. Every thirteen steps or so, they came to a landing and an iron door leading to the inner core of the building. The doors were rusted shut. Tendai noticed they didn't have handles on the outside.

At the landings, the She Elephant stopped to catch her breath. "Damn Blue Monkey," she muttered. She had Rita under one arm and dragged Tendai along by the hand. She was panting with exhaustion, and Rita's regular kicks didn't improve her mood. When she rested, Trashman perched on a higher step and waited.

"Go find Mama," Tendai whispered. Trashman looked up.

"Do that again, and I'll throw your precious sister down the stairs," said the She Elephant.

Once, after the fourth or fifth rest, they startled a flock of bats. The creatures erupted from a crevice and filled the air with their jittering bodies.

"More! More!" cried Kuda, clapping his hands.

Other, less innocent things scuttled out of their way as they climbed. A rat watched them from a crumbled hole by a light; a scorpion danced from under their feet; a huge baboon spider squatted in a crack with its fangs resting on the edge. It lifted its mouthparts as they approached.

"Come *on*," said the She Elephant, jerking Tendai past the spot. At last they came out into a dim antechamber near the roof. It was lit only by the cold green panels. Above was a stone ceiling. Before them was another of the iron doors, only this time it was topped by a camera that creaked as it swiveled to watch them.

"Who is that man?" demanded a deep voice from the camera.

"A simpleton," the She Elephant replied. "He's no problem. Doesn't remember what he had for breakfast." The camera looked at Trashman, who smiled and patted it. The She Elephant put Rita down. The camera observed them one by one, pausing when it got to Tendai.

"He looks like his father."

"Why . . . so he does," said the She Elephant in surprise. "Funny, I didn't notice that before."

Tendai heard the sound of many locks being undone. Whoever was in there didn't like company. But of course he knew who it was. He patted Trashman on the shoulder and whispered, "Kuda wants Mama."

"Shut up!" snarled the She Elephant, whirling around. Tendai put himself in front of Rita as Trashman turned toward the stairs.

"Kuda wants Mama!" Tendai shouted. The She Elephant, instead of attacking him as he expected, lunged at Trashman and plucked the little boy from his shoulders. Trashman babbled anxiously with his hands out.

"Mama! Mama!" screamed Kuda. The She Elephant backed away. Trashman grabbed the boy's legs. Tendai was terrified they would have a tug-of-war, but Kuda twisted his body

around and pounded the She Elephant's face with his fists. She was so startled, she let go. Trashman did a victory dance in the dim antechamber.

"No! No! Kuda wants Mama!" yelled Tendai, seeing the man had already forgotten what to do.

"Hurry!" shrieked Rita, but the iron door had shrugged off its last chain. It swung open. The noise attracted Trashman's attention, and the moment was lost. He trotted inside before Tendai could stop him.

A stream of hooded shapes swarmed out and surrounded them all. "Hey! I'm on your side," cried the She Elephant.

"She's on our side! She is, she is," hissed the shapes, whisking them through the door. "Is that the *out*side or the *in*, O She Elephant? Are you riding *on* the hyena or *in* its gut?"

"Don't talk like that! I'm here to do business."

"Businessss," sighed the shapes, doing up the many locks, chains and bolts that secured the door. The room was almost black, and a rank smell sent flutters of panic along Tendai's nerves. It reminded him of dogs' teeth and rats' fur, of fresh bones and old scabs. The shapes moved around in the gloom, ceaselessly and hypnotically, in a kind of dance. The shuffle of feet told him the room was crowded. They were all around. He had to see what they were or scream.

They laid hands on him, and he struggled wildly. A murmur of laughter went around the walls. He could see humps of shadow, moving and dancing. "Let me go!" Rita shrieked, not far away.

Someone lit a match.

Tendai watched it move down a row of black candles. The light dipped and bobbed and sent confusing shadows across the floor, but he was able to see. Tacked to the walls were dried bats, owls and shriveled lizards. Bunches of gray herbs hung like diseased fruit from the ceiling. Over an altar crouched the body of a stuffed hyena.

"It's a witch's den!" screamed Rita.

The laughter was louder now. The humps of shadow suddenly threw off their hoods. Beneath were swollen faces with slitted eyes and bulging foreheads. Mouths dripped with the teeth of crocodiles. Heads sprouted ape fur and lion's mane. Cheeks were blotchy gray. Behind the slits, Tendai saw glittery eyes moving back and forth, back and forth. He lost all hope then. They could never escape. They would never be found. They had been carried, body and spirit, into the secret killing ground of the Masks in Mufakose.

34

When Ear, Eye and Arm arrived at Twenty-five Horsepool Lane, it looked as if the garden had exploded. Teapots lay smashed, gnomes were trampled flat, chairs had disintegrated into splinters. A pitchfork was embedded in a jacaranda tree.

"Oh, dear, oh, dear," whimpered an old woman by the fountain. "Your very best tea service."

"Piffle. I was tired of the old stuff," said Mrs. Horsepool-Worthingham. Arm recognized her from the picture the General had provided. The Mellower's mother poured the old woman a drink of some amber-colored liquid. "Here. Down the hatch. It'll do you a world of good."

"Do you think I should?"

"Everyone else is."

The old woman glanced around. Every one of the women in the garden had been provided with something to fortify her nerves. "You're so strong, Beryl. To think of attacking that monster with a pitchfork."

"I wish I'd had the Nirvana gun." Mrs. Horsepool-Worthingham suddenly noticed the detectives, who had been waiting patiently in the shade of the wisteria vine. "No tradesmen!" she called.

"We aren't selling anything," said Ear.

"No charities either! We've had a perfectly dreadful afternoon. Go on! Shoo! I am not donating to the Handicapped Fund."

"Sorry-sorry-sorry," said the robot, lurching toward them. Its head stuck out at a right angle, and its eyes blinked fitfully. It fell over a wisteria root and lay there with its wheels spinning.

Mrs. Horsepool-Worthingham closed her eyes. "Please state your business and be done with it."

"We're looking for General Matsika's children. They were kidnapped." Arm watched the woman's face closely.

"Yes, yes. I heard about it from my son. Poor things. I do hope you find them. Now, if you don't mind—"

"Oh, Beryl, did he say 'children'?" said the old woman by the fountain.

"My dear, you must lie down. You look ever so shocked."

"But, Beryl, I saw—"

"Don't argue. Sherry goes straight to the brain." Mrs. Horsepool-Worthingham steered her toward the house. "I wouldn't want you to have a heart spell. I'd never forgive myself." They disappeared inside.

"She's lying," Arm said.

"Even I could tell that. Let's look around while she's busy covering up." Eye nodded politely at the members of the Animal Fanciers' Society. The women pretended not to notice, but Arm saw several of them watching from the corners of their eyes.

"Boo!" he cried, whirling around. They shrieked and dropped their sherry glasses.

"Shame on you," said Ear.

"I make a great bogeyman." Arm bowed courteously, and the women turned their backs.

They continued prowling. A pair of Dobermans peered nervously from a gooseberry hedge. When they saw Arm, they retreated into the leaves with howls of despair.

"See?" said Arm.

"We'll rent you out on Halloween. Hello, what have we here?" Ear picked up a scrap of black cloth. It was a ripped-off pocket, and inside was a matchbook.

"Starlight Room. Well, well. Someone's living high. And look!" At the foot of a toppled garden gnome, Arm picked up a small cloth bag. "It's a copy of the one we found in the subway. The children are here!"

"Wonderful! Shall we hunt for them?" Ear waved his ears at a woman in tight riding pants. She winced.

"Let's leave that to the General. Our job was to find enough evidence to give him a search warrant."

They saw Mrs. Horsepool-Worthingham emerge from the house. "I'm afraid it isn't convenient to talk now. We've had the most awful burglary."

"Oh, yes," said another woman. "It was an enormous lady dressed in black. She gave me palpitations."

"My head aches," called the woman in the tight riding pants. "Might I have another drop of that medicine, Beryl?"

Mrs. Horsepool-Worthingham urged the detectives toward the gate. "I do hope you find the poor lost lambs. Such a tragedy." She saw them into the street and raised her hand as though to close a door. Then, realizing the gate was missing, she turned and walked briskly back to the house.

"I have a bad feeling about that burglar," said Arm.

Eye approached the ring of police, riot officers and SWAT team members that had sealed off the area. He gave the little bag from Resthaven to General Matsika, who was brooding like a thundercloud at the edge of Mrs. Horsepool-Worthingham's property.

So close! Arm could have torn his hair out. The She Elephant must have left minutes before the police arrived. The members of the Animal Fanciers' Society had quickly given up whatever information they had. Mrs. Horsepool-Worthingham was on her way to Waa Waa Prison. The

Mellower had locked himself into a closet, and even the cries of Sekai couldn't lure him out.

"I'm not surprised," Arm told Mother, who was lying on the sofa in the detectives' office. "He wasn't father material. Too wishy-washy."

"Now, now," said Eye.

Mother raised her woebegone eyes to look at Arm. "I was so sure we had them. Now it's just like the first day."

"No, it isn't," Arm said firmly. "The children have proven strong beyond our wildest expectations. They escaped from Dead Man's Vlei. They got in and out of Resthaven. They eluded the Masks in the subway. According to Mrs. Horsepool-Worthingham, after they recovered from the chicken pox, they practically ran her house."

"That evil woman!" burst out Mother. "Did you see the Kiddie Koop?"

"What was left of it. The point is, at every turn the children have behaved with courage and intelligence. I'm sure they'll keep on doing it."

Sekai stirred in a pouch Arm wore on his chest. She was replete with a sense of belonging. *You never really liked the Mellower, did you?* thought Arm.

Bad man. Not you, she agreed loyally.

Ear stirred the cup of tea he was fixing for Mother. He didn't want to give her the stuff they usually drank: Mr. Thirsty had sent over a packet of Black Dragon tea. Eye donated a gold-rimmed cup inherited from his grandmother. Arm hoped the roach family would postpone their happy hour until later.

"Mmm! This is good," Mother said as she drank.

"What would the She Elephant be doing at the Starlight Room?" remarked Eye.

"Sh!" warned Arm.

Mother put down her cup. "It's all right. I don't have the luxury of falling apart like the Mellower. Anyone can go up and down the elevators of the Mile-High MacIlwaine, provided she doesn't make a nuisance of herself. The She Elephant probably stole the matchbook as a souvenir."

"Or got it from someone who ate there," Arm said.

"Yes," admitted Mother. "I can't imagine *her* knowing anyone respectable."

"She has so-called 'respectable' customers." As soon as Arm said it, he was sorry. Mother's mouth turned down, and her eyes filled with tears.

"I—wouldn't mind—so much—if I knew the children were being taken care of. That's the only thing that matters to me. To know they're safe and happy."

"It's not a comfortable idea, but the She Elephant *is* in the business of selling children. The people who buy must want them very much." Arm didn't mention what he had heard about the Masks.

Mother cheered up a little then and even ate one of the cookies Eye placed temptingly by her cup.

"We'll have to check out the Mile-High MacIlwaine," Arm said. "The problem is, where to begin?" He thought about the trip to the Starlight Room.

Sekai started screaming. Arm remembered too late how closely his mind was linked with hers. She must have seen the ground drop out from under his feet as the elevator shot up like a rocket. He tried to shift his thoughts, but Sekai's terror was too great. Her fear trapped him. "Take her," he gasped. Mother plucked the baby from the pouch and carried her to the other end of the room. Ear splashed ice water in Arm's face.

"Ahhh," he breathed, shaking himself free of the hurtling elevator. Sekai settled down in Mother's arms.

"What happened?" Eye said.

"It was like being in a room full of mirrors. I thought of something frightening, Sekai reflected it back at me, which made me more frightened, which upset her even more—I don't want to know how far that kind of thing can go."

For a moment everyone was silent. Then Mother hesitantly said, "I wouldn't mind keeping the baby for a while."

"It's an excellent idea. You know, until Tendai and the others are found," said Ear.

Arm went to the window and looked out. Evening was falling, and the beggars were returning to the Cow's Guts. They were building a cook fire, and a legless man, who propelled himself on a little cart, was ferrying vegetables to a large stew pot. A pair of blind children peeled potatoes and sang lustily to the gathering people. It wasn't fair! Even the beggars had children. Even Mr. Thirsty went home to three adoring daughters who probably didn't know what Daddy did for a living.

Eye and Ear could look forward to finding wives who would accept their unusual looks and abilities. Only he could not fall in love. Sekai told him that. If he and another person got their minds locked into a frightening thought—and who does not have one now and then?—they would mirror it back and forth until they died or went insane.

"I'd like you to have her," he forced himself to say. "Only you mustn't let that slimy Mellower near her."

"Now, now," said Eye.

"There's no chance of that. He locked himself away when his mother was taken to Waa Waa Prison." Mother wrapped Sekai in a blanket and thanked everyone for tea. As she climbed into the limo, she said, "Tomorrow is Tendai's birthday. I wonder if he'll be able to celebrate it."

35

Arm curled up on the sofa with the blanket pulled over his head. He heard Eye and Ear tiptoe out the door. They were probably going to eat at one of the soup kitchens that plied their wares in the Cow's Guts.

Leaving me all alone, he thought bitterly. They'll talk to the waitresses and tell jokes. About me. I hope they have indigestion. Grumbling and fussing, much as Sekai was doing in Kuda's old crib at that moment, Arm fell asleep.

He was walking along a forest path. Arm often dreamed of the countryside around Hwange, where he grew up, but this place was different. The forest was much wilder than anything he had ever seen. And it felt old. The trees towered far above his head. They were dotted with woody fungi, as big as dinner plates, and parasitic orchids. Throughout the canopy flitted night-apes that melted into the shadows when he tried to look at them. Arm realized that no ax had ever been laid to these trees.

Therefore, it was a sacred grove.

The brooding spirit of the trees surrounded him like the coils of an electric dynamo. Even the air seemed to flow with power. The place was aware of him. From the shadows of the canopy to the rustle of Matabele ants in the dry grass, the whole grove vibrated with watchful attention.

255

Arm remembered stories his mother had told him about a giant serpent that inhabited such places. You never saw it. All you detected was a springing shadow as the thing uncoiled to sink its fangs into the back of your neck.

Arm whirled around. The night-apes froze in the shadows. Flicker, flicker, rustle, rustle—always just out of sight.

"Enter a strange part of the forest with praise," his mother had told him. "You don't want to anger something you can't see."

"What beautiful trees," said Arm as he jumped. What *was* that large shape behind those bushes? "The grass is so thick, the kudu must go to sleep with round bellies every night." And so do the lions, he thought. Arm continued to praise the sacred grove, and presently he became aware that he was not alone. He turned and cried out.

A man was on the path.

He was very tall. He wore a knee-length bark cloth with a zigzag pattern. His legs were ringed with gold anklets, and around his neck he wore a large, almost luminous *ndoro*. But what most got Arm's attention were the weapons. The man had a short sword at his waist, an ancient but efficient ax slung over his shoulder, a bow with a quiver of arrows next to the ax, a club covered with a filigree of copper wire, a pouch of darts that might or might not be tipped with poison and the most businesslike spear Arm had ever seen.

It was clearly someone who was used to unfriendly neighbors.

Arm stood hypnotized as the person approached, moving with an easy hunter's gait. His mouth was set in a grim line, and his eyes were steady: lion's eyes. *I wouldn't give a bent pin for your chance of survival if we were alone on a jungle path*, they said. It was the man in the General's book: Monomatapa, founder of the Shona Empire.

Arm sank to his knees. He understood in whose presence he really was. The *mhondoro*, spirit of the land, had chosen to show himself in the shape of the ancient king.

"Great chief," Arm whispered.

"*Nyaokorefu*," the spirit said in a deep, commanding voice. "One Whose Reach Is Great."

"What do you want of me, lord?"

"Our people are in danger. Alien spirits invade. They come, hiding their true nature, but their purpose is to eat us."

Arm's mouth went dry. He didn't know what to say.

"They seek to enslave our children and make them messengers of their will. You must prevent this."

"Me? How—"

"Go to the highest place. Look down and you will see them." The spirit took off the *ndoro* and placed it around Arm's neck. It felt as though live snakes were writhing all over his skin. It was unbearable! Arm reached up to tear off the necklace—and the sensation vanished. He stared at the *mhondoro*, unable to speak.

"Come the worst, we must perish together, *Nyaokorefu*," the spirit whispered.

And then the whole sacred grove came apart. Leaves swirled, trees snapped, and night-apes fled with cries of woe. The forest broke open with a great crack, and Arm fell into darkness until—

—he was shaken awake by Ear. He felt for the *ndoro*, but it was gone.

"Some nightmare!" Eye said. "I could hear you on the street."

"That's what comes of sleeping on an empty stomach," said Ear, setting down a selection of takeout. "Garlic soup, curried prawns, avocado salad—if these don't give you nice dreams, I don't know what will."

But Arm didn't want to eat. He paced up and down as he described his vision to the others. He was in a fever to go somewhere and do something. "The *mhondoro* spoke to me. Me! A nobody from the Cow's Guts."

"We always knew you had talent," said Eye.

"Lots of people are contacted by family spirits, but only two or three in each generation can speak to the *mhondoro*!

He told me the country was being invaded by alien spirits who hid their true nature."

"Sounds like they're wearing masks." Ear helped himself to garlic soup and passed the ladle to Eye.

Arm stopped pacing and stared at his friend. "Ear, you're a genius. He was talking about the Masks."

"I have talent, too, you know." Ear licked curry sauce off his fingers.

Arm continued his restless progress around the office. "The Masks were the first and most destructive gang, and they set the pattern for the rest. When the General restored order, the Masks survived. They're *not* like the others. They don't really care about money. Terror is what they feed on." Arm struggled to form his idea. "They're like an invading army."

He went to the window and watched the beggars. They had finished their meal. They sat by the fire and listened to a pickpocket tell a story. Even from the office, Arm could see their dreamy, contented expressions. Across the street, Mr. Thirsty stood in his doorway in a white bartender's apron. He seemed to be enjoying the evening breeze.

And Arm understood that when you had ten million people jammed together in a city, you always had a few troublemakers. Some were violent like the She Elephant, and some were dishonest like Mrs. Horsepool-Worthingham. Some were weak like the Mellower, and quite a lot were simply greedy like Mr. Thirsty.

You also had good people. The good and bad bubbled around like vegetables in a huge stew pot. General Matsika scooped out the bad vegetables when he found them, but he didn't attempt to get them all.

Only *Mwari* had the wisdom to do that.

Mr. Thirsty's head turned as a bottle smashed through his window. He signaled to a man built like a hot-water heater. The man dragged the bottle thrower to a parking lot to discuss his antisocial behavior.

The bartender's brand of trouble felt normal. The Masks' didn't. That was the key. The Masks were a form of spirit pollution, spreading poison from top to bottom in the country. They were trying to kill the *mhondoro*, the spirit of the land. And then the soul of Zimbabwe would be dead.

"I was told to go to the highest place," Arm said, turning over the matchbook from the She Elephant's pocket. "Unless I'm very much mistaken, that means the Mile-High Mac-Ilwaine."

Eye fainted again when they went up in the elevator. Arm felt queasy from his friend's fear. He and Ear dragged their comrade to a couch outside the Starlight Room. Down the hall they saw an immense, nail-studded door and five villainous-looking guards with weapons.

"Those aren't Nirvana guns," whispered Ear.

Arm studied them carefully. "They're called Soul Stealers. I've seen pictures in books. People say it's like getting hit by lightning. They're also illegal."

When Eye woke up, they helped him into the restaurant for tea. "Look at these prices!" cried Eye, who seemed ready to faint again, but the maître d' insisted on serving them for free.

"Any friend of the General is a friend of mine," said the round little man.

"Who are the apes down the hall?" Arm asked.

"Them!" The maître d' pursed his lips. "Gondwannans. May *Mwari* protect us from such neighbors! Our business has fallen by half since they moved in. They're rude and insulting—"

"And stingy," added a passing waiter. "Never leave tips."

"If they didn't have diplomatic immunity, I'd have them arrested as thieves. They take silverware, glasses, even"—the maître d' quivered all over with anger—"my *wallet*. I saw one of them slip it into his pocket, but do you think I could do anything? Once they're inside the embassy, it's Gondwannan territory. The police are helpless. If that's how they behave as guests, I'd hate to see them at home."

"Interesting," said Arm. He carefully noted the position of the Gondwannan Embassy before sitting by the panoramic window that made the Starlight Room famous.

The sky was clear except for a few clouds that now and then drifted below the window. Arm could see all the way to the edge of Harare, where city lights gave way to farmland. Streams of traffic moved on the airways between tall buildings. A dinner party arrived on the elevator and was placed at tables not far away. The men were dressed in expensive *dashikis*, and the women wore long classical Ethiopian gowns.

Arm felt a ripple of lazy good humor from the dinner party, a surge of greed from the waiters as they sized up the clothes. And something else. It wasn't an emotion but the absence of it. To Arm, the world was a seething ocean of human desires that he tried to block out. This was a hole in the ocean.

Intrigued, he turned his attention to it. It pulled at him. *Come inside,* it said. *It's peaceful here. No more decisions. No more struggles.* Arm felt his mind drifting toward the opening. How wonderful it would be to rest.

No! said a voice inside him. *It's not a hole but a mouth.* Arm jerked back so abruptly, he knocked over a pitcher of water on the table. It splashed over the carpet, making the women at the next table squeal. A waiter hurried over at once to sponge off their gowns.

"What's wrong?" said Ear. Eye stood up at the table he was occupying, far from the window.

"I don't know. I never felt anything like it before, but it was coming from there." Arm pointed at the Gondwannan Embassy. After apologizing to the people at the next table, he went back to gazing out the window. This was the highest point in the city: all he had to do was wait.

Nyaokorefu, if you're going to keep acting like a fool, I'll have to find someone else to possess, said the voice inside.

Mhondoro? Arm said, aghast.

Of course. Why else did I give you my ndoro? *Sometimes I think the intelligence of people gets less every generation.*

I'm sorry, said Arm.

The Mile-High MacIlwaine has a roof. Go look there.

"Yes, sir," Arm murmured unhappily.

"What did you say?" asked Ear, but Arm was already on his way to find the maître d'.

"When the hotel was built, they put an observation deck on the roof," explained the little man. "They expected it to be a popular attraction, but . . ." He gestured at a dark stairway with boxes stored on it.

"Scary, eh?" Ear said.

"I only went there once." The maître d' shuddered.

"I'm going to be sick," moaned Eye.

Arm phoned General Matsika to tell him about the *mhondoro* and the strange presence in the Gondwannan Embassy.

The General waited so long before he answered, Arm thought the connection had broken. Finally, he said, "I don't want to be discouraging, but at present, only two men are able to contact the *mhondoro*. Both of them studied years before they were successful."

"I tell you, he spoke to me."

"You're asking me to invade the embassy of a foreign government because you felt a hole in the astral waves. What kind of evidence is that?"

"I'm going to get you evidence now. All I want is for you to wait outside," said Arm.

"People see strange things when they're under stress."

"I am not making this up!" Arm shouted so loudly Ear, Eye and the maître d' jumped.

"Calm down. I'm willing to believe you saw your family spirit. But the *mhondoro* doesn't concern himself with everyday problems, no matter how important they seem to us. He's only concerned with national emergencies—"

"This *is* a national emergency!" shouted Arm. The maître d' turned gray with fright. He reached for the holo-phone cord, but Ear and Eye grabbed his hands. "This goes beyond the disappearance of your children. They are only the means by which alien spirits intend to conquer us. The Masks are involved and probably the Gondwannans, too."

"Control yourself," the General said coldly. "I have no evidence the Gondwannans are implicated."

"I *felt* something in the embassy. That's why the *mhondoro* told me to come here, you glorified truant officer!"

"Please," said Mother, suddenly breaking in. Her picture appeared in a little square at the bottom of the screen when she picked up the extension. "Everyone take a deep breath. I know of a case exactly like what Arm is suggesting."

The General and Arm glared at each other like a pair of lions standing over the same antelope, but they kept quiet.

"Once, long ago, Zimbabwe was attacked by spirits from Mozambique," Mother explained. "I read about it in a history book. A group of Ndau people moved next to a Shona vil-lage. The Shona began to have the most terrible dreams. They fought with one another and mistreated their elders and children. Their culture broke down until someone real-ized the Ndau spirits were waging war on the Shona spirits. Once this was understood, the Ndau were forced to return to Mozambique."

"I can't believe what I'm hearing," said the General. "Are you suggesting I commit an act of war because this man has a hot line to the spirit world?"

"Yes," said Mother.

"I think both of you should take aspirin and lie down before anyone else catches what you have!" The screen flicked off just as Mother was opening her mouth to argue.

"*Maiwee!* Did you have to call him a truant officer?" said Eye.

The maître d' rocked back and forth. "I'm ruined! The General will never come here again. I'll go out of business, and my children will beg in the streets."

"Oh, be quiet," Arm growled. "And get me a long piece of rope." Ear and Eye watched warily as he tied a series of knots in the rope that the trembling maître d' fetched from a storeroom. "Stay here, Eye. You'd only faint. Ear, come with me."

"You—you don't sound like the Arm I'm used to," faltered Ear.

"Well, of course not. The *mhondoro* is in here with me." Arm patted his chest. He went up the stairway to the roof of the Mile-High MacIlwaine, with Ear unhappily following behind.

I n the flickering light of the candles, the Masks were like creatures from an evil dream. They crowded around the terrified children, who clutched the She Elephant for want of better comfort. Kuda wailed and hid his face in Trashman's grain-bag shirt.

"That's enough, see," said the She Elephant. "I'm not one of your chickens on the subway. I have business to discuss."

"Businesssss," hissed a large Mask with warthog tusks protruding from his mouth. "We know what happened to your business in Dead Man's Vlei. The police were there! They closed up your little *shebeen* and took your slaves away. You have no business, She Elephant."

"You promised me fifty thousand dollars for the little one. I'll throw the others in for nothing."

"Why should we pay when we can take what we wish? But you may have the money. One little goat was all we asked for. We are pleased to have three."

"Goat? What are you talking about?"

"The keeper of the Big-Head Mask was shot by the police—curse them!" replied the Warthog. "We need to install a successor, but for that we need a goat to sacrifice."

"I don't understand." The She Elephant's skin turned gray under the dancing candlelight.

"The Big-Head Mask needs food to make it powerful. We will send the children as messengers to our gods. The children will lead them to the heart of the Shona spirit world."

"No!" roared the She Elephant. "I didn't bring them here for that!"

"Beware! Beware!" snarled all the Masks together as they moved in a dizzying dance. "You are not safe. Oh, no! You can be found at the foot of the stairs with a broken neck. No one would cry!"

"I don't like it!" she cried.

"She doesn't like it. Oh, dear!" said a Mask with baboon fangs and fur.

"Poor She Elephant!" mocked another with the speckled snout of a hyena.

"Lying at the foot of the stairs with her head turned backward," finished a third bristling with porcupine quills.

"I didn't say I *wouldn't* sell them." The She Elephant shook off Tendai's and Rita's hands. They slid to the floor, too terrified to stand.

Kuda uncovered his face and looked at Trashman. Tendai saw the little boy's expression change from fear to surprise. Then he, too, saw that the man was staring at the Masks in openmouthed delight, just as he had watched the soccer matches on Dead Man's Vlei. Kuda immediately copied his hero. This was fine entertainment! These creatures must be clowns. The little boy laughed out loud.

"So, little goat. You think this is funny," hissed the Warthog, thrusting itself at Kuda. The boy impulsively grasped the tusks protruding from the mouth. He yanked the mask right off, and it clattered to the floor.

"*Don't look behind a mask!*" the others shouted, swooping to retrieve it. They swiftly returned it to its owner, but in that instant, Tendai saw a human face. He had expected something horrible—a skull, perhaps, or a bundle of snakes.

Instead, he saw a middle-aged man with sagging jowls and pouches under his eyes.

"You're people!" he cried.

"People, yes," said the Porcupine. "Without the Masks we are men, but with them we take on the powers of the spirit world. And the powers must be fed!"

"We're wasting time," the Warthog said. Tendai and Rita were snatched up, and their hands were tied. Kuda was plucked from Trashman's arms. The man immediately tried to get him back. He was brought down with a rag soaked in chloroform, like the ones Knife and Fist used at Mbare Musika, and rolled into a corner. The Masks packed suitcases with the things they would need: herbs, dried animals, noxious oils and an assortment of knives.

"I recognize the Warthog," whispered Tendai to Rita. "It's Obambo Chivari, the Gondwannan Ambassador."

"Are you sure?" she whispered back.

"I saw him at the Starlight Room."

"I remember. He tripped the soup waiter as a joke—oh!"

"What is it?"

Rita nodded at the calendar. It was tacked among the dried creatures on the wall. A picture of Zimbabwe Ruins, with a knife driven through it, was at the top, but the days were crossed off in a perfectly orderly way. Tendai saw it was the day before his birthday.

"At midnight, you'll be fourteen," said Rita.

Tendai swallowed. So much time had passed! He saw himself on his last birthday, a spoiled, ignorant child. He had got a model village kit and toy spear. Tendai flushed with embarrassment. Had he really been such a baby? And when he blew out the candles on the cake, hadn't he made a wish? *I want an adventure.*

"On your feet," said Obambo Chivari. They were led to a landing platform and put into a limo. The Masks prodded and pushed the She Elephant into another. Then they all took

266

off into the night sky. The windows were shaded and the hoods decorated with flapping Gondwannan flags. These were embassy cars, and no traffic policeman would dare to stop them.

They raced through the Zimbabwe heavens, black on black, blaring sirens that meant "Make way! Or we'll run you down!" They sideswiped a taxi and sent it spinning almost out of control. The Masks crouched in their hideous disguises, hidden behind their tinted windows.

Tendai looked down on the beautiful crisscross of streets that made up his city. A year ago, he would merely have admired the view. Now he saw how fragile it all was, laid open to its enemies at its heart. He understood, as Rita and Kuda could not, what was involved in becoming a messenger to the Gondwannan spirit world. They had not listened to the conversation between Father and the martial arts instructor in the library so long ago.

Becoming a messenger meant death.

It meant dying in such pain that one's spirit was charged with dreadful energy. Only then could it gain the attention of the sluggish Gondwannan gods.

Tendai was terribly afraid. He saw how he had blundered—and taken Rita and Kuda with him—into one bad situation after another. *Just look how you behaved at Mbare Musika,* a voice inside his head told him. *You were supposed to take care of your siblings, but no. You had to have fun.*

And what about Dead Man's Vlei? Wasn't it you who gave up and Rita who kept fighting? In Resthaven, you basked in everyone's approval instead of finding a way home. Worst of all was how you behaved at Mrs. Horsepool-Worthingham's. You should have confronted her the minute you learned about her treachery. You were afraid to. Admit it! That's why the She Elephant had time to find you. You were a baby last year, and you're still a baby—

Stop it! cried Tendai to all the thoughts crowding in on him. *I know what you are. Go back, you filthy Gondwannan spirits! I'm a Shona warrior. My* mutupo *is the lion; my* chidao *is the heart. Beware!*

As he thought this, he remembered a poem the Mellower used to recite to them in the nursery. It was a traditional boast of a fighter before he went into battle. The Mellower strutted up and down, aiming punches at the shadows and scowling ferociously.

> I am one for whom dangers are playthings!
> One who empties men of their strength
> As a nut from its shell.
> The charms you use I chop up
> For relish on my porridge.
> Beware!
> I am a deadly mamba,
> Wrestler of leopards,
> A hive of hornets,
> A man among men!

The old war song filled Tendai's chest with warmth, radiating from the *ndoro* that still nestled under his shirt to his fingers and toes. The evil thoughts fled away like shadows from a bonfire. They were still out there, waiting for his courage to fail, but for the moment Tendai gave himself up to the feeling of strength.

The limos swooped down toward a private dock near the top of the Mile-High MacIlwaine. Tendai was amazed the Masks would hide in such a public place, but of course it wasn't public. It was the only spot in Zimbabwe beyond the reach of the law: the Gondwannan Embassy.

The dock wasn't very wide. Around the edge was a low railing, and beyond, the wind howled as tatters of cloud blew between the landing area and the great city of Harare. The She Elephant cursed as she was forced from her limo.

The dock was moving!

With a vast creaking, the Mile-High MacIlwaine swayed like a huge flower on its stem. Slowly the dock crept forward and eclipsed a pattern of buildings far below. As the landing area creaked back, the buildings reappeared. The wind tore at the Masks' robes and fluttered the quills of the Porcupine. Tendai suddenly snaked out his foot and tripped the Warthog, who was grasping him by the arm. They went down together. The Warthog mask, perhaps weakened by Kuda's earlier assault, came off. It bowled over and over in the wind until it came to the railing and fell off.

A collective wail went up from the Masks. The Warthog tusks were outlined briefly against a patch of cloud in the dock lights. Then it was gone. "My power!" shrieked Obambo Chivari. He dragged Tendai to the railing, but the other Masks pulled them back.

"Don't be a fool!" shouted the Porcupine over the wind. "The boy will make an excellent messenger. The braver he is, the more force he will have when we break him down."

"Anyhow, you were going to be possessed by the Big-Head Spirit tonight," yelled the Baboon. Tendai's head was pulled back from the rail. He was shoved through a glass door and onto a Persian carpet in an astonishing room.

Gold-inlaid tables were crowded with jade and ivory statues of the most exquisite workmanship. Silk curtains decorated the walls. Fine furniture was draped with leopard and tiger skins, and real plastic bowls glittered with jewels.

"If you ask me, it's overdone," sniffed Rita. The Mask behind her gave her a shove. Kuda wandered up to one of the bowls and dug in his hands. Emerald, diamond and ruby necklaces draped over his stubby fingers. He put a large black pearl earring in his mouth, but Rita made him put it back. "You don't know where it's been," she said.

At the far end of the room was a black curtain. Obambo Chivari yanked it back to reveal the second half of the room. Gone were the carpets and golden tables. Gone were the exquisite works of art. Tendai saw a dull cement floor on which was bolted a chair. All around the walls and on the floor was the evidence of the lowest impulses to which humans could sink: one could not call the cruel remains of sacrifices bestial, for beasts have dignity. Whatever was twisted or diseased in the human soul was present in that room.

Rita turned away with a cry. She hid Kuda's face against her T-shirt. The She Elephant sank to her knees and gathered both children into a bear hug.

The thing that most commanded Tendai's attention lay against the far wall, beyond the chair. The lights of the first part of the room barely touched it. It was large and shifting, as though composed of shadow and the ominous stench that pervaded everything. Tendai walked toward it, hypnotized by its eerie presence.

"Don't," sobbed Rita.

It was a mask.

Twice as large as any of the others, it had a human face, but one so twisted with agony, it was unbearable to look at. The mouth was rimmed with many teeth. They were too small to have come from an adult human. The head was covered with scalps stitched together to form a wig. The cheeks were streaked with a sticky blackened substance. The eyes—

—were hollow. At least for the moment. But Tendai had the feeling that somewhere the Presence that inhabited the mask was prowling. It was waiting for the moment when it would take up residence. And then the eyes would open.

The hands of the Masks reached out to him from all sides and carried him to the chair in the middle of the room.

37

The wind struck them the instant they came onto the roof. Arm ducked and crawled along the cement on his hands and knees. Ear folded his ears. The traffic beacon at the top of a metal scaffold cast a fitful red light as it blinked on and off.

"Imagine changing *that* light bulb," shouted Ear over the howling wind.

"It looked so peaceful from inside," Arm shouted back. "This is a problem I hadn't expected."

"Are we—are we *moving*?" Ear flattened himself on the cold cement.

"Yes! The Mile-High MacIlwaine is built to sway. It has something to do with structural stability. Nothing this tall can survive unless it bends in the wind."

"I'm going to be seasick."

Arm moved away from Ear along the platform. He was extremely glad he hadn't dined on garlic soup, curried prawns and avocado salad. After a few moments, Ear recovered. "The Gondwannan Embassy is over here," called Arm from the railing. He looked down the mile-long drop to Harare. About sixty feet below was a landing dock.

Ear crept up behind. "If the building tips, won't we slide off?"

"We won't fit between the bars. Hold on to the railing like I do. Can you hear anything?"

"The building creaks. It's so strange. It sounds like the sailboat my father used to take out on Lake Kariba. I wish I was there now."

"Pay attention. I've got to know if anyone's in the embassy."

Ear extended his ears slightly, but the wind blew them shut. "I can hear dishes clinking in the Starlight Room. The cook just cut his thumb. He says—"

"Not there! Can't you open your ears more?"

"I'm afraid the wind will tear them." But Ear tried again. This time he heard a guard test the safety catch on his Soul Stealer outside the Gondwannan Embassy. "I don't think anyone's inside—whoa!" The building tilted, and Ear slid up against the railing. His feet went off the edge. He kicked wildly as he clawed his way back to safety.

"See? Your shoulders don't fit between the bars," said Arm.

"I'm going to be sick again."

Arm watched the clouds pass between them and the city. The wind was picking up: the Mile-High MacIlwaine creaked back, and the landing dock jutted out slightly. If he climbed over the railing, he could almost slide down the side of the building to reach it. "I hear something whirring."

"It's only a taxi. Can we go inside now?" Ear said.

"The taxi stands are on the opposite side of the building. Isn't listening supposed to be your job?"

Ear miserably crawled back to the railing. He opened his ears slightly, backing them with his hands for protection. The dock lights came on.

"Well, well. Company's coming," said Arm. From the night sky came a cluster of black limos. They dipped through the rushing shreds of cloud, and the traffic beacon painted their windows red. The limos swooped in a tight pattern to settle on the Gondwannan landing dock. Arm pulled himself to a standing position and leaned over the railing. "Come up here."

"I can't," moaned Ear.

"You must!" It was not Ear's comrade who spoke now but the *mhondoro*. The spirit was roused by the sight of his enemies. He was made up of the dreams and memories of the Shona people, but he was also the spirit of Zimbabwe. A thousand generations of men and women who had cherished the land gave power to his voice. Ear could no more have disobeyed than he could have sprouted wings and flown off the Mile-High MacIlwaine. He stood up against the railing and opened his ears wide. The wind bellied them like sails.

He'll get hurt, Arm said to the *mhondoro*.

Be still, commanded the tribal spirit.

The two detectives looked down, each with his special ability. The She Elephant, hurling insults at her captors, was pushed from one limo. Tendai, Rita and Kuda were dragged from another.

"At last," murmured Arm. The stream of Masks that now swept onto the dock appalled him. Eye could have seen their hideous shapes, but Arm could feel their malevolence. The men were brutish, but the spirits that flitted about them were far worse. They were bloated with cruel animal sacrifices. Rage and cringing fear had created these monsters. All the noble aspects of the sacrificial animals had gone, with their deaths, into *Mwari*'s country. Only the evil was left, like a twisted natural force.

Arm felt faint as he watched the human and inhuman spirits gather.

Courage, Nyaokorefu, whispered the *mhondoro* inside his mind.

Suddenly, Tendai tripped the man who was holding him. They both fell. The man's mask was caught by the wind, and it barreled away over the cement. Arm could sense the spirit: an old, corrupt warthog grown fat on the flesh of its young. The mask rolled into space with the spirit snarling after it. The man howled and dragged Tendai to the railing.

"No! No!" shouted Arm, but the wind tore his voice away. Fortunately, the other Masks prevented the man from throwing Tendai to his death.

"They say the boy will make an excellent messenger. The braver he is, the more force he will have when they break him down," reported Ear. "Someone's going to be possessed by the Big-Head Spirit—ah!" Ear screamed and fell back onto the roof. Arm watched long enough to see Tendai and the others hustled inside. He knelt by his comrade.

Ear huddled on the cold cement. The light of the traffic beacon showed that his magnificent ears had been split by the wind. Blood oozed from the tears. "Oh, *Mwari*," whispered Arm.

"Now can I go inside?" said Ear.

"Oh, Ear. I'm so sorry."

"I think they have bandages in the Starlight Room. The cook asked for one after he cut his thumb."

Tears poured down Arm's face. He knew how close Ear was to going into shock. He called down the stairway for help. The maître d' and two waiters carried the detective inside. "Call the General and tell him we have evidence," Arm said. "The children are inside the Gondwannan Embassy and so are the Masks."

"The Masks!" gasped the maître d'.

"Tell him to hurry. They're going to sacrifice Tendai."

"Where are you going?" the little man cried as Arm grimly climbed back to the roof.

"I'm sneaking in the back door." Arm uncoiled the rope from the storeroom and crawled out again into the howling wind.

Mother thought she would faint. She had just come into the Starlight Room, after a stormy departure from Amadeus and a high-speed ride to the hotel. She wasn't sure what Arm had meant when he said the children were to be messengers. She did understand that important clues were hidden in the Gondwannan Embassy, and that Arm was going to find them.

Amadeus could shout at her until he was hoarse. She wasn't going to stay home. She was tired of waiting while other people carried her children anywhere they pleased. As far as Mother was concerned, if Arm wanted to blast a hole in the side of the embassy, she would help him.

The wind had been perfectly awful during the flight. The limo had to fight its way through the gusts, and paramedic cars were everywhere. The glass elevator actually hitched a couple of times on the way up. But that wasn't what had frightened Mother.

The maître d' burst in with a flock of waiters carrying Ear. Eye jumped up to help them. They laid the injured detective on a sofa. "Call the General! Call the General!" yelled the maître d'. "The children are in the embassy! It's full of Masks, and they're going to sacrifice Tendai!"

That was what almost made Mother faint. But she took a deep breath and went straight to the holophone. The screen was blank. The computer was down.

"It's the swaying of the building," cried the maître d'. "It sometimes pulls the power lines loose. Someone has to go down in the elevator."

Two or three waiters volunteered, but the elevator refused to budge. The maître d' pulled sacks of potatoes and onions out of the service elevator and climbed in himself. The power was out here, too.

"Why do we still have lights?" asked Mother.

"We have an emergency generator," panted the man, crawling out of the potato dirt and onion skins. "The designers of the hotel figured we only needed electricity for that and the stoves. Cursed bureaucrats!" He kicked a sack of potatoes.

"Hey, waiter! How about some service?" called a man from the dinner party by the window.

"Throw him a box of crackers!" shouted the maître d'. "Listen, you rich, spoiled people. We've got an emergency here. The Masks have holed up in the Gondwannan Embassy, and they've got General Matsika's kids. They're going to *kill* them if we don't get inside. If you want anything to eat, go to the kitchen and find it!"

A shocked silence followed this outburst. The elegantly dressed diners in their *dashikis* and Ethiopian dresses stared goggle-eyed at the little man.

"Well—why didn't you say so before?" stammered the man who had asked for service.

"Of course we want to help," said a woman in a silk robe embroidered with little diamonds.

"Oh, good! This is so much more interesting than a dinner party," another woman cried.

Suddenly everyone was bustling around. A doctor bent over the now unconscious Ear and dabbed him with antiseptic. The waiters came out of the kitchen with meat cleavers, toasting forks, iron pots and frying pans to arm everyone. With them was the chief cook, the three undercooks, the sauce cook, the salad master, the soufflé maker and a dozen dishwashers. They rushed to the door.

"Wait!" shouted Eye. "The Gondwannan guards have Soul Stealers."

Just as quickly, the waiters, cooks, salad master, soufflé maker and dishwashers skidded to a halt.

"We need strategy. Does anyone have a gun?" Mother asked.

"I have a Nirvana," said Eye. "So does Ear, but he won't be able to use it."

"Give it to me," Mother commanded. "Now. We need a diversion."

"Leave it to us," said the chief cook and the salad master. The cook, who was built like a five-course dinner, chased the salad master, who was as light as a lettuce leaf, down the corridor toward the Gondwannan Embassy. "I'll teach you to leave snails in the spinach!" roared the cook.

"Don't hurt me! *I* didn't wash it!" The salad master raised a frying pan in self-defense.

"You good-for-nothing! You were only hired because your brother works at the desk!" The cook swung his meat cleaver through the air with a whistling sound.

"Look at that," said one of the Gondwannan guards, laughing.

"I put my money on the cook. He's bigger," a second Gondwannan offered.

"No, no. The little one is faster. Nice footwork." All five guards followed the men down the hall.

"A hundred dollars says the cook gets the runt!"

"Two hundred on the runt! I like his style."

Eye crept into the hall and put himself between the guards and the embassy door. Mother moved silently along the wall.

"Now!" shouted the chief cook. Eye and Mother fired bolts at the Gondwannans. They brought down two. The chief cook banged one on the head with his big fist. The salad master brought his man down with the frying pan. The remaining guard flung himself behind an ornamental vase and fired at Eye.

The Soul Stealer produced a noise like a thunderbolt landing in the hall. The waiters and diners in the Starlight Room fell over one another as they scrambled for safety. The salad master dropped his pan, and the chief cook lost his grip on the cleaver. The shot from the Soul Stealer landed on the wall by Ear's head. It snaked out in all directions, forming a brilliant flash that burned through the wallpaper and melted the paint underneath.

Eye dropped his gun and flung up his hands. "I can't see!" he screamed. The Gondwannan guard laughed and rose from behind the vase. He aimed at the bewildered detective—

—and was felled by Mother on the spot.

"Hurrah!" cheered the waiters and diners from the Starlight Room. They swarmed out at once to tie up the guards. The chief cook and salad master gave each other the high sign. The doctor and the woman in the diamond-spangled dress rushed over to Eye, who was rocking back and forth on his knees.

But Mother coolly studied the door of the Gondwannan Embassy. She was deeply sorry for Ear and Eye, but they were being cared for as well as could be managed. Her battle was only beginning. The metal door of the embassy fitted snugly into the wall. There were no cracks in which to thread razor wire and no hinges to remove. It was as solid as the vault in the Bank of Zimbabwe.

Now what? said Mother to herself.

ell, I guess this is it, said Arm as he tested the rope tied to the railing.

That's right, agreed the *mhondoro.*

Tell me. What happens if I—you know, if I fall? What happens to you?

Nothing. I am already in the spirit world.

Arm looked out over the swiftly rushing clouds. The wind blew his shirt back against his chest so that it almost looked glued there. It was cold and getting colder. *What happens to me?*

You join your ancestors. You become part of mudzimu, *your family spirit. You know that.*

How much of me will be there? I mean, do I remember this life? Will I be able to look in on Sekai?

Nyaokorefu, *are you stalling for time?*

I suppose so. Arm tested the knot once more. He looked back at the roof of the Mile-High MacIlwaine. It seemed a haven of safety now, and it had been so frightening earlier.

Nyaokorefu, *if it's any consolation, I'm taking as big a risk as you. Falling won't hurt me, but the Gondwannan gods can. They can twist me into a slave for their hateful and perverted designs. Then parents will abandon children, elders will be left to starve. Brother will kill brother, and the land itself will decay. What kind of world would Sekai have then?*

You're right. We have to fight, said Arm.

She's asleep right now and having a really fine dream.

Thank you, Arm said. He waited for the building to creak back. The sloping side of the Mile-High MacIlwaine with the attached landing dock lay beneath him as he went over. His feet rested on one of the knots tied in the rope.

The wind! The wind struck him when he was only a few inches from the top of the building. The warmth was whipped from his body as fast as it was produced. His body was so much longer and thinner than anyone else's. He hadn't an ounce of fat to protect him. His hands began to tingle and grow numb.

The Mile-High MacIlwaine groaned back in its cycle. The rope swung out to hang over a mile of empty space as the wall and dock retreated out of range. Arm continued to edge downward, knot by knot. The feeling had completely gone from his hands, and he had to concentrate to keep them closed. His foot slipped on a knot, and he slid sickeningly to the next.

Very good. You're halfway there, said the *mhondoro.*

The wind swung Arm like a pendulum. Out, out, out he went, then back again, each time with a wider arc and more dizzying sweep. His hands—were they still holding on? They must be or he would have fallen by now. His whole body ached with the effort. He didn't have the strength to look up.

Waste of time anyway, remarked the *mhondoro.*

Out, out, out. A vast creaking. In, in, in and then *slam!* Arm struck the side of the building. His hands opened. His feet lost their purchase. The rope slithered past him as he fell. He slid along the incline of the building. Its rough surface tore his shirt and grazed his skin. Faster and faster he went until he came to rest with a jarring crash on the Gondwannan landing dock.

Tendai heard Rita and Kuda weeping as they crouched in the embrace of the She Elephant. He was firmly bound to the chair bolted to the floor. "Look, you don't want war with Zimbabwe," said the big woman. "Why don't I find you a nice goat to sacrifice? I won't ask a penny."

"The Big-Head Mask doesn't like goats," said Obambo Chivari. In the background, Tendai heard the scrape, scrape, scrape of a knife on a whetstone. "The Zimbabweans will never find out what happened here. They're a silly, trusting people." *Scraw, scraw* went the knife. Metal clinked as though someone were riffling through a box of instruments.

"I don't like it!" the She Elephant cried.

"Oh, she doesn't like it," said the Baboon Mask. "She wants to take a little walkie on the landing dock."

"I didn't say I'd cause trouble!"

"Very wise," Obambo Chivari said. The Gondwannan Ambassador tore open Tendai's shirt and jumped back as though he had been scalded. "What's *that*?"

The She Elephant leaned forward. "Oh, it's only an old *ndoro*. The spirit mediums in the villages wear them. Supposed to have power, although if you ask me, it's only superstition. It's unusual-looking, though." The woman came closer. Tendai stared back at her with the cold, steely gaze he had learned from Father. "That's the real thing! The ancient kings wore *ndoros* made out of shell. Even then they were valuable. Why don't you sell it and let the brat go? I could help you—"

"You stupid woman! When will you get it through your head that we don't want money?" snarled Obambo Chivari. "The boy is an ideal messenger to our gods. He's the son of General Matsika. He's got the heart of a lion, and he's wearing the symbol of Zimbabwean spirituality. Nothing could be more perfect! When we break him down—and we will—his soul will glow like a hot coal in the dark country of our gods. Oh, they will certainly notice him."

Tendai shifted his steely gaze from the She Elephant to Obambo Chivari. "See that?" said the Gondwannan Ambassador. "Looks just like his father." He placed a box of instruments on a stand where Tendai could see them. The long, the jagged, the hooked surfaces picked up the light from a rack of black candles against the wall.

> Beware!
> I am a deadly mamba,
> Wrestler of leopards,
> A hive of hornets,
> A man among men!

Tendai chanted the war song in his head. The warmth of the *ndoro* spread through his body. Even though he couldn't move his arms or legs, he was still a warrior. His spirit would fight them. He would never carry their loathsome messages.

"Excellent!" Ambassador Chivari said with a chuckle.

Something crashed on the landing dock. The Masks all turned at the noise. "One of the limos must have broken loose," said the Porcupine. "It's the wind. The building's really dancing tonight."

"Fix it," Obambo Chivari commanded, but at that instant an amazingly tall man in torn clothes threw open the glass door and began firing into the room.

Arm was shaken up by the fall, but the *mhondoro* immediately ordered him to rise.

Get moving! They're alert as a pack of hungry hyenas in there!

Arm staggered to his feet. His body throbbed with cold and scratches. He drew the Nirvana gun, threw open the door and began firing as rapidly as he could. There was no lack of targets. He brought down three Masks before they rallied to attack him. The hatred of a thousand angry animal deaths boiled out at him from the bloated spirits of the Masks. The room was filled with roars and howls and snarls and bleating—but only Arm could hear it. The spirits circled, nipping at his heels. They blew their hot breath in his ears and dripped their poisonous saliva on his skin. He turned, bewildered.

Fight! Don't let them confuse you! shouted the *mhondoro*.

Arm saw Tendai tied to a chair. Rita and Kuda crouched at the feet of the She Elephant, and the Gondwannan Ambassador stood at her side. The detective raised his gun, but something shifted in the shadows beyond the chair and captured his attention.

It was the hole in the ocean of desire Arm had noticed in the Starlight Room.

No! You fool! the *mhondoro* shouted.

Hello, Arm, said the Presence behind the mask leaning against the wall. This mask was large and curiously indistinct, but Arm suspected he wouldn't want to see it clearly. *You've never known peace, have you?* the Presence whispered. *Always listening to the emotions of others, always feeling their petty yammering on your nerves. What you need is a rest.* The Presence looked out at him like a kind old grandfather.

It's a trap! cried the *mhondoro*.

You? said the Presence. *You squeaking little goody-goody. You can't even keep your own people in line. They don't even fear you.*

Shoot the Gondwannan Ambassador! commanded the *mhondoro*.

Arm took a step forward, but he felt tired, so tired. The hole hovered before him, inviting him with its cool, restful depths. The gun slid out of his fingers to the floor. He moved toward the hole, with the voice of the *mhondoro* growing ever weaker inside him. Too late, he saw the eyes of the Big-Head Mask open. Too late he remembered what the *mhondoro* had told him earlier: it was not a hole but a mouth.

39

Tendai saw a strange man enter through the door. He was long and skinny, like a wall spider, but he was definitely a friend. The man shot three Masks with a Nirvana gun. Tendai had practiced with one at the police firing range and recognized it.

The strange person aimed his gun at Obambo Chivari and suddenly stopped. He began shaking as though he had a high fever. Please, please don't stop now, prayed Tendai. The man seemed hypnotized. He was looking beyond Tendai at the location of the Big-Head Mask. No one moved.

Tendai realized a silent struggle was taking place. He had no idea what it was, but everyone seemed to feel it. The candles spluttered, although there wasn't a breeze at this end of the room. A murmur of sound rose just beyond the level of his hearing. Tendai felt his skin prickle.

The tension snapped. The man dropped his gun and fell to the floor. His head struck with a terrible crack, but Tendai was certain he was already dead before he reached the ground.

Before he could despair at this turn of events, something happened inside his chest. The heat spread out from the *ndoro* a hundred, a thousand times stronger than before. The strength of it frightened him, but it was a clean fear such as one might have before a magnificent force of nature—a volcano, for example.

You're a little young for a spirit medium, but you'll have to do, said a voice inside him.

P-please, stammered Tendai. *Who—who are you?*

The mhondoro, *my young warrior. Aha! I recognize this* ndoro. *It was worn by Monomatapa himself. It feels good to get inside it again.*

Tendai was filled with wonder. The *mhondoro!* And it chose him! He was so filled with awe, he almost forgot the desperate situation he was in, but the tribal spirit soon woke him up.

No time to pat yourself on the back. You know what they're up to here, don't you?

Yes, sir, said Tendai.

I have to act through humans, as spirits always do, so both of us will have to look for a weak spot in the Gondwannan defenses. If the worst happens, you're going to die. You do know that.

Tendai swallowed. Yes, he knew it, but that was what warriors sometimes had to do. The important thing was to die for the right thing, and with dignity.

That's right, little lion. I can see I made the right choice.

Tendai's heart swelled with pride. He looked up at the encircling Masks. They were apparently waiting for the effects of the Nirvana gun to wear off the Gondwannans who had been shot by the strange man.

"Let them wake up fully," said Obambo Chivari. "We can't do this ceremony with too many missing."

As the moments ticked past, Tendai caught a glimpse of what the *mhondoro* really was. It—for the spirit was both male and female—stretched back to the first human who raised his—or her—shaggy head from the immediate business of finding food. She—or he—became aware of the land. He saw the good red soil and clean water flowing through it, the plants that sprang up and the animals that bounded through them. And he knew that this was where he belonged. This was *home.*

Ever since that time, all the men and women who had cared for the land added their voices to the *mhondoro*. Tendai saw, in a distant, shadowy way, the country of Zimbabwe with its millions of souls. As his attention was drawn in from the larger landscape to the room, his vision became sharper. He saw Kuda sitting on the floor with Rita's arms around him. His little brother was planning to trip the Mask next to him. Rita was thinking about how to reach the Nirvana gun.

Last of all, Tendai came to the She Elephant. *Her?* he said. *She can't be one of your people.*

They are all my children, said the *mhondoro.*

With the tribal spirit guiding him, he saw the She Elephant as she once had been: a fat, unwanted child. Nobody cared for her. Nobody was her friend. Ignorant, graceless and rough, she ran away from home. "The only way you get by in this world," said the young She Elephant, "is to bash people before they bash you."

Tendai saw her build an empire in Dead Man's Vlei. The *vlei* people were her real family. She didn't lure them out there: they came willingly. She bullied and exploited them, but to the mournful, unwanted *vlei* people she represented *home.*

He gazed at her in wonder. It was difficult to understand the feeling the *mhondoro* had about her. The closest he could come to describing it was: *she belongs.* At that instant, the She Elephant noticed him watching her. Her eyes widened. Tendai felt a smile break out on his face. It was a good, friendly, *belonging* kind of smile. The big woman shuddered and turned away.

"It's time for the ceremony," said Obambo Chivari. Reverently, the Gondwannans carried the Big-Head Mask from the shadows to place it before Tendai. The darkness flowed along with it. Even in the light of the candles, its form seemed incomplete. Tendai could focus on a part—the little teeth or scraps of scalp—and another area would collapse. When he shifted his eyes, the mask seemed whole, and yet an instant later something else would grow dim.

It isn't completely in this world, explained the *mhondoro.*
The ceremony will give it substance.

"The Big-Head Mask is the most ancient and powerful of our fetishes," Obambo Chivari said in a deep voice. "It has passed from man to man for a thousand years. It has been called up by the other Masks and by countless sacrifices. Only it has the power to rouse the Gondwannan gods from their long sleep."

"*They're not asleep. They're bone-idle,*" remarked the *mhondoro.* Tendai grimaced. He wished he felt as cheerful as the *mhondoro.*

"You, Child of Zimbabwe, will be the messenger of our will. Look upon the mask and know terror."

"I'm not carrying any of your messages," said Tendai.

"That's telling him—ow!" cried Rita as the Porcupine Mask pulled her hair.

"Good, good," Obambo Chivari said pleasantly. "Be defiant. It will make your eventual surrender that much more powerful."

Tendai glared at him with hate, but his heart was beating very fast. Now it was going to be real. Now it would hurt.

The Masks formed a ring around the chair. Obambo Chivari wasn't able to join it because he had lost the Warthog Spirit. The Gondwannans began to chant. It was like nothing Tendai had ever heard. It started low, a mutter of angry bees in an underground hive. It rose to the surface, coming nearer. Tendai knew the men were making it, but it seemed to hang in the air without direction or source. It was exactly—he broke out in a sweat—the kind of sound ghosts would make as they gathered in a dark forest.

Stop that! You're too old for ghost stories, said the *mhondoro.*
Sorry, Tendai said.

But the noise was unnerving all the same. Gradually, one after the other, the spirits that attended the Masks took up residence. The men jerked as they were possessed. The sound grew louder. Barks, yowls, grunts and hyena laughter filled the air. It was the animals trapped as messengers. They circled the chair, calling for their Master, who fed only on humans. The Presence that had lurked in the shadows began to awaken in the Big-Head Mask. Its shape became clearer. But just as it seemed to come into focus, something would fade.

It's because you destroyed the Warthog Mask, said the *mhondoro. The animals' voices are weakened. That was a good trick, Tendai. What made you think of it?*

I don't know. I just didn't want them to have it all their own way, Tendai replied.

Obambo Chivari wrung his hands as he watched the Big-Head Mask struggle to take shape. The animal messengers went faster and faster; their panting filled the air. The spirit-ridden men writhed as though stricken with disease. The Big-Head Mask suddenly leaped into sharp definition. It came alive, more terrible than any nightmare. The eyes opened.

Tendai cried out.

You again, said the Presence. *Fine warrior you've got this time. The last one was delicious, by the way.*

It's not over till it's over, said the *mhondoro.*

Brave words! If the only soldiers you can come up with are freaks and children, Zimbabwe deserves to be eaten.

Obambo Chivari selected one of the knives and approached Tendai. He raised it to make the first cut. The eyes of the Big-Head Mask followed the blade greedily.

Snap!

For one horrified instant, everyone in the room seemed turned to stone. Everyone, that is, except the She Elephant. She tossed the two halves of the Big-Head Mask to the floor and dusted off her knee.

Women can be warriors, too, the *mhondoro* said with satisfaction.

Then everything went berserk. The Masks whirled in panic as their spirits abandoned them. The animal messengers fled with cries of woe. Rita tried to grab the Nirvana gun, but Obambo Chivari knocked her away. In revenge, she yanked a rug out from under the Baboon Mask, who tumbled to the floor. Even Kuda ran around aiming punches with his little fists. The She Elephant gathered an armful of statues and was using them with great skill as missiles.

The She Elephant couldn't destroy the Big-Head Mask until it was entirely in the real world," explained the *mhondoro. That's what I was waiting for. You communicated with her very well, by the way.*

I did? Tendai said. The Masks appeared demoralized by the destruction of their most powerful fetish. They crouched on the floor with their hands on their heads. Obambo Chivari tried to shoot at the She Elephant with the Nirvana gun, but so far all he had managed was to dodge heavy gold statues.

When you smiled at her, you reminded her of something she forgot a long time ago. It's her land, too, and her people.

The Gondwannan Ambassador struck the She Elephant with a blast, but she shook it off like a gnat bite. She roared and barreled straight for him. "We need help!" yelled the Porcupine, rousing himself from his paralysis. He ran to the door and flung it open. Instantly, he tried to shut it, but it was too late.

In poured a crowd of excited waiters, cooks and dishwashers brandishing mallets, cooking forks and other unpleasant weapons.

"Dirty child killers!" shouted the chief cook.

"Murderers!" yelled the salad master.

"Stingy tippers!" screamed the waiters.

The Masks ran around frantically. "Ambassador Chivari, please wake up," they implored. But Obambo Chivari lay on the floor with his head at a funny angle. The She Elephant calmly stuffed her pockets with jewels as the battle raged around her. A pair of elegantly dressed women knelt by the strange man who had come in from the landing dock.

I'm going to leave you now, said the *mhondoro* to Tendai. *You ought to think about becoming a spirit medium. You have a real talent.*

I'll miss you, Tendai said.

I'll always be around, young lion, for as long as the land of Zimbabwe exists. And then it was gone.

Tendai felt so lonely he could hardly stand it. The *ndoro* grew cold. It was only a lump of seashell. Tears rolled down his cheeks.

"Now's a stupid time to cry," said Rita, busily using a sacrificial knife to cut through the ropes that bound her brother. "Everything's turned out fine."

40

Mother could hardly believe her good fortune when the door opened. She already had her makeshift troops ready. They swarmed inside, hitting right and left. Mother brought down a few Masks herself. Then she saw what she had been waiting for all those long months. Rita was cutting Tendai free from a chair. Kuda was trying to help with a wicked-looking steak knife. Tendai struggled to stand, but his knees sagged.

Mother was there in a flash. She caught him before he fell and was surprised by his weight. He seemed to have grown several inches, too. She lowered him to the floor, from where he watched her with a dazed expression.

"Mother! Mother!" shrieked Rita, hugging her.

"Mother?" Kuda said. And this was the bitterest moment of all: her younger son didn't even recognize her.

"Of course, you booboo head," Rita snapped. "I suppose you think Trashman's your *father*."

"I knew who it was all along." Kuda hugged Mother cautiously.

Presently, Tendai's wits returned; he tried to rise. "It's all right," Mother said. "You don't have to get up." But Tendai insisted. Behind them, a frying pan clanged as the last Mask slid to the floor. A large woman moved toward the door. Mother stiffened and raised her gun.

"No!" cried Rita, hanging on to her arm. The shot went wild, and the She Elephant bolted.

Knocking waiters and dinner guests from her path, the big woman threw herself at the elevator. It opened—and out streamed a squad of policemen! The elevator was working at last. They pounced on the She Elephant, and when the dust had settled, she was tied up as neatly as a bale of cotton. A pile of necklaces, bracelets and rings from her pockets was heaped at the side. Mother walked around and admired the knots.

The elevator opened with a second load of passengers— paramedics this time, with Amadeus glowering at the rear. Mother almost laughed out loud at his amazement when he saw the corridor.

Waiters were dragging groaning Gondwannans to a heap in front of the Starlight Room. Their costumes had been torn off, and they were merely a group of foolish-looking men. The waiters stood guard over them with cooking pots. The walls were scored by the Soul Stealer. Eye and Ear were being fed snacks by an elegant woman in a diamond-studded robe. Another woman clapped her hands and cried, "Isn't this exciting? I haven't had so much fun in years." The maître d' went around with a tray of mango juice to celebrate the victory.

"What in *Mwari*'s name is going on?" said Father.

"You mean you didn't get a message?" Mother asked.

"What message? When you stormed out of the house, I thought it was a good idea to follow, to be sure you stayed out of mischief."

"And those policemen and paramedics?"

"Oh." Father looked sheepish. "I thought they might double-check the security and health systems of the Starlight Room."

"Daddy!" yelled Rita. "Come *on,* you loon." She yanked Kuda after her as they ran from the Gondwannan Embassy.

Mother thought Amadeus in full battle dress with weapons bristling from his belt and strapped to his arms and legs looked like the last person anyone would call Daddy. But Rita and Kuda didn't care. They threw themselves at him, and he knelt and gathered them into his arms. The policemen hid their smiles.

"You won't *believe* where we've been," Rita said. "We met a blue monkey and were slaves in a plastic mine. Tendai and I were accused of witchcraft. Oh! And we had *chicken pox*."

"I used a man's shovel by myself and ate termites and jumped up and down on a Mask!" Kuda pointed at the group of sorry-faced men guarded by waiters.

"Wait, little lions. I have to greet my other child, too." Father rose. Tendai stood in the doorway of the embassy. They stared gravely at each other. Mother's heart gave a hitch. Her son had gone away a boy and returned a man.

"Father, someone tried to help us a few minutes ago. I think he's dying," Tendai said.

How exactly like his father, thought Mother, to put aside a joyful reunion for duty.

The two went to a couch where paramedics were busy. It's Arm, Mother thought sadly. His eyes were open and staring. Father closed them gently.

"I can't find a pulse," said a paramedic.

Tendai removed the *ndoro* from his neck—it was the first time Mother noticed it—and laid it on Arm's chest. He put his hands over it and closed his eyes.

A chill went through Mother. Exactly what had been going on in this room? Now that the battle was over, she had time to observe it. She saw the loathsome masks stacked in a heap against a wall. On the floor was a—was a *thing*. It lay in halves, but the two parts seemed to be crawling toward each other. Of course it was a trick of the candlelight.

What horrible candles! They gave off a sweet rotting smell as they burned. The gap between the two halves was smaller—

or had she forgotten? Whatever the halves were intended to be, they were made of things she couldn't bring herself to name. The candles were making her drowsy. If you fit the two parts together, she thought, wouldn't you get—

"Hah!" shouted Father, kicking the almost-joined face. The halves flew in opposite directions. At once they began to disintegrate. The sewn-together parts broke up; the bits feathered into dust. All the other masks began to crumble.

Father threw open the door to the landing dock. The wind howled through the Gondwannan Embassy. It swirled the dust in a gray tide across the floor. Mother jumped back to keep from being touched by it.

Above the wind tumbled the voices of animals: yips and barks, growls, bleats, caterwauls and roars. With them were the voices of men, women and children. They weren't angry. Rather, they rejoiced as though released from long slavery.

"It's the people and animals who were sacrificed to feed the Masks," said Tendai.

The gray tide swirled around the room and fled out across the landing dock and into the sky. Into *Mwari*'s country.

"Now I've got a pulse," said the paramedic. "That's funny. Why couldn't I find it before?"

Arm opened his eyes and looked up at Tendai. "I'm hungry," he said.

"What you need is a nice hot garlic soup," said Eye as Arm was settled into an easy chair in the corridor.

The maître d' shuddered. "I don't know what kind of swill they serve where you live, but *no one* eats garlic soup in the Starlight Room."

"It's their loss."

"I might have a tasty *potage d'haricots* in the kitchen, however," said the little man.

"He means bean soup," translated Ear. The maître d' scowled.

The Gondwannans and the She Elephant were packed off in police vans. Obambo Chivari was flown to the prison hospital to see if someone could straighten out his neck. Tendai tried to help the waiters arrange chairs in the corridor, but they told him to sit down.

"You're our guest of honor," they told him. So he, Rita and Kuda were placed at a table with Mother and Father. Ear, Eye and Arm were allowed to stay in easy chairs because of their injuries. The dinner guests and workers from the Starlight Room settled down wherever they could find seats.

"My eyes are almost back to normal," said Eye. "Normal for me, that is. I'll have to put on dark glasses soon."

"My ears hurt, but the doctor says they'll be good as new in a few days." Ear was bundled up in thick bandages that doubled as muffs.

"You're lucky I had my first-aid kit with me," said the doctor. "How do you feel, Arm? I'll admit I don't know how to treat you."

"It's strange. All my life I've felt the emotions of others. Now they're gone."

"Is that bad?" asked Mother.

"It's . . . lonely."

"What happened inside the country of the Masks?" Father said. Tendai wished he hadn't asked that question. Even the memory of the Presence behind the Big-Head Mask made him sick.

Arm stared down at his long fingers before answering. "There's nothing like it in our world," he replied slowly. "Imagine fire that burns but has no warmth, darkness that blinds you but is no relief from light. All I can say is that it was like being dropped in a vat of acid. Whatever makes real things *real* was eaten away. I can't describe it! Only that it was horrible!" He hid his face in his hands.

"If you can't read minds anymore," Mother said quietly, "you can keep Sekai."

Arm looked up. "Yes. That's true. By the way, who's looking after her?"

Mother looked embarrassed. "Well, the Mellower came out of his room for the first time today—"

"That does it! He'll put salt in her formula. He'll let her roll off a table." Arm tried to get up, but he was still too exhausted.

"I'm sure the Mellower knows how to take care of children. After all, he raised mine," Mother said.

Tendai didn't care to mention all the times he, Rita and Kuda had found him asleep with a newspaper over his face.

"Who's Sekai?" asked Rita. When this was explained, she did a celebration dance, as the Resthaven girls had done when Tendai was carried home in triumph from his fight with Head Buster. "Yea! Hurrah! The story has a happy ending!"

The old-fashioned clock by the elevator churred as its gears began to turn. It chimed sweetly. "It's twelve o'clock!" cried Rita. "It's your birthday, Tendai."

"Really?" the maître d' said.

"I'm fourteen years old," Tendai replied.

"Then we have to celebrate!" The maître d', the cooks and the waiters scurried off to empty the pantry. They brought plates of cold ham and chicken, bowls of fruit salad, caramel pudding and ice cream. Tendai was presented with a cake and fourteen candles.

"Make a wish! Make a wish!" chanted Kuda.

Tendai remembered his last birthday. It seemed one shouldn't make wishes idly. Who knew which spirits were listening? He considered a moment and then thought, I wish for courage. Because with courage, you weren't afraid to look at the truth. You weren't afraid to ask questions or do the right thing.

Good choice, young warrior, whispered the *mhondoro* from far away.

"And now we have to sing 'Happy Birthday,'" Rita announced. Tendai groaned. His sister stood on a chair and directed the singing. Everyone joined in, from the youngest dishwasher to the maître d'. Father sang loudest of all. His deep bass voice threatened to drown everyone else out. The song was so successful, they did it again. A late dinner party arrived from the elevator.

"This place is a mess," complained a man. "Look at the furniture higgledy-piggledy in the corridor."

"The kitchen staff is eating with the guests," exclaimed a woman. "Bad management is what I say."

"And what *I* say is, you can go home and open a can of beans," shouted the maître d'.

"Well! I never!" huffed the woman. The late dinner party got back into the elevator and left.

"What about Trashman?" Kuda asked suddenly.

Everyone stopped talking and looked at him. "He's right. We've been so busy celebrating, we forgot about him," said Rita. So Father phoned the police and arranged for a squad car to pick them up on the Gondwannan landing dock.

Father, Tendai and Kuda flew off to Mufakose, while the rest went on with the party. "It was a tall building, not far from the central market," said Tendai as the squad car came in low. Mufakose was dark now. Its citizens were tucked into bed, and the noisy market was still. "That's it!" Tendai cried, pointing at an unusually tall tower in the bright beam of the car. "See? There's a landing dock at the top."

They set down, and two policemen got to work on the door with crowbars. "I hope he's all right. He didn't have any food," Tendai said.

"I brought him a big piece of cake," said Kuda. The policemen peeled back the opening.

"Phew! It smells! Set out lanterns by the door." Father shone a flashlight around the room.

"It—doesn't look the same." Tendai saw that the stuffed hyena, dried owls and mummified bats had been pulverized. The black curtains lay in shreds on the floor. The altar was smashed to kindling, and the dried herbs were reduced to dust. Trashman was curled up in a corner, sound asleep.

"I think he had a temper tantrum," observed Kuda. "I get them, too, sometimes."

"He ate the candles," a policeman said in disgust.

Kuda went up to Trashman and prodded him. "Have some cake."

The man awoke. "Kuda," he said with a big grin. Then he and the little boy shared the cake and babbled the doings of the past few hours to each other.

"This building is full of stolen property." Father shone his light through a trapdoor, and Tendai saw a king's ransom of gold, jewels and money. The whole tower was loaded with the ill-gotten wealth of years of crime.

"What will we do with it?" he asked.

"Find the original owners if we can," said Father. "The rest . . . well, you know how many poor people exist in this country: the beggars in the Cow's Guts, the *vlei* people, the thrown-away children. And the honest hard-working people—they need things, too. It'll be gone in no time."

Tendai nodded. He was proud his father was speaking to him as an adult.

"No thanks. I'm full," said Kuda as Trashman offered him the stub of a candle.

EPILOGUE

Obambo Chivari and the other Gondwannans were shipped home. They met unpleasant ends at the hands of their own people for losing the masks.

The She Elephant, in view of the help she gave, was only sentenced to two years in prison. She enrolled in a cooking course and perfected her considerable skills. When she was released, she went back to Dead Man's Vlei. After a stay in the new shelters General Matsika built for them, the *vlei* people began to join her.

When Tendai was sixteen, he got his first pilot's license. He flew low over Dead Man's Vlei. The cooking pots were steaming. Knife and Fist, recently finished with their prison terms, were lounging in easy chairs, but Granny wasn't with them. She had entered a convent in Mozambique, where she spent many happy hours listing people's sins and praying for them.

Of the *vlei* people there was no sign. Perhaps a shimmer of the ground indicated when one of them moved. The She Elephant came out of her burrow and shook her fist at the little sports car. Tendai flew away.

Mrs. Horsepool-Worthingham was allowed to go home after she promised to do a thousand hours of public service.

She was assigned to a clothing charity in the Cow's Guts. She watched carefully to be sure no one got more than his share. Trashman had somehow memorized his way to her garden. He drifted through every few months in search of T-bones and guavas. Mrs. Horsepool-Worthingham let him in because she was afraid of General Matsika. As Trashman munched his way through the garden, she retired to the Invalid's Room with a glass of sherry.

Trashman was impossible to reward. He simply accepted whatever was given him, whether he deserved it or not. No matter how kind the Matsikas were to him, they would awaken one morning and find him missing from the heap of grass clippings he preferred as a bed. He wandered throughout the city. Sometimes he disappeared altogether. Tendai thought he had found a way into Resthaven.

Tendai occasionally visited Resthaven Gate, at which he listened intently. He never heard anything. The entrance never opened. The bell went unanswered. No one, with the possible exception of Trashman, even knew if the people inside were still alive. But Tendai thought they were.

Monomatapa's people went on in their timeless way, farming, hunting and thatching their round huts when the season of long grass was upon them. And at night, they gathered in the *dare* to tell tales. Or so Tendai believed. Someday, when the spirit of Zimbabwe stumbled and the *mhondoro* grew faint, the gate would open again and remind the rest of the world of what it once had been.

Tendai himself studied medicine when he was old enough for college, but he also spent time with the Lion Spirit Medium in the Mile-High MacIlwaine. That person agreed to train him in the special discipline that would allow him access to the *mhondoro*. Having once been accepted by the spirit of the land, it seemed likely he would be chosen again.

Rita became a prizewinning math student, and Kuda, to no one's surprise, was possessed by his great-great-granduncle, a famous fighter pilot, and was taught military strategy from the inside out.

Eye very quickly got back his wonderful sight. Ear's wounds healed until you could hardly see a mark, unless he opened his ears wide, and only then with the sun behind them. But Arm never recovered his psychic abilities. He was certainly more sensitive than most people, but he never again was able to read minds.

The President awarded the three detectives the People's Medal and gave them lifelong pensions. After all the publicity, they suddenly had more clients than they knew what to do with. They became moderately rich. They were able to buy a house in Mufakose, which was a better place than the Cow's Guts to raise Sekai.

The Mellower was given new duties. He accompanied the children to and from their new public school. He held the students spellbound with tales of old Zimbabwe, and the teachers competed to lure him into their rooms. He was not permitted to Praise there or at home, however.

General Matsika said they all had been listening to Praise too long, and it made them blind to real problems. But now and then, because it made him so happy, the Mellower was allowed to visit the detectives.

He Praised the wise farseeing eyes of Eye and the keen hearing of Ear. He recited the virtues of Arm and described the fantastic cleverness of all three. Ear, Eye and Arm listened until they were so filled with happiness, not another kind word could slip in.

As Arm said, too much Praise was bad for you, but a little was like a vitamin. It was necessary for healthy, happy spirits. And besides, he said as Sekai clambered over his skinny knees and looked up adoringly at her father's face, it was fun.

GLOSSARY

antigrav pad   An antigravity unit used to dock a flying bus, taxi or limo.

baboon spider   A large hunting spider with businesslike fangs.

Batonka   A group culturally akin to the Shona; also called the Tonga.

blue monkey   A genetically engineered monkey composed of the worst aspects of monkey, human and pit bull.

bonding   An emotional tie formed between a parent and an infant in the first few days after birth.

bush baby   A small, nocturnal primate that resembles a squirrel with long toes.

caldo verde (Portuguese)   Portuguese soup made of cabbage, potatoes and lots of garlic.

chidao (Shona)   A totem from the mother's side of the family.

chidoma (Shona); zvidoma (plural)   Monsters created by witches from dead children; akin to zombies.

chili-bites   A delicious fried bread, somewhat like a dumpling, made of lentil and rice flour with shreds of chili peppers.

dare (Shona)   A men's meeting and dining area.

dashiki (Yoruba)   A loose, often brightly colored tunic worn by men.

Dead Man's Vlei   A large area in the middle of Harare used to store toxic waste in the early twenty-first century.

doek (Afrikaans)   A head scarf.

dwaal (Afrikaans)   To go into a trance state; to daydream.

force screen   A semipermeable force field that allows air in but keeps mosquitoes out.

frangipani tree   A tropical American shrub with showy, fragrant flowers.

garden gnome   A fetish used by the English tribe to make plants grow.

Gondwanna   A large country carved out of northern Africa by bloody wars in the late twenty-first century.

holophone   A telephone with a three-dimensional viewing screen.

holoscreen   A three-dimensional viewing screen in which the image appears to be physically present.

holovision   A television with a large three-dimensional screen.

hoopoe   A medium-sized bird with a crested head and a mellow *hoop-hoop* call.

jacaranda   A Brazilian tree with abundant lavender flowers.

kachasu (Shona)   Moonshine brandy made from almost anything.

kraal (Hottentot)   An enclosure for cattle commonly made from thornbushes.

kudu (Xhosa)   A large antelope with a brownish coat, narrow white vertical stripes and long spirally curved horns in the male.

Lake Kariba   A large artificial lake between Zimbabwe and Zambia caused by damming the Zambezi River.

loofah pod (Egyptian Arabic)   A fibrous spongelike fruit of the loofah vine used for bathing.

magnetic rail   An early form of antigravity travel in which a train is floated over a magnetic ceramic pipe that is cooled to near absolute zero.

maheu (Shona)   A sweetish, slightly alcoholic drink made of crumbled porridge, millet and water left out overnight to ferment.

mai (Shona)   Mother; a polite form of address.

maître d' (French)   Short for *maître d'hôtel*; chief steward in charge of a hotel or restaurant.

maiwee (Shona)   Literally, Oh, mother!; Good grief!

mamba (Zulu)   A venomous snake found in tropical Africa.

mangwanani (Shona)   Good morning.

Matabele   The second most populous tribe of Zimbabwe; an offshoot of the Zulus; also called Ndebele.

Matabele ant   A large and aggressive driver ant; akin to the army ant.

mbira (Shona)   A hand piano made of a sounding board or gourd and flat metal keys that are twanged with the thumb.

mealie (English)   Corn or maize.

Mellower   A combination of a traditional Praise Singer and a psychiatric therapist.

mhondoro (Shona)   The lion spirit, or the spirit of the land.

Mile-High MacIlwaine Hotel   Built over Lake MacIlwaine in 2150, this mile-high structure, the showpiece of Africa, contains the essentials of an entire city.

Monomatapa   The legendary fifteenth-century founder of the Shona Empire.

mopani flies   Stingless bees that like to drink moisture from the
    eyes, nose and mouth; very irritating.
msasa (Shona)   A handsome shade tree whose leaves turn red
    in the spring.
mudzimu (Shona); vadzimu (plural)   Family or clan spirit.
munynguna (Shona)   Younger sister; used by a senior wife for
    a junior wife.
muramwiwa (Shona)   An abandoned child.
mutara (Shona)   A small tree with beautiful waxy white flowers
    and a delicious scent.
muteyo (Shona)   A poison made from the bark of the *Erythro-
    phleum suaveolens* herb that is used in a trial by ordeal.
mutupo (Shona)   A totem from the father's side of the family.
Mwari (Shona)   The supreme god.
mynah (Hindi)   A blue-black bird with a yellow bill that can be
    trained to speak.
ndaba (Matabele)   Discussion; debate.
Ndau   A tribe related to the Shona, but with its own distinct culture.
ndoro (Shona)   A spiral-shaped, heavy white circle hung around
    the neck; its significance has been lost to urban Zimbab-
    weans, though once it had great spiritual value for them.
nganga (Shona)   A traditional healer.
ngozi (Shona)   A vengeful spirit.
night-ape   A very small species of bush baby with large ears
    and eyes.
nightjar   A nocturnal bird with a harsh cry.
Nirvana gun   A weapon that emits vibrations that stimulate
    the sleep center of the brain; the effects last about fifteen
    minutes.
nunchucks, originally nunchaku (Japanese, Okinawan
    dialect)   Weapons of defense consisting of two hard-
    wood sticks joined together by a strap or chain; the
    Teenage Mutant Ninja Turtles carry nunchucks.
Nyaokorefu (Shona)   Long-Armed One; a traditional Praise
    Name.
pamusoro (Shona)   Excuse me; the polite way to begin a
    meal, to show respect for the cook and the other guests.
quelea bird   A devastating grain pest.

rapoko (Shona)   Millet.

robocycles   Robot motorcycles that are directed by the voice; they can also be sent alone on simple errands.

rooibos (Afrikaans)   A fragrant noncaffeinated tea made from a shrub.

sadza (Shona)   A stiff cornmeal porridge.

sekuru (Shona)   Mother's brother or father.

Shaka Zulu   A famous Zulu king of the early nineteenth century.

shave (Shona)   A wandering spirit of someone who didn't receive proper burial rites.

shebeen (Irish)   An illegal beer hall.

Shona   The dominant tribe of Zimbabwe, made up of a collection of related tribes.

shooper (Shona)   To say the one thing calculated to keep an argument going.

Soul Stealers   Weapons based on the laser that creates a plasma burst similar to the interior of a lightning bolt; illegal in 2194.

synth-food   Food made from bacteria grown in tanks of sewage; the bacteria are creamed off the top and processed into fake hamburgers, hot dogs, etc.

tokoloshes (Xhosa)   Small imps or demons.

totem   An emblem or symbol of a clan.

triple-hardened titanium-molybdenum razor wire   A very thin wire used by housebreakers in 2194 to break through locks; General Matsika had locks made of quadruple-hardened titanium-praseodymium metal, which breaks razor wire like straw.

tsotsis (Xhosa)   Hoodlums.

vababa (Shona)   Honored father.

vakoma (Shona)   Elder sister; the correct title for junior wives to use for the senior wife.

vlei (Afrikaans)   A marshy wasteland.

wall spider   An alarmingly large but harmless spider.

weaverbird   A small yellow bird that builds ingenious basket-shaped nests.

Xhosa   A South African tribe with a language akin to Zulu.

APPENDIX

The Ndoro

The original meaning of the *ndoro* has been lost, but it was certainly an important symbol of rank and authority. Monomatapa wore one on his forehead. One of the ancient kings of Zimbabwe won a battle because he ordered his warriors to wear *ndoros*; the rival king was demoralized by this show of power.

The original *ndoro* consisted of the flattened whorl of a marine mollusk with the scientific name *Conus virgo*. Ceramic versions were mass-produced by the Portuguese in their Indian colony of Goa and traded for gold.

Ndoros are sometimes demanded by ancestral spirits before they will agree to possess a descendant. Broken *ndoros* are used as a form of *hakata,* or divining tablets.

Spirit World of the Shona

This is extremely complicated and often misinterpreted in books on Zimbabwe. It is probably wrong to break the religion down to a simple system, because each tribal group has a variation on the beliefs. I will do so only to make it possible for non-Africans to have some understanding of the religion.

Mwari is the supreme god, but he (or she) could better be described as Natural Order. A disturbance in the Natural Order brings evil results and must be corrected, but *Mwari* is not concerned with day-to-day problems.

A *mhondoro,* or lion spirit, is concerned with a land and its people as a whole. Because the Shona people are actually made up of several tribes, each one has a *mhondoro* and a lion spirit medium. In Zimbabwe of 2194, I have combined these into one. The *mhondoro* is concerned with general problems, such as rainfall and famine.

A *mudzimu* is a family spirit who can be approached to solve arguments and to cure illness. One contacts a specific male or female ancestor through a spirit medium. Certain family spirits may become interested in their descendants and teach them skills. This is why particular skills run in families.

An *ngozi* is an angry spirit who can cause madness, illness and death. A murder victim, a parent mistreated by his children or anyone else who has a grievance left over from life may turn into an *ngozi*. The wrong must be corrected before the spirit will agree to depart.

A *shave* is someone who died far from home and therefore couldn't receive proper burial rites. A *shave* can possess anyone he or she likes, to impart knowledge. This is what happens when an unusual skill shows up in a family, for example, a computer expert in a family noted for hunting. Race or tribe is unimportant in this possession.

Witchcraft

Witchcraft is said to run in families, but it can be learned. There are cases of people who don't want to be witches, but who are overwhelmed by an ancestral spirit.

It is a serious crime to accuse someone of witchcraft in Zimbabwe, because the results can be so devastating. The accused sometimes commits suicide. It is possible to be a witch and not know and therefore to feel responsible for whatever illness and deaths have occurred.

Among many other activities, witches create monsters called *chidoma* (singular) or *zvidoma* (plural) out of dead children. These are a cross between zombies and the familiars (such as black cats) used by witches in Europe.

Witches are discovered either by a professional finder who can smell them out or by undergoing an ordeal by poison. *Muteyo*, the ordeal poison, is frequently lethal, and death is taken as proof of witchcraft.

Slavery

For those surprised to find slavery in Gondwanna, please consider a report in the *Sudan Democratic Gazette*, March 1993, published in Great Britain.

For the past three and a half years, according to the *Gazette*, the Nuba Mountains area of South Kordofan province in Sudan has been singled out for destruction. The government in Khartoum has been carrying out an ethnic cleansing program designed to remove the Nubian people from rich agricultural lands and to re-settle those lands with nomadic Arab tribes.

More than sixty Nubian villages have been destroyed, and twenty-five thousand children have been forcibly taken away and relocated to concentration camps. These children have then been distributed as slaves to fourteen Arab towns and villages across northern Sudan, including Khartoum.

Praise Singing

Praise Singing was and is important in many African cultures. Most of the praises used in this book are traditional, including the ones Fist and Knife use to describe the She Elephant. "A beauty whose neck is so long, a louse has to rest before it can climb it" may not seem like a compliment to us, but three hundred years ago most people considered lice a normal part of the world. Women today might not care to be called She Elephants either. A female elephant is a noble creature with a graceful stride—not a surpris-ing subject for a Praise Name. It is only very recently that plump-ness has become unpopular. Most civilized people throughout history have considered it attractive as well as a sign of good health and prosperity.

Tribes of Zimbabwe

SHONA: The ancestors of the Shona arrived from the north between A.D. 1000 and 1200 as a collection of tribes with a com-mon language. The whole group was not referred to as Shona until the nineteenth century. Histories of several royal lines were preserved in oral poetry, but the most famous king was Monoma-tapa. When Zimbabwe gained its independence in 1980, the Shona, who made up 80 percent of the population, became the most pow-erful political group.

MATABELE, or NDEBELE: Mzilikazi, one of Shaka Zulu's generals, was allowed to leave the Zulu tribe with three hundred warriors. He built up his own tribe (the Matabele) but was driven out of South Africa by encroaching white settlers. He moved into southern Zimbabwe around 1836. Mzilikazi brought with him the powerful military organization of the Zulus and was able to establish a kingdom at the expense of the resident Shona. At the time of independence, the Matabele made up about 19 percent of the population. The two tribes, Shona and Matabele, have had a long history of mutual hostility.

BRITISH: The British tribe is composed of several subgroups: Scots, Irish, Welsh and English. One of these, the English, has been dominant for several centuries. The British gained control of Zimbabwe around 1890, but not without violent dissent from the Shona and Matabele. Several uprisings occurred before 1965, when the British lost control of the country. From 1965 to 1979 Zimbabwe was ruled by a small minority of English tribesmen.

PORTUGUESE: The Portuguese first settled in East Africa in the fifteenth century. They pursued a policy of conquest and trade with the interior for five centuries and developed the slave trade from around 1600. In the twentieth century, a great number of Portuguese immigrated to colonies in Africa. After Mozambique and Angola became independent in 1975, many of these people moved to South Africa, Zimbabwe or back to Portugal.

OTHER TRIBES: Several small tribal groups exist in Zimbabwe. Some of them are immigrants from other countries. These include Indians, Afrikaners, Tonga, Xhosa, Tswana, Venda and an interesting group known either as Brown or Cape Colored. The Brown People originated in the Cape province of South Africa. They are of mixed race, and some of their forebears were Malay indentured servants imported to South Africa many years ago. The Brown People have made important contributions to music, literature and fine cooking. In the book, Eye is Brown.

Great Zimbabwe

This ancient city was constructed between the eleventh and fourteenth centuries. No one is absolutely sure who built it, but most people attribute it to the Shona. The ruins are located on a hill. It is nearly invisible from below and must have been easy to defend. Around it lies good farmland with adequate rainfall. The area has always been free of tsetse flies, a crucial consideration for any economy dependent on cattle. The ancient Zimbabweans mined gold, which they traded for glass beads, porcelain and silk from as far away as China.

Several statues of birds perched on pillars were unearthed from the ruins. It is not clear whether these were eagles or vultures. In some cases a crocodile was carved climbing the pillar. The Zimbabwe bird is the symbol of the modern country.

Great Zimbabwe is only one of several ancient cities in the area. Ruins are found from Mozambique to South Africa, but it is unknown whether they were all part of a large kingdom or represent the remains of several small ones.

Monomatapa

Monomatapa lived in the fifteenth century, and tales of his splendor reached the first Portuguese traders on the coast of Mozambique. He was supposed to rule a vast kingdom from the Kalahari Desert in the west to the Indian Ocean in the east. The size and grandeur of his country were exaggerated, but no more so than that of Camelot in the tales of King Arthur.

Vlei People

In the early twenty-first century, a marshy wasteland in Harare was used to dump toxic chemicals. These formed a witch's brew that had unpredictable and dangerous side effects. The chemicals spread far beyond the original contamination site and permanently ruined a large area in the middle of the city. The area became known as Dead Man's Vlei.

Ordinary people shunned the place. Others, rejected by the normal world, found it to their liking. Every year a few of these individuals would drift into the melancholy wasteland, and every year a few of the older inhabitants would die and add their bodies to its gray mass.

In time, the *vlei* healed itself. Plants and animals moved back, but only these rejected humans dared to live there—if they could be called humans anymore.

Years of isolation and exposure to strange chemicals had wrought a change in them. They seldom spoke, but understood one another's thoughts. When one *vlei* person was angry, the others sensed it. They had evolved a kind of group soul like that of an ant nest. Only one thing was missing to complete their metamorphosis: a spiritual center. This the She Elephant supplied. Her vitality drew them like winter-chilled bees to the sun. She enslaved them, but she also gave them a sense of *home* and *family*.

For the first time in their long, dreary existence, the *vlei* people experienced something akin to happiness. And the She Elephant, for the first time in her life, felt needed and perhaps even loved.